Gordon Greenwood has spent much of his career in the transport industry, as a driver and as a transport manager for firms in Britain and Ireland. He has bred and reared greyhounds and is also a qualified counsellor. Gordon has two daughters, Dawn and Kelly, and lives in County Wexford, Eire.

BLOOD AND FREEDOM

Gordon Greenwood

Book Guild Publishing
Sussex, England

First published in Great Britain in 2013 by
Book Guild Publishing
The Werks
45 Church Road
Hove, BN3 2BE

Typesetting in Baskerville by
Ellipsis Digital Limited, Glasgow

Printed and bound in Great Britain by
CPI Group (UK) Ltd, Croydon, CR0 4YY

A catalogue record for this book is available from
The British Library.

ISBN 978 1 84624 922 8

The city square was vibrant in the lunchtime heat; a beautiful day to be alive, people rushing from shop to shop or meandering along gazing wistfully, business people leaving their offices for their one hour escape from duty, mostly heading toward the far side of the square, to the homely cafe on the north-east corner, dodging the hustle and bustle of people and the statuesque trees in the square's centre like a runner on his way to a touchdown.

The cafe was unusually busy; the first day of the sales had brought the shoppers out in their droves. Now people were taking time out from the rush, people inside and people on the pavement outside, all partaking in refreshing replenishment. It was a hectic adrenalin rush of a time for the staff serving food and drink. Until the bomb detonated.

Time stood still as the explosion ripped through, forever shattering the everyday life of the people in and around the cafe. Everyone in the square stopped, frozen in horror and amazed disbelief. Then people began screaming, running from the cafe and from the falling debris and shards of glass which crashed and jingled and danced to the ground. Clouds of smoke and dust billowed from the abyss which moments earlier had been the cafe. Minutes seemed eternal before the dust settled, to the sound of sirens and flashing lights. Police were quick to cordon off the mangled wreckage of the once thriving business. Paramedics strived to help the injured but for many, their help was no longer needed. Firemen doused the flames. As the panic died down and the screams subsided, an uneasy calm began to creep in. Among the people killed were a woman and her daughter.

⟫⬦⟪

Through wars and, more recently, government covert assignments, McNeill the sniper and Fitzpatrick, his spotter, had been together for almost ten years. This was their last job; retirement was now theirs. The mission had taken six long arduous months overseas to complete. Now, they were on the army flight home, its only cargo, and the two sat in the belly of the transport plane. No first-class passenger airline here; no gorgeous hostess to wait on your every need; no comfortable seat either, for that matter, just steel and netting, the bare essentials. But McNeill and Fitz were on their way home, McNeill to be reunited with his family and Fitz to try to patch things up with his ex-girlfriend, Carla. McNeill and Fitz were laughing and smiling, happy with excitement. So what if the debriefing took a few hours – what was a few hours or a day, even, compared to the last six months of sweat, humidity, grime, mud, flea- and fly-bitten, no sleep for days, crawling around in dense undergrowth and stifling heat in the jungle?

'Well, Fitz, what's the first thing you'll do when you get out?' asked McNeill.

'A cold beer followed by another cold beer,' Fitz replied. 'Join me?' he added.

'No, Fitz, as much as I like your company, I prefer my wife and daughter. I can't wait to see them,' replied McNeill.

The plane touched down in the afternoon sunshine at the army base located to the far north of the city, and taxied to a halt in front of a small tower. The doors opened and Fitz and McNeill were ushered off. Fitz noticed the time on the tower clock: 3.30

p.m. Soldiers appeared either side of Fitz and McNeill and shepherded them inside the base to a room with a desk and four chairs, two either side of the desk, and gestured for them to sit down. Coffee promptly arrived and the two men helped themselves while two soldiers stood guard at the door. There were no windows to the room. A lone fluorescent light lit three walls; the last wall was made of glass – one-way, and not the way Fitz or McNeill looked at it.

Nice five-star homecoming for heroes, thought Fitz. Suddenly, he heard footsteps marching purposefully, and two men came in. They sat down opposite and the younger of the two produced a tape recorder from his satchel and clicked the on button before it reached the table, whirring it into action. Debriefing had begun.

Sometime later, McNeill was taken from the room and brought along a corridor flanked by two armed guards, with two more behind. McNeill recognised the AK-47s – light, easy to use, rapid fire, very reliable and very deadly. A steel door opened and McNeill was led through into a sparse room with a mahogany desk and one chair facing the desk 6 feet away, another tucked nicely behind the desk. No windows, a radiator behind the desk, and an overhead fluorescent light. A television was bolted to the wall high on McNeill's right as he sat down facing the desk. 'Major General Alexander Byron', read the nameplate on the mahogany desk. McNeill sat, an armed guard standing to each side. An officer of authority strode in. McNeill stood to attention, then was told to sit as the guards were dismissed. He heard the steel door shut. The officer spoke, his voice calm, matter-of-fact but assertive.

'Major General Alexander Byron,' he said as he put a small file down on the desk and sat down. He opened the file and read the first page in silence. Stamped in bold black letters was the following:

'Under no circumstances let McNeill out of confinement after relaying the news. McNeill has a history of extreme violence followed by deep depression or vice versa and is extremely dangerous. One year ago he almost killed two civilians, severely injuring two more, and four military police officers had to restrain him. Keep confined in the hospital wing until he is deemed safe to society.'

Major General Byron read no more, closed the file, bent down to his right and opened a drawer, taking out two tumblers and a bottle of Scotch. McNeill looked on silently as the major general poured the whisky into the tumblers and offered one to McNeill. McNeill sat motionless.

'You may need that after you have heard what I have to say, McNeill,' said Byron. He then told McNeill of the explosion in the city square earlier that day, and as he sat down on the edge of the desk he informed McNeill that his wife Jane and sixteen-year-old daughter Deborah had died in the blast. McNeill slumped. The air in his body gushed out, his stomach wrenched. Byron turned on the television in the corner and a voice announced the latest update:

'Death toll stands at fifty-six, which may well rise as over a hundred and fifty more people are injured, some critically. Some of the dead have been identified. Hospital services are at breaking point trying to cope, emergency services are trying to make safe the area of the bomb blast and forensic scientists will move in later. It is believed an Islamic terrorist splinter group has claimed responsibility for the bomb which caused the bloody mayhem—'

McNeill heard no more. He was dazed, numb, dumbfounded, a man in his own time and the time seemed motionless. He lifted his head and his wet eyes stared emptily at the television, then at the major general. The numbness turned to shock, then to despair. His face paled, his head bowed. His hand felt the tumbler and he raised the glass to his mouth, downing the whisky in one swallow. He replaced the tumbler on the table and his head now sank to his chest as his mighty fists clenched, the muscles in his arms beginning to tremble. His fists battered against the solid desktop. Time passed.

Major General Byron went to the door and knocked on it. The steel door opened and two soldiers entered.

They helped the ashen-faced McNeill to his feet and took him to the base hospital as ordered by the major general, where McNeill was undressed, showered, put into a hospital nightgown and given a bed in a room. The door was locked and guards remained outside. McNeill was in oblivion, totally unaware of everything happening to and around him.

Initially he was kept under twenty-four-hour observation, but as the hours became days, days became months, the round-the-clock surveillance subsided. Rehabilitation was long and arduous. Never before had McNeill imagined living without his wife and only daughter. He had to realise they were no more, to let go, to move on and to live again. Begin to learn how to live or to learn how to die – that was his choice.

⇒•◇•⇐

It was early March when McNeill was discharged and deemed safe to enter society. Nineteen months had passed. He stood outside the hospital, gazing back, remembering the major general telling him of his wife and daughter's death, then nothing till waking up in a hospital bed in a standard-issue military nightgown. He had missed months of his life, his body became wilted and weak, his face made gaunt by the weight loss, his fitness evaporated. He thought back to the punishing training regime he had undertaken to return to full fitness. Now he was now back to 250 pounds of solid muscle, and at 6 foot 3 he cast quite a shadow. He let his green duffle bag fall to the ground as he looked at the hospital wing, the part of the building with no windows for the first three floors, barred windows on the next two levels. Memories of padded walls came flooding back, the hours, days and weeks of solitude. His thoughts of hatred and revenge rose. The smell of disinfectant that lingers in your nostrils, the first thing you smell when you wake, the last smell before you sleep. People in white coats carrying clipboards scurrying about, keeping what is written secret. He drew in the cold, crisp daylight air and looked around.

I need to get out of here, I need transport, and I reckon Uncle Sam should provide that free, he thought as his eyes fell upon a jeep outside the officer's mess. McNeill picked up the duffle bag and made his way over. He opened the driver's door and found the keys left in the ignition. *After all*, McNeill thought, *who would expect someone to steal a jeep from a military base?* He threw his duffle bag on the passenger seat, climbed in, started the engine, reversed and promptly drove out of the base.

McNeill knew where he was heading. He began the drive to the country home he had shared with Jane and Deborah, set in woodland with a long, tree-lined driveway, idyllic in its isolation. Jane had fallen in love with the log cabin at first sight. Deborah hated it. He bought it. Some long hours later, McNeill slowly drove the jeep down the potholed lane, stopping 100 yards short of the cabin. He killed the engine, got out, stretched and looked at the lawns, and the trees surrounding the cabin, keeping it safe. A rope dangled from one, a tyre tied to its end. Memories of himself and Deborah swinging came flooding back. He looked around and could now see his beloved wife Jane everywhere; from the bluebells to the lawns, to the solitary weeping willow nearest the cabin which they had planted together. McNeill could feel his wife and see his daughter swinging on the rope swing, grazing her arm as she fell to the ground, then running to him with her arms outstretched, sobbing.

McNeill drew in a deep breath and walked up to the door. It was locked. He stooped to the flowerpot at the side, the spare keys as usual underneath, now a little rusty. Jane was terrible with keys, putting them down anywhere and never remembering where, and her way to make sure she was never locked out was to have a spare set under the flowerpot. One of her endearing traits, McNeill recalled. He unlocked and opened the door and went inside. The cabin he remembered as so warm, loving, homely and vibrant was now a sad, empty, life-less shell.

McNeill wandered around inside. He could still smell her, Jane, his beautiful wife, still taste her cooking in the kitchen, still hear her laughter, still see her in the bedroom undressing in the soft twilight. McNeill shook himself, clasped his eyes shut, opened them and went to the wardrobe. He packed a travel bag, then removed the wardrobe's false floor and took out his Beretta pistol, spare magazines, plastic money pouch, false driving licence and passport. Putting these into the bag, he got up, turned around and returned to the kitchen. He saw the kitchen now as it was then, just as she would have left it – spotlessly clean, but homely and lived in. A tear came to his eye and slowly rolled down the contours of his right cheek, finally dripping from his chiselled chin to the floor.

He tried the gas cooker, which to his surprise lit, then turned it off and went outside to the shed. McNeill searched in the shed and returned to the house with a large can of petrol, doused the cabin, turned on the gas and went outside, where he part-filled a large bottle with what was left of the petrol. He dipped one end of a rag in the petrol, then stuffed it into the bottle neck, leaving as much out as in, lit the end of the rag with his lighter and then threw the Molotov cocktail through the kitchen window. There was an explosion as the cabin erupted into a blaze. Flames licked lovingly at the timber, smoke bellowed to the sky. McNeill returned to the jeep, flung the bag in the boot and jumped in. He started the engine and drove slowly away.

He turned right at the end of the lane, heading east towards the city, not knowing why. He drove through the afternoon and before nightfall he booked into a roadside motel, showered and went to bed. Sleep did not come easily to McNeill now, not since the day of the explosion at the cafe. Sleep was now a numbing, eyes-wide-open coma. Nights were not easy – the solitude, still-ness and silence had turned to loneliness and dismay.

Morning came and McNeill rose early. He showered, shaved, dressed, and with the Beretta now in its holster under his jacket, he went outside to greet the sun. He strolled across the road to the diner and ordered ham and eggs over easy. A mother and teenage daughter came in, reminding McNeill of Jane and Deborah – of his loss. McNeill paid for breakfast, then hopped into the jeep and headed for the city centre. Just inside the city limits he joined the exhaust-fume-filled stream of traffic slowly commuting to work. He felt out of place amongst the cars, trucks, buses, people, skyscrapers, buildings of every shape and size. There were people everywhere, hurrying about, walking briskly, striving to get where they were going in a mad panic. The city was springing to life. McNeill felt claustrophobic and turned off the highway, heading for the park. He parked up, got out and walked into the park, where people were walking their dogs or jogging, and found an empty bench. He picked up a newspaper which had been left there, sat down and began to read.

He did not take any notice of the figure jogging towards the bench, nor did he hear the figure shout his name enquiringly as it passed before turning. McNeill just wanted time, time to be anonymous, to be alone. The jogger slowed to walking pace as he got nearer and shouted his name again. McNeill never stirred. A hand gripped his arm.

'McNeill, McNeill,' a voice called.

McNeill looked blankly up at the man dressed in a tracksuit standing in front and slightly to the side of him.

'Hey buddy, you OK?' came a voice.

'Fitz, you look terrible,' McNeill said, recognising him eventually. McNeill stood and the two men hugged, each glad to see a friend and comrade.

'What brings you here, McNeill?' asked Fitz.

'Dunno,' came the reply.

'Hey, man, sorry about Jane and Deborah,' said Fitz remorsefully, adding, 'Hey, you got a car? Fancy coming over to see my apartment?'

McNeill nodded his agreement. They walked to the jeep and McNeill followed Fitz's directions to his apartment. Once there, Fitz showed his friend around, then left him in the kitchen with the coffee pot and clicked on the television while he went to take a shower. McNeill changed the channel on the television to CNN news, poured a coffee, then sat down. A live report came through about the kidnapping and murder of a politician's wife and two children. An Islamic terrorist faction had held them hostage for ransom, the same group responsible for the bombing of the cafe which had left 78 people dead and many more injured almost two years ago. The ransom had not been met, and the reporter told of their brutal deaths, recorded on video, of how explosives had been strapped to them and then detonated. McNeill turned away and was physically sick in the kitchen. He felt dazed horror, anguish, bewilderment and sorrow, but this turned to hatred and anger.

Fitz finished his shower, dressed and entered the kitchen. He could see his buddy was in a sorry state. 'Gee, looks like you could do with a proper drink,' he said, pouring himself a coffee.

'Yeah, sure thing,' came the reply.

'OK, Parnell's bar it is,' replied Fitz.

They left the apartment and turned left onto a street where people of different cultures mingled, wearing yashmaks, turbans, saris, burkas, long black dresses. McNeill looked on, confused.

'Yeah, it's Mohammed Street, this. We'll turn left in a minute, down a side street to Parnell's,' said Fitz. Before the two men turned, McNeill saw a building where people were removing their shoes, leaving them on the steps outside before going in; he did not see anyone come out.

Fitz and McNeill entered Parnell's bar, where Fitz ordered Scotch on the rocks twice and a Bud for himself. The two friends and war veterans drank the whisky and ordered another. A few more war veterans entered the homely bar, and friendly banter of past war skirmishes ensued, until the conversation soured with talk of the kidnap victims. Parnell's bar had filled, and the crowd inside was increasingly uneasy. McNeill began to steel himself, to harden, becoming tense and angry. At 6 foot 3 inches and 250 pounds, he loomed over Fitz's 5 foot 10 inches and 190 pounds. McNeill began to drain the whisky bottle.

Parnell himself was serving behind the bar when a member of his bar staff turned on the TV. The topic: the brutal murder of the American senator's wife and children. At the same time, an eerie cry was emanating from the building McNeill had seen earlier – the muezzin had begun his call to prayer. The sound stoked a fire of hatred amongst the war veterans in Parnell's bar. The television reran the video clips. McNeill looked at Parnell, who was now watching the TV behind the bar, then behind Parnell to a framed picture – a picture of Parnell's wife and teenage daughter.

Fitz left McNeill's side and went to the men's room. McNeill continued to stare at the photograph. He could hear the anger-filled conversation of the people in the bar, feel the tension, resentment and anger rise, but all he could see in the photo was his wife Jane and daughter Deborah. Parnell's bar was fast approaching fever pitch. All had ideas of what should be done with the terrorists – with all Muslims, for that matter. The muezzin's call went on unabated. It was too much for McNeill. His head was bursting, his mouth was dry, and cold sweat seeped from his brow as he focussed on thoughts of Jane and Deborah.

Abruptly, McNeill stood up and left. He turned right outside and 20 yards later made another right into the mosque, pulled out the Beretta pistol and began shooting all around him. He emptied the magazine and stocked another, walking forward and firing again indiscriminately. Fitz came in running. McNeill turned 180 degrees and through crazed eyes somehow recognised his friend, then turned back and began firing again. The screams and cries died with the prayers. Fitz surveyed the carnage and as he did a young boy ran in with a rifle. Fitz drew his gun and shot the boy in the chest, killing him instantly. 'Oh, shit!' Fitz yelled as he went over and grabbed McNeill, who was still firing his now empty Beretta, and ushered him into the street, reholstering his gun.

McNeill was in a daze. Fitz yelled at him to holster his pistol and they ran across the street into a gathering crowd, turned down a subway and jumped onto a train, disembarking at the next stop. They walked out of the subway station and back onto the street; they could hear the faint sound of sirens. Fitz knew he had to think and work fast, for the both of them. McNeill had saved his skin many times and it was now down to him to save his. They walked the streets, diagonally crossing, checking in the reflections of shop windows for any signs that they had been spotted or the police were on the lookout. Fitz was full sure a description of himself and McNeill would be in police hands and he needed to get somewhere safe, out of the public eye. He also knew family members were out of the question – they would be the first place the police would go. More sirens, more anxious edginess from Fitz. McNeill just seemed dazed and impassive.

Then Fitz remembered Carla. He found her a few hours later in a drug-induced stupor, slumped in her bedsit. *Lovely, bloody lovely, she can't help in that state, but neither will she recognise us*, thought Fitz.

Hers was a single-room bedsit in a downtrodden part of the city. McNeill just lay on the bed. Carla curled in a ball against the wall at the foot of the bed, rocking to and fro, mumbling softly to herself. Fitz moved to the phone, turning on the television as he did so. There on the news was a report of a massacre at the mosque where at least twenty people had been killed and some wounded as crazed gunmen began shooting at people as they prayed. Police had descriptions of the two men seen leaving the scene. The descriptions fitted McNeill and himself perfectly; he knew they had to get out. He made a phone call.

'It's me, Fitz, I will take that job you offered.'

'You left it late, we leave in a few hours. OK, Fitz, you are in,' said Sergeant Cronin.

'Wait: McNeill comes with me,' demanded Fitz.

11

'What? Hold on there,' said Sergeant Cronin as he turned to Lieutenant Colonel Mahon.

'Problem?' inquired the lieutenant colonel.

'Fitz wants in but he wants to bring his mental buddy McNeill with him. I am not sure.'

The lieutenant colonel rubbed his chin in contemplation. 'Hmm, McNeill, best shot in the army but a loose cannon.' Long moments of deliberation followed as Fitz held the line. 'OK, two it is. Tell Fitz he has total responsibility for his buddy and I want no mess-ups!'

Sergeant Cronin relayed the message. Fitz agreed, informed Cronin of their whereabouts, disconnected the line and sat down to wait.

Two hours later a black sedan pulled up outside. Fitz grabbed McNeill and they went outside and got into the back seat. The driver drove for three hours through the late afternoon and into the evening, on into the beginning of night, out of the city, into the suburbs and on into countryside. Fitz dozed. McNeill just stared out of the window in a trance-like state. Light rain fell as the driver pulled off the road onto a dirt track. About a mile later shapes came into view. Fitz squinted. They were hard to visualise, almost invisible in the moonless, starless night —more so with the light rain falling and the windscreen wipers working – but he could see the black-clothed forms were industrious in their work. The sedan stopped short of a large cabin and two men opened each rear door. Fitz and McNeill got out, a syringe found both, and soon they were fast asleep.

—=◆•◆=—

McNeill woke first. It took time for his vision to steady, but there across from him was his sedated buddy Fitz. He heard something but couldn't make it out – what was the buzzing sound? His eyes narrowed and his vision widened but it was still blurred. With each passing minute his hearing returned. He felt around him.

He could hear a language being spoken: English. They were aboard a military helicopter, destination unknown. Fitz stirred, beginning to awaken.

The two men sat facing each other, flanked on each side by armed men. Fitz and McNeill had no idea how long they had been unconscious. The helicopter banked to the left and began to descend, touching down in what seemed to be a disused airbase which was now full of life. Fitz and McNeill were bundled from the helicopter and into a transporter, a military goods plane loaded with munitions and a hundred men.

The doors shut and the big Boeing engines droned into life. The fasten seat belts light went on, the plane taxied and took off. Once again, for Fitz and McNeill, destination unknown. This had no effect on Fitz or McNeill; on assignments, orders would be passed out and opened in flight. Only this time, there was no envelope for either of them. Apprehensive and tired with a headache, the aftermath of the drugs, Fitz looked at the blank expression on McNeill's face. He just seemed oblivious, no emotion, a blank stare, a vacant shell of a man. He dropped off to sleep. Fitz slept for what seemed hours and woke to see McNeill asleep and the soldiers alongside sleeping; his mind flashed back to the day's events. For killing the young boy, he knew returning home was never going to be an option. As for McNeill, he felt for him – his best friend's future life was totally lost. No home, no family, no country.

The plane taxied to a standstill and everyone disembarked. The sky was dark and unforgiving and a chill was in the air. Fitz glanced round; he could see men fussing around the plane, offloading its contents. The men were billeted into makeshift barracks. Fitz and McNeill bedded down and slept. At 8.00 am, everyone was woken. They dressed and went outside along with the hundred others. Fitz and McNeill recognised Lieutenant Colonel Mahon and Staff Sergeant Cronin, the man Fitz had called from Carla's telephone. They were what the rest were to become: mercenaries.

Cronin called for Fitz and McNeill; both stepped forward. Cronin took the two to another barracks, gave out uniforms and directed them to a small simple cabin containing ten bunks, of which eight were occupied. 'Showers are across,' said Cronin, pointing. 'Mess is... well, you will smell it,' he added, laughing. McNeill and Fitz showered, changed, went to the mess to eat and returned to find Browning sniper rifles propped against their beds. Cronin entered and explained that they were to spend the next few weeks back in army training and sharpening their aim.

McNeill, as ever, was able to hit dead centre up to and at a range of 650 yards. Fitz, although admirable, was not up to McNeill's standard; but then in yesteryear Fitz finished third in the army shooting competition which McNeill won with ease. They realised they were about to go to someone's war, but on who's side and for how long? Would they survive, and what did the future hold?

Fitz and McNeill became exceptionally fit, but the dry humour, cheeky wit, boyish charm and talkativeness of McNeill had vanished. Few words were spoken by him now. Fitz would not desert his friend, just as in days gone by McNeill had not deserted him.

They were loaded with eighteen others into a transport helicopter and dropped into war-torn Yugoslavia. An elite squad of men under the command of Sergeant Cronin.

There was a noise to the right of the clearing where they landed and everyone crouched, assuming a firing position directed at woodland where the noise came from. A white flag was being waved and two men came out dressed in the same uniforms as themselves; grey and light blue berets with light blue bandannas.

'At ease,' called Cronin, who walked over to greet the men.

The group were taken to the command post. Here they were fed with black bread and soup. Fitz, McNeill and the other professional soldiers looked around at the ramshackle amateur army of men speaking a foreign tongue. Worse still, very little English was understood or spoken.

What have I got us into? thought Fitz, but he remembered there was no way back for him and McNeill. Soon they were introduced to their Croatian comrades. All was quiet.

Sporadic firing broke the silence. Fitz looked up. Nothing to fear, it's too far away. Shells began to creep closer. The men were split into two groups of ten and loaded into battered cars, a jeep and a truck. Hurriedly they left the post. Inside the Nissan Patrol jeep sat McNeill and Fitz. As it passed over raised ground the small convoy came under hostile fire. The driver of the jeep slammed the accelerator to the floor just as a rocket exploded into the leading car, rolling it off the road in a ball of flame. He overtook the burning wreck and turned into a hollow, hoping they could not be seen by the enemy, and killed the engine. The four men jumped out, rifles at the ready, and ran back to the roadside. They reached the road just in time to see the occupants of the second car had got out and the truck taking a direct hit from a rocket. Moments later the stationary car itself was hit, lifting it off the ground, burning it in mid-air.

McNeill could see the four men and beckoned them to use cover and regroup at the jeep, then he hit the floor. Single shots rang out and two of the four fell, wounded or dead, he would never know. He attached the sight to his rifle, peered through in the direction of where he thought the shots came from. He saw one man running. McNeill took careful aim, squeezed the trigger and watched through the sight as the man fell backwards, arms outstretched. McNeill adjusted, saw another, aimed and squeezed off another deadly bullet. Fitz, to McNeill's left, was doing the same. Twenty minutes had passed. In that time McNeill and Fitz had located the rocket launcher and peppered it with bullets, bodies sprawled around it. An uneasy silence then followed. McNeill and Fitz scouted the surroundings through telescopic sights – they were a team, each knew how the other worked – starting at twelve o'clock, one working clockwise, the other anticlockwise. McNeill and Fitz remained still for a long time after the other soldiers went to the jeep. Then they slowly retreated back to the jeep, which was now ticking over. Once in the jeep the driver sped off down the rocky terrain. The two soldiers from the car turned out to be French. Fitz smiled. Two Croats, two French, McNeill silent by choice – no word of English, no conversation.

Fitz and McNeill both realised Sergeant Cronin had died in the lead car. In his case and most of the others' that died that day they would not appear on the death lists, just victims of war, and Fitz and McNeill were well and truly trapped in it, fighting for a cause alien to them, and not knowing who they were fighting. A lot of questions with no answers.

The jeep pulled into the next base and everyone got out; men carrying jerry cans fuelled the Nissan jeep. The driver brought the survivors to a makeshift tent, ushered them in and pressed his outstretched palms towards them, a signal to wait, then turned and left. Shortly afterwards he reappeared carrying a hot flask and some mugs, accompanied by three men. One spoke Croatian, one translated into French, the other to English. McNeill and Fitz were now members of the Croatian army fighting the Serbians who were trying to annexe Croatia and ethnically cleanse it. McNeill and Fitz's location was somewhere between the city of Banja Luka, which was almost surrounded by Serbs, and Tuzla, near the mountains. They were under the direct orders of Captain Bogdanovic, the commanding officer here; the translator pointed him out as he walked towards them. The captain introduced Dmitri the driver to McNeill and Fitz, then to the two Frenchmen, Jean and Laurent. The captain eyed Fitz and McNeill. 'You shoot well, Dmitri tells me, deadly accurate.'

McNeill and Fitz just nodded, went outside the tent and began to tend to their weapons, oiling, cleaning, dismantling, rebuilding, reloading – ready for the next time. Then they ate and slept.

Hours later, in darkness, Dmitri left the captain's tent with his orders. He collected Jean and Laurent before picking up Fitz and McNeill and they drove out of the camp. After driving for some hours, Dmitri killed the lights, drove a little further, pulled off the road and killed the engine. Dmitri turned to them, pursed his lips and put his forefinger to them – the sign for silence. Then, with the index finger and middle finger he made the sign for walk. They got out of the jeep and Dmitri led the way.

They walked uphill carefully, silently leaving the jeep below them, across a small plateau and eventually up onto high ground overlooking a Serbian camp. Fitz checked his watch: it read 9.30 p.m. He realised he had forgotten to adjust the time and figured it was 3.30 a.m. They were in complete darkness, no moonlight, just an empty, dark, cold sky. He counted eighteen tents below. Dmitri showed two tents which were to be the targets, and the four sharpshooters lay down, adjusted themselves to comfortable firing positions, adjusted their telescopic sights, and waited for Dmitri to give the signal to fire. Dmitri looked down at the target through binoculars. He came around behind Fitz and McNeill and showed them their target, then did the same with Jean and Laurent. The four sharpshooters emptied half a magazine each on their chosen targets. The bullets ripped through the canvas, leaving their deadly message behind. Pandemonium broke out in the camp as the alarm was raised. Dmitri and the four snipers retreated into the dark, the Serbian soldiers firing wildly in panic at anything and everything.

Dmitri and the snipers reached the jeep without hindrance. Dmitri started up and returned to base.

And so the war trudged on. The Croatians held the town of Banja Luka. McNeill and Fitz went on many forays, spent most of the day eating and sleeping, and the nights as silent messengers of death. Base became the town. It wasn't long before Fitz realised that the forays were becoming more frequent and not as deep into enemy territory. He realised the Serbians were getting closer and closer.

They had been in Banja Luka some ten weeks now, and McNeill had uttered as many words. Fitz looked at his friend in the daylight. McNeill's face was pale and gaunt, his lips super-glued shut unless eating and drinking, his eyes hollow and distant. Fitz felt the weight of McNeill's sadness. The rest of the day, Wednesday, came and went. Thursday morning – nothing. Dmitri appeared early that afternoon. He had news of a ten-man Serbian patrol to the east and closing. His orders were to destroy it. Dmitri gathered the four snipers, McNeill, Fitz, Jean and Laurent, and they headed out of the base, travelling north-east in the Nissan jeep.

The sun was overhead, the air warm and humid, the tar on the road shimmered with the heat. All the windows were down in the jeep. Dmitri drove steadily past lush green fields on either side, which rolled off then climbed to the mountains in the distance. He continued for over an hour, passing sporadic cottages, abandoned sheds, the odd farm house. He stopped to check his map, then drove on before veering off the road onto a dirt track which after a mile began to climb. McNeill looked round, a worried expression on his face. Fitz read his thoughts.

'Jeez, we are sitting ducks now,' said Fitz. McNeill nodded in agreement. Dmitri drove on.

Trees began to take over from grass as the dirt track levelled out.

'Less chance of somebody spotting dust clouds in here,' said Fitz to McNeill, trying to make conversation. McNeill silently nodded as the dirt track began to wind and climb. Dmitri stopped the jeep. *We walk*, he signed. The men got out. Using the woodland cover they moved ahead, reaching a hilltop. Fitz knelt down first, took his rifle from his shoulder and began looking through the telescopic sight, slightly to the sun's right. McNeill did the same except he went to the sun's left. Fitz spotted them and he pointed with his left arm. Jean and Laurent looked in that direction. The soldiers were a mile away at least, lounging.

'We need to get closer,' Fitz said. 'Maybe that hill there,' he added, pointing. 'How many do you count, Jean?' Six, came the reply. Laurent was now counting – *cinq, six, sept* – then shrugged his shoulders.

'OK, Fitz, you are best, you take point, then me, then these two,' came a stern voice.

'God, he talks – McNeill, he speak,' said Fitz and he moved off ahead stealthily. Intermittently Fitz would squat, shoulder his rifle, look through the telescopic sight and count the enemy. *Eight, maybe more*, he signalled to McNeill, who squatted the same instant Fitz did before relaying the message to Jean and Laurent.

The trees gave way to long wayward grass and for the last 200 yards the four men spent most of it on their bellies, crawling using elbows and knees, reaching the vantage point of the lower hill unseen. Fitz looked towards the patrol. The patrol had found a small lake. Three men were swimming in it, three men were on the shore, and four men were lounging over the bonnets of two of the three jeeps. Fitz signalled to McNeill to come up. Fitz pointed to the four men. *One man for each of us, we take the swimmers last.* Fitz picked his targets and moved off lower down to get better shots. McNeill called up Jean and Laurent, designated each their targets, and they moved off. McNeill made ready on his targets, but kept a watchful eye on Fitz, who held up five fingers twice. *Ten seconds.* Five seconds later McNeill also held up five fingers to Jean and Laurent.

At the countdown's end the four snipers opened fire. The first volley hit the four men lounging on the jeep bonnets; the next volley hit the men on the shore. The men in the lake were frantically swimming, trying to reach the shore as the assassins trained their sights on them. Four more shots and the water around the swimmers began to discolour from blue to red. Arms and legs stopped thrashing. McNeill looked through his sight at the lake. The gentle water lapped at the lifeless bodies. He checked the area around the shore and the three jeeps parked on the beach, saw no movement and signalled to Fitz and Laurent to go and take a look. McNeill and Jean stayed ever watchful while Fitz and Laurent checked the bodies. Laurent turned over two dead soldiers lying face down, who moments earlier were lying over the jeep bonnets smoking. Fitz and Laurent moved to the three men on the shore, all face down, all shot in the back, one twice. They turned them over to face the sky; all had large gaping holes in the centre of their chests where the bullets had exited. Fitz looked at the lifeless bodies in the red water. His head bowed into his chest as he turned and signalled the all-clear.

McNeill and Jean rose up and walked down to Fitz and Laurent. Fitz was looking at the bodies once again. Six of them, it appeared, were barely out of their teens. Sadness and remorse gripped him as McNeill arrived. McNeill looked at the four bodies by the two jeeps, each struck once through the head. Fitz watched McNeill. As McNeill moved towards him Fitz looked into his eyes – they were hollow, unfeeling, guiltless, blank, no sign of emotion or care, and he thought of McNeill as a robot. Jean and Laurent took the guns and ammunition from the dead, and the four began the walk back to Dmitri.

Dmitri was waiting patiently, drawing on his cigarette. The four men put the acquired weapons and ammunition in the back of the jeep and climbed into the seats. Dmitri drove back to the base steadily without mishap. He reached the sentry post he had left earlier that afternoon in Banja Luka and the sentry opened it: Dmitri drove through smiling. Fitz looked out of the rear side window, saw lookouts posted high on buildings and walls and wondered, did he see them there earlier? Dmitri drove on to the town centre and Captain Bogdanovic, stopping the jeep at the entrance to the hall. The men got out. Jean and Laurent went to the bar for a drink; Fitz grabbed McNeill, who was swapping his Browning for an M21 sniper rifle. Fitz did the same.

'Did you see the sentries as we came in?' he asked.

'No, why?' replied McNeill.

'The ones on the wall all had their guns pointing into the town. They should be looking out,' said Fitz.

'Fitz, you're getting paranoid. Come on, let's get something to eat and some target practice, so we can adjust these rifles to our liking,' said McNeill.

———⊰◆⊱———

Patrols were sent out that night. McNeill and Fitz were not involved and they slept. The next morning Fitz woke early, left McNeill asleep and went outside. The air was cold and moist, refreshing until he saw the remains of the last night patrol, shot to pieces as it passed by. He took out a cigarette, lit it, and walked to the mess for a coffee. McNeill surfaced later and joined Fitz in the mess. Fitz was agitated and uneasy, McNeill could see it.

'Buddy, if I go for a walk around this town will you come along with me?' Fitz asked McNeill.

McNeill just nodded a yes and continued to drink his coffee. When McNeill was done the two men left the dance hall that masqueraded as the soldiers' mess, turned eastwards out through the town centre, down a main thoroughfare. Small houses and shops interspersed with large ones adorned each side. The further away from the centre, the more dilapidated the houses became. Just before they reached the outer perimeter roadblock they turned to follow the machine-gun posts to the north side. The east side of the town was slightly elevated over the forest about a mile away. Open ground divided the forest from the machine guns. When McNeill and Fitz reached the north side roadblock they had passed through the previous day, they turned and looked back. Once again Fitz noticed the soldiers on the apartment rooftops were looking into town as well as out. He showed McNeill.

'Something's amiss here,' Fitz said.

They moved on to the west side. Once again, from the west side you could see for miles across open country; however, it had a more relaxed feel. Lookouts posted on all the tall apartment blocks looked out onto emptiness.

'Not expecting an attack from this direction,' commented Fitz.

McNeill and Fitz moved to the south side, where the town

21

sprawled from the concrete apartments across a green to a perimeter fence. They passed a sentry post and came to a sheer drop, then no-man's-land, a mass of rubble, burned out cars, overturned jeeps, twisted metal, lumps of concrete, and no vegetation, no grass, no trees, no nature. There was one road which ran through the concrete jungle, also littered with debris, and habitable and uninhabitable apartment blocks rose on the far side. Graffiti adorned the walls of three of the four-storey blocks, and some windows were covered with wire mesh, while other apartments had no windows and curtains flapped where glass should have been. Gaping holes where rockets and missiles had hit and bullet marks riddled the outside plaster. The only thing that linked the divided town was a small wooden walkway, wide at the beginning in the concrete mangled mess, rising and narrowing to the concrete bunker to the left of Fitz and McNeill.

A soldier stood outside the bunker smoking a cigarette. Fitz turned round; a sniper was on the roof of the apartment behind him, scanning below them, watching the walkway. McNeill and Fitz approached the lookout and examined the walkway. It started wide, then the narrowing began at a fence put across the walkway like a dam on the river, or locks on a canal, and again near the top, all to slow down anyone who was coming up. Fitz glanced to his left. There, high on an office block, was another sniper, his rifle also trained on the walkway. The concrete bunker contained a machine gun, Fitz surmised – that's how the wall had become so riddled. He looked down the wooden walkway and saw tin cans at the side by the locks, and guessed the snipers used them for target practice. He turned to the soldier and asked, 'What's on that side of town?'

'That Serbia, this Croatia.' He spat as he said Serbia. 'Don't go there – the snipers shoot on sight.'

McNeill and Fitz pulled out their cigarettes at the same time, offered the sentry one, and they all lit up. A stray cat walked the edge of the wooden walkway and the sniper on the office block opened fire, killing it.

'Target practice,' said the
yesterday – that evens up the s(

As Fitz watched the walkway
view with a ribbon attached belo
floating over the walkway. He s
years of age trying to catch it,
behind. The balloon floated ov
haired boy began to climb over

'No! No, go back!' shouted F
been fired. It hit the boy full in h ___ ... The boy rocked backwards and fell, dead. Fitz put his head in his hands. The little
girl screamed, and people appeared at the apartment windows,
began screaming, yelling, remonstrating. Fitz was bent over. He
felt dismay and genuine hurt for the boy. He rubbed his eyes with
the fingers of his cupped hands, then stood erect, dropped his
hands to his sides, and turned to look at McNeill. He had witnessed
the same thing Fitz had just seen, but he just stared, blank and
emotionless, in another time, at another place. Fitz realised, then,
that McNeill's world had ended the day of the explosion in the
cafe where his wife and daughter had perished. He watched
McNeill take the last drag from his cigarette, drop the butt to the
floor and crush it with his right boot.

A burst of machine gunfire had Fitz pull McNeill to the ground.
A car with four people inside below on the road in the Serbian
quarter were driving alongside no-man's-land firing indiscriminately and wildly. Almost level with Fitz and McNeill but below
on the road, the car came to an abrupt halt. A rocket fired from
a flat-roofed house above and behind the concrete bunker struck
the right side of the car, which burst into flames and was lifted
skywards, its occupants still inside. The car spun back to earth,
and the snipers and sentries in the concrete bunker emptied their
magazines into the blazing car where it rested. No survivors.

Fitz and McNeill slowly clambered to their feet and went back
to the base. McNeill wanted something to eat, and Fitz felt queasy
as they made their way to the mess. McNeill ordered two large

sh, gave one to Fitz and sat down opposite him. ked in. Fitz thought of the violence and pointless a young boy's life, the pointless waste of the four car nts' lives, brutal and unnecessary killings which turned s stomach. He could not eat. McNeill finished his bowl then tucked into Fitz's with relish.

Nothing happened for the rest of the day and like all good soldiers, they both tucked in to sleep early. In times of war, eat when you can, sleep when you can.

Nothing happened the next day.

The day after Jean was on duty in the bunker, and he shot both cat and dog for practice.

Dmitri came looking for McNeill and Fitz early the next morning, found them awake and called them outside. There waiting was the Nissan jeep, accompanied by a Ford Escort with a driver. Jean and Laurent were sat in it.

Fitz looked on. 'There goes the comfortable ride, McNeill, lost to two Frenchies,' he said.

Dmitri explained in broken English that the driver spoke French.

'Ain't that a bugger – all this army and they can't spare a driver who speaks English, but have found the only driver in it that speaks French, and because of that, Jean and Laurent get to sit on nice leather seats, well padded for their backsides, and we, McNeill, we get Spartan covered metal seats for our backsides, no padding unless it's your own. The cheap version for us, pent-house edition rear seats for the Frenchies!' exclaimed Fitz.

Fitz and McNeill got into the Nissan jeep, Dmitri got into the driver's seat. Fitz noticed there were provisions for two days at least. The two vehicles left the centre of town and headed north, out past the sentry, then turned east.

'Going out on holiday, are we?' Fitz asked Dmitri, pointing to the provisions.

Dmitri smiled. 'Is no holiday, Fitz, is no holiday,' he said. They drove in silence for two hours. Fitz recognised the road as the one they came out on when they shot the patrol at the little lake, the lush fields on either side, the sporadic buildings, abandoned cottages and sheds. A light breeze brushed the green grass which swayed in unison.

A land at peace to be wrecked by war, thought Fitz.

This time they didn't turn down the dirt track. Instead, Dmitri drove on and the lush green grass began to fade into harsh wild grass, bushes and shrubs, rocks and trees.

When Dmitri pulled off the road, Fitz and McNeill got out and scouted ahead, always alert, always watching and looking, eyes darting in every direction. They were deep into enemy territory. Fitz and McNeill were on opposite sides of the road, Fitz circling left and McNeill right. They returned to the Nissan as the Ford Escort approached.

'All clear,' said Fitz, throwing the M21 over his shoulder. Dmitri smiled and gave them both soup in a mug. They ate and drank. Dmitri checked his watch and then looked at the map. They were on schedule, he thought. The sun was slightly to the left of centre overhead. Its heat rays beamed down, visible through the trees. Fitz looked ahead to where the road ran pretty centrally through the wood. Grass met tarmac on either side, with boulders and rocks of all sizes and shapes making an uneven surface just out from the trees. Jagged tree stumps pointed skywards where the trees had been cut down to make way for the road. He could see the road rise; perfect ambush country. Dmitri looked uneasy. The soldiers finished their food and drink. Fitz went over to Dmitri. 'What's up?' he asked.

'Last patrol was ambushed here, badly beaten up,' he replied.

'Then we scout. Two Frenchies over the far side of the road, myself and McNeill this side, you behind and wait for our signal to advance,' said Fitz.

Fitz and McNeill took the road's left side, Jean and Laurent the right side, and they moved ahead. Shortly, both pairs entered the wood. They moved slowly, assuredly, through bracken and gorse onto the forest floor, with its few leaves and fallen branches. Halfway in, and nothing. Fitz was thinking of signalling. He stopped, then carried on to the edge of the forest using the trees as cover. He looked up the road through his rifle sight. The road was no longer on the level, but had begun a steady uphill climb. He signalled McNeill to come up. McNeill began to make his way cautiously to Fitz. Fitz looked round and located Jean and Laurent a little further behind on the opposite side, and signed to them to wait. McNeill reached Fitz, who pointed ahead. 'What you think?' he said.

'Perfect for an ambush – that hilltop looking straight down a channel,' replied McNeill.

Fitz signalled to Jean. McNeill and Laurent would wait here, while he and Jean scouted the hilltop from either side. Once there, and it was clear, they would give the OK to McNeill and Laurent, who would pass it on to Dmitri, to bring the transport. McNeill watched Fitz move off and keep left, aiming to use the forest cover before entering the waist-high grass. He could see his intentions of circling the hilltop. Laurent watched as Jean did the same.

Progress was slow, painstaking, crouching, crawling, edging along on hands and knees at times, using whatever cover was available – trees, boulders, even hollows – not to be seen. In one such hollow Fitz looked at his watch; he had been gone forty minutes. Fitz paused and looked ahead. The waist-high grass did not carry through to the hilltop; short grass took over, fifty yards of it. Open country. He looked over to his right. The scene was much the same on Jean's side. Fitz wondered if Jean was, like himself, eyeing the open ground. Fitz took the sight off his rifle and scouted the hill and its surrounds. Seeing nothing, he crouched and waited.

Suddenly, he exploded into a sprint, swerving, side-stepping in a zigzag pattern up the hillside. Blood rushed through his veins with each turn. Panting and gasping for air he made the hilltop. What had begun as a steady climb was almost perpendicular from halfway. The backs of his calf muscles ached, his lungs burned in his chest. *I'm getting too old for this*, he thought. He scanned ahead and around; nothing moved. More forest below, empty road, more hills, a lot more hills, short grass leading to the forest and boulders. He signalled the all-clear to where he thought Jean would be, and Jean broke cover.

McNeill saw the signal too, and he passed it to Laurent to signal Dmitri to bring the cars. McNeill and Laurent moved to the road.

The vehicles stopped and McNeill got into the jeep, Laurent into the car, before moving on to approach Fitz and Jean, stopping just shy of the hilltop. McNeill made his way to Fitz, and Jean, Laurent and Dmitri joined the pair.

'Well?' asked McNeill.

'Same again, déjà vu,' said Fitz and they all scanned the road below which ran through open country before it sliced the forest ahead into two, a small line of hills right and left, an embankment where the road cut through a hill.

'Valley beyond?' enquired Fitz.

McNeill looked at Fitz through hard, cold eyes and shrugged his broad shoulders. *There's more emotion in a statue,* thought Fitz, and he once again suddenly exploded into a sprint, down the hill to the forest.

'*Loco,*' Laurent heard Jean say, as they watched Fitz run to the forest. '*Stupide,*' he commented.

Fitz was now stepping over fallen branches at pace and a large thick tree stopped the mad dash. He sucked at the air. Deep breaths followed, an inner calm restored. He scanned the forest, signalled Jean, Laurent and McNeill to join him. The three men wasted no time. Once again Jean and Laurent took the far side of the road. Dmitri watched through binoculars and waited, but soon the four men were out of sight in the wood. The four men moved stealthily from tree to tree. Forty-five minutes passed.

Sunlight illuminated a patch to the left of McNeill. He moved around it, avoided standing in it, but on its left side as he looked up he could see tall grass, about 20 yards away. *The ridge of hills – must be,* he thought and he motioned Fitz to come over. Fitz joined McNeill. McNeill jerked his head in the direction of the grass, Fitz nodded agreement and they moved towards the grass. The forest thinned as the grass took over and the sun shone through. The long grass grew between fallen tree trunks, then there was grass and brambles, before short grass and stones.

Fitz was in front, with McNeill fifteen to twenty paces behind. They moved to the left side of the hill, where Fitz broke cover and began the 60-yard climb. Dmitri spotted him, McNeill waited. Fitz made the climb very easily, lay down at the top and viewed the scene in front through his telescopic sight. McNeill began the climb on Fitz's all-clear, and soon lay down beside him on the hilltop. Dmitri looked on through his binoculars then slowly moved to his right, hoping to see Jean and Laurent, but there was no sign of the two Frenchmen. Fitz turned and saw Dmitri through his telescopic sight, then lowered it.

'Shall we bring up the cars? Or do we wait till we look from the third of the four hills on our side?' he asked McNeill, knowing what his answer would be.

'We will get a better view from there, so wait,' McNeill confirmed. The two men moved off. They kept to the east of the hills and passage was easier away from the road. They rounded the second slightly smaller hill and ascended the larger one, Fitz on point. At the top, once again he lay down. The last hill in front was slightly smaller, and moulded itself into the valley below. Trees joined rocks and grass alongside the road. There were no hills on the far side of the road. Slight mounds had taken their place, and behind one of these Fitz saw the two Frenchmen. Directly in front and slightly below Jean and Laurent, 300 yards ahead were disused farm buildings. Between the buildings and the two Frenchmen lay 300 yards of short grass – no cover! Fitz checked the road and he saw craters in it, mostly in a stretch 50 yards to Jean and Laurent's left. McNeill arrived.

'Look, McNeill, seems like Jean and Laurent are stuck, three hundred yards of no cover to the farm buildings. From where they are they have a good view of the road which turns to our left slightly. Those buildings are close together and about one hundred yards beyond them looks like waist-high grass or some-thing, but it's not like what we have met so far.'

'Wait here, Fitz – after your last suicide run, I'm going. Get Jean's attention; I'm going to the small copse on the last hill. Wait for my signal before calling Dmitri or Jean.'

Daylight was ebbing into darkness when McNeill entered the copse. He surveyed the scene in front of him and gave the all-clear signal to Fitz, which he relayed to Jean, and the two Frenchmen moved off warily and passed the signal to Dmitri. Dmitri drove the jeep and the Ford Escort followed. The two vehicles entered the forest, where potholes in the road made progress slow. Dmitri manoeuvred round some of the craters then drove the jeep off the road, many yards short of Fitz.

McNeill was frantically signalling Fitz. He had spotted a patrol moving up the road towards the buildings – the same ones Jean and Laurent were headed for. He counted eight men. The patrol fanned out from the road into tall grass and disappeared from McNeill's view. Eventually Fitz contacted Jean and relayed the message. The two Frenchmen ran the final hundred yards to the buildings. Fitz turned again to see Dmitri, way below on the road, looking through his binoculars at him. Fitz relayed the message: patrol eight strong, 1 mile plus away and closing, McNeill up ahead, Jean and Laurent plus 300 yards in buildings on right. Move closer quickly.

Dmitri reached the forest edge, and turned around to face where he had come from. The Ford Escort followed.

McNeill kept looking, searching for any sign of the patrol. Time passed. Then he saw them, in the waist-high grass. He hadn't been sure at first, but he was definitely sure now. Six, seven, eight, in an arc. Then further over to the right a field of a crop he had never seen before, tall and thick and umbrella-like in the half-dark. McNeill moved position, going deeper into the copse. He wanted a clear shot, and found a tree which allowed a panoramic view of the closing patrol. He took out a piece of elastic cord with clips at each end, wrapped the cord around the tree trunk, clasped the clips together, then he threaded the nozzle of the M21 rifle barrel up between the elastic cord and the tree, put the stock in his shoulder, looked through the sight and waited.

Fitz moved position. He looked through his sight at the buildings where Jean and Laurent waited, then to the maize-like field ahead and on their right, then to the partially visible patrol. He trained his rifle on the patrol's centre. More minutes passed and the patrol moved closer. All four men waited.

McNeill squeezed the trigger of his M21 sniper rifle, the bullet finding its target with unerring accuracy. Fitz squeezed the trigger of his own M21 sniper rifle, sending its own messenger of death. Jean and Laurent began shooting; McNeill and Fitz fired again. McNeill looked on as the bullet hit its target in the chest, knocking him backwards, his arms outstretched. Then machine gunfire peppered the copse and the farm buildings.

McNeill dived to the ground, pulling the M21 free of the elastic cord as he fell. Jean and Laurent hit the floor as bullets struck the walls in front and burst through the open windows to the walls behind. Fitz shot aimlessly into the maize-like field. The machine gunfire riddled the building housing Jean and Laurent and splintered the trees in the copse. McNeill crawled, Fitz kept firing. Jean and Laurent were pinned down by enemy fire. McNeill escaped the copse and, crouching low, he ran. Fitz was still firing into the maize-like field, no specific target. McNeill headed up a small incline to get through the division in the hills. Bullets smashed into the earth to his left, but he made it unscathed.

Dmitri could hear the fierce gun battle. He went to the road and looked through his binoculars to see Fitz still shooting. Dmitri took out his pistol and fired into the air. Fitz looked down, saw Dmitri and signalled that two of their men were surrounded to the right, then he continued shooting into the field. Dmitri ordered the two cars deeper into the forest. The machine gunfire was intense and now concentrated on the buildings housing Jean and Laurent, who were lying prone on the floor, unable to return fire, unable to retreat. Fitz continued shooting at the maize-like field.

McNeill joined Fitz and they both fired into the field, while the enemy continued their assault on the buildings. Then there was a lull, but McNeill and Fitz kept on. Jean and Laurent made their exits out of the rear of the first and second buildings and began running for the forest. Dmitri was shouting but the driver of the Ford Escort did not hear; he was heading towards the two Frenchmen. Fitz saw the car, caught sight of the two Frenchmen running for their lives, saw red flashes in the maize-like field, then saw soldiers on the second hill on the right shooting at Jean and Laurent. Fitz pointed and he and McNeill began shooting at the soldiers. Two fell dead.

The machine gunners still peppered the buildings with bullets, while more soldiers on the hill shot at the running Jean and Laurent, the earth spitting at their heels. McNeill and Fitz took deadly aim at the soldiers and fired. Soldiers erupted from the maize-like field, running the 250 yards to the buildings. Bullets began to hit the ground on the hill around Fitz and McNeill as they continued shooting. The Ford Escort screamed on through the short grass to Jean and Laurent. Dmitri fired his pistol three times into the air. Fitz and McNeill stopped shooting and ran down the hill towards Dmitri. Dmitri now sat in the jeep, scared, perspiring, engine running. The Ford Escort swung round and Jean and Laurent jumped in. Fitz and McNeill were running to the jeep when BOOM, a red flash lit the night sky. Fitz and McNeill hesitated for a split second only, then ran harder to the waiting jeep, jumped in and Dmitri sped off.

'What do you think hit them – rocket? Bazooka? Tank?' Fitz asked McNeill.

'Whatever,' came the cold reply.

Dmitri drove the jeep expertly around the craters and potholes, his two passengers thrown from side to side as he did so, but he was scared and his innate flight mechanism had taken over.

As they approached the comparative safety of the base Fitz had a sobering thought – of all the men in the plane who came here, only himself and McNeill were still alive. Fitz eyed McNeill.

McNeill used to be so talkative, the life and soul of the party, a joker and prankster, a jovial, lovable rogue. Now he hardly uttered a word, looked out from cold eyes, alone and empty in himself.

⟹◆⟸

Bright sunlight came in through the windows when Fitz woke the next day. McNeill was already awake, just lying there, hands behind his head, a blank expression on his face. Fitz looked around. All the beds were now empty except two. He felt a lonely stillness of alienation. He again looked at McNeill and his open, vacant eyes. *Doesn't look like he slept at all,* thought Fitz. Fitz got out of bed, showered and dressed. McNeill did likewise. Not a word was spoken. They went to the mess with rifles slung over their shoulders, and ate breakfast. On returning to their billet, the two men began dismantling their rifles to clean, oil and reload them.

The M21 sniper rifles, their beloved compatriots; M21s, made by the Springfield Armory Incorporated, with their gas-operated, semi-automatic or single-shot rotating bolt action, weighing in at just over 11 pounds, were beautiful and light for a rifle some 44 inches long, its barrel length half its total length, with 5, 10 or 20 detachable box magazine firing 7.62 x 51-mm bullets, capable of shooting through a block wall. The two-stage trigger, pressure at first when aiming, then squeezing to fire, made it deadly accurate up to 900 yards. Both the telescopic sights were Redfield and Leatherwood, a 9x multiplication ranging scope. Fitz and McNeill loved these rifles for reliability and accuracy. They reassembled their rifles, got coffee and went to the munitions store.

Then a rocket entered the base, shattering the peacefulness of the day and blowing to smithereens the barracks where McNeill and Fitz had just slept.

Fitz and McNeill rushed out of the munitions store and onto the street. Another rocket exploded some distance behind them. The base was under attack. Soldiers were running now, and another rocket blasted into the road to their right. Bodies were tossed like paper on the wind. Fitz looked to his left, saw the Nissan jeep about 80 yards away, and the pair ran towards it. There was a loud bang behind them, and they were showered with wood splinters and dust, then the after-blast forced them to the ground. Fitz and McNeill hauled themselves back up and ran the last 30 yards to the jeep.

Dmitri came crashing out of a now chaotic large stone building 20 yards above the jeep. McNeill, Fitz and Dmitri reached the Nissan at the same time. Dmitri jumped into the driver's seat, McNeill and Fitz in the back. Rockets were now streaming into the base, seeking and finding any target. Dmitri started the jeep and floored the accelerator, heading north. He swerved to avoid running soldiers and overturned cars. Buildings were in a state of collapse, others on fire. Soldiers and civilians lay prone in the street, weeping and bleeding from wounds. Dmitri drove on, not bothering to slow down. He reached the sentry gate at the north side, crashed right through and sped away.

There was gunfire 100 yards out and bullets thudded into the Nissan, shattering the windscreen, missing Fitz and McNeill by millimetres as they dived for the floor. As the jeep thundered on more bullets hit, penetrating the outer shell, but not the reinforced interior. More glass shattered, and the next few minutes seemed like hours – the whistle of bullets through the air, the thud of metal on metal. Dmitri drove on. Soon the noise stopped. Fitz and McNeill gingerly sat upright, but Fitz had seen it – telltale red spots on the floor near the gear lever, and the gear stick had a red smear on it. Blood ran down Dmitri's hand.

Fitz climbed into the front. Dmitri was perspiring. Fitz looked at the crimson patch on his right arm, looked again and saw another crimson patch just below his left shoulder at his upper chest. Fitz shouted to Dmitri to pull over. Dmitri slowed the jeep to a halt on the grass verge.

McNeill jumped out, pulled Dmitri from behind the steering wheel and laid him on the verge at the side of the road, propping him up in a sitting position with his back against the jeep. Dmitri looked at his legs in front of him and felt the blood flow, felt the heat, and continued to perspire. He was startled when Fitz ripped his shirt open. Fitz, who had found the first-aid kit in the jeep, was looking at a half-inch hole in Dmitri's left shoulder above his chest and the same in the bicep of his right arm, oozing blood. He pulled Dmitri to him, searching for a hole in Dmitri's back, and did the same with his arm. Fitz found an exit hole twice the size of the entry hole in Dmitri's arm, but no hole in his back.

'Bullet went straight through his arm, but there is no exit hole for the one in his upper chest. That bullet's still in him,' Fitz said to McNeill as he gently eased Dmitri back against the jeep. As Fitz looked at Dmitri a slither of blood exited his chest; blood ran down his right arm more consistently, like a tributary seeking its mother river. Fitz ripped Dmitri's shirt further and used the arm of the shirt as a tourniquet. The rest of the shirt he used as a pad for the chest wound. Fitz turned to McNeill.

'He's losing a lot of blood, and he looks like he could pass out, poor bugger. We can't leave him – he's the only one of us who knows this country and where to go.'

Fitz and McNeill hoisted Dmitri up as best they could. Dmitri screamed in pain, his wounds gushed, and then they laid him across the rear seats of the jeep. McNeill elected to drive. Fitz went to the back, opened the door and looked in. There was a small first-aid kit, a gallon of diesel oil, some 2-litre bottles of water, one half-empty packet of cigarettes, which he placed in his pocket, and a travel blanket. Fitz brought the travel blanket and a bottle of water. He covered Dmitri with the blanket and offered him some water. Dmitri drank, then Fitz drank and offered the water to McNeill.

'Save it.'

Fitz sat in the passenger seat, opened the smaller first-aid kit and said, 'OK, drive.'

'Drive? Drive? Drive to where?' said McNeill.

'Exactly, McNeill, but for now, in broad daylight in a shot-up jeep, bullets and rockets behind us – anywhere!' retorted Fitz.

A voice uttered from the back, 'North, north-east.'

As McNeill drove off, Fitz checked both first-aid kits, the small one on his lap and the one on the floor at his feet – bandages, loaded syringe, plasters, scissors, lint pads, alcohol, safety pins and headache tablets by the packet. He looked at Dmitri, who was now drifting in and out of consciousness. The travel blanket had fallen off to reveal reddening cloth, and Fitz realised they needed to bandage him up better, but that it might be best to leave him for a while.

'He needs a doctor,' Fitz said as he put the blanket back over Dmitri.

McNeill drove on, trying to miss the potholes and bumps in the road, seeming to locate each one with effortless ease. The road shimmered in the afternoon sun. The sparse vegetation on either side began to get fuller and lush. As the hours passed, derelict and deserted buildings became less frequent, bushes and trees more prevalent. McNeill stopped at the roadside. He was looking ahead to where the road ran between hills and into a valley – once again, perfect ambush country. Fitz appeared at his side, took one look and knew what McNeill was thinking. They went back to the jeep for their rifles and both reconnoitred the journey ahead. After fifteen minutes Fitz spoke.

'We go to there,' he said, pointing, 'park up, climb the hills on either side from the side or rear and take a look.'

'OK,' agreed McNeill.

They returned to the jeep. McNeill drove ahead, pulled off the road into a hollow and stopped the engine. Fitz and McNeill alighted with their rifles and set off on either side of the road towards the hills, both men moving further and further away from the road itself. They circled the hills and climbed to the hilltops, where they lay down, surveying the valley and hills below and in front. Both satisfied, they returned to the jeep.

Dmitri was unconscious; Fitz looked at him and decided to redress his wounds, starting with his arm. McNeill held Dmitri's arm up slightly. Fitz washed it as best he could with alcohol and dried off the arm, put lint gauzes on the bullet entry and exit holes, padded cotton wool on top of the gauze then applied a bandage, leaving the tourniquet in place above the wound. He then removed the shirt pad on Dmitri's chest, crimson now from Dmitri's blood, and repeated the process, putting plaster strips over the cotton wool and attaching the ends of the strip to bare flesh. Dmitri moaned. McNeill laid Dmitri's arm to rest across his stomach and Fitz covered him with the travel rug.

'He is losing a lot of blood,' Fitz said to McNeill, who nodded in agreement.

After two painstaking miles and twenty minutes of avoiding potholes in the road, McNeill stopped again.

'Time for another look?' enquired Fitz.

Both men got out.

'Looks like some kind of a road to the left over there, beyond that line of small mounds. Seems to be clear to there,' said Fitz.

They returned to the jeep, got in and McNeill drove off slowly. Dmitri stirred.

'Where are we?' he asked, trying to sit up.

'Lie down,' ordered Fitz, who then described the terrain ahead and the journey past.

'If the road you saw ahead is a dirt track with a big rock on the left-hand side which you can only see when you get near the entrance to the track, turn into it,' said Dmitri softly.

'How would he know?' asked McNeill abruptly, adding, 'He's been out of it for ages.'

'I was raised in this part of the country. I'm sure,' Dmitri muttered in reply.

McNeill drove on, eventually coming to the dirt track described by Dmitri. The air outside was beginning to cool; soon daylight would fade and surrender to dark. The jeep bucked and bumped its way along the dirt track. Dmitri moaned in pain, progress was slow. The dirt track cut into the hillside and eventually the hills gave way to a plateau, green fields on either side.

An hour later and darkness had taken over. McNeill approached a T-junction, tarmac road to the left, more of the same dirt track to the right.

'Dmitri, which way?' asked Fitz.

There was no reply. Fitz and McNeill both turned their heads to look at Dmitri. Dmitri was of no use, he had returned to his unconscious state. Fitz opted for the tarmac road, on the basis that travelling on the tarmac would be easier on Dmitri. McNeill took the left fork. Night was drawing in fast.

'We need somewhere to sleep,' said McNeill.

'Yeah – and maybe dress his wounds again,' added Fitz.

McNeill drove on slowly. The road was uneven and bumpy, the tarmac only sporadic. They began to pass deserted ramshackle buildings.

'How about one of those for the night?' asked McNeill.

'Nah, keep going,' replied Fitz.

McNeill drove on further and spotted a cottage; small, isolated, set off the road. Without hesitation he turned up the uneven potholed lane towards it. The jeep rocked to and fro, sometimes lurching forward as McNeill drove up the lane in the darkness. He stopped the jeep behind the cottage and turned off the dimmed headlights. The moon gave light to the night sky. McNeill and Fitz got out of the jeep and McNeill went off round to the cottage front, sneaking a peek inside through the two front windows on either side of the door and listening.

He joined Fitz at the rear door.

'Looks deserted,' whispered McNeill.

Fitz went up to the door. The bottom half was solid wood, the top half had 6-inch square panelled glass in it. He tried the handle. It moved but the door was locked. He took out his pistol and smashed a glass square nearest the door's handle with the butt of the pistol, reached in and undid the lock from the inside. Once inside he moved from door to door and room to room, pistol pointing in front of him. The single-storey cottage was empty. He made his way to the rear entrance and walked outside, tucking his pistol inside his belt at his back. McNeill appeared.

'Everything OK out here?' asked Fitz.

'Grand,' came the grunted reply.

'Let's get Dmitri inside,' Fritz suggested.

They moved the semi-conscious Dmitri the best they could to avoid giving him more pain. Once out of the jeep they propped him upright and McNeill put his right arm round Dmitri's waist and Dmitri's left arm around his own left shoulder and half walked, half carried him into the cottage. Fitz collected the rifles and first-aid kits and followed inside.

McNeill manhandled Dmitri onto a wooden table in the cottage kitchen where Fitz tended his wounds. Dmitri moaned in pain. McNeill then searched the kitchen for food. There was a cupboard above the sink. He looked inside and found a tin containing tea leaves, two cups and a small pan. He removed them from the cupboard. Fitz had bandaged Dmitri.

'Let's get him to a bed,' Fitz said and the pair carried Dmitri out of the kitchen, through the main room into one of the two small rooms at the end, laid him on the single bed and covered him with blankets, then returned to the kitchen. Fitz grabbed the pan, went outside to a large tank which he had seen earlier, filled the pan with water and returned to the kitchen, where McNeill was making a fire in the stove. Fitz gave him his cigarette lighter to light the fire and placed the pan on top of the stove. The two men waited for the water to boil before making tea.

'I will take first watch,' said McNeill.

Fitz was taken aback. *He speaks without being spoken to, the iceman melts! Four to five spoken words – gee, welcome to the Plaza.*

'OK,' Fitz replied.

McNeill went outside. Fitz went to rest.

Fitz felt a jab in his ribs; his four hours were up. Fitz and McNeill changed places. Dmitri slumbered. Four more hours passed in silence and Fitz went inside the cottage to make tea.

McNeill was already up. The water in the pan was boiling and McNeill had already made his own tea and was sitting down now drinking it.

'Morning,' said Fitz; a nod of the head in silence was the reply. After drinking the tea, they again manhandled Dmitri, this time into the jeep, laying him across the rear seats as best they could. Fitz returned to the cottage and killed the fire in the stove and carried out the rifles and first-aid kits. McNeill returned to the cottage and brought two more blankets, which he placed over Dmitri. Fitz gave Dmitri a drink of water. McNeill started the engine of the Nissan then rocked it to and fro down the lane to the road.

The air was moist and daylight had broken the night sky. McNeill turned right out of the lane onto the road. Soon the tarmac gave way to stone and cinder and more hills began to appear, taking the place of the green fields on either side. McNeill drove on; Fitz was half asleep, Dmitri groaned with pain. Fitz woke and reached to touch Dmitri's now sweaty forehead. A fever was beginning to take hold of him; delusion approached. Fitz removed the syringe from the first-aid kit and injected half of the morphine it contained into Dmitri, who was immediately lulled into a slumber. The stone and cinder road became bumpy and rocky.

'We are not making good time,' said Fitz.

'Good time?' enquired McNeill coldly. 'Good time? To what and where?' he added stonily.

'Exactly,' came Fitz's reply.

They drove on; McNeill driving, Fitz half dozing, half awake, Dmitri hallucinating on a morphine-induced trip. Fitz and McNeill were hungry but Dmitri was out of it, away in his own mind with no need for food.

'We will come across some friendly town or village somewhere, get Dmitri a doctor and then we can eat,' Fitz said to McNeill. Thinking positive made him feel better, until McNeill retorted, 'Yeah, only if it's friendly,' as he drove slowly over holes in the road.

Some hours later McNeill could see the outskirts of a town; he stopped the jeep and got out. A cooling breeze blew over the side of his face from the hillside to the left, refreshing him. McNeill peered through the rifle sight at the town below then returned to the jeep and jabbed a sleeping Fitz in his ribs. Without a word Fitz got out and looked through the sight at the town below. There was a roadblock just outside the town, the guards on duty dressed in the same uniforms as themselves.

'OK, let's go,' said Fitz. McNeill drove on slowly and they approached the roadblock, stopping short of it. A young man in his early twenties approached and barked in some unintelligible tongue. McNeill wound down the window then looked at Fitz. Fitz pointed to the prone, wounded Dmitri in the rear seats. The sentry looked in, saw Dmitri and shouted. Another soldier ran from behind the roadblock, jumped onto the side of the jeep alongside McNeill, holding himself by the frame where front and rear doors met by his arm through each window and he began pointing furiously. The roadblock was lifted; McNeill drove through, following the soldier's finger prompting directions, and arrived at the hospital tent. Dmitri was carried in and unceremoniously dumped onto a slab in front of a doctor. McNeill and Fitz watched the operation performed there and then in a room where hygiene was non-existent, full of the wounded, with bloodstained towels, floors and walls. A nurse bandaged Dmitri and he was taken to a bed. The two men walked outside for a breath of fresh air, then lit cigarettes. They smoked and looked round.

The town was rather quiet and mundane. Although the hospital was full of wounded, there seemed a definite lack of urgency. Both men sensed the war had a somewhat lackadaisical edge to it here – either the war hadn't reached here or it had passed it by. They began thinking of food and rest when from their right side approached three men, two of whom spoke. Fitz and McNeill looked at each other quizzically, not understanding a word, until the third man, about 5 foot 10 inches in height, over 14 stone, with slick black hair, piercing blue eyes and two-day-old-stubble, politely asked, 'Come with me, Americans, please.'

McNeill and Fitz followed on and were led to a small house. Parked outside was their Nissan jeep. They entered the house and were shown into a dimly lit room; a small man sat alone behind the huge desk, the rest of the room was empty. On the desk in front of the man were McNeill and Fitz's M21 rifles and ammunition. The little man spoke and the other three men stood immediately to attention. The man with the slick black hair interpreted for McNeill and Fitz.

It was an amateur debriefing compared to the ones Fitz and McNeill had had to endure in the past, but nonetheless quick and thorough. McNeill and Fitz were given back their rifles and taken to a barn that served as a food hall. After eating they were shown to a small house with two beds in it. McNeill and Fitz sat down and cleaned, rebuilt and reloaded their rifles. Fitz began recounting aloud their escape, but after ten minutes realised he was talking to himself. McNeill was there opposite, but far away, his eyes sullen and sunken, his mind detached from this world, lodged in his past, stuck at the time of the explosion in the cafe which took his beloved wife and daughter, the explosion which shattered and ended his world.

———≈·◆·≈———

Two days passed, two relaxing days, two boring days, that led into a third. No news of Dmitri. On the fourth day two men came and brought Fitz and McNeill to the little plump man. Here they were assigned to the command of Yiddich, the man of the slick black hair and piercing blue eyes who spoke English. Fitz and McNeill were ushered into the rear seats of the Nissan jeep. Yiddich sat in the passenger seat next to the driver. Two cars in front and one behind accompanied them.

'How's Dmitri?' asked Fitz.

'He'll live,' came the droll reply from the passenger seat. There was a pause before Yiddich continued, 'He also says you, Fitz, are an extremely good shot, but you, McNeill, are deadly accurate; the best he has seen. I wonder?'

The small convoy exited the town on the south-east, stopping a few miles out at a ramshackle rifle range. McNeill and Fitz both sensed a test of their prowess. All occupants got out of the cars. McNeill and Fitz were shown targets and ordered to fire. Both men hit perfect bullseyes, firing five rounds each at 300- and 400-yard targets, and again at 500 and 600. Fitz then hit four perfect and one inner at 900 yards, McNeill five perfect. The men watching applauded.

'Nice shooting,' said Yiddich, adding, 'Dmitri was right. Welcome to my team.'

They returned to camp. That night they were sent out on night patrol, and the same for the next two nights. This followed a day inside the town, doing nothing.

Yiddich's patrol were then moved 80 miles south-west. They arrived at the new camp in the afternoon heat, and were given barracks. McNeill and Fitz slung in their gear then decided to look around.

The camp was on an elevated plateau with nothing to the north-east or west, only grassland and the road on which they had arrived, but behind it and to the south was a small town. Between it and the camp existed a no-man's-land. Barbed wire ran along the rear of the camp. A sentry post was at the centre in front of another two posts in tall buildings. Fitz looked on. He could see pockmarked houses and apartments across a short grass and shale area below where he stood. Where he stood was the same height as if he was looking into the fourth floor of the six-floor buildings in the town.

He saw a distant road which ran alongside the apartments; some were windowless, and the road had overturned cars on it. Between the road and the fence for the end of no-man's-land was a grass verge, where children were playing football, amongst other games. When the football went over the fence into no-man's-land they stopped and looked towards the sentry outpost and pointed in unison at the ball. The children waited as the sentry raised his binoculars and looked through, then raised a blue flag. A sniper behind him took aim as the child climbed over the fence. The sniper watched, the sentry watched, Fitz watched, the children watched as the child retrieved the ball, kicked it back over the fence, then climbed the fence to his friends. The sentry lowered the flag, the sniper relaxed and the child returned to his game. Fitz lit up a cigarette as he and McNeill walked to the sentry post.

The post was made of iron sheets nailed to timber, a makeshift shed with filing cabinets, red material, two desks, two chairs, telephone, radio and the flag, blue cloth clipped to a broom handle. Fitz and now McNeill were calmly smoking their cigarettes. Fitz offered a cigarette to the sentry who took it and lit up. Fitz asked to look through his binoculars, gesturing with his hands to make himself understood. The sentry passed him his binoculars. Fitz looked at the town below. He saw a wooden walkway from the town up the steep slope to the plateau, but it didn't come up in a straight line, it was purposely made to zigzag up the slope and it stopped 50 yards short of the sentry post with a gate across. Fitz returned the binoculars to the sentry, then headed back to the barracks with McNeill where they ate and slept.

The next day saw the men in the barracks respond to a shooting in the town. Nothing was found, but a little girl gave Fitz a small doll. She smiled a toothless smile and waved at him as she went away, her pigtails bobbing up and down. *Lovely,* thought Fitz as they returned to camp. Fitz stopped at the sentry post, took the binoculars from the sentry and looked back at the town. The pockmarks in the apartment walls were bullet holes, which explained the glassless windows with boards on them; the overturned cars had bullet holes in them too. He gave the binoculars back to the sentry and headed towards the camp. He reached the tall buildings and went silently past, lighting up a cigarette. Three shots rang out from the building alongside him. Turning, he saw a red flag elevated at the sentry post. He ran back to it.

The sentry was laughing as he lowered the red flag. Fitz grabbed the binoculars and looked through.

He looked at the buildings across – nothing – then to where the child climbed the fence – nothing – then he looked at the bottom of the zigzagged walkway. He felt a tightening in his stomach. He saw a dead cat, two dead dogs, shot for target practice. He moved the binoculars up the wooden walkway, and there he saw the bodies of two children, a boy and a girl, neither above six years of age. He took his head away from the binoculars, moved it to one side and retched. The sentry laughed. Fitz threw the binoculars at him and stormed into the camp.

Fitz joined McNeill in the barracks. He looked at McNeill, and the caring compassion of Fitz was met by the empty stare of McNeill, void of emotion and feeling. Fitz went for a shower. The next two nights saw uneventful night patrol duty for both of them. The next three days and nights passed slowly.

━━━►◆◄━━━

One day saw Fitz posted to sentry duty at the south side. McNeill was his sniper in the building behind and on his right and one other of Yiddich's men behind to his left. A lovely sunny day passed with Fitz eating fruit and listening to music on the radio. Once relieved they returned to the barracks. The next day once again saw Fitz on sentry duty. McNeill, who was on night patrol, slept in. Fitz once again sat with radio on, eating oranges and occasionally peering through binoculars.

Fitz saw something shaking, passed it by, and then returned to look again – a figure waving a makeshift flag on the edge of no-man's-land at the beginning of the walkway. The snipers behind saw it and moved their fingers to the triggers of their rifles. Fitz looked at the little girl carrying a stick with a white piece of cloth attached to it. Fitz lifted the blue flag and the snipers stood down. The little girl came up the walkway, past the dead dogs and cats, past where the children were shot. As she came up the wooden walkway Fitz recognised her as the girl with the pigtails and tooth-less grin who had given him the doll over a week earlier. He smiled.

McNeill had showered and was dressing himself. Once dressed, he went out into the sunshine, lit a cigarette and looked at the lighter he had used – it was Fitz's, so he decided to return it to him and began to make his way to the sentry post.

Fitz looked on as the little girl came closer, her left hand holding the stick with the white piece of material on, and her right hand behind her back as she began to skip towards the gate, singing. Fitz sat in the chair, put his booted feet on the desk and with the charred book he had found in the desk drawer waved the little girl over the gate. She pushed the stick through the mesh on the gate, climbed over, collected the stick and began to cross the 50 yards towards Fitz.

McNeill was approaching the buildings where the snipers were stationed. Fitz stood, a gentle smile met his lips as the little pig-tailed girl stopped just a few yards from him. She smiled at him, dropped the stick from her left hand and threw something at Fitz from out of her right hand, waved to him, then turned and ran. The snipers opened fire. Something metal hit Fitz's chest and fell as he looked and saw the girl fall, shot in the back, her body life-less before it hit the ground. Fitz looked down, and saw it just before it exploded. BOOM! A blinding shock of light, a deafening bang, a shock wave pulsation all at the same time. Shrapnel flew in all directions, hundreds of red hot tiny pieces of metal whizzed through the air, pinging off and ripping through the metal sentry post. Fitz fell to the ground along with the dust and debris.

McNeill was less than 50 yards away and the whirlwind of the aftermath spun him round then to the ground. He got to his feet with the realisation that Fitz had been blown to smithereens and he ran to what remained of the sentry post. He clawed at the twisted metal, throwing it behind him; what he saw was unrecog-nisable as Fitz. McNeill stood and looked at the cigarette lighter with the realisation of losing everyone and everything, emptiness ebbing through him. The fact that he was now totally alone in a foreign country, a foreign war, fighting for a foreign cause, hit home. What did he face – survival or death? To learn how to begin to live or to learn to begin to die – his choice.

Seconds later soldiers were bundling him into the camp, back to the barracks, where Yiddich was waiting. McNeill was bewildered, dazed, trying to think, but thinking in a void as they bundled him into the Nissan jeep along with his pack and rifle. They were moving out: new orders, new assignment.

The Nissan jeep and two cars, a Ford Capri containing four men and a Ford Cortina containing two men and rations, left the base heading south-east. They drove till nightfall then pulled off the road. Eight men bedded down under the cold night sky while two others stayed on guard. McNeill was one of the eight. He was in the numbness of shock. He could hear and see Fitz laughing, joking, smoking, pointing. The words 'eat when you can, sleep when you can' echoed in his mind. The guards changed four hours later. McNeill watched through half open eyes. Two hours later the call to get up and move out came. Dawn had not yet broken, there was a damp chill and rain was in the air. McNeill had not slept. His senses were still paralysed. He climbed into the rear seat of the jeep and stared blankly out of the window.

The small convoy rejoined the tarmac road for little over half an hour before it took off on a dirt track road to the right. Rain began to fall heavier and heavier as they began to climb, the Capri in front of the Nissan jeep, the Cortina behind. The higher they went the worse the dirt track became. Potholes became small craters, large stones barred their way and slowed progress. Rain lashed the cars. Rain lashed the dirt track. Thunder bellowed in the sky. In the jeep Yiddich was becoming agitated, annoyed. He checked his watch compulsively. McNeill stared an empty stare, locked away in his despair and self-pity, but the soldier in him was beginning to awaken and become fine-tuned. The convoy climbed the mountain dirt track road, a sheer drop on one side. Rain drops hit the road and cars like hailstones.

The convoy stopped. Yiddich got out in the lashing rain and stormed over to the driver of the Capri.

'What's up? Get a move on, we are falling further and further behind schedule. Move it!' Yiddich yelled.

The driver of the Capri complained, saying in this rain and on this road and with no windscreen wipers he was going as fast as he could. Yiddich drew his pistol, narrowed his eyes

'Drive or die,' he said through clenched teeth.

The Capri roared off. The rain pelted down. Yiddich returned to the jeep and they drove off. Yiddich saw the brake lights of the Capri, then saw it lurch to the right. In the heavy rain the driver hit a large rock, and then plunged into a pothole, snapping the steering rod underneath. The rear end of the car moved round to the right, dragging the front with it just where the road gave way before a 180-degree hairpin bend, slipping the Capri over the edge and down the sheer drop. It fell down the rock face, down to the valley below, the grit and stones from where it slipped over accompanying it. The jeep stopped and the Cortina behind nearly rammed into the jeep.

All the men except McNeill got out. In the music of the dancing rain they heard the last screams of the men in the Capri, heard the thud of metal on rock, then rock and stone on metal. The screams died. The Capri was rolling over, crushing itself and whoever was inside it, the rain tumultuous. The soldiers returned to the jeep and Cortina. Rain battered both vehicles incessantly. Yiddich ordered the driver to pull the jeep away from the sheer drop and stop. The driver pulled over and killed the engine. The incessant rain sounded like machine gunfire on the jeep's roof. McNeill closed his eyes, sleep took him.

He woke to the noise of Yiddich screaming at the driver outside the jeep. The rain had abated. McNeill got out and stretched. The other passenger in the jeep was talking to the two men in the Cortina. McNeill walked over to Yiddich and the driver.

'What's up, Yiddich?' McNeill said, looking up the road towards where the Capri had slid to oblivion. The rain had washed most of the shale which made the road off down the mountainside with the Capri, leaving a wide deep hollow across the road.

'The driver says it's impossible to cross. He wants to go back, which is also impossible. He says the cinder will shift under the weight of the jeep and it will slide over the side. We have many miles to go and we are way behind schedule. We have to cross that gap somehow,' explained Yiddich.

McNeill walked the few yards to the cutting. Near the edge, the shale was extremely loose. It was firmer nearer the inside verge bordering rock, although the cutting was deeper and narrower. McNeill bent down on one knee, looking at the cutting and feeling the shale, then got up and returned to the men, where he found Yiddich, pistol drawn and pointing level with the driver of the jeep's head as he sat behind the steering wheel.

'What's up, Yiddich?' asked McNeill again.

'He says he will not drive the jeep any further, says it's impossible to cross over and refuses to go on. I told him I would shoot him if he disobeys my orders. He says go ahead, death is easier by the bullet than to be crushed like the Capri. I'm deciding whether to shoot him or not,' Yiddich replied.

'Save your bullets, I'll drive,' said McNeill.

'Get out!' Yiddich yelled at the driver. 'Let the American drive,' he added.

The driver got out, handed McNeill the keys, looked at him then at the other men, making a clockwise circular motion with the index finger of his right hand at the side of his temple, then pointed to the whereabouts of the Capri in the valley somewhere below. The other men laughed. McNeill calmly got into the jeep's driver's side, put the keys in the ignition and turned on the engine. He selected four-wheel drive, put the gear lever in first gear, gunned the accelerator to the floor at the same time holding the clutch and handbrake, spinning the wheels, showering the men and Ford Cortina behind with shale and dirt. Then he dropped the handbrake and sped up the hill, slamming the gear lever into second gear.

McNeill headed for the cutting and its 10-foot wide gap, driving the driver's side wheels onto the grass verge bordered with rock. Potholes and rock jolted the jeep. McNeill drove on, undeterred. He hit the cutting, at the same time tugging the steering wheel to the right, bringing the front wheel down from the verge and into the cutting, then he jerked the steering wheel to his left. 'Bite and grip,' he swore at the front wheels, the road edge coming closer. The rear wheel bounced off the verge, lifting the left front wheel off the ground. McNeill kept the accelerator pedal pressed to the metal floor; the left front wheel span frantically in the air while the right front wheel fought tooth and nail to grip the shale underneath it. Oblivion loomed via the mountainside. The men below looked on, the driver smiling. The left front wheel returned to the ground and spun shale under the jeep's floor rapidly, before finding grip and pulling the other wheel up and onto the road on the cutting's far side. The rear wheels followed the front ones, bouncing up onto the track road at the far side. Shale slipped away from the passenger side rear wheel and the jeep began to sway but McNeill soon corrected and controlled the jeep. Shale spluttered down the mountainside. Stones flew backwards until McNeill stopped, got out and walked back to Yiddich and calmly asked, 'Have you got any rope?'

'In the Cortina,' came the reply. 'Why?' he added.

'Drive the car to the trench on the left near the verge. I'll be on the other side with the jeep. Then pass me the rope,' McNeill said, and walked off.

Yiddich ordered the driver to drive to the trench. The driver stopped at the trench, got out and threw the rope to McNeill. McNeill tied the rope to the rear of the jeep, then, throwing the rope back to the driver he motioned to him to tie the rope's end to the Cortina. Yiddich joined McNeill.

'What's next, American?' he asked.

'Heaviest men sit in the jeep while I drive. As the Cortina's driver is the lightest he draws the short straw and drives the car; no passengers. We roll the car back and the jeep back, so the jeep is at the trench, take the strain on the rope, then it's pedal to the floor and we drag that car over if we have to, but he must drive exactly like I did. We can't pull if he is head first in the cutting as the Cortina will just bury itself in this side of the cutting here,' McNeill explained.

Yiddich went back to the Cortina driver and explained the plan. The men got into the jeep. Yiddich decided to watch.

The Nissan jeep and the Cortina rolled backwards, and when the rear of the jeep was almost in the cutting Yiddich gave the signal to go. The Cortina driver and McNeill took off driving forward at the same time and the rope remained taut. The Cortina mounted the stony verge on its driver's side then slewed into the cutting, as the jeep had previously done. The rear of the jeep was pulled from left to right again as its wheels fought against the loose shale for grip, spinning and gripping, sliding, spinning and gripping. The Cortina driver yanked the steering wheel to the left and its front rose. McNeill felt the jeep judder backwards and forwards but climb steadily. The men alongside, anxious, sweaty, saw the front of the Cortina pull up but not over the cutting edge. Another judder from the jeep, and its rear wheels slewed perilously close to the sheer drop. Its front wheels spun, roaring and gnarling at the shale underneath. The rope reached breaking point, the men inside sat, ashen-faced.

McNeill focussed intently and pressed the accelerator pedal to the metal floor. The jeep recovered and started to pull the Cortina up and over the cutting, its engine screaming, its rear wheels fighting for grip, its driver with his boot ramming the accelerator to the floor. The shale wanted to deposit the Cortina with the Capri. Its rear end slid towards the sheer drop. The driver, now white with fear, pressed harder on an already-rammed-to-the-floor accelerator. Cold sweat ran down his face and his hands locked on the steering wheel. The Cortina's rear end was slipping towards the edge, oblivion clawing at its boot.

McNeill in the jeep was pushing against the steering wheel, urging the jeep onwards and upwards, willing the jeep's tyres to grip in the shale then pull, pull before the Cortina went over the edge and pulled them backwards and over too. The Cortina and the jeep both skidded around in the shale in a tug of war with oblivion, but the jeep kept pulling, its wheels clawing at the shale until they gained purchase and pulled the Cortina on, its rear wheels franticly spinning in their quest for grip, its rear end now over the edge. The jeep clawed its way up slowly at first, the rope sinews stretched to breaking point, then finally clear of the drop. The Cortina roared after the jeep on finding grip.

McNeill drove on, rounding the hairpin bend, and pulled the Cortina bumpily over a smaller cutting before stopping. The radiator in the jeep was close to boiling over, so McNeill left the engine running, put the heater on full blast, pulled the handbrake and got out. The men in the jeep got out. The Cortina driver left the car engine running, handbrake on, door open and threw up on the roadside. The knots on the rope were so tight that Yiddich had to cut the rope to separate the two vehicles. Yiddich checked his wristwatch and a scowl met his face – hours lost, four men and a car lost.

'Load up!' he yelled. 'Move, we have no time.'

McNeill returned to the rear seat of the Nissan and went to sleep. The climb of the shale mountain road eased at the summit, and eventually they drove on a dirt road across a lush short grass plateau. The rain had now ceased entirely and the sun broke through the clouds. The mountains and hills receded. McNeill slept. The two vehicles sped on, occasionally passing people. McNeill woke and looked through the window to see people tending crops in a field. Some waved; nobody waved back. Yiddich checked his watch yet again, his features stone-like, impassive.

A man in a hurry is a dangerous man to be around, thought McNeill.

The dirt road ceded into tarmac.

'Faster, faster,' Yiddich said to the driver through clenched teeth. McNeill looked on.

The Cortina began to fall behind. Fields and outbuildings and occasional cottages flashed by, then the tarmac on the road ended, returning to dirt and stone, and daylight began to fade. The driver slowed and Yiddich glared. The road became even more uneven and the driver slowed down further. Night was beginning to overtake day. Yiddich admitted defeat.

'Find somewhere to pull over. We bed down for the night,' Yiddich ordered. The Cortina caught up, stopped, and the hungry men bedded down to sleep. McNeill was on first watch with one other. Four hours later Yiddich relieved him, telling him to sleep. McNeill was hungry and restless.

The men were called two hours later. McNeill was already awake. The men packed their things into the two vehicles and set off. Daylight had not yet crept into the night sky and progress was initially slow, but once dawn broke they began to move quicker. It was overcast, the air fresh and moist when the two vehicles entered a small village at the foot of some hills some three hours later. The village had one road in and one road out. The road was level enough as it ran through the village, then rose to a fork in the road just outside where a large house sat overlooking the domain below. Yiddich ordered the driver to stop at the village end and everyone got out. Yiddich climbed into the jeep driver's seat and drove the rest of the way to the large house.

McNeill looked round. The Cortina pulled up a short distance behind and the driver ran into the house alongside. McNeill scanned round; six houses on one side quite close together with two more behind, five on the other with hills to the rear, one lone house at the opposite end of the village to the large house, nestled on the road fork. The road was tarmac. McNeill eyed the big house – good vantage point, able to see the whole south approach. McNeill knew whoever was in the house was higher ranking than Yiddich and that they knew they were coming into the village long before they arrived. Some of the villagers came out of their houses. It was then McNeill realised he was alone; the rest of the men had all gone into different houses.

A teenage girl wearing a headscarf and green coat walked towards him, stopped, took his arm and brought him to a small cottage near the big house, in the fork but below it and on its left. They entered and McNeill was greeted by a woman whom he took to be the girl's mother but he didn't understand her. The cottage was neat and tidy and McNeill glanced around. A picture of a proud man with his arm around a young soldier in uniform was on the mantelpiece over the open fire, which was lit. Either side of the fireplace were two doors. It came to McNeill's knowledge later that these were bedrooms. The kitchen was off to the left of the door they had just entered as he looked back at it; more pictures of the soldier in uniform adorned the far walls. The girl closed the front door, removed her scarf and coat to reveal a fine figure and ash blonde hair. A beautiful girl in the last stages of her teens.

McNeill left his rifle by the front door and was shown to a chair at the kitchen table. He sat down and the girl gave him stew and bread while the mother made tea. McNeill was hungry. The stew was appetising and tasted gorgeous. He ate up, and the girl brought more. Tea arrived. McNeill ate and drank his fill and turned to watch the girl tend the fire. Her mother appeared from behind a door on the fireplace's right and beckoned to McNeill. He walked over to her and she showed him the room with the freshly made bed, then put the palms of her hands together and brought them up to her cheek, tipping her head slightly. The sign for sleep. McNeill went to the front door, collected his rifle and returned to the bedroom. He placed his rifle down alongside the bed, took off his boots, put his pistol under the pillow, his knife under the bed, removed his clothes and climbed into bed. Sleep came and took hold.

⇒◆⇐

McNeill woke in the evening to the sound of raised voices and the smell of tea. He got out of bed and dressed quietly before entering the main room. The voices stilled at the sight of him. McNeill poured tea for himself and offered a quiet hello to the young soldier sat at the kitchen table. The young soldier, the girl and her mother eyed McNeill as he raised the mug of hot tea to his lips. The young soldier had been shouting at the girl and her mother, who were now apprehensive.

'What's wrong?' McNeill asked the girl, who replied, 'The soldier is here to bring you to the general, and you were to be woken immediately. My mother and I wanted you to sleep a little longer as you looked very tired. I see we have woken you, I'm sorry.'

'Thanks,' said McNeill as the soldier began to shout.

McNeill turned to the soldier. 'Tell the general I will be along after I have drunk my tea.'

'Nobody keeps the general waiting,' the young soldier retorted.

'Go,' said McNeill. 'Before I spank your arse,' he added.

The girl laughed. The young soldier gave her a look of hatred and anger as he left.

McNeill finished his tea, collected his rifle, thanked the girl and her mother and began to make his way to the general's house. He stopped before the fork in the road and looked up at the gable end with the door in the centre. There were windows either side and two more windows above, and a small decked area in front of the door. McNeill stood there and pondered. He guessed that right now, right at this very moment, two rifles were trained on him. He put the rifle across the back of his head, resting across the tops of both shoulders, his right arm over the barrel and his left over the stock. He walked slowly to the front door, which opened as he approached the decking, confirming his suspicion.

A young soldier and another much older, battle-hardened soldier met him. 'Please, leave your weapons here,' the war veteran said. McNeill rested his rifle, took out his pistol and hung it on a nail on the balustrade, then the knife, which he deposited in the handrail. The young soldier searched McNeill and found nothing; McNeill entered the house. There were stairs immediately in front of him about 4 feet wide going straight up to a balcony, with rooms either side behind. A hallway ran behind the stairs to a kitchen, but before the kitchen were two closed doors on his right, guarding what was behind. A door on McNeill's left opened, and he was shown into the room by the war veteran.

Behind the desk sat a balding man of about fifty years of age, thick set with dark piercing eyes and a strong jaw. Yiddich was standing on his right. McNeill was given a chair and told to sit. The general stood, breathed in to his sturdy, broad frame and drew himself up to his full 6 feet 3 in height, then turned to Yiddich. The conversation started in Croatian then turned to English.

'This is General Tomelsky of the Croatian Army, my commander in chief, and he does not like to be kept waiting, McNeill,' Yiddich began, looking distastefully at McNeill.

The general stared at McNeill through dark, venomous eyes. Voices shouted outside, followed by a knock on the door. The general nodded and the war veteran opened the door, letting a soldier in. 'A car is fast approaching and the snipers have their rifles on it and are awaiting orders, sir,' he said.

'What kind of car is it?' asked the general sternly.

'Bashed up Land Rover, grey,' came the reply.

A wry smile met the general's lips. 'Snipers to stand down. Let him through,' he boomed.

The Land Rover careered to a halt outside the house. A young man got out and opened the passenger door. He dragged a heavily pregnant young woman out, and as she resisted he shoved her through the front door. He brought her straight into the general's office. The general looked with eyes of hatred to the woman and back. 'I see you found her,' he hissed, 'my disgrace of a daughter,' he added with contempt. Suddenly, an older woman burst into the room screaming in Croatian, tears streaming down her face, throwing her arms round the pregnant daughter.

'Get them out of here, NOW!' the general boomed, slamming his fists onto the desk. 'I will deal with them later,' he added icily.

The two women were quickly manhandled into the kitchen and the older woman began to shout. McNeill looked at the general, whose dark eyes began to narrow, his jaw locked, teeth now grinding. Rage was taking over as he stormed out of the room. The powerful brute, who must have weighed about 16 stone, dragged the two women from the kitchen and into a room off to the side of the stairs. McNeill heard the door slam shut and the general's voice reverberating with anger, then what sounded like a slap. A chair moved, a young woman's raised voice called out, then there was a definite slap. Shouting began then, and ended with the women's tears.

'What's going on, Yiddich?' asked McNeill.

'No business of yours, American,' came the reply, with a hooded look.

The general left the room like an enraged bull, slamming the door shut and leaving the two crying women inside. He re-entered the room where Yiddich and McNeill were. He paced round to the desk and leaned forward, resting his weight on his strong arms to face the seated McNeill. The general spoke, his anger now controlled. His dark eyes danced.

'McNeill, you are now under the command of Yiddich here. Yiddich is from this village, an admirable officer, and he serves me loyally.' His stare intensified before he continued. 'All that Polish wife has ever given me is grief and two daughters, but if I had a son I hope he would be like Yiddich,' he said, pointing at Yiddich. 'Now go – go to the house from where you came,' he said slowly, his stare locked on McNeill.

McNeill rose from the chair, saluted, turned and left the room, closing the door behind him. He made sure he had shut the door properly then looked up, and out of his left eye he glimpsed the pregnant girl now across from him leaving the room. She had been weeping and had a red mark on her left cheek. She looked at him with distaste. McNeill nodded his head in respect and went outside. The front door closed behind him. McNeill collected his pistol, knife and rifle, took out a cigarette and lit it with Fitz's lighter. He looked at the lighter as he ran it through his fingers. He heard more shouting in the house behind him, half turned, then thought of the soldiers on duty behind the door, more in the house, sentries and snipers upstairs. He returned to the little house where the blonde teenage girl was waiting with the door open. He went in and the girl asked him what had happened.

Her eyes lit up as McNeill told her of the heavily pregnant girl, and when he told her of what had happened to her the light in the girl's eyes went out. She then told McNeill that the pregnant girl was Alina, the general's daughter, that the other woman was her mother, the general's second wife, and how Alina used to babysit her when she was younger, playing games and having fun, and what a wonderful woman she was. The blonde girl's mother gave McNeill stew and bread and brought tea. Again, McNeil ate his full then retired to the bedroom to sleep.

McNeill was restless and woke early. He tried to go back to sleep but couldn't, and as dawn broke he got up and went to the kitchen, put the teapot on the lit stove and made tea. He went outside, lit a cigarette and sat down, cigarette in one hand, mug of tea in the other. He looked towards the general's house, thought he saw something move and looked more intently. A grey Land Rover crept towards the general's house and stopped. A figure got out and walked slowly to the house. The door opened and Alina, the general's heavily pregnant daughter was shepherded to the Land Rover and manhandled into the passenger seat. The figure then got in the driver's side and McNeill made out one more figure sat in the back. McNeill watched the Land Rover go uphill to the right of the general's house. He took a pull on the cigarette, watched the doors close on the general's house and everything became still. McNeill smoked the cigarette then looked at the village and its surroundings, so peaceful and serene. He drank the rest of the mug of tea, went inside, stoked the fire, then sat down and dozed off.

The blonde teenager came into the room and McNeill woke. She looked happy and cheerful and was putting clothes into a large bag. She turned to McNeill, saying, 'Please could you give these to Alina the next time you visit the general's house.'

'Don't bother, she left earlier,' said McNeill, looking at her.

The joy in her face evaporated to sadness instantly.

Hours later McNeill was taken to the general's house. The general was in a hurry. The Nissan jeep was brought to the house. The general and three others ran to the jeep, got in, and the jeep roared off to the left of the house. Yiddich casually came into McNeill's view.

'I see you have brought your rifle. You are going to need it,' Yiddich said with sarcastic undertones.

A Ford Cortina arrived at the house and the driver got out. McNeill, two others and Yiddich went towards the car. The soldiers put their rifles in the boot. McNeill looked at the two sniper rifles before adding his own. McNeill sat in the passenger seat and Yiddich drove off to the right of the house uphill for a while through a small copse then onto open road. Yiddich continued for an hour, checked his watch, drove for another hour, then slowed and pulled off the road. He stopped the car and ordered everyone to get out and take their rifles from the boot, then drove off, returning some twenty minutes later. He strode up, sucking his teeth.

'Your target will be arriving in a couple of hours or so – two cars. Find positions and no, I repeat, no survivors,' he stated coldly.

McNeill did not move. He took the sight from his rifle and surveyed the road and terrain. He saw a small cluster of trees and thick bush 50 yards further on slightly to his left. 'Perfect,' he said. Yiddich overheard.

'What? Explain,' said Yiddich.

'The cluster of trees is on higher ground to the road's left, and will give good cover if anything goes wrong. Let's go there and take a look,' McNeill said.

The four men went to the trees and bushes. McNeill surveyed again. 'Look – just below, the road comes out of a bend. There would be a clear clean shot here, but only for a couple of minutes. What we need is a spotter further down to say what's approaching and whether it's the target. Yiddich, as you are the only one who knows the target, that's going to be you,' said McNeill.

'Off you go,' said McNeill, taking out a piece of elastic and clasping it to a tree trunk. A twisted smile pursed Yiddich's mouth. He turned to one of the other soldiers and sent him to act as spotter. McNeill put the rifle barrel through the elastic, down, up, over, down and through. He played the scene in his mind, looking through the sight which was now attached to the M21 rifle. He reckoned the distance to be 700 yards. He removed the rifle from the elastic cord, sat down and opened his cigarette packet: two cigarettes left. He lit one and began to draw in the smoke. After he had smoked the cigarette he looked below at the spotter in the grass looking up the road, then McNeill lay down.

'Keep an eye on the spotter, one of you,' he said, looking at Yiddich. An hour passed. Yiddich took out his cigarettes and offered them round. McNeill smoked a cigarette and lay on his back. Almost an hour later the spotter lifted his arm.

'This is them,' cried Yiddich excitedly. 'Look!'

McNeill sprang up, slipped the rifle through the elastic as before and adjusted it. The other sniper lay in a prone position a little further in front and to the left.

'OK. What's he saying, Yiddich?' asked McNeill.

'Two cars approaching with hostiles inside,' Yiddich relayed.

McNeill swung the rifle and watched the spotter through the telescopic sight. The spotter was now slipping down into the grass and aiming his rifle. He was 250 yards in front of McNeill to his right. McNeill trained his sight on the exit of the bend in the road and waited. The black front of a Volvo car appeared. Without hesitation, McNeill fired two shots at where the driver would be sitting, then after a slight adjustment two more bullets left the M21 barrel aimed at the Volvo's passenger side. The windscreen shattered, the four death projectiles found their victims and the car shuddered to a halt.

The dark blue Zephyr behind crashed into the rear of the stricken Volvo just as its rear doors were opening, lunging it forward. Shots from the spotter and the other sniper entered the Zephyr. McNeill fired off two more at the man leaving the rear passenger side of the Volvo and watched him fall. Yiddich was now running down the incline towards the immobilised vehicles. Reaching them, he sprayed firstly the Volvo with pistol bullets then the Zephyr, laughing. Psychopathic joy was etched on his face and he never heard the click, click, click of the empty magazine. He opened the driver's side rear door of the Volvo and a lifeless body flopped out. The mayhem and slaughter was all over in a matter of minutes.

The spotter was next to arrive at the bloodbath, then the sniper, and finally McNeill. They pulled the dead from the cars, laid the corpses at the roadside, then dragged the soldier McNeill had shot leaving the Volvo and stretched him out beside his comrades. A mesmerising delight shone on Yiddich's face as he looked at the corpses − six dead soldiers all in their late twenties/early thirties, two dead older men in their late fifties. McNeill eyed the bodies; all wore the same uniform as he did, the two older men high-ranking officers. He eyed Yiddich, now searching the two cars, and saw him collect a briefcase from each one then turn and come alongside him.

'You are extremely good shot − two to the head, two to the chest, one more each to the chest and head of a moving target,' Yiddich said with an avaricious grin.

The spotter searched the two cars and found two jerry cans filled with petrol. They then pushed the cars off the road.

'Shall we burn them?' the spotter asked Yiddich.

'No, leave them, get back to the car.'

Yiddich brought the car a few moments later and took a makeshift funnel out of the boot. He undid the cap on the car's fuel tank and then released the cap on the jerry can. The spotter then poured the contents of one jerry can into the Cortina's fuel tank. He placed the other jerry can into the boot alongside the briefcases.

'Rifles in the boot and get in − we go. I'll drive,' said Yiddich.

This time McNeill sat in the rear behind the spotter, who occupied the passenger seat. They drove on past the dead men and around the bend. Yiddich beamed as he drove on for an hour in complete and utter self-satisfaction. No one spoke. McNeill wound down the window of the car door and gazed out at the grass-land, the hills left far behind. *Lovely country,* he thought. The other men began to talk among themselves. As time passed McNeill became locked away in his silent thoughts of his wife and daughter, and Fitz, all gone: his heart felt loneliness. Another hour and once again hills began to take the place of grassland. McNeill felt the hairs on the back of his neck prickle. Yiddich veered the car to his right, taking another road off the main route. The three other men began laughing and talking loudly. Yiddich drove on. Hills on either side rose majestically out of the ground. Unease began to grip McNeill. Then he heard, above the sound of the laughter in the car, three pistol shots in the distance.

'Stop the car!' McNeill shouted. Yiddich laughed and accel-erated. McNeill pulled his Beretta pistol with his right hand from behind his back, and removed the knife from his boot with his left hand, then jammed the muzzle of the pistol into Yiddich's ribs, the knife to the neck of the sniper sat alongside him. The soldier in the back seat at his side froze as McNeill's ice cold stare met his eyes.

'Pull over. Now,' McNeill said icily.

An enraged Yiddich stopped the car then turned to face McNeill with the look of a wounded animal.

McNeill stared and coldly said, 'One ambush is enough for one day and I don't intend to be the victim of another, and tell your spotter friend, one false move and I shoot you, Yiddich. Now everyone out, slowly.'

They all got out of the Cortina; a nervous tension filled the air. Yiddich glared at McNeill, until the eerie silence was broken by a piercing scream which brought Yiddich back to his senses, and the men too. They got their rifles from the car boot.

'I go left,' said McNeill. 'You,' he said, pointing to the sniper, 'you go right. We climb the hills and go round. They can only be past that turn to the left just ahead,' he added.

The hills on the left were steeper and the sniper to the right made better progress. Yiddich and the spotter moved to the car. McNeill wished for eyes in the back of his head. His dislike of Yiddich was now immense. He watched the sniper on the far side in front of him hold out his left arm and motion to the ground. The sniper stopped, knelt down on one knee and aimed through his telescopic sight, the barrel pointing further up than McNeill's position and to his left. McNeill stopped, readied his M21, looked through his telescopic sight and saw what looked like a woman, her arms raised aloft, her back in full view. He moved the rifle to the right and saw a man pointing his pistol at her.

Crack, crack! The other sniper had sent two rounds. The soldier with the pistol moved to his right on the stony ground. The woman sank to her knees, hands now on the back of her head. Clouds of dust shot up from a point 5 yards in front of the soldier. The sniper had missed his target. McNeill saw his opportunity and squeezed the trigger, sending a messenger of death on its life-taking journey. A hole appeared in the soldier's chest. He rocked back, fired a round from the pistol that missed the woman and fell. McNeill and his fellow sniper gradually moved forward. Yiddich brought the car. The woman on her knees prayed with arms outstretched. As he moved forward McNeill caught a glimpse of a grey Land Rover off the road, its doors open.

The sniper and McNeill reached the woman with Yiddich in close attendance. McNeill gestured to the sniper to go ahead and check. McNeill now recognised the woman as Alina, the general's daughter. Yiddich and the spotter arrived just as the sniper returned.

'Tunnel ahead, sir,' he said to Yiddich.

McNeill was trying to calm Alina. He figured he needed an ally, and none better than the general's daughter, especially with Yiddich now... McNeill looked at her frightened eyes, tried to console her, but she was looking directly past him at Yiddich and shaking uncontrollably with fear. McNeill was desperate, the general's daughter was desperate. McNeill gripped Alina's shoulders in his powerful hands and looked at her. Her mouth was trembling. Yiddich arrived and barged into McNeill, shouting in his native tongue, then drew his pistol and pointed it at her forehead. Without a thought McNeill drew his Beretta and pushed the barrel against Yiddich's head. The soldiers looked on; they, too, had recognised the woman.

'You shoot her, I will kill you,' McNeill said coldly, adding, 'Are you mad? She is going to have a baby and that's the general's daughter, your commander-in-chief.'

'Stay out of this, American,' Yiddich snarled. A sick smile grew on his face. Yiddich lowered his weapon. Rain began to fall and dark clouds filled the sky. A distant rumble of thunder echoed.

'Get into the car,' Yiddich ordered the soldiers. 'You, McNeill – you take the woman to the tunnel on foot.'

Yiddich went back to the Cortina and sped off towards the tunnel. McNeill watched, then turned and went back to the Land Rover. He saw a dead body on the far side of it; bullet holes riddled the engine. A woman's coat was on the rear seat. He retrieved it, took it to Alina, who was now standing, and placed it around her shoulders, then motioned her forward towards the tunnel. Rain poured down. She stood there frozen, gripped by fear as the rain lashed the ground. McNeill went to her and pushed her forward.

Yiddich stood in the centre of the mouth of the tunnel, hands on hips, flanked by his two soldiers. McNeill approached, slightly behind Alina and to her right. Her steps faltered the closer she came to Yiddich. Once in the tunnel Yiddich grabbed Alina and threw her to the ground to his left, glared at McNeill and, sneering, said, 'If you ever pull a gun on me again, I will shoot you the next possible moment.' Then he turned to the two men and yelled in his native tongue, 'If he steps out of line, kill him. We need him, but soon he will become expendable.' They laughed.

Alina looked up from where she had been thrown, straight at McNeill. McNeill looked at her, then at the two Croatian soldiers. He saw their eyes and smiling faces as they made guns out of their fingers, pointing at McNeill, then he saw the hateful scowl on the face of Yiddich. McNeill surmised what Yiddich had said to the two Croatians in their native tongue that instant.

Thunder roared, lightning flashed and lit up the sky, rain pelted the ground. Yiddich yelled, 'Get some sleep – we wait till the storm passes.' McNeill eyed Yiddich, who now sat with his knees pressed into his stomach and chest by his arms. Yiddich visibly shook as again the thunder roared and the lightning cracked and danced across the dark sky.

He's scared, scared of the thunder and lightning, McNeill surmised as he retreated to the side of the tunnel so he could see Yiddich below and slightly to his right and the other two above slightly to his left. Alina was just below the trembling, rocking Yiddich, just out of the rain. An uneasy silence fell inside the tunnel as the storm raged outside. McNeill was on edge, irritable. His gut instinct told him not to sleep – he may not wake, his throat slit from ear to ear, his body left to rot. Just what inside him made him think of survival? Maybe that's what the human mind does? The disquiet in him grew.

Alina was talking to Yiddich quietly, and had been for at least fifteen minutes. *She is goading him, she too knows Yiddich is afraid,* McNeill thought as he looked on. Yiddich spat at her, then grabbed her, dragging her to her feet. He crossed the tunnel from side to side. She fell and Yiddich dragged her along the floor, picked her up and rammed her into a niche in the tunnel wall 10 yards away from McNeill, between McNeill and the tunnel's mouth. Yiddich then threw her to the ground. The two Croatian soldiers looked on. The sniper had dismantled his rifle and was now cleaning it and the other looked away in disgust.

Yiddich kicked Alina's legs, started yelling at her then bent down and smashed a clenched fist into her face. She rolled away and blood began to pour from her nose. She looked up at Yiddich and spat at him. He slapped her across the face, then stood again and kicked her legs. She rolled towards him and he kicked her stomach, shouting 'WHORE!'. She screamed in agony. McNeill jumped up, ran and rugby-tackled Yiddich to the ground. Yiddich began to kick and dig his elbows into McNeill. McNeill rolled. Yiddich pulled his pistol, but McNeill grabbed the pistol-laden hand and the two men wrestled. Neither compromised, no quarter given. Shots were fired from the pistol indiscriminately as the two men grappled.

The two Croatian soldiers now stood, reaching for their weapons. More shots exploded from the pistol and the Croatian sniper fell forward. McNeill wrestled the gun from Yiddich's hand, then smashed his face into the tunnel wall before thumping him in the kidneys. A crack, and a bullet whistled past McNeill, distracting him. Yiddich turned and smashed his right hand into McNeill's stomach. McNeill bent forward to see Yiddich's knee aiming for his face. McNeill grabbed Yiddich's right leg, pushing him backwards. Yiddich buried his right elbow into McNeill's back just below his neck, before his own back crashed into the tunnel wall. Another bullet whistled past McNeill. Then crack, crack, crack, crack, click, click. Out of the corner of his eye McNeill saw the Croatian soldier fall.

Yiddich sank two elbows into his back, and smashed his right hand into his left ribs. McNeill winced as Yiddich's left hand caught him on his right cheek. McNeill staggered backwards, releasing Yiddich. Yiddich reached for his lower leg and pulled his knife, lunging at McNeill. McNeill deflected Yiddich's arm across his own body, turning Yiddich in one movement and pulled his own left arm around Yiddich's neck. Yiddich was now with his back to McNeill's chest. McNeill held Yiddich's fist and brought the knife back to face Yiddich's undefended chest. McNeill was stronger. Yiddich pulled his left arm through to push his right wrist away, to keep the glistening steel away from his torso. McNeill released his neck hold and held the back of his right hand with his left, pulling towards him.

Yiddich's eyes burned wide. He felt his own knife, its sharp point penetrating his skin at his solar plexus, felt droplets of blood as the knife sliced, felt his mouth open, an intake of one short, sharp breath, a slow exhale as the knife sank deeper. Yiddich's resistance failed. He began to cough, his eyes to stare, unblinking. Blood trickled from the side of his mouth. The cough ceased, his body jolted then was still and his breathing stopped. McNeill let him go. Yiddich fell forward, dead, his head resting on the floor. Open unseeing eyes stared at the woman. McNeill looked around.

Yiddich dead, the sniper dead, the spotter dead. He went to the stricken Alina, the empty gun still in her right hand, her face bloodied, her legs wet and bruised. McNeill began to lift her. She screamed in pain, and then started to breathe heavily. Her waters had broken. McNeill looked down at her legs where a trickle of blood showed on her right thigh just above her knee. At that moment her contractions began in earnest. The baby was coming. McNeill felt helpless, powerless, transfixed by her situation. He could not leave her, wanted to help her. Her baby was coming, and it wasn't about to wait for anyone. She breathed heavily, rapid intakes of breath, before one long exhale. She tried to lift her skirt then pointed to the knife in Yiddich's chest. McNeill gave her his own, and she clasped the knife with both hands, pointing the blade at her heart.

McNeill was horrified. He knew she was about to take her own life and that of her unborn child. He grabbed her arms, stopping her, then calmly took the knife from her, raised her skirt, and used the knife to slice through her knickers at the top of both thighs. Pain gripped Alina; her head went backwards. She took two short breaths and one long one escaped from her mouth. Again she screamed in pain and her knees rose up, her legs apart.

McNeill stood up, went over to the dead Croatian sniper, removed his light jacket and placed it between Alina's legs. He then ripped the leather belt from Yiddich, folded it and shoved it across her mouth, telling her to bite hard. She widened her legs, her head went backwards once again, her arms outstretched, her fingers gripping at the tunnel floor. She screamed as her body contracted again.

'Push – push harder,' said McNeill.

The contractions released their grip on her body. Her breathing now was heavy. She began panting, then bit hard on the leather belt. Her body contracted again. McNeill propped her up from behind, then rushed to open her legs. He didn't know what to do, where to be, confused but willing as she pushed and screamed and pushed again. McNeill was now kneeling between her legs. Alina pushed, screamed, sweated, then gripped McNeill's arms and pushed. She let go of McNeill, screaming, and stopped herself from falling backwards by propping herself up. McNeill looked down. The baby's head had appeared.

'Push,' he yelled, 'it's here.'

Again the same procedure, only this time McNeill was excited. He cupped his two hands around the baby's head, supporting it. Alina pushed one more time and the baby eased itself free of her body and slipped gently into McNeill's hands. McNeill then cut the umbilical cord from the placenta, folded it and held it, and rubbed the newborn, which greeted life with a cry. McNeill offered the newborn to Alina, who looked at what she had conceived then looked away in disgust. McNeill did not understand as he held the baby, the perfect beautiful baby – he had no idea what to do next and was getting no help from the baby's mother as she was both too exhausted and refused to acknowledge her baby.

McNeill ran to the car, opened its boot, found a towel and laid the baby on it, all the while rubbing her gently with his powerful hands. He found two bottles of water and gently washed the baby and dried her, then placed the baby on the rear seat. He went to the dead soldier Alina shot earlier, removed his shirt and jacket, and wrapped the baby in them. The baby cried.

McNeill left the baby and returned to Alina, who had now dragged herself to the far wall. *Christ, what is she doing? It's her child,* thought McNeill. Alina was now slumped against the wall, oblivious to her crying child. McNeill bent down and began to clean her, gently dabbing the moist towel on her upper legs. Her skirt was soaked. She was of slim build and so was the soldier she had shot. McNeill got up and removed the dead man's trousers, returned to her and took off the wet skirt, washed and dried her the best he could, then he physically lifted her up, made her stand, supported by the tunnel wall, and moved her away from the mess. He bent down and began massaging her legs to help her skin dry and to get her blood to flow. She had lost one of her shoes. McNeill removed the other then placed her right leg into the right trouser leg, then her left into the left and pulled the trousers up. Alina slumped, the baby cried. McNeill sat Alina down. She was exhausted. Then he remembered the morning – when she was pushed into the Land Rover she carried a bag and he remembered seeing it on the floor of the Land Rover earlier. McNeill dashed through the pelting rain to the Land Rover, grabbed the bag and ran back to the tunnel.

Alina had moved. She had somehow crawled over to the dead soldier and was almost touching his pistol. McNeill ran towards her just as she was trying to free the pistol from the dead hand. McNeill dropped the bag and jumped onto her. In her exhausted state his weight on top of her made her stop and release the pistol and scream in pain. McNeill took the pistol, got up to his knees, rolled Alina away from the dead soldier and onto her back. McNeill returned to the small holdall and opened it.

'Thank God!' he cried. There were towels, baby clothes, cloth nappies, bottles and teats, a tin containing milk formula, and a change of clothes for a woman – trousers, underclothes, skirt, blouse and jumper. McNeill looked at Alina. A wet red patch was now visible at her crotch. He removed the trousers and she never stirred as he dried her again with the towel. He then ripped one of the dry hand towels from the bag in half, put new knickers on her then put the half towel inside her new clean knickers, put the new trousers on, removed her blouse and put on the clean one. Her trousers were too big – he realised this after he lifted her to her feet and they began to slip down – so he carried her to the Cortina and placed her into the passenger seat.

He picked up the leather belt she had bitten on earlier and put two new holes in it with his knife point, then ran the belt around her trousers and fastened it. He removed the boots of one of the dead soldiers – size 42 – and put Alina's size 36 feet into them. *Perfect*, he thought, as he went to the holdall and removed the bottle of milk. He tried to warm the bottle between his hands, and brought the bottle and baby to its mother. She turned her head away from it, her expression and eyes blank. The baby cried. McNeill put the teat of the bottle into the baby's mouth and the newborn sucked.

'Take her, help her,' McNeill begged, but no help was forth-coming. McNeill cradled the newborn in his arm as the baby contentedly sucked on the bottle. He put the baby on the rear seat.

McNeill was a soldier. He surveyed the scene, and realised he was in deep trouble. A whole elite Croatian patrol wiped out, including the general's favourite, one survivor, himself, missing grey Land Rover outside, driver and soldier dead, woman passenger who just happens to be the general's daughter missing. A newborn baby and a mother who wants no part of it. How could he explain that the woman shot the soldier, Yiddich shot the sniper and he killed Yiddich in self-defence? What would happen if a Croatian patrol picked him and Alina up? How would he know what version she would be telling? He couldn't speak the language, nor could he read it, and what about the two carloads of dead Croatians by the roadside at the ambush?

McNeill knew it would only be a matter of time before the general got suspicious at Yiddich's non-return, then he would send another patrol out to find out why. Yiddich was on a mission – whatever was in the briefcases was enough to be killed for. Dressed like they were, he could not surrender to the Serbs, either – he would be shot and so would she. *What a mess – deep shit*, he thought. The only piece of good luck was the thunderstorm; at least no one would be out in that.

McNeill realised they had to move quickly. He collected his

M21 rifle, put the clothes and contents back into the holdall and placed them in the Cortina's boot. He then went to the body of Yiddich, turned him over, removed his cigarettes from his pocket, lit one, and carried out a search of his pockets for anything – pieces of paper, orders, map co-ordinates – but found nothing. Then he collected the dead sniper's rifle and put that into the Cortina's boot.

The baby cried. McNeill wrapped her in the jacket, climbed into the driver's seat, closed the door and leaned across Alina, who just stared ahead as he pushed down the little black door-lock button, locking her in. The baby still cried. McNeill searched for and found the baby's bottle, then lifted the newborn and deposited it between his legs. He started the Cortina's engine, switched the headlights on and headed deeper into the tunnel, put the bottle in the baby's mouth with one hand and held it there as the newborn sucked.

McNeill knew that the milk would not be enough for the child – maybe her mother would oblige? *I'll leave that for now,* he thought, as he drove on. Soon light began to filter through dark, a murky light – they were nearing the tunnel's end. But where were they going to? Anywhere away from here. McNeill exited the tunnel and was met with what proved to be the last of the daylight. It was raining still, but the thunderstorm had abated. The wind-screen wipers coped with the downpour efficiently and effectively. Thankfully, the baby was asleep on his lap. Alina stayed silent and still, staring blankly ahead.

'Speak English?' he asked softly as he lifted the newborn and settled the child on the rear seat in one movement of his right arm. She never flinched.

'Speak English?' he asked, this time with more force. Still no response from the general's daughter. McNeill looked at her, at her shoulder-length black hair, and guessed her age as late twenties/early thirties. She had high cheekbones, was of slim build, with blue eyes, a small mouth and a dainty nose – not overly beautiful but attractive nonetheless, a girl-next-door type, the kind your mother would want you to bring home. A lot going for her but not very good with newborn babies.

McNeill drove on. The hills had given way to flat fields and the tarmac road had given way to dirt and stone miles before. McNeill just drove on in silence, never too fast for the road conditions – the car was now of major importance. He had stopped a couple of times to tend to the baby, cleaning it, trying to feed it, showing it to its mother – her child. He offered the baby to her, trying to get them to bond, but was always met with a blank empty stare and a motioning refusal like she didn't care, the baby non-existent in her world.

He drove for a further half an hour in silence, until the cry of the newborn broke it. McNeill tried to calm the child as best he could, but he knew that without mother's milk the chances of survival for the child were minimal. He knew refusal to bond from mother to child could not be ongoing – the baby would surely die. Food was also a must for both Alina and himself: she would be weak after delivering her baby. He had passed a number of abandoned cottages and buildings, and he began thinking where in hell he was going. *What direction am I and should I be driving in?* Lots of questions with no answers.

The rain eased in the night sky, and off to his left McNeill spotted a cottage. He turned off the road and headed for it. He looked at his watch: 9.45 p.m. He'd known it was late, but he hadn't realised it was so late. Events had taken a hold on him and time had flown. McNeill drove the Cortina up to the cottage door searching for signs of life inside as he did so. He looked at the solitary window and front door. There were no lights, the window was shut and no smoke came from the chimney. He passed by the front door and parked the Cortina at the cottage's gable end, opened the car door and got out. He took the baby from the rear seat and nestled the child in the crook of his arm, then moved to the passenger side and lifted Alina out with his free arm. She stood unsteadily, saying nothing. McNeill figured that like all the others, the cottage would be empty and he helped her walk to the cottage door and propped her up beside it.

He pressed the door latch. The door, to his surprise, was unlocked and opened inwards, and McNeill found himself face to face with a double-barrelled shotgun held by a wizened old woman. She was small, dressed untidily in well-worn black clothes, her wrinkled face granite-like. She barked at McNeill in a tongue foreign to him. Alina slipped into view. McNeill caught her before she fell to the ground. The baby began to cry and McNeill froze. The old woman dropped the shotgun and moved to support the mother. McNeill gave the child to the old woman, and then carefully lifted Alina into his arms and carried her inside. The old woman watched closely as she beckoned them through and into a bedroom. McNeill laid Alina on the bed then wrapped her in a blanket, turned and held out his big hands towards the old woman, who promptly gave him the child, looked into his eyes and smiled.

McNeill held the child once again in the crook of his right arm and pointed to his ears with his left hand, shaking his hand slowly, a hand sign for deafness. He then gestured with his fore-finger, tapping his tongue and pointing to the baby's mouth and his. The old woman took McNeill by the arm and led him to the unlit fire, gestured to it and took the baby and laid it in an armchair. She went to her kitchen stove, lit it and put a kettle full of water on to boil. McNeill went outside and returned shortly with kindling and an armful of wood blocks which he dropped by the fire, then went back outside to a small shed. The shed's roof leaked and a tarpaulin was stretched over a stockpile of wood to keep it dry. He returned to the fire with more timber blocks, dropping them in a large basket by the fire, and some by the wood-burner in the kitchen. He built a fire and lit it, then removed his jacket and unholstered his Beretta pistol. The old woman turned to face him just then and when she saw the pistol in McNeill's hand she stopped dead in her tracks. Her hands began to shake and her mouth to quiver. McNeill looked at her, then at his pistol and waved with his free hand the sign for no. He tossed the pistol onto his jacket and sat down in the vacant armchair. The kettle of water behind the old woman began to whistle.

McNeill got up and went to the bedroom. He looked at Alina; her eyes were closed in sleep. Then he went outside to the car and returned with the bag which contained the empty baby's bottles and the formula. The old woman looked into the bag and removed the tin of formula and a bottle, made a feed for the baby, then passed the bottle to McNeill, who fed the newborn. The baby sucked at the teat with relish. Minutes later the old woman put soup and tea on the table. She took the baby from McNeill, inviting him to eat. The baby cried as the old woman nursed it. McNeill finished the soup and tea then retrieved the baby from the old woman and continued the feed. Again, the baby drank.

The old woman took soup to the baby's mother, who woke at the sound of her voice but did not want to take the food, so the old woman left the soup on the ground beside her. Then she lifted the bedclothes off Alina and began removing her trousers. She looked at her bare legs and returned to the kitchen, where McNeill was rocking the baby. The old woman smiled, went to a cupboard and selected two towels. She filled a large bowl with lukewarm water, put the towels over her shoulder and carried the bowl into the bedroom. The baby cried. McNeill put the baby over his shoulder and gently patted its back and the baby burped, then burped again. He lowered the baby into the crook of his arm and gently rocked her to sleep.

He ventured over to the bedroom and looked in. The old woman was tending to Alina, gently washing her legs, dabbing them dry. McNeill turned away to put some logs on the fire and sat down in the armchair. He listened as the two women began to speak gently in their native tongue. He got up, made his way to the shotgun, unloaded it and replaced it. He returned to the armchair and sat down, this time resting his pistol on his stomach and pulling the jacket over it. The old woman exited the bedroom, the soaked towels over one arm, carrying the bowl of water. She emptied its contents down the sink, left the two towels at the side of the sink and returned to the cupboard, from which she removed two large tea towels and a facecloth. She renewed the tepid water in the bowl, then deposited it beside McNeill in front of the fire and pointed to the baby then to the water. McNeill gave her the baby and the old woman smiled a friendly smile, placed his jacket, under which was his pistol, on the table and promptly washed his soup bowl and empty mug at the sink.

The old woman sang to the child as she bathed it. McNeill went to the bedroom. The door was slightly ajar, so he opened it further and looked in. Alina had returned to slumber. He collected her now empty soup bowl and half-drunk mug of tea, then gently placed his left hand on her forehead and touched her cheek with the back of his fingers. The sleeping mother murmured. There was a sound in front of him and McNeill looked up to see the old woman coming towards the doorway carrying the baby girl. She stopped short of entering and beckoned to McNeill to come out. As McNeill moved towards her she smiled.

McNeill went and stood in front of the fire. He looked round, saw that the now empty shotgun was still in the same place, his jacket unmoved, the kettle humming on the stove. He went to the sink and washed the mug and bowl and looked at his watch: 12.15 a.m. He felt tired. The old woman looked at him and pointed to the bedroom. *Hmmm, sticky, sticky situation*, thought McNeill. On the one side, a woman in bed whose only words to him were a sleep-induced murmur a few minutes ago, or an old woman, baby in her arms, in the company of a shotgun and loaded pistol. He went to the cottage door and locked it, took the baby from the old lady, placing her in the crook of his left arm, then led the old lady to the bedroom by her arm. He pushed her inside, tilted his head to the left, placed the back of his right-hand fingers to his left cheek, making the sign for sleep, and pulled the bedroom door closed. He went and sat in the armchair.

Soon, the baby slept, and McNeill closed his eyes and went to sleep.

He woke to the cries of the baby. He looked down and there at his right side was a new bottle of milk. He picked it up and placed the teat in the baby's mouth. As she sucked he glanced at his watch: 4.55 a.m. After feeding the baby he stood up, placing her in the armchair, and went to the cottage door and unbolted it and went outside. No rain, a chill in the air, with a slight wind. Turning to his left he saw a large barrel overflowing with water from the drainpipe above it. He went over, cupped his hands and threw cold water onto his face. He wiped his hands on his trousers, took out a cigarette and lit up with Fitz's lighter. He rolled the lighter in his hand, looked at it, smiled, and put the lighter back in his pocket. He eyed the makeshift road both ways: nothing, still, silent, empty. Nothing disturbed the last of the night. He went back inside the cottage. All was quiet and peaceful. He sat down and began to think of yesterday's events.

Something bothered him. When Alina was at the Land Rover, her mother had run out of the house and thrust the holdall into her arms and run back to the house. Was she being smuggled to safety? The Land Rover was a recognised car. It was easy to slip up to the house in darkness and the driver always kept his head low. The Land Rover had left the house very slowly then turned right, carrying the driver, Alina and the soldier. Could there have been a struggle in the Land Rover before it crashed? Did it crash when the driver was shot? Was the soldier a planted assassin? The driver was shot at close range – she had obviously tried to escape and she had been cornered by the soldier... *who looked like he was about to shoot her before I shot him.*

The general turned left when he left the house. Yiddich came for him and took the right fork. Yiddich had been continually looking at his watch and pushing. The ambush – whatever was in those briefcases, the people in the cars were killed for it, and Yiddich was adamant: no survivors! The sniper, a very good sniper, had missed an easy target. The soldier had pointed his pistol at the girl – did he deliberately miss? Were they warning shots? Was he supposed to be collected by Yiddich after shooting Alina? The fear on her face when she saw Yiddich, the seething hatred in his screaming words and remonstrations, the brutal beating he gave her... What then happened in the tunnel? More questions than answers, but the conclusion to McNeill was simple. Both he and she were now thrust together, not wanted alive by either side. The ambush assasination would be squarely put on his shoulders. Those briefcases were now in his hands and they would kill them both to get them. No way back.

The soldier in him again took over. *Move out,* it cried, *pull yourself together. Start to think but get moving.* He got up, went to the bedroom and began to shake the baby's mother. The old woman woke and shouted, 'Alina, Alina!' She woke and McNeill lifted her from the bed, carried her out of the cottage and put her in the passenger seat of the car, then went back inside and collected the holdall and the baby. The old woman followed and gave Alina a blanket and tore the holdall from McNeill's grasp. She opened it, took out the empty bottle and returned to the cottage. She returned with a full bottle, the tin of formula and a small bag of fruit. McNeill thanked her by nodding his head. The old woman smiled a knowing smile, went inside the cottage and closed the door behind her. McNeill got into the car and deposited the baby girl on the mother's lap, put the ignition keys in and started the car. The Cortina sprang to life. McNeill drove to the road and turned left.

⇒•◇•⇐

An hour later General Tomelsky sent out a small patrol in a Nissan jeep. Yiddich was long overdue; the motorcade had not arrived either, something was wrong. The general was irritable. What could have gone wrong? It was a beautiful, well thought out, simple plan. What had messed it up? Yiddich was a loyal soldier and would die for him. He despatched four of his best soldiers to find out why and bring back those briefcases.

Just after midday the Nissan containing the four soldiers arrived at the scene of the ambush. They spotted the dead bodies, searched for the briefcases and found nothing. They drove to the grey bullet-ridden Land Rover, found the driver dead and their comrade spreadeagled on the floor, a gaping hole in his chest. They sped to the tunnel mouth and stopped short, disembarked and in two-by-two formation they entered the tunnel, one to the right, one to the left, AK-47s at the ready. They saw the dead bodies – the soldier, the sniper, Yiddich, his knife buried in his chest. The other two came up and looked around – trousers and shirt missing from one man, shirt from another. One spotted a discoloured patch on the ground and called the others. One of the soldiers, an ex-intern, knew from the stain that the woman had given birth here.

'Anyone find the American?' one of the soldiers asked.

'No,' the others said in unison. 'Let's take a look around to see if the woman is still here – she couldn't get far,' said the ex-intern.

No sign. They loaded the bodies onto the jeep and began the drive back.

'The general is not going to be happy. Yiddich is dead, the briefcases are not recovered, and the American and his daughter are missing,' the leader said to the group.

⋙◆⋘

McNeill drove steadily for a couple of hours. Every attempt to spark conversation was met with silence. He was not speeding, registering around 90 kilometres per hour to maximise fuel efficiency. The baby slept in the back seat where Alina had put her shortly after leaving the old woman's cottage. He came to a junction. *Which way,* he asked himself. There were no road signs. He got out, taking the ignition keys with him, looked both ways, then

77

returned to the car and reached in through the passenger side window to open the glove compartment and searched for a map. He didn't find one. He looked hard at Alina, who returned his stare twicefold. The baby woke. McNeill took off his jacket and placed the baby in it to protect it from the morning chill. The baby was restless, uncomfortable with the pistol holster and kept squirming. McNeill took off the holster and left it on the car bonnet.

Alina watched from inside the car. McNeill moved to the middle of the road, baby in arms, then froze when he heard the car door open and close behind him. He knew he was too far away from the car, knew he was defenceless. Baby in arms, he slowly turned, horrified. He saw Alina looking at him a few feet from the front of the car, pistol in hand, pointing it at her right temple. He moved slowly towards her, her baby in his outstretched arms, his eyes pleading with her not to do it. *Stay alive and we will help each other stay alive.*

Alina looked at him, at the baby girl and back at McNeill, getting still closer, his eyes continually pleading, his thoughts only of his need for her to remain alive, she alone could understand and speak the language. McNeill edged tentatively closer. His heart sank as Alina squeezed the trigger… but the pistol did not fire. Then, like a rugby player, more than 250 pounds of solid muscle slammed into her. McNeill sent her sprawling backwards over the car bonnet, her right arm flopping over the edge of the car and dropping the pistol. The gun hit the road. McNeill pulled Alina up with his right hand. Face to face, his eyes burned into hers. The baby began to cry. McNeill shoved the baby into Alina's lap, went around to the side of the car, retrieved his pistol and looked at it: the safety catch was still on. He returned to face Alina.

'Feed her,' he said. Nothing happened.

'Feed her,' he said more forcibly, his eyes scorching hers. Nothing. He stared into her blue eyes. There was a stony silence.

'Feed her!' he shouted with venom. Alina jumped and muttered in Croatian.

'Speak English, I know you can. I have seen your eyes when I have cursed you,' screamed McNeill, his face flushed with anger. She shook her head.

'Feed her. Speak English,' McNeill said sternly and coldly.

'No,' whispered Alina.

'Oh, so we understand, and we can talk – that's an improvement. And while you are talking, which bloody way do we go from here?' he yelled at her.

'I will not feed the baby,' Alina stubbornly screamed.

McNeill took the child, put his angry face within touching distance of Alina's nose and through clenched teeth hissed, 'Which way? Which way?', his voice rising. He grabbed hold of her blouse at the neck in his big fist and drew her close, until their noses touched, then he shook her furiously. 'Look, I aim to get out of here and you *are* going to help. I am your only chance to live,' he spat.

Alina looked at McNeill. She could smell both his breath and anger, feel his eyes burning hers, sense the violent power. She closed her eyes and pointed right.

McNeill fed the child with the bottle of milk the old woman had given him and the baby drank heartily. McNeill winded her and laid her comfortably in the back seat. Alina watched. McNeill pushed Alina into the passenger seat, shut the passenger door, took the magazine out of the Beretta, took off the safety and checked the firing mechanism. He replaced the fifteen-round magazine, put the safety catch back on and reholstered the pistol. 'Careless, bloody careless,' he cursed himself as he got into the driver's seat and started the car. He looked at the baby, open-eyed, arms waving. He was sure she smiled at him. He smiled at her, moved his head to face front and as he did so his left eye glimpsed Alina's head also revolving round to face front. McNeill put the car into gear and turned right at the junction.

The Nissan jeep arrived at the general's house. General Tomelsky was pacing the room impatiently as the four soldiers walked in. 'Well?' he boomed. The general's wife came out of the kitchen quietly and began to eavesdrop on the conversation as a soldier began his report.

'Soldiers and two high-ranking officials assassinated, briefcases missing. Driver of Land Rover dead, our soldier also. Your daughter is missing. Yiddich and two others dead. American plus one other sniper rifle missing. It would appear your daughter has given birth, sir. The bodies of Yiddich and his men are in the jeep, sir,' he added.

'That means there is a car is missing,' added another soldier.

The general's wife clasped her hands together, relieved that her daughter and now grandchild were alive. She prayed the American would take care of them both. She returned to the kitchen silently as soldiers came in, poker-faced on the outside and smiling contentedly on the inside.

In his office the general flew into a rage, his eyes narrowed as his huge fists thumped into the mahogany desk. Moments later he bellowed, 'I take it my hussy of a daughter is now with this cursed American. Bring me a map.'

Another soldier appeared with a map and set it down on his desk. Tomelsky stood as he eyed the map. 'There is the tunnel, there is the main road,' he said out loud, his finger jabbing at the map.

He turned to the veteran soldier who had brought the map. 'Get some of my men from this town here, my special guard. Tell them to kill the American, kill my daughter if she gets in the way, bring the baby, but – and this is imperative – bring me those briefcases. Set it up, report to me, use my phone. I want those briefcases in the hands of my special guard before night-fall and in mine before dawn.'

Thirty minutes later, there was a knock on the general's office door.

'Well?'

'Four soldiers is all we have from your special guard in the next town. They are some fifty miles away and have been despatched with orders to kill and others as suggested, sir.'

There were flat fields on either side of the road and the sun was beginning to shine as McNeill drove on slowly, pondering about his reliance on Alina. He could neither read nor speak Croatian. Where was she going to lead him? Could he trust her? When he spoke to her civilly, she ignored him, staring blankly at the road ahead. When he yelled at her, she answered defeatedly, often just pointing the way. McNeill took out one of Yiddich's cigarettes, lit it with Fitz's lighter, and after two long ecstatic drags offered the cigarette to Alina, who looked at McNeill with disgust and dismay.

'Sorry,' he said and he finished the cigarette before flicking the butt out of the window.

'So you speak English,' he said to Alina, who just scowled at him silently.

If looks could kill, I'd be at my own funeral now, he thought. McNeill drove on at 90 kilometres per hour in total silence. The road ahead veered to the left. Once again a stretch of hilly country beckoned. McNeill drove on, unperturbed. The baby began to cry, then cry more. McNeill waited, waited to see if Alina would pick up her child, waited till he could wait no more, then swung his right hand around and picked up the little girl, resting her on his lap. Hills began to appear on the passenger side of the car. Alina looked at McNeill, at the baby, looked aloof and straight ahead, but McNeill thought he saw her smile.

'Are you OK? Look, I'm sorry if I scared you, but I intend to get out of this mess, I can't speak the lingo and you are all I've got.' She looked at him, into his eyes appealing for her help.

'What have you got to lose? Nothing, and you just might survive, it's a win-win situation for you,' he pleaded. She glared at him, her eyes wide, her body taut. Silence followed as she looked into his eyes full of compassion and digested his words but her staring eyes began to blink, her head bowed. McNeill wondered had his words resonated with her, had they broken her stubborn resolve. Was the ice lady beginning to melt?

Suddenly the rear passenger window behind Alina smashed and something hit the rear seat with a small thud. McNeill gunned the accelerator and threw the car off the road to the left down into a dip and halted. Another bullet hit the door behind Alina, pinged with a metallic sound. She ducked down, let out a scream and shook her head. He opened his door, lifted the baby in his left hand and dragged Alina down and out his side of the car with his right hand, then sat Alina by the front wheel and gave her the baby. His eyes met her stare, but something in them had changed, she looked at him, frightened. Staying low, he then went to the boot, opened it and ducked down. His hand found the two sniper rifles as two bullets hit the raised lid of the boot. He took out the rifles and returned to the front wheel as two more bullets entered the roof of the car on the corner behind the driver's side.

McNeill figured the front of the car, being lower in the dip, was out of sight, but he could not be sure: all hits were to the back of the car. He looked ahead – 20 yards on he saw two large rocks, in front of them a trench 2 feet or so below the road, running parallel with it. He strapped the two rifles to his back and slid into the trench, inched the 20 yards to the boulders, left his M21 there, moved around the rocks and slid back into the trench. He stopped 20 yards on and effortlessly took the sniper rifle from his back, then turned through almost 120 degrees in one movement and pushed the rifle barrel out over the roadside. He looked through the sight at the terrain.

The road was single carriageway both ways, but wide, then a drop before a flat space of 20 or so yards, after which small grass-covered mounds gave way to grassy hillside. As the sun rose, he counted how many bullets had hit the car, trying to work out from where they were fired. He counted six hits. McNeill lay motionless, searching through the sight. *How many? Come on, show yourselves,* he willed then waited. *Surely you will come to take a look-see, surely.* He waited, eye glued to the telescopic sight. Then he saw it – the glisten of sunlight on metal or glass. He made adjustments to the rifle, set the distance for the required 400 yards and moved slightly to his right. There in the distance on the far hill another soldier was half stood. McNeill looked over, below and slightly to his left. There, a lot closer, 300 yards away, was another. McNeill did a sweep round, counted three. Three did not seem enough.

He looked again. The first soldier was getting up, the second guy was walking down the hill. He concentrated on him. Slow, deep, inhaled breaths, held then exhaled. Breathe in and hold, squeeze the trigger twice in succession, exhale, breathe in. Eyes glued to the sight, he saw the soldier being hit twice in the chest, throwing his arms wide as he fell backwards. McNeill trained his weapon on the second guy, despatched two more messengers of death. No time to look –machine gunfire hit the ground behind and to either side of him. He wheeled to his left and found his target running towards him, firing his AK-47 semi-automatic rifle. He stopped in his tracks, slumped to his knees, hit by two perfect shots to the chest from McNeill. So cold, so effortless and so accurate. He sprawled forward, lifeless. Bullets whistled past McNeill's head as he slammed his face into the dirt. More bullets just missed his boots. Three bullets smacked into the ground at the left side of his head. McNeill left the rifle peering just above the roadside and rolled off to his right and into the trench. Bullets screamed into the earth on the far side of the trench where he was positioned only moments ago, more peppered the road. McNeill hauled himself back, snake-like, to the two boulders and his beloved M21 as bullets hammered into and around the rifle on the roadside 20 yards further on.

McNeill reached the comparative safety of the boulders and his trusted M21. Alina saw him and half stood. Two bullets passed through the roof of the Cortina and into the earth in front and to the side of her. She screamed. McNeil spun round and pushed the palm of his right hand to the floor and pumped it up and down, beckoning her to get down. Alina fell to the floor. McNeill waited. *He shoots to my left at the rifle, then the car, then the rifle. One man, probably one man left,* he thought. *He can hit the roof even though it's below the road, he can hit the road and the far side of the trench but he cannot see the trench as I would have been targeted coming back to the boulders. He has to be quite high because he is missing maybe 400–500 yards away.*

He set the sight for 500 yards and scoured the hills around the upper sections. Two shots hit the ground just above the abandoned rifle muzzle 20 yards further on. McNeill purposefully looked through the sight. Then he saw it – the flash, the flash of bullet leaving rifle barrel. The bullet hit the decoy sniper rifle, sending it backwards off the ground. McNeill waited; two more flashes. McNeill looked through his sight, the M21 rifle barrel rock steady, peering out from the boulders. He inhaled slowly, held his breath. Two more flashes. McNeill squeezed the trigger, then squeezed again and again and again, all aimed at the flashes. His eyes were now glued to the spot from where the flashes of light came and he fired twice more. Through his telescopic sight, with his breath held, his body motionless, his finger poised on the M21 trigger, he saw his adversary throw one arm into the air then the other in quick succession, then slump.

McNeill smiled, the corner of his upper lip becoming a smirk. He waited, looked over to Alina, who was lying face down but slightly humped over. She looked at McNeill, whose hand went up, signalling her to wait and stay where she was. McNeill scoured the hills, looking for another assailant. Nothing. Ten minutes passed: still nothing. He left his position and returned via the trench to the sniper rifle further up. He took off his jacket, lay down on his back and covered the rifle muzzle with his jacket, then held it up above ground, let the soft breeze fill it, then lifted it higher. No shots, only stillness. He lifted the jacket higher:

nothing; took it down and put it back up again: still nothing.

McNeill admired the hole in the rifle stock left by his one-time adversary. He returned to the car and Alina, crouching down all the way. He was amazed, overjoyed, relieved – Alina was lying on top of the child, using her body to protect the baby girl and clutching her to her chest. McNeill sat her up and told her to stay there and wait. He went to the rear of the car, then sprinted up the incline across the road and on in zigzag fashion through grass and sparse bushes, sparse trees, thicker, taller grass and more trees to the hills. At the foothills he stopped, caught his breath then went off uphill sprinting again, where he located the body of his last kill. He recognised the rifle – an M21 similar to his own. The user's body was sprawled and twisted forwards, hit once in the left shoulder, once through the head. He pulled the M21 free and looked through the rifle sight. He looked towards the car; he could make out the corner of the roof behind the driver's seat but could not see the front. Then he moved and saw two bodies spread on the earth like Da Vinci's Vitruvian man. He then located the fourth below. All the men were dressed in the same uniform as he.

McNeill returned to the car with his own M21 and the sniper's M21. He put both rifles into the boot and closed it. McNeill just stood there. A minute passed, then more. He realised they had just survived an assassination attempt from Alina's father. He shuddered and opened the boot, looked at the pair of M21s. His beloved friend and trusted companion was his M21 sniper rifle made by Springfield Armory; American, of course.

He shut the boot and went to Alina. She was still where he left her, back at the driver's door, baby now in her lap. The baby began to cry. He took the baby from her and the crying stopped. The baby's eyes beguiled McNeill. She looked as if she smiled at him. He smiled back then looked at Alina, who was watching him, but there was a difference. There was no self-pity, no scorn; she was watching a loving bond between two unfortunate souls. McNeill sat alongside Alina. Relief was what McNeill felt – heartfelt, alleviated relief. He gazed at the baby girl, unharmed, then gazed at Alina, unharmed. He put his right arm around her and hugged her, then whispered into her ear, 'Let's get the hell out of here, what do you say?' She nodded in agreement.

They got into the car and McNeill started the engine, found reverse and slammed the accelerator to the floor. The car lurched, skidded and slewed its way back to the road. He then drove forward.

'Stop!' shouted Alina. He pulled over and she got out of the car and walked over to the body of a soldier on the right, face down, clutching his AK-47 even in death. She turned the body over and looked at the face, the face of a man who in her teens she used to date, the face of a man from her village, the face of a man who had tried to kill her, a member of her father's private army. She felt a shiver run through her body, returned to the car and sat beside McNeill, her face white.

'OK, drive please,' she muttered in perfect English.

McNeill nearly ran the car off the road in surprise. *She spoke to me.* McNeill drove on and the road became bumpy, the scenery dull, unless you like green fields that stretch as far as the eye can see. The baby broke the monotony when she began to cry with hunger.

Suddenly Alina reached over and took the baby onto her lap, undid her cardigan and blouse, displaced her bra and began to breastfeed her baby. McNeill, gobsmacked, watched in amazement, utter embarrassment, joy and shyness. He looked away and kept his eyes on the road ahead. He slipped back to his past, fondled Fitz's lighter in his pocket, thought of his wife and daughter – that tragic day, the torching of his home, his rampage at the mosque, Fitz's smiling face, Fitz's terrible death. His retraction from society and how he had alienated himself from it, his own solitude and loneliness; his silence and the depths of despair. His days like leaves on a tree waiting to fall.

The past lies in the shadow of our lives, endlessly patient, secure in the knowledge that all we have done, all we have failed to do, must surely return to haunt us in the end. In younger days we cast aside each day like seeds on a wind as we move along a path towards sunset and home. Nothing regretted – there are many more days to come. Now, as I reminisce about the path we have chosen, it's overgrown where seeds of past actions and half-acknowledged sins are tangled and have taken root. The growth is catching up as life steadily moves forward. The undergrowth of briars around my ankles, weeds brush my fingertips and the ground I walk on crackles with the leaves of dead days. A monster of my own creation, my past is waiting for me, McNeill mused, staring blankly out.

Alina finished feeding her baby, covered herself and proceeded to change her child. The makeshift nappy made from the old woman's tea towel and safety pins was wet, dirty and smelled. Her original nappy, the one in her mother's holdall, was dry, so she took it out and put it on. She finished changing the baby, then wrapped a blanket around her for more warmth, lifted her and began to sing a Croatian lullaby. The baby was soon fast asleep. McNeill looked at Alina. He was dumbfounded, relieved, didn't quite comprehend how such a turnaround had happened, but he was sure glad it had. McNeill knew she had recognised the dead soldier; he stared at her rocking her child then broke the silence.

'OK, where are we headed, where are you taking us, and why did your mother smuggle you out of your father's and why is he now trying to kill you?' he asked.

Alina reached for the bag of fruit the old woman had given them, took out two apples and gave one to McNeill.

'It's a long story,' she said.

'Start at the beginning, I'm going nowhere,' came McNeill's reply.

Alina shuffled in her seat and began.

'Before the war, I grew up in the village. My childhood sweetheart was Yiddich. We went everywhere together; everyone in the village thought we would marry one day. My father doted on Yiddich as if he were his long-lost son but Yiddich began treating me badly, taking me for granted, seeing other girls and denying it and beating me occasionally. As we grew up, my father's influence on Yiddich changed him from a quiet, gentle man to an obstinate, power-mad bully.

'I dated that dead soldier while I was still seeing Yiddich for a while. Slavan and his family moved into the house at the far edge of town, opposite father's. His family were Serbian. I grew to like Slavan – he treated me with total respect when I was beginning to feel like Yiddich's possession, under his total control. Slavan never took me for granted, was always there, always gentle and kind. If we ever had arguments, he would turn up the next day with a forgive-me token, flowers he picked from the garden and fields, chocolates he stole from his mother. I began to see more of Slavan and less of Yiddich. This did not sit kindly with Yiddich or my father, though my mother adored the gentleness and trustworthiness of Slavan.

'One day, against my father's wishes, I spent the whole day with Slavan. I sneaked out of the house while father was meeting some politicians. Father wants to be a war hero and a great politician, but he is so corrupt and will stop at nothing to get what he wants, and that includes murder. Anyhow, Slavan and I were kissing at the edge of a cornfield. Yiddich, with some of his thugs, had been sent by my father to find me, and they caught us. Yiddich began pushing Slavan. I began screaming at Yiddich. Yiddich hit me full in the face, knocking me to the floor. Slavan flew at Yiddich, knocked Yiddich onto his back and began beating him. Slavan was yelling, "Don't you ever hit her, scumbag!" and was thrashing Yiddich. Yiddich was rescued by his four thugs, and they attacked Slavan. Slavan was totally outnumbered and had no chance; there were too many of them. I tried to help him but I was swept aside. Slavan was on his hands and knees, blood pouring from his lovely face. Yiddich caught him square in the ribs with a full-force kick just before Slavan's father came over, looking for his son. I was dragged away by Yiddich who said that Slavan deserved all he got for hitting me in the face in the first place. Yiddich was declared a hero by my father. No one believed Slavan. My father always believed Yiddich, never believed me.

My mother believed me, but I was banned from seeing Slavan. Slavan was ostracised by the village and his family too. His young sister was badly beaten and continually bullied. I used to sneak away to see him.

'Time passed and Slavan wanted to marry me, and I him. He came to our house to see my father and he asked for my hand in marriage. My father flew into a rage, said I was betrothed to Yiddich, and threw Slavan out. Eventually he squeezed out Slavan and his family, I know he threatened them. Slavan and his family left the village one night and never came back.'

'Did your father have them killed?' asked McNeill.

'I don't know, I'm not sure. At that time I would have been a loss to my father, and a wayward daughter would only interfere with and in his ambitions. I became a prisoner in my own house, only allowed out under Yiddich's guard. I ran away to try to find Slavan, my true love. I found myself in Serbia, then war broke out. A Croatian woman in the heart of Serbia, can you imagine? I was very lucky. I had befriended a Polish woman named Paulina who came from Gdansk, my mother's home town, who helped me escape. I knew Slavan had been called up to join the army. I had located and spoke to his mother some days before. She gave me his regiment and address. I was on my way to find him.

'Paulina and I caught a bus heading north out of town towards Slavan, or so I thought. The bus turned off the main north road and went to a small wood, where everyone was ordered off. We were all grouped together. I was at the centre with Paulina. Soldiers encircled us and they just began shooting. Paulina pushed me to the floor, lay across, stopped me from getting up. The shooting stopped. I heard voices and laughter, then the roar of engines, then nothing. I managed to get out from underneath Paulina, who lay motionless. She'd been shot a few times, like all the others, dead in pools of blood. I stood and walked. I walked over bodies and through puddles of blood. My clothes were stained with blood, blood was on my hands, on my face, my legs and in my hair; their blood. I ran into the woods.

'Every time I wiped my tears, I smeared more blood. I cried and cried. I realised I could not go back to the town, it was too dangerous and I had to get out of Serbia. I went back to the massacre, searched the bodies for money, found some but not enough. I was alone, frightened. I hid in the woods. Flies attracted to the stench of stale blood were my only company. I found a small stream, washed myself in it, took off my clothes and washed them the best I could. I put them back on wet and waited for the clothes to dry whilst wearing them. Eventually I plucked up enough courage to leave and passed myself off in towns as a beggar. My clothes had begun to smell rancid so people kept their distance. I travelled on trains, farm tractors and trailers, stole pedal cycles, never set foot on a bus, but I was caught almost at the Croatian border by four soldiers, two young and two old. They kept me prisoner, fed me, washed me, repeatedly raped me. I became pregnant and they abandoned me near the border, told me to go. I found my way back to my mother. My beautiful mother never lost faith in me. I told her what had happened to me; my father said I was a disgrace to him, a major disappointment. Yiddich despised me.

'I was just glad to be with my mother. House arrest suited at the time, until Yiddich delighted in telling me of Slavan's death at the hands of his Croatian patrol. His sniper had shot him. They brought Slavan's body back, forced me to look. The chain and locket I had given him a year earlier was still around his neck. I cried, I wept for my Slavan: Yiddich threw me inside the house, that house. There I lived, loved by my mother, abandoned and spurned by my father, hated by Yiddich. I'm so glad you killed him.

'Yes, the night you saw me I had run away and they brought me back. I am a nuisance and a liability to my father and his dreams. This baby is a result of being raped by Serbians, my father knows it has a Serbian father, but like me doesn't know the baby's true father.

'Yes, American, this war has taken everything from me, and

given me this – a Serbian baby from a Croatian mother watched over by an American.'

She stopped speaking as tears ran down her face.

McNeill looked at Alina and saw her in a different light. She had steel in her inner strength. She was a survivor – she had shown it through capture, through endurance to survival. His respect for her grew there and then. He looked ahead. They were coming to another junction.

'Which way, Alina?' he asked.

'I am not sure,' she replied.

'Alina, we need food, shelter in a safe place, water – you know these people of your country. Please, which way?' pleaded McNeill.

'Turn right,' she said apprehensively. McNeill followed her instructions. A while later a little smile replaced the tears on her face.

'What's the smile for?' asked McNeill.

'This is the road which leads to my mother's sister's place – my aunt. She is also my godmother. Surely she would not betray me?' she asked McNeill tentatively.

'I should bloody well hope not, but it's one of the places your father would look for us. We may not have much time. His patrol will be expected to make contact back,' replied McNeill.

Again McNeill noticed that most of the houses were deserted or abandoned. He had passed through destitute villages – empty of young males, only children and grandparents to be seen – while Alina was telling her story. McNeill had just driven through; there was no resistance, and he didn't want to stop either. As McNeill drove on, Alina comforted her baby girl when she cried, shared the last of the fruit with McNeill, an apple and a banana each.

McNeill glanced at Alina a few times over the next hour. He was warming to her. He drove and stared; Alina dozed and gazed. He looked again and she was dozing with her little girl sleeping. Yes, typical girl-next-door type with a sensuous mouth. Alina woke and McNeill smiled at her. Alina nodded, then paid eager attention to the road; McNeill knew she was looking for something, a landmark. He slowed the Cortina down. The fuel gauge was now reading empty. He pulled over, took the jerry can from the boot of the Cortina and put all its contents into the car's fuel tank, then replaced the empty jerry can in the boot and drove off slowly, one eye on the road, one eye on Alina. A further half-hour passed and they neared a small town.

Alina looked at McNeill. 'Do you think the men from the ambush came from here?' she asked.

'More than likely,' replied McNeill. 'But you recognised one, so tell me,' he added.

'Yes, one of my father's assassins. My father sends people out to kill people, especially ones who stand up to him, or get in his way, and you will be top of his hit list after today, McNeill!' she replied.

'How comforting to know, thank you,' said McNeill and they both laughed. McNeill went on, 'OK, and these assassins – are they planted in other regiments or are they his special forces deployed only by him?'

'His most trusted are immune to other people's orders. They report only to my father and do his bidding only. Many people, many politicians, have been murdered by those professional killers. Other people believe my father is a saviour; he loves this. Yes, they are his special forces and they serve and are loyal only to him,' Alina replied.

McNeill digested what she had said; his brain had begun to compute the moment he asked the question. 'What are your own beliefs?' he asked.

'My father is a brutal dictator, has murdered many good, innocent people. He is a bully, a corrupt bully. He will ruin this country, rape it for its own wealth. He is a power-hungry control freak,' she said sternly.

McNeill drove into town, drew the Beretta pistol and placed it comfortably on his lap. The town was almost deserted apart from a few soldiers, smoking, resting and eating. McNeill drove steadily on. He passed shops open but with no customers. A one-stop town, blink and you miss it. Once you have been there, you will instantly forget it. McNeill drove on through steadily; even the few townspeople did not look up as he passed. He exited the town as easily as he entered and drove on.

⇒·◇·⇐

But McNeill and Alina were seen, recognised, timed. They passed by the rundown hotel, and there in the reception hallway stood an elderly man with grey hair, who walked with a limp, dragging his right leg. He saw the Cortina, recognised the woman, went to the reception desk, used the telephone and rang General Tomelsky. He got through to the general in his house office almost immediately.

'General, sir, your daughter and the American have just passed through in a brown Cortina, which means the four soldiers have been eliminated.'

'Thank you, Dracek, you are a good servant,' said the general calmly before disconnecting the phone. He flew into a rage, throwing and smashing ornaments, lamps and drinking glasses. His face was a blazing red.

'Damn you, Alina, damn you, American. Damn you both to hell!' the general hissed through clenched teeth, his eyes black and narrow.

Alina's mother heard the smashing of furniture, heard her husband's curses and smiled, outstretched her arms above her head and said softly, 'Thank you, Lord, Thank you for the American.' Then she smiled again.

The door crashed open. The general stormed out of the room, bellowed to two soldiers in the next room, 'Get me Rasik, immediately.'

⇒·◇·⇐

McNeill drove on steadily. Alina once again breastfed her child, cleaned and changed her, but this time, instead of returning her to the back seat, she held her. McNeill looked at the two of them then looked away and smiled. Alina began to pay more attention to the road then asked, 'And McNeill, how did you get into this war?'

McNeill gazed into his past, regressed into loss and depression. He didn't want to go there. He looked at Alina. Alina gazed into eyes of hurt, shame and sadness. McNeill began to speak. Alina listened, listened to him tell her of his heartfelt loss of his wife and daughter, his depressed stay in the mental hospital for recuperation. She heard him tell of how an explosion took the best parts of his life, his burning of their home to try to release the shackles of connection to his wife and daughter. Then, not knowing what to do or where to go, he had bumped into his best friend and fellow war veteran of many missions together, Fitz. Then he told her of the massacre at the mosque at his hands, and how Fitz had smuggled them out of America. Two fugitives who became mercenaries overnight. Then Fitz's death and how he blamed himself for getting him into this mess in the first place. If it were not for him, Fitz would still be alive. Finally, he explained how he came to be assigned to Yiddich.

McNeill spoke from the heart for nearly two hours. At times Alina wanted to hold him, to hug him; at times she wanted to punch and kick him; at others she wanted to cry, and sure enough on occasion a tear escaped her eye. *Two lost souls,* she thought, *thrown together to sink or swim. My baby is a retribution, a form of repayment for him, and hence so am I.* She looked at McNeill. He looked so sad, so down; a heavy heart made a great weight. She looked ahead.

'Take the dirt track just off to the left,' she said.

McNeill turned. 'Then that one just off to the right.' McNeill turned again, and the Cortina bucked and rolled but eventually made the house at the lane end. Darkness was beginning to fall. Alina went to get out of the car. McNeill stopped her, removed his Beretta and opened his car door slowly, remembering the last time he walked into a cottage and was met by a double-barrelled shotgun. He got out and looked around. The house was directly in front of him, door in the centre, two windows to the left of the door, one to the right. The house was single-storey. *Any one of those windows could have a rifle pointed straight at me right now,* he thought. McNeill raised both hands above his head, moved away from the car. The next two minutes seemed like an age. Blood pounded around his body, his mind thumped and whirred like an over-worked computer looking for answers to every scenario. Nothing happened. He moved towards the door, now only 10 feet away. He noticed a derelict small building to his left. He heard a bang to his right and behind and spun round, right arm outstretched, loaded Beretta in hand.

'Don't you point that thing at me!' shouted Alina as she moved towards him. McNeill relaxed. The front door of the house thudded open and out rushed an elderly woman. She ran past McNeill, stretching out her hands and calling Alina's name, sobbing at the same time. The woman threw her arms around Alina, who did likewise. Alina looked at McNeill, a smug degree of self-satisfaction nestled on her face. McNeill felt like an idiot as the two women passed him by. McNeill reholstered his Beretta, returned to the car, brought the baby, the holdall and began walking to the house where he was met by Alina. She took the baby from him and told him to bring all the clothes from the car and to bring himself in. McNeill turned and did as he was told, then he walked through the door.

'Let me introduce my Aunt Sasha, my mother's elder sister,' Alina said, smiling.

McNeill looked on at a greying woman holding the baby girl, about 5 feet 2 inches tall, a little shorter than Alina. The baby girl began to cry. Alina's aunt took the baby into the kitchen, undressed her, bathed her lovingly in the sink and dried the naked baby in a towel laid on the table. Then she put some water into a pan, put the pan on a lit stove and spoke to Alina in Croatian.

Alina rushed into the kitchen and began preparing food and tea. McNeill joined them, took the knife from Alina, and chopped onions and tomatoes. The two women looked at McNeill, watched him for a moment, looked at each other and smiled.

Alina's aunt took the baby to a bedroom, opened a large blanket box full of old keepsakes and found some baby clothes, dressed the child and returned to the kitchen. Alina had prepared the formula milk. Aunt Sasha took it and fed the child. Alina and McNeill made soup and tea. They all ate and drank whilst the baby stayed awake, watching. After the meal was finished, Sasha took hold of Alina's arm and led her to the bathroom. She made her take a bath. Whilst she bathed, Sasha took her clothes, went outside and burned them. On returning to the house, she once again went to her bedroom, took clothes from a chest of drawers and took them to the bathroom. Alina got out of the bath and her aunt saw her bruises and looked at Alina in shock.

'No, no,' said Alina, 'he is a gentle man, it wasn't him who did this.' And she began to explain all. Her Aunt Sasha wept and hugged the naked Alina. Then she helped Alina choose what to wear from the handful of clothes she had brought in. Alina knew the clothes belonged to her two daughters, both of whom, along with their father, had left when the war began, gone to serve their country. Sasha left the bedroom and returned to the kitchen. McNeill had kept the stove burning and he had also lit the fire in the living room. Sasha began to speak to McNeill in Croatian, realised he had not understood a word, and spoke to him the best she could in broken English. McNeill felt comfortable. He took out his Beretta pistol, dismantled it and began to clean it.

Alina entered the room dressed in a black skirt and white blouse, her wet shoulder-length hair hanging down. McNeill looked up and gazed at her, his gaze turning into a stare. Alina smiled at him. Her aunt caught McNeill's arm gently but firmly, leading him to the bathroom. She pushed him in and pointed to the bath. McNeill bathed and relaxed.

Sasha returned to Alina, looked at the baby, who was now asleep, and brought Alina into her bedroom, selecting more clothes for her and her baby and putting them into the holdall. They exited the room. McNeill finished bathing and dressed in the same clothes. He could hear laughter coming from the kitchen-dining room.

Alina had made tea and was chatting brightly with her aunt. His dismantled pistol was still on the table where he had left it. Alina rose from her chair, went to the hot teapot on the stove and poured tea for McNeill. McNeill eyed Alina. She looked stunning in a black skirt just above the knee, white blouse open at the neck, and a figure-hugging black woollen jumper, with her hair swept to one side from the left of her head. McNeill sat down and Alina sat beside him. He could smell her, touch her. He liked it, and so did she; they felt safe with each other, reliant on each other. Alina's aunt looked on and smiled. McNeill reassembled the Beretta and drank more tea.

Hours passed. The fire died down and the cold chill of night began to make its entrance. Alina's Aunt Sasha yawned, as did Alina. They both stood and Alina left. McNeill stood, a little anxious and apprehensive. He was thinking of the sleeping arrangements. He knew there were two bedrooms at the end of the house. Sasha collected the sleeping baby gently and passed her to McNeill, then showed them to the room. Alina was already there. McNeill entered and saw two single beds. He turned to face Sasha, who just smiled at him then said, 'It's all right, you are safe here.'

Alina's Aunt Sasha then closed the door behind them and went to her bedroom. McNeill waited, heard the click of the latch on her door to open it, and heard the click to close it. Alina took off her jumper, turned to McNeill and said, 'Please sleep. Rest yourself, please.'

McNeill looked around the room. The two single beds were separated by a locker with a small lamp on top. The door was to the left of the nearer bed and there was a window on the far side where the roof began to slope down. A small wardrobe was against the wall beyond the foot of the beds and a chest of drawers on its left side, a small chair to the wardrobe's right.

Alina opted for the bed nearest the small window, saying, 'If you take this one, you will bang your head getting up.' She smiled and giggled. She then pulled out the bottom drawer of the chest, rearranged a blanket into it, took the baby from McNeill and placed her gently into it. McNeill watched her. Alina turned and shook her hair loose. It fell around her shoulders and neck, encompassing her face. He looked into her blue eyes, two lovely blue eyes, so clear, so sharp, like two endless pools. She spoke. 'Please, McNeill, make yourself comfortable and get some sleep.' He looked at the bed then at her, then sat down on the bed with his back to her, removed his boots, jacket and jumper, placed the Beretta under his pillow and lay down. He looked over and watched Alina in bra and panties climb into bed. She turned to him, smiled and said, 'Goodnight, McNeill, sleep well. I will look after the baby when she wakes.' McNeill looked at her from his single bed, smiled at her, remembered his lovely wife Jane and closed his eyes. But sleep did not come till later. He tossed and turned, looked at Alina, so beautiful, so peaceful in her slumber. Eventually sleep took him.

He never heard the baby cry, never heard Alina get up, never felt the bedclothes being put over him. Never felt the lightness of her finger against his cheek, never heard her leave the room.

<hr />

McNeill woke with a start and looked around. No Alina. No baby. The bedroom door stood open and he was alone. He felt defenceless, trapped in emptiness. His blood raced through his veins. He heard footsteps, reached for his pistol and grabbed it. Alina entered carrying a tray with tea, bread and jam on it. McNeill hid his pistol under his back and watched Alina move round the bed and remove the lamp from the locker, setting it on the floor and placing the tray on top of the locker. She looked good, she smelled ravishing. McNeill exhaled a long breath.

'You OK?' she asked as she poured his mug of tea.

'Yeah, sure,' he replied. 'What time is it?' he added.

Alina finished pouring the tea, got up and went to the tiny window and drew back the curtain. Sunlight made its entrance quietly, nonchalantly and serenely. McNeill guessed it was mid-morning.

'It's OK, you were tired. I didn't want to wake you. Everything is fine.' Alina tried to reassure McNeill.

Sasha appeared at the doorway holding the baby and winked at McNeill, then turned and went back to the kitchen.

'Today is Sunday,' said Alina. 'Everyone in the village will go to church shortly,' she added as she passed by him and returned to the kitchen.

Village? thought McNeill. *Christ, how the hell are we to remain unseen?* He drank the tea, ate the bread and jam, got dressed and strode into the kitchen. Alina and her aunt were sat at the table, waiting. They both smiled at McNeill, who smiled back. He went to wash himself in the bathroom and then stepped outside. He rushed back into the house; he had been outside less than a minute. He walked over to Alina and held her right arm in his left hand's firm grip.

'Where's the car?' he whispered to her sternly.

'I hid it in the far shed, out of sight, while you slept. The keys are there on the table.' She pointed. 'Now take your hand off me.' Her blue eyes were now cold and piercing.

McNeill let go, took the keys and went to inspect the far shed. Sure enough, just like she had said, the car was well and truly hidden. McNeill went over to the Cortina, climbed into the driver's seat, put the keys in the ignition and checked the fuel gauge. It registered just under a quarter of a tank. McNeill realised fuel was now a priority; as they probably had a long way to go. His thoughts turned to the sheds – farm tools, tractors, machinery of kinds... He got out of the car and started looking for petrol.

He left the shed housing the car and burst into the next. His search was halted by the sight of Alina in the doorway.

'Leaving?' she enquired.

'What?' replied McNeill.

'Are you leaving? You cannot leave us here. My father's assassins will find us and we will all be killed. You cannot go alone, you need me, you cannot leave us here.' A forceful desperation was now in her voice.

McNeill looked at her. 'Yes, you are right, I do need you. We are on the run from your father and yes, who knows what lies ahead. You speak the language, you know the routes we must take to get out alive, you must guide, and yes, you are a fugitive. We do need each other and NO, I wasn't thinking of leaving you behind, but we need petrol for the car, or shortly we will be walking. Happy?' McNeill looked at her and then said softly, 'Now help me look.'

Alina just walked straight up to McNeill, threw her arms round him, kissed him once on the lips and then on his cheek, then hugged him. McNeill was slightly taken aback. A beautiful woman had just kissed him and was now holding him tight, her lissom body pushed against his. He smelled her hair, her fragrance and he liked it!

They both searched the shed and found nothing, then continued the search in the yard outside. Alina found an empty petrol can. Alina's aunt held the baby and watched Alina and McNeill intently through the kitchen window. She had seen them embrace, then search from shed to shed. *Only a matter of time before they return here,* she thought.

McNeill's search ended when Alina found the empty petrol can. Alina and McNeill returned to the house. The patiently waiting Sasha rocked the sleeping baby in her arms.

'You need petrol, I see,' she said.

'Yes,' came McNeill's reply.

'Petrol is rationed and is in very short supply here,' Sasha replied. 'Look after your baby, feed yourselves, use whatever you need,' she added as she took her coat and exited the door. McNeill watched her through the window as she collected the empty petrol can and headed across the fields to the right of the shed. Seeing her leave made McNeill feel uneasy. He went outside and stood watching her, the house to his right, the two sheds to his left. He looked at the house and saw the window he looked through the night before situated on the back. The road was behind him. He looked on at the fields of knee-length grass which Sasha was walking through. He circled the house, bedroom, kitchen-living room, bathroom and on the road's side, living room, front door, kitchen. The bedroom with a window – Sasha's – gave a panoramic view of anyone approaching from the road. *This is where Sasha spotted and watched us approach from.* He walked round again and realised the two gable ends had no windows. *Vulnerable,* he thought.

He went inside via the rear door. Alina was making tea and she had already prepared a stew pot, which was now simmering away. They looked at each other and smiled. Alina spoke first.

'It will be OK, please trust her.' She offered McNeill a mug of tea, which he took, but he still had the knot in his stomach, still had that irksome itch. The hairs on the back of his neck began to prickle and stand. 'I don't like this,' he said.

'Why?' asked Alina.

'An old woman, without any machinery, is going to ask for and bring petrol, plus probably more food than is enough for one. We are putting her in danger, therefore putting ourselves in danger too. Your father's assassins know where we have been, but don't know where we actually are, although that should be easy to figure out, Alina,' McNeill explained.

'I agree. My father will soon realise we are here. My aunt's is too close to where you left the four dead soldiers, and I suppose by now he knows they are indeed dead. He will send others. We cannot stay here much longer,' Alina replied.

'Yes, you are right, if Sasha is not followed or if we do not have company before your aunt returns, we can take it your father has been informed and the next lot are on their way. It will be an uneasy wait.'

McNeill drank the tea, then went to the shed housing the car, reversed the car out, turned it around, then reversed the car back into the shed and removed his rifle from the boot. He walked outside into the afternoon air. The sky was overcast but no rain fell. He sat down, dismantled his rifle, cleaned it and assembled it, then walked round looking for a vantage point, one that gave him an overall panoramic view of the approach to the house, the rear of it, the rear of the sheds and the open fields beyond into which Sasha had walked. He looked, waited and thought. If Sasha was followed, if she returned the way she went, then the attack would begin on the front and rear of the house simultaneously. If unwelcome visitors came before she returned, they would drive up to the front of the house as they had done. McNeill looked again for a vantage position, but he could not find one which gave him an overall view of the house and its circumference. Smoke filtered into the sky from the chimney. McNeill walked to the rear door, propped his rifle alongside, turned and collected firewood from the shed for the stove and fire and went inside. He deposited the wood by the fire and retrieved his rifle. Alina looked at a pensive McNeill.

'What's bothering you?' she asked politely.

'Do you have any idea of how long she will be or where she has gone?' asked McNeill.

'I'm not sure as to which friend she will go, but to have a guess, it is a forty-five-minute walk for her, maybe another thirty minutes for a rest, chit-chat and to get the petrol, then forty-five minutes back, maybe a little longer as she has to carry the weight,' Alina informed McNeill.

'That's two hours. How is the baby?'

'She is fine and sleeping now after a bath and her feed,' said Alina.

'OK, pack up the bags, just in case,' instructed McNeill.

He went back outside, rifle in hand. He went through the

whole routine as before, searching for the best possible vantage point, and realised there wasn't one. He sat and watched the approach to the front of the house for an uneasy hour. Nobody came. Alina exited the rear door. From where he sat he watched her go to the shed housing the car carrying a holdall. She left the shed empty-handed. She spotted McNeill, who was now walking towards her, and smiled at him. He smiled back, a heart-warming, friendly smile. He was beginning to like her. She was growing on him emotionally, and by her childish grin he knew he was growing on her.

'Do you want tea?' she enquired. 'I have the kettle on and the stew will be ready in about an hour.'

'OK, tea it is.' They went inside together. Alina sat McNeill down at the table, and then fussed over him with tea and a sandwich. McNeill liked the attention. He looked round the kitchen. It was spotlessly clean. Alina had busied herself cleaning and mopping the whole room. The baby slept contentedly. McNeill smiled at Alina then said, 'I see you have been very busy. Your aunt will be pleased, and that stew smells good.' Alina smiled back.

McNeill went outside and moved to a position where he could see the field between the house and sheds at the rear, and the approach lane to the front door from the road. He settled down and waited. Half an hour passed: nothing. He got up and moved off behind the sheds at the rear, and entered the field to the left of the one Sasha had crossed. He moved into the field's heart and crouched down, looking through the rifle sight. He saw nothing, waited and rechecked. Just over half an hour later he saw her, Alina's aunt carrying a bag wrapped round her shoulders and two cans, one in each hand. He watched and his mind raced.

Trust her, Alina had said, *trust her.* But what if she is being followed and doesn't know? What if she is a part of the general's private army and Alina did not know it? What if she has left word that Alina and the American are at her home? McNeill did not like it, did not like it at all. He scanned behind Alina's aunt for anyone following her but saw nothing. Sasha made her way slowly but surely through the fields, but unknown to her a rifle sight followed her every step.

The lone figure carried the two petrol cans in either hand, just one lone figure crossing the field. McNeill scanned the skyline behind her for more figures, found none. He then searched as much of the front of the house as he could through his rifle sight. He found nothing. Then behind him and to his right: nothing. He went through the same motions again: nothing. Sasha had now crossed the field and was in the clearing between her house and sheds. McNeill watched as she went to the shed housing the car and laid the two petrol cans outside the door. He watched her adjust the bag back around her shoulders, watched her make her way over to the house and go inside.

McNeill checked all round, searching for more figures through the rifle sight: he saw nothing. He waited ten minutes, twenty minutes, thirty minutes, checking all the time: nothing. He moved to where he could see the approach to the house from the road, checked again: nothing. He raised his rifle, looking through the sight into the field between the sheds and the rear of the house from where Sasha had walked. The door of the house flung open and McNeill swung to aim the rifle. Alina stepped out, arms waving aloft. He could see her, she could not see him. McNeill relaxed when Sasha appeared outside holding the baby girl. He did one more check and, satisfied, he broke cover and headed for the house.

Stew was laid out on the table for him. Alina and her aunt had almost finished theirs. A small fire burned in the fireplace; now hungry, he sat down to eat. Alina and her aunt finished their stew. Alina pulled a chair up to the fire and invited her weary aunt to sit. Her aunt accepted gleefully and gratefully she sat down. Alina made tea, and began to wash the dishes. The baby cried and Alina went and took her into her arms, and as her aunt turned she gave the baby to her, returning to finish washing the dishes but McNeill was already there, doing the washing-up. She picked up a towel to dry them. McNeill took it from her, then dried the dishes with it. As he did so he caught sight of Alina's aunt watching him. He looked over. Sasha smiled and slowly nodded her head. Alina began to tease McNeill.

'How could such a big man, a clumsy, strong man, do such a gentle chore without breaking anything, and what about your hands becoming soft in the water with the washing-up liquid in it?' she giggled.

She then cupped some of the lather from the top of the washing-up water in the sink and playfully pushed her hands onto his cheeks. She walked over to a drawer and took out a pinafore and made several attempts to wrap it around McNeill, all to no avail. Alina's aunt began to laugh, Alina began to laugh, and McNeill finally laughed. Alina moved towards McNeill and threw her arms around him. McNeill held her supple body close, so close it felt so good against his. He could smell her perfume, her lovely black hair, felt the soft skin of her face against his. He kissed her cheek, marched her to a chair and sat her in it. 'Stay there,' he commanded and went to finish drying the dishes.

McNeill finished the dishes and then sat with Alina and her Aunt Sasha. Still, silent time passed. The three glanced at one another, each hoping the other would speak. Eventually, McNeill broke the ice.

'We have to move on, Alina, we cannot stay here any longer. Not only are we at risk but your lovely aunt is, too. It is better for her that when they come here, and your father's henchmen will, that we are not found here. We have to leave.'

Aunt Sasha knew McNeill was right. She looked at the baby in her arms, smiled at her and then passed her to Alina. McNeill stood, went outside and lit a cigarette. He looked around and saw nothing, then walked around the house. He saw nothing, but he was seen. He returned to the kitchen.

An old man waited for McNeill to enter the house, watched

the door close behind him, waited a bit longer. As silently as he could he stood up, limped to the road, mounted the small motor-bike he had hidden there earlier, started it and headed back to the town, a thin smile on his face. *General Tomelsky will be pleased, he will pay me well.*

It was late afternoon, early evening. 'When are you leaving?' Sasha asked McNeill. McNeill looked at her.

'Just before dark; that way, if someone is watching, we can hopefully slip away unseen,' McNeill said.

'You think someone is watching here?' Sasha enquired.

Alina turned to look at McNeill to see if McNeill mistrusted her aunt. Her eyes narrowed, her thoughts beginning to race, thoughts of being watched by a spy of her father's, thoughts of who would be coming to kill them, wondering if she would be killed, knowing McNeill would not be spared, not knowing the future for her baby girl and her Aunt Sasha. A shiver ran up her spine.

'Go on, McNeill,' she said forcefully and inquisitively.

'The bodies of the four men should have been found by now. They will search for anything near there. Alina, you recognised one of them as one of your father's killers. That means as we are still here, either there were only four of his special army in town and all were despatched to terminate us, and if so it's only when they do not check in or are stumbled upon that the alarm will be raised; or there were more than four – four sent out, one lookout or maybe two left behind, maybe one or both in the town. I would say two; one to remain in town, the other to see why the unit did not return and probably to hide their bodies. Either way, they know they are dead. Then they report to your father, who as you said, Alina, knows the proximity of your aunt's house to the town. It is only a matter of time before more of your father's henchmen arrive, and so one of the lookout men will have been sent out to make sure we are here then report back to your father, Alina,' McNeill stated.

'So that's why you were late for dinner – you thought my aunt would be followed and you planned to shoot him. You used her as bait!' said Alina angrily.

'No, Alina, I did not use her as bait. Yes, as a good soldier doing his job I checked to see if she was followed, but I checked all around the house, checked the roadside, and I saw nothing. But it is not to say that as careful as I was, I was not seen, or, in fact, that you were not seen outside either,' retorted McNeill.

Aunt Sasha spoke then. 'He is right, we both know he is right, Alina. You must leave.'

McNeill made the last mug of tea. Sasha and Alina fed and changed the baby, and Sasha held her for the last time. Then they drank the tea in silence. McNeill decided to leave now and took his rifle to the car, collecting the two cans of petrol on the way. He drove the car out of the shed and up to the door. He entered the house. Sasha had given Alina a three-quarter-length black-and-white checked coat, under which she wore a calf-length black skirt, black polo-neck sweater and sensible heeled shoes. She carried her baby. Just before the door Alina turned. Sasha ran to her, embraced her, kissed both cheeks, tears streaming down her face. McNeill picked up two bags, carried them over to Alina and Sasha and dropped them to the floor. He took Aunt Sasha in his big arms, hugged her, kissed both her cheeks and her forehead, said 'Thank you' and meant it. She whispered to him, 'Go north,' as he hugged her. McNeill then collected the two bags, went out the door and got into the car. A teary-eyed Alina followed soon after, holding her baby. They set off down the lane to the road. On reaching the road they turned right and headed north.

⇒◆⇐

The old man with the limp opened the hotel door and hobbled through the lobby to the reception telephone and began to dial. He did not recognise the voice that answered but said, 'Get me General Tomelsky, quickly. I have news of the American.' The next voice he heard was that of the general. 'Who is it and what is your news?'

'Dracek, sir. Located your daughter and the American at your wife's sister's, as you thought they would be, sir.'

The general, with a crooked smile on his face, answered, 'Ah ha, you have done well, Dracek. Rasik will be there to pay you.'

There was a click and the line went dead. The old man felt a cold shiver of fear run up and down his spine when he heard the name Rasik.

⋙⋘

McNeill turned left off the dirt track and onto the main road. The dark sky had no moon so he clicked on the dipped head-lights and broke the silence in the car.

'Your aunt is one super lady,' he said, trying to promote conversation, at the same time knowing the chances of seeing her alive again were very slim.

'Yes she is,' Alina replied. 'Now shut up and drive,' she added as she wiped a tear from her eye.

McNeill drove steadily, past the occasional dimly lit house or cottage on either side of the road, mostly with their curtains drawn tightly shut. The odd oncoming car would drive by and McNeill passed dirt track lanes which separated fields until no more cars came their way. The night air began to chill. Alina huddled into her coat, the breeze from the shot-out window somewhat icy as it swirled around inside the car. McNeill switched the heater on to full heat. The baby was wrapped up in blankets and even she did not disturb the silence.

A further hour of silence passed before McNeill slowed down. Visibility was becoming poor, a fog or mist was descending. Alina stirred. 'Where are we?' she asked.

'No idea, somewhere in Croatia,' was the reply from McNeill, who then began to laugh.

Alina tilted her head towards him slightly and made a face,

sticking her tongue out and screwing up her nose. The road began to go downhill. There was a break in the fog.

'See – see that shed roof over there on our left?' said Alina, pointing. 'It's a hay shed, an old one. Why don't we stop there in the hay shed and sleep for a while, let the fog lift? We will make better progress in the early morning then,' she added.

'Makes sense,' replied McNeill. He parked up behind the shed, making sure the car wasn't visible from the road. Alina entered the shed carrying her baby, McNeill carrying a bag and a rifle. They climbed a small ladder to the loft.

McNeill took out a blanket from the bag and laid it over the hay. Alina lay down, the baby at her side. McNeill covered them with hay to keep them warm then lay down beside Alina. Shortly Alina turned to him, rested her head on his shoulder and put one arm across his chest. McNeill looked at her and smiled. She looked at him through wide eyes. She felt safe, secure and needed. Not since Slavan had she felt so safe. The fingers of McNeill's hand traced her hairline, then caressed her cheek. She looked at him with her mouth half opened. He wanted her, but kissed her forehead before saying, 'Get some sleep. We start early in the morning.'

McNeill woke just before 4.30 a.m. and gently eased himself away from Alina's sleeping grip. He picked up his rifle and went outside. It was still dark, misty and moist. He looked around then sat between the car and the shed and smoked a cigarette. He returned inside the hay shed and woke Alina. McNeill carried the sleeping baby to the car and placed her on the back seat. Alina brought the bag and blanket, placed the bag in the back of the car and the blanket over the baby. They got into the car and drove off. The darkness combined with the intermittent fog slowed progress, but it would be the same for everybody, thought McNeill. By his side Alina slept curled into her coat in the passenger seat.

The road headed north, past sparse houses on either side enveloped in darkness and drizzle. The windscreen wipers swished to and fro. The broken window let the cold damp air in. Alina stirred and her eyes opened.

'What's in the other bag, Alina?' McNeill asked.

'Food and water, you hungry?' she mumbled.

'Yeah, slightly,' replied McNeill. Alina produced an apple from her coat pocket and gave it to McNeill. 'This should fill your slight hunger, then!' she replied with a giggle and half-smile.

The houses began to become more frequent, the roadside fields became smaller.

'Town ahead?' he asked Alina.

'Why, what makes you think there is a town ahead?' she asked.

'A lot more houses,' McNeill replied.

'Where are we?' she asked.

'I dunno, you're supposed to be the guide,' he replied, 'and whatever town it is I hope that it's friendly. It's time for me to take off this jacket and jumper. You hide it under your seat,' he added. McNeill took off the jacket and jumper. Alina leaned over and held the steering wheel as he did so. He handed the two items of clothing to her, saying, 'Wait, give me a cigarette and lighter from the pocket, please Alina.' Alina gave McNeill the cigarettes and lighter and hid the clothes under her seat. McNeill lit the cigarette and drove on into the town's boundaries. 'Any money?' he asked.

'Some, but not much,' came her reply.

McNeill entered the town. The road ran right, then left, a passage with houses on either side. McNeill's eyes scanned the area. There were very few cars, no people – perhaps they were a little early. No mortar or shell damage to any buildings, no soldiers – the war had not fully arrived here yet. He drove on slowly.

'Recognise anything, Alina?' he asked.

'No, nothing,' she said.

He drove on slowly, past more parked cars. Some people who were outside a house paid no attention to him. Ahead of him the door of a jeep was left open. McNeill pulled up, got out and walked ahead. Alina watched as McNeill walked to the jeep and bent down, as if looking for something he had dropped onto the road. He then took something out from the side of the door, stuffed whatever it was under his shirt and walked back. The whole episode went unnoticed by any of the people. McNeill got into the car and removed a map from under his shirt and handed it to Alina. 'Hide it,' he said as he drove on up the street.

The road turned left, then right, then widened beyond, but before it widened there it was – the very thing McNeill had thought was missing: an army checkpoint. Alina saw it, smiled apprehensively and immediately looked at McNeill through horror-filled eyes. If McNeill turned around now, it would be a dead giveaway, and the men would come after him with bullets flying or perhaps there was now a rifle pointed straight at them. So he drove on straight ahead, straight into the lion's den. Alina, horrified, stared at McNeill, her stare met by the calculating blank expression on his face.

'Get the baby and a bottle,' he ordered. 'Wake the baby when I almost reach the guard and make her cry, then get out and create a holy stink about anything and point to me when I stop the car, you understand?'

Alina understood and nodded. She reached into the rear of the car and removed a bottle from the bag and collected her baby from the back seat.

They approached the sentry, who halted them and began to walk from the front of the car towards McNeill. The baby cried. The sentry bent down and looked at McNeill. McNeill's heart pumped the blood through his arteries. His pulse raced, yet he remained calm and in total control. Alina thrust the baby onto McNeill's lap, thrust the bottle into McNeill's hand, got out of the car and promptly gave the sentry a lecture on how he, her no-good husband, never does anything. 'Any time and every time the baby cries, it's me – ME! – who has to feed and change her, wash her, dress her, nurse her, make the food for her. All he did was father the useless brat!' She demonstrated her point with an animated forefinger. McNeill looked at the sentry and threw his eyes to the sky. The baby cried more at the sound of Alina's raised voice.

'Get in the car, woman, and go!' shouted the sentry as he backed away from the car and gave the order to raise the barrier. Alina got into the car. McNeill gave her the baby and drove through.

'Brilliant. Absolutely superb, what an actress, give this lady an Oscar!' exclaimed McNeill with a broad smile on his face.

She raised her eyebrows and dropped her chin slightly, exhaled through puffed out cheeks and said, 'I was shitting a brick.' McNeill laughed.

The town became busier. More uniforms and guns became visible, more everyday townspeople going to the shops for food. Some just stood smoking, others gazing at nothing and some talking in small groups. McNeill saw a small cafeteria and pulled up in a parking space just beyond it. 'Bring the baby and an empty bottle,' he ordered as he got out.

He went inside the cafe and Alina followed. Two tables of four were in each window either side of the entrance door. The sandwich bar extended down the wall on McNeill's left to the end wall. Booths, each with two benches designed to fit four people, ran down the right-hand side, four in all. Two more tables of four were at the cafe's rear. Alina ordered milk for her baby and two teas. McNeill picked a booth near the front, one which gave him a good view of the entrance and would enable Alina to eavesdrop on the eight soldiers talking at the two tables at the rear of the cafe. Alina sat opposite McNeill, gave her baby the bottle of milk and watched as she suckled contentedly. The attendant brought the two teas. McNeill took the baby from her and continued with the feed, only this time the baby sucked contentedly with wide open eyes. Alina, nervous, watched and began to eavesdrop on the soldiers' conversation. McNeill calmly fed the baby and drank his mug of tea. Alina had almost drunk her mug of tea when, startled, she kicked McNeill's right leg. McNeill casually looked at her.

Alina gestured to the car with her hands. McNeill sat and fed the baby. Alina kicked his leg again. McNeill calmly finished his tea, then stood. Alina stood and they walked casually and slowly out of the cafe and over to the Cortina. McNeill gave her the baby before they got into the car. McNeill started the car and gently pulled away from the kerbside. People were queuing at the bakery for bread, the same at the butcher's. The main street of the town stretched for almost a hundred yards, shops on either side. A cobbled walkway separated the two traffic flows, trees surrounded by black painted iron railings dotted its centre. McNeill noticed that some of the shops were in dire need of a lick of paint. People milled around a small supermarket entrance. All the bars were closed but the two hotels had their doors open. They passed another cafe. The chairs and tables outside were occupied by soldiers eating and drinking. All the restaurants were closed and litter blew down the street. More people were joining the street from walkways on either side. McNeill drove through. The main street's cobbled central walkway ended and McNeill found himself driving on a single file road. An army jeep raced up towards his rear bumper. McNeill pulled his Beretta out of its holster and placed it on his lap as he pulled over. The jeep raced by. He turned to Alina. 'OK, let's have it – what were the soldiers talking about?'

Alina began to blabber. 'Slow down, take a deep breath. Talk slowly and calm down,' said McNeill as he stopped the car.

'They know I have my baby. They found the dead patrol in the tunnel and the other on the hills. Another patrol is on its way to my aunt's to kill you and capture us. There is a reward for my capture alive, and a reward for you dead only.' Alina then began to become hysterical. 'He will find us and get us...'

McNeill forcefully gripped her, shook her then stopped her from saying anymore by placing his right hand over her mouth. He leaned over, let his right hand slip to her shoulder, kissed her gently on the cheek and whispered into her ear, 'No, they won't, everything will be OK, they think we are still at your aunt's.'

McNeill had barely spoken the word 'aunt' when Alina began shaking and shouting.

'Sasha, my Aunt Sasha, OH NO…!' The 'no' tailed off as she began to wail.

'Pull yourself together. We have made it this far. I will look after you,' said McNeill. Alina looked at him through crying eyes, still shaking. 'Pull yourself together,' McNeill said forcibly. Gripping her he kissed her forehead, then went on, 'Now, let's take a look at that map and see which is the best way to go. You choose, Alina – your tyrannical father and his henchmen, or freedom.' McNeill loosened his grip.

'Let's get out of town, somewhere safe and quiet before we take this map out. It may look a little too conspicuous here.'

McNeill smiled. He had his answer. He sat back into the driver's seat and drove away slowly. He drove to the end of the single-file road with buildings and sub-let apartments on either side and was forced to stop. An army convoy roared past from right to left, then turned right, heading out of town. Trucks with soldiers, jeeps pulling field guns and heavy machine guns, petrol tankers, a munitions truck, a hospital truck, more men in cars and jeeps, supply trucks, more men in two cars. McNeill turned left and tagged along.

'What the hell are you doing, McNeill? Soldiers are looking for us and you ride along with them?' Alina screamed at him.

'Listen, this convoy is heading out of town. It will drive straight through any roadblock. Quick, pass me my rifle from under the blanket stretched all along the back seat under the baby, and my jacket. Then get down in the back between the seats and try to keep out of sight,' McNeill ordered in a commanding tone of voice. Alina did as she was asked. McNeill, after putting on his jacket, pulled out, accelerated and overtook the last two cars, the last two trucks and two more cars before pulling in to join the convoy. It powered through the sentry outpost at the north end of town.

A couple of miles flashed by, then McNeill slowed down and

pulled off the road. The two cars and trucks passed by, the next car slowed. McNeill was now around to the passenger side of the Cortina, his back to the soldiers. They shouted and he waved them on with his left hand. The last car slowed. McNeill pretended to take a leak. There were jeers from the car. McNeill waved them on. Its occupants laughing, the car roared away. McNeill held up the solitary middle finger of his left hand, turned and watched them go out of sight. Alina was laughing and sat up.

'OK, what's so funny?' asked McNeill.

'You sure you want to know?' Alina enquired, teasing.

'Yep, what did they say?' asked McNeill.

'OK,' she said, 'you want to know.' She tried to stop herself from smiling. 'Big man, big chest, big muscles... small pecker,' she said. 'Is that true?' she asked cheekily.

'Wouldn't you like to know!' replied McNeill. And they both laughed.

⟫◇⟪

The old man with a right leg limp fell four storeys to his death. Seconds later, Rasik left by the hotel front door.

Later, he arrived at Alina's Aunt Sasha's, ransacked the house looking for the briefcases, said nothing, found nothing. He had his men tie Sasha to a chair. 'Leave! Get out!' he barked at them. Then Rasik lit a cigarette and took a few delightful puffs before watching the slow burning tobacco redden as he exhaled the smoke onto the smouldering cigarette end held by his fingers a short distance away from his mouth.

'Where are they?' Rasik hissed menacingly into Sasha's right ear. Sasha said nothing. Rasik put the lighted cigarette onto the back of her right hand. Sasha screamed as it burned her flesh. He put it to his mouth and took a pull.

'Where are they?' Rasik hissed again.

Still no answer from Sasha. Rasik took the pan full of boiling water from the stove and poured some on her legs above her knees. Sasha screamed and almost passed out with the pain, but Rasik stopped pouring; he wanted her conscious.

'Once more, where are they?' he hissed as he moved to the back of her and pushed her head forward and lifted her hair to reveal the bare skin of her neck and shoulders. Sasha could feel the heat of the saucepan, sense the steam off the boiling water.

'They're gone, gone,' she whispered as her head rocked, the pain from her blistered red legs excruciating.

'Gone where?' Rasik asked in a low voice loaded with intent as he moved to face her. He bent down, putting the pan onto the floor, then slapped her scorched legs. Sasha screamed in agony. 'Talk!' Rasik venomously demanded, raising his hand to slap her thighs again.

'Gone. The American decided it was not safe to remain here and they left early this morning.' She moaned with the agonising pain and her head sank.

'Where have they gone? Who have they gone to? Which way did they go?' Rasik asked firmly, now gently picking at his teeth with a matchstick on bended knee.

Sasha replied with silence. Rasik put the pan back onto the hot stove, then asked the same question again. Sasha, summoning all her reserves of courage, remained silent. Rasik removed the pan, went behind Sasha, lifted her hair and let droplets of boiling water drip onto her bare neck at the join with her shoulders. He could smell the burning flesh. Sasha screamed and squirmed on the chair. The binds on her wrists cut into her skin, blood began to ooze and drip to the floor. Again Rasik ceased before she slipped into unconsciousness.

He asked again, 'Where have they gone? Who have they gone to and which way did they go?'

A now broken Aunt Sasha whimpered, 'I don't know where or who, but they turned left onto the main road. '

'And of this you are sure?' hissed Rasik as he let more droplets of boiling water hit her tortured skin.

'YESSSSsss, aarggh!' she screamed. Her body fought the binds on her wrists and ankles as she squirmed in agony, the binds now cutting deeper into her flesh, releasing blood to run and drip to the floor, the binds holding her captive to the torture as she rocked the chair.

Rasik put the pan down silently, took out his pistol, placed the barrel at the back of Sasha's head, said thank you and pulled the trigger. He stormed outside and yelled, 'Load up! Load up and drive, drive to the next town,' as he climbed into his jeep. The jeep in front sped off down the lane. At the road Rasik hissed through a twisted, contented smile. 'Lying bitch. Turn right.'

<hr />

Alina got out of the car, walked around and stretched her legs, then turned to McNeill and said, 'I'm hungry, are you?'

'Yes, a little peckish,' was his reply.

Alina went to the car boot and opened it. There, between the two briefcases, was the bag of food her aunt had given her. McNeill helped her take it out. Alina opened the bag and McNeill looked at the briefcases. 'Whatever is in those briefcases people are dying for?' he said to Alina. Alina tucked into ham, cheese, tomato and onion sandwiches and offered one to McNeill, who ate then drank from a bottle of water. He got the map and spread it out on the floor using stones to keep it flat.

'OK, where are we, Alina?' he asked.

She pointed to approximately where they were and then showed McNeill her father's village some way below. McNeill then asked, 'Which would be your father's strongest areas and his weakest?'

Alina began drawing circles with her index finger, speaking as she did. 'Mostly my father's strongest areas are in the south, with strong links east, north-east and west.'

'Mmm, that's why your aunt told me to head north, she also knew this,' said McNeill.

Alina went on, 'Yes, but the north of the country is very mountainous with very little population apart from scattered large towns.'

'All the better – easier for us to hide, easier for us to remain unseen longer,' said McNeill.

'But there are very few places to find food or shelter to sleep, and the weather will be colder. What about the baby?' asked Alina.

'True, and it might be easier to cut us off knowing the direction we are taking, but if we are quick enough and with luck we may be able to outrun and outmanoeuvre your father, especially as you say his loyal factions are not as strong in depth this way,' countered McNeill.

'That does not mean to say he hasn't got his fanatics up there,' replied Alina candidly.

'Yes, also true, but if we use speed and stealth and if they are spread out and thin on the ground then he might not be able to mobilise them quickly enough to catch us,' said McNeill calculatingly.

'It doesn't matter – that's Serbian territory, that's where the main war is. If we go north, we have father's henchmen snapping at our heels, and the whole Serbian army to get through,' Alina replied with desperation.

'I would rather take my chances fighting the Serbians. At least you know who the enemy are,' said McNeill dryly, adding, 'So when you get a chance, you read what's in those briefcases.'

McNeill folded the map. Alina folded the uneaten sandwiches away into the bag, put the bag into the well behind the passenger seat and took out one of the briefcases from the boot. Once settled in her seat she began to go through the documents. McNeill drove on. Half an hour passed. Alina had said nothing, she was immersed in the documentation. The blood had drained from her face and she was as white as a ghost.

'Nice reading material, hey?' asked McNeill.

Alina never said a word. She was totally oblivious to what McNeill had said, and tears began to slide down her cheeks. McNeill slowed down. Another twenty minutes had passed and Alina was now weeping. He passed her his handkerchief, put his hand on her left arm, gently squeezed. 'You OK?' he asked. She broke down and wept uncontrollably. McNeill pulled off the road, then put a comforting arm around her. 'Anything you want to tell me?' he asked quietly and with concern.

'McNeill, if you knew what was in those documents my father would have you killed,' she said.

'Aren't you forgetting something there? He already wants me dead, according to the soldiers back there, so come on – fill me in,' he said matter-of-factly.

'These documents list times and dates of killings, murders, assassinations – all done on behalf of my father. They list monies received for favours, bribery, embezzlement, prostitution, protection rackets, gunrunning. My father is corrupt to the core, an evil, power-hungry dictator, who when anyone stands up to him has them brutalised, tortured, or eliminated, and whole families too. He has been selling stockpiled Croatian army munitions to the Serbians and now our supplies of arms are running low. Many Croatians will die in this war while he makes a substantial profit, and Croatian people think he is a war hero. He has had political enemies, their wives and children blown to smithereens by bombs planted by his most loyal fanatics, then framed someone else for his criminal acts,' said Alina with a weeping heart.

'Nasty piece of work, your father. Now take it easy, put the papers back into the briefcase and get the other one and read what's in there – maybe it will not be as bad,' suggested McNeill.

Alina exchanged briefcases, settled in the passenger seat and began to read. McNeill drove on. Once again the colour drained from Alina's face, until she broke down and wept uncontrollably, her body heaving and her head in her hands. McNeill again pulled off the road.

'Hey,' he said, holding her in his arms. 'Hey, it can't be that bad. Tell me, c'mon, tell me.'

'He paid the Serbians to deliver Slavan's patrol to him, they had no chance – dates, time, whereabouts and where they were headed…' Tears billowed from her eyes as she spoke.

'And the rest?' asked McNeill.

'Yes, he pays for information. And some high-powered government officials are in his pocket. Those men you assassinated were on their way to arrest him, to charge him and to bring him to trial. Obviously his spies found out and told him. Not only that, there are war crimes, rape, pillaging, murders, large homes and land being suddenly signed over to him or his trusted soldiers from his own side, people disappearing...' Her voice tailed off and merged with her tears.

'Quite a large can of worms, then!' McNeill said sarcastically. Minutes of silence followed uneasily for McNeill; he knew he had upset her and thinking of his comments he felt stupid. 'Sorry, that was rather crass and unsympathetic of me, I did not mean to upset you, I'm sorry,' he said.

⇒◆⇐

Rasik entered the town. The thin, wiry man made his way, after speaking to several soldiers, to the cafe, the one McNeill and Alina visited earlier that day. He already knew that the brown Cortina which belonged to Yiddich was spotted in the town earlier; now he wanted to be sure, doubly sure of its occupants, before reporting to his boss, Alina's father. The cafe owner was more than willing to talk.

'The only couple with a baby were in earlier – a big man. My wife saw them get into a brown car and head north out of town,' the cafe owner said.

'Just the two adults and a baby in the car, nobody else?' enquired Rasik, his low voice tinged with menace.

'No, no, just as you say – man, woman and child,' replied the cafe owner. Rasik despatched two of his men to the roadblock on the town's north side, turned and ordered coffee.

Shortly, the two men returned and informed Rasik how the car was part of the convoy and had been let straight through. Rasik scowled (idiots), then a wry smile crossed his face; smart,

American, very clever. Rasik got up, left the cafe and marched to the hotel, demanding to use the telephone. The woman behind the desk refused. Rasik took out his pistol and shot the mirror just behind her in the reception booth to pieces. He rang General Tomelsky. He told him that McNeill and his daughter and baby passed through hours previously. He listened and heard the general's voice reach fever pitch. Rasik's lips curled into a smile.

'Get them, Rasik. Get them at all costs, do whatever it takes, bring me those briefcases.'

Rasik put down the phone, left the hotel and returned to the cafe.

'Eat quickly. Two men, get fuel – top up both vehicles,' he barked. Two men sprang to their feet and ran out the door past Rasik. The thin wiry man sat down at the table and checked his watch. 'Bring me a map,' he ordered; his brain began to calculate. He estimated they were two hours behind, and that McNeill wouldn't dare drive too fast; the convoy was in front and he would not want to catch up with it, and he would sleep for a few hours. Neither would McNeill drive too far at night as he would be seen for miles using headlights, so any night driving would be done on side-lights. Progress would be slow by side-light driving and the smart thing to do would be to park up and set off at first light and follow the convoy at a safe distance. *Whereas we can drive as fast as we dare, change drivers and keep going.*

Rasik estimated contact somewhere between twelve and fifteen hours if they did not stop; however, that was unlikely. The convoy was ahead, and they would stop for a few hours to sleep. The American would not dare to pass it; they would have roadblocks. With four to six hours' sleep they should spot the American in six to eight hours. But it would be dark then – his chances of finding the American would be slim, as he would pull off somewhere safe to sleep. He looked at the map, checked his watch. 'Eat, then sleep. We leave in five hours. Midnight,' he commanded. Rasik smiled. Four to five hours' sleep, five to six hours to catch up in daylight, convoy in front, them behind, nice little trap, and soon the trap would be tightened.

Rasik eyed his men: two drivers, very accomplished, two ruthless, battle-hardened warriors who had served him for years, a spotter for his Croatian sniper, one of the best in the world, and the incredible hulk of a man just in case of close-hand combat, his speciality. Rasik was happy, smug in the knowledge that his crack crew had the element of surprise. He guessed the American would expect someone to come after them, but not know when or how, or how soon. He broke into a vicious, sadistic laugh – it was only one American, a woman and a baby his crack crew were after. Kill the American, bring the briefcases to the general along with the baby, and his daughter would be their plaything before she died. Rasik began to laugh as he considered. 'Do whatever it takes.' He laughed louder; he liked the odds.

⋙◆⋘

McNeill soothed Alina, took the documents from her and replaced them in the briefcases. He dumped both briefcases into the boot, got behind the steering wheel and drove off. The baby woke and Alina breastfed her. McNeill looked at her, watched her feed her baby. All she had was the baby and him, and at this point all he had was her and her baby. She was growing on him; he liked what he saw. Her faced glowed when she laughed, she gave his heart a lift.

The soldier in McNeill took over, told him he had to keep going, survive, close up to the convoy, close enough to use it for his advantage. Documents like those would make sure someone was coming and approaching as fast as they could. He accelerated. An hour later he made out the dust clouds from the convoy up ahead. *Keep a safe distance, camp when they camp, move when they move,* he told himself. He turned to Alina, saying, 'We may have to sleep under the stars tonight and it may be cold, try to sleep now.'

He drove on. The baby slept, Alina slept and the day began to darken. McNeill looked at the terrain; the flat fields had given way to hills, mountains now in the far distance. Trees clumped together adorned the hillsides, set back from either side of the road. The road carved its way through the hills, and the hills deepened further on. He could see the lights of the convoy in the distance. He was sure they could see his dimmed headlights. In the twilight the convoy began to slow and he could see that he was closing on the convoy. *They are stopping,* he thought. McNeill slowed and killed his lights, watching the convoy pull off the road ahead. 'Making camp for the night,' he said to himself as he stopped the car off the road. The bumping of the uneven ground woke Alina. 'Wait here,' he said as he got out, taking his rifle with him.

A little over an hour later he returned. 'Where the hell have you been?' asked Alina sternly.

'Cold, are we?' asked McNeill.

'Freezing. I did not start the car because I was afraid to,' she said.

McNeill climbed in, started the engine and put the heater on, but no lights, and drove back to the road, going slowly down a long decline, his eyes searching. Suddenly he swung the car to the left. The nearer hill protruded further than the lower hill. The division between them rose steadily, wide enough for a car. He drove through and reached the top of the rise dividing the two hills, then he levelled out before a slow descent, using the edges of both hills, sometimes zigzagging to keep the car balanced. They levelled out into a small field, a disused barn shed at the far side. McNeill drove over to the barn at the far side, opened the hanging barn door and reversed the car inside. There was just enough room for the car to fit into the barn. He squeezed himself out of the car, closed the barn door and looked up at the roof. Shafts of light from the stars entered through splinters in the wood and gaps in the rusted corrugated sheets of metal. It was murky inside, but warmer than the cold chill of night outside, and there was an upstairs loft on his right. He poked around and found a ladder. He ushered Alina to the loft and climbed after her carrying the baby and his rifle, then descended the rickety ladder and retrieved the two holdalls from the car.

'Are we safe here?' Alina enquired.

'Think so. This field and barn cannot be seen from the main road, you have to be on the second line of hills to see this and there will be no patrols from the convoy coming out this far either,' said McNeill.

'What's behind us, McNeill?' asked Alina.

'Don't you mean what's in front of us, Alina?' McNeill questioned.

'Don't play games with me – the convoy is in front and you seem OK with that, but you constantly checked your rear-view mirror, as if expecting someone, so what's behind us, McNeill?' she asked, somewhat agitated.

'Your father's henchmen. They will come, they will not rest until they have those briefcases,' McNeill replied in a matter-of-fact fashion.

'Thank you, McNeill, thank you for your honesty… Eventually,' Alina replied.

'Let's eat,' said McNeill.

Alina opened the bag containing the food and drink while McNeill spread out a blanket.

'Sandwiches, fruit or both?' she asked, adding, 'With water, I presume; the milk is for the baby.'

McNeill looked into the other bag: more clothes and cotton nappies for the baby, a jumper for Alina, two hand towels and two facecloths. He thought of Sasha and hoped she was OK. Alina passed the sandwiches to McNeill then fed and changed her baby, humming a tune as she did. McNeill took one sandwich and passed the rest back to Alina. He watched her, then made a makeshift bed out of gathered straw for Alina and her baby and said, 'Get some sleep.' Alina lay down as McNeill climbed down the ladder, his rifle on his back.

McNeill went out the barn door, closing it behind him, and out into the chill of night. He walked away from the barn and climbed the hills, circumnavigating the barn before returning, opening and closing the barn door behind him. On the way to the ladder he collected Alina's coat from the car, then climbed to the loft. Alina was half awake and shivering with the cold. The baby was sleeping, clothed and wrapped in a large towel on the straw beside her. McNeill put the coat over Alina, put some loose straw over her legs and lay down beside her. She turned towards him. Her eyes seemed to be willing him, beckoning him. McNeill looked at her; the ice in him began to melt. He stroked her hair, pulled her to him. His left arm moved to the small of her back, her head tilted slightly backwards as her lips parted. The baby woke, crying. McNeill looked at Alina, then at the baby, who was now wailing; he knew sound travelled farther by night, so he moved his left arm away from Alina and scooped the baby up, placing her between himself and Alina. The baby looked at them both, and seemed to smile at them as she moved her arms and legs.

'She is laughing at us,' Alina said to McNeill, who began to laugh. He wrapped his arm around both baby and her and said again, 'Get some sleep.' McNeill could not sleep. He dozed, lay awake, dozed, woke and began to think. His mind raced back to his wife and daughter, then the war, to his best friend Fitz. How he was now caught up in a race for survival. Survival for a baby girl, her mother and himself. How could he escape capture? He thought of Fitz, how would he handle it? On missions he always got them in and out. His way would be the best way. Sleep eventually came to him.

———⟫◆⟪———

McNeill woke with a start. Alina was bent over him and had been shaking him. She told him he had been dreaming, talking and shouting in his sleep, and how she had woken when the baby cried for a feed, which she had given. 'But it's now heading for six by my watch and a lot later than you wanted to leave, McNeill.'

'Shit,' said McNeill emphatically as he sat up. He took a mouthful of water, sloshed it round his mouth and spat it out. 'The bags and the baby, Alina, where are they?' he asked.

'In the car,' came her reply. McNeill grabbed his rifle and water, Alina the blanket and they climbed down the ladder to the car. Alina threw the blanket into the back of the car over the child. 'Open the door, I will drive,' she called to McNeill. Surprised, he opened the barn door. The sun had not yet risen from slumber either and the sky was dark and murky. Alina drove the car out through the barn door. McNeill shut the door then, more to his surprise, he climbed into the passenger seat. 'No lights,' he said to Alina.

Alina drove through the field, then upwards using the slopes on the hills just like McNeill had done the night before, and onto the level ground. Soon she began to drive down the small incline to the road below between the hills. With no dimmed headlights to light up her way she had driven with a lot more care and was a lot slower. Suddenly she braked hard, the Cortina coming to a dead stop. McNeill saw it flash past. Alina could go no further, horror was written all over her face. McNeill grabbed his rifle, ran part way down to the road then walked the rest of the way. At the roadside he peered right, saw nothing, looked left and saw a huge cloud of dust rising. *Those cars are definitely on a mission and we are that mission,* he thought as he turned and started the climb back to Alina.

'Two vehicles, one jeep and one car – doesn't matter, that's four in each, eight in total, not such good odds,' he mumbled, thinking aloud. McNeill arrived at the Cortina and climbed into the passenger seat. 'Follow the cars,' he told Alina.

'Are you mad?' she replied.

'Follow the cars at a safe distance and let me think,' McNeill replied in a stern tone.

Alina drove down the descent and turned left onto the road

and accelerated. McNeill watched the dust clouds intently as he sat there, his mind whirring like a computer. Alina was hard pressed to keep up and not slip too far back in the distance. *Whatever or whoever is in front is certainly in a hurry*, thought McNeill. He thought of Fitz, cold, calculating, watchful, a master planner. He would have turned to follow, he would watch, formulate and watch some more. It would not be long before those two vehicles caught up with the convoy. If they had new orders for the convoy, they would pass them on, then either stay with the convoy or turn around and drive back slowly. McNeill smiled. He checked his weapons, checked his pockets for spare magazines, making sure his weapons were fully loaded. McNeill's smile became a smug laugh. He was thinking of Fitz, and remembering. Alina watched McNeill in horror. Was he enjoying this game of life or death? Did it excite him, she wondered. Once again her father and the war had ensnared her.

A time filled with tension and anxiety for Alina was broken when she heard McNeill's voice telling her to slow down and stop as they were stopping ahead. McNeill got out and looked around: flat fields on both sides. He raised his rifle and peered through the sight, and made out the convoy and what looked like raised ground in front of it. McNeill thought, then jumped onto the car bonnet, then the roof and looked through the sight again. He shouted to Alina to move ahead slowly. Then he yelled 'Stop!' and stood erect on the car roof and looked through the rifle sight. He waited. The car inched slowly forward; he slammed his right boot into the Cortina's roof to reinforce the stop command. He watched, his mind calculating.

Alina sat in the driver's seat worrying, her foot on the brake, contemplating McNeill playing a game with their lives, the what ifs. What was she doing? Why drive closer, why not turn and run? But she trusted him. McNeill watched as the convoy began to move. The dust cloud was huge. He peered and he waited. Two more dust clouds exited the larger one and merged into one smaller one: then a gap developed between the smaller dust cloud and the larger one. McNeill figured they were on their way back looking for them. He weighed up the options. Either the convoy had new orders and the cars were going to return – so if he and Alina pulled off the road somewhere they would just drive past – or they really were looking for them, and in their haste and with some good fortune for Alina and himself they had now caught the convoy, asked to see if they had passed by and been told no. Now they had turned around, but the hunter was now the hunted. *We shall see.*

McNeill looked at the terrain. He was watching and thinking. The odds were still more favourable for the hunted. He tapped the car roof, telling Alina to move on as he sat down on it. McNeill watched the dust cloud ahead. He yelled to Alina to stop, stood up once again and peered through the rifle sight. The dust cloud had divided. McNeill watched as the dust clouds disappeared. Pulling off the road, planning an ambush? He embedded the location in his mind, waited and watched. Stillness descended ahead. McNeill got down from the car roof and got in.

'Drive on the other side of the road. They are behind that rise in the ground,' said McNeill, now pointing to a hilltop, adding, 'They have less chance of seeing you on this side, but get to that bend ahead very quickly and pull in just before it.'

Alina followed the orders. 'What are our chances?' she asked. McNeill explained their situation with an air of calm and authority.

'OK, it's like this: they do not know we have seen them, only that we are behind. I think they are laying an ambush ahead, expecting us to waltz right in. They know how many of us there are; we don't know how many there are of them for sure – two cars might mean eight, maybe. We know where their ambush is. Eight professional soldiers against one sniper, a woman and a baby. Not good, is it? But we cannot turn around and run. They will wait there only for a short while then come after us and then in the daylight it's just a matter of time before they catch us, and this terrain is worthless to us. At least where they are planning to ambush us gives us good cover too. Still, the odds are better but not great, though.'

McNeill tried to assess the force ahead. Eight men – one officer, one sniper, one spotter, two drivers, both competent soldiers, each probably with semi-automatic machine guns, probably AK-47s, that's five – three other specialists. A formidable unit. Alina switched off the car engine.

McNeill got out and went to the car's boot. He took off his black jumper and put back on his jacket, took the half-empty bottle of water and drank some, offered the rest to Alina. 'Drink,' he said. Alina refused at first, but McNeill was adamant. She drank her fill. McNeill tipped the remainder out, and half filled the bottle with petrol from the can. He opened a bag and ripped a facecloth in half, stuffed both halves in his jacket pocket and put the top back on the bottle, then put the bottle into another pocket. He took out another bottle from the bag and did the same. Then he unholstered his Beretta pistol, took off the safety and gave it to Alina.

'Now listen and listen carefully,' he said. 'I reckon we have one hour or maybe a shade over, especially if they think I have been keeping far behind the convoy so as to avoid being seen, or I am a slow driver. In one hour and fifteen minutes you drive the car round this bend. They will see the dust cloud and know a car is approaching. I will show you through this rifle sight where you will pull in for only a few minutes in a moment. When you round this bend they will have a full view of the car. The officer will have his binoculars trained on the exit. Come, I will show you where I want you to stop.'

They walked alongside the road, then moved to some large rocks near the bend, crouching now. McNeill poked the rifle over the rock, checked the roadside and the incline far ahead, then aligned his rifle back down the road.

'Here, Alina, look.' There was a small jut in the hillside, where it almost touched the road. Alina looked at it through the rifle sight. McNeill spoke. 'In one hour and fifteen minutes you drive the car to there, you stop, you make it look like you have to go to the toilet, anything, but you take your baby out unseen and leave it there. You leave your baby there. Are we clear?' he asked.

'Yes,' said Alina.

'OK, then you get back into the car. At this point you are out of range for sniper shot, just. You drive off slowly.' He took the rifle, looked through the sight and moved it along the road. He showed Alina the spot through the sight. 'You drive to here, but you wander all over the road like you have had a puncture. You turn the car so the passenger side of the car faces them, faces down the road, so you can get out the driver's side, and if you have to you crawl all the way back to your baby. Are we clear? You crawl if you have to but you do not show yourself at any moment, understand?'

'Yes, I understand,' came Alina's reply. McNeill shouldered his rifle.

'Check your watch. One hour and fifteen minutes from now, understand?'

'Yes, McNeill, yes,' she imparted, 'I UNDERSTAND!'

'Good,' said McNeill, adding flippantly, 'I have to go now, and don't be late.'

McNeill turned, walked back to within touching distance of the car, then climbed the west side of the first hill with ease and disappeared from Alina's view. McNeill made good progress along the sides of the next two hills, moved to the bottom of the next before sprinting through short grass for 30 yards. He checked his watch. He calculated forty-five minutes to get into position and a further half-hour to assess and flush them out. He climbed the hill slowly, not making too much noise and as he approached the top. He lay down just before the ridge and looked round through the now detached rifle sight and back up the road towards Alina. He figured one sniper would be high with a perfect shot just before the left bend after the quick right-hand turn in the road: there the car would be going slow. Once around that left-hand bend all hell would break loose and the car would be shot to pieces. Just one problem for you, boys – the car isn't going to get that far. McNeill allowed for two machine guns either side of the road around the left-hand bend, one straight ahead – that's four – an officer somewhere on that hill to get a good overall view of the road, maybe the spotter off on the hill in front of him to the right. That way, when the car makes the right turn it's open to both snipers, front and rear. That made seven men. Where would number eight be? Not much time to guess. Good planning, perfect ambush, one problem – the car isn't going to get that far and that means the only sniper with a clear shot at Alina is the one on the officer's right ahead on the next hill. He must be taken out first.

McNeill now formulated his moves. He retraced his steps down the hillside and moved stealthily around its arc at the bottom. The sun was rising. *Good, if I stay low, my shadow will be cast away from me, making it easier to approach and find the first kill; however, across open country my shadow will be a giveaway to the other sniper.* He would have to be extra careful. He checked his watch: twenty-seven minutes had passed. He pictured the road in his mind, hills on either side, steeper ones on its right. The road cut the hills in half on the right-hand bend. There was level grassland to the hills in front before the road bent left to once again cut through the hills. He briskly walked, hunched over, along the side of the hills away from the road. The sniper would be visible from behind, invisible from the front. He stopped. Trees, bushes and tall grass were over to his left. He entered into them; a further ten minutes passed.

He moved into a thicker cluster of trees, peering to his right every few paces. He saw the expanse of level grass and stones from the right turn to the line of hills and he kept moving, approaching the hill where he thought the first sniper would be. He went round the back of it. A smaller hill was behind, connected to another small hill, then a mound which grew out of where the hills met level ground. He could see the road moving off to the horizon. He made his way to the edge of the trees, checked the hills, saw nothing, checked them again. *Where is the officer? He should be on that hill over there, overseeing, but I don't see him.* McNeill checked his watch; ten more minutes had passed. *Time is beginning to ebb away,* he thought, *don't do anything stupid or rash, everything is OK, so far, so good.* He was trying to calm himself. He eyed the middle-sized hill and surmised that the sniper would be on the other side. He looked round again, double-checked and saw no one.

He left the cover of the trees, staying very low. He made it quite easily to the middle-sized hill and began to climb just off centre, keeping his back in line with the trees. As he stealthily neared the top he began to crawl. Fifteen minutes later he reached the top, crawled over the flat hilltop and at the far edge looked out over the road. There, below and to his left, about 80 yards away, were three men with machine guns. A monument of a man stood in the road with another machine gun – that's four counted for – and maybe two others on the far side, two snipers. He slouched back, removed the two bottles from his pockets and the two pieces of ripped facecloth, wet both pieces of cloth with petrol, stuffed one in each bottle, then set down Fitz's lighter and his sniper rifle.

McNeill crawled to the higher hill on his right and made his way silently up its right side. He reached the top. Adrenalin was now pumping through his veins as he peered over the edge. There, lying in a perfect little hollow not 10 feet below, his rifle pointing out at the road, eye peering down the sight, his left hand on top to shield the sun, his right forefinger near the trigger, motionless, hardly breathing was McNeill's first kill. McNeill slipped his right hand into his boot, pulled out his knife, his heart now pounding against his ribcage, a cold sweat on his forehead as he slid over the ridge towards the sniper. *If he turns round now, I'm dead,* thought McNeill, but the sniper was intent on looking through the rifle sight at the road.

The sniper heard a twig snap behind him and he turned, releasing the rifle stock from his right shoulder, bringing his finger away from the trigger. He thought it was Rasik, but death came in the silent form of McNeill. In half-turning, the sniper had shown his soft underbelly. The thrust of McNeill's blade pierced the solar plexus, moving upwards behind his ribcage into his heart. He silently let out his last breath and left this world behind. McNeill took the rifle and searched the body, finding a pistol, then turned the body to face the earth; that way, the metal of the knife would not glint in the sun. He returned, crawling, to the flat mound where he had left his rifle and two bottles.

He set the sniper's rifle pointing to the far side of the road, just in front of the three men below, so that he would not be caught in any crossfire. He checked his watch. Exactly one hour and thirteen minutes had passed. *Shit, hurry McNeill, she will be on her way any minute now. Come on, McNeill, one dead and four definite identifications, c'mon!* said the soldier's voice in his head. The skin on the back of his neck began to tingle, the hair on it to prickle and stand up, his own telltale signs of something's not right. *Jesus, I hope I haven't fucked up. Alina could be driving to certain death. Where is the officer? Too late now, you're stuck in it up to your neck,* he thought. He rolled over to his trusted friend, his M21.

⤜◈⤐

Alina had started the car by now and was approaching the first stop point. McNeill peered through the sight of his M21 and watched as the man mountain dropped onto one knee holding his AK-47 in front of him. McNeill, his adrenalin pumping, drew a deep breath, held it, squeezed the trigger one notch, then added a little bit more pressure, sending a messenger of death into the incredible hulk's chest. He repeated the sequence. There was a moan from the man mountain as the first bullet struck; no blood was secreted before the second bullet located its target. He fell backwards. The three machine gunners saw him fall and turned towards the hill. The one closest to McNeill fell, hit in the head by McNeill's bullet as he turned round, his finger on the trigger of the AK-47, spraying bullets skywards before he hit the ground. McNeill aimed and sent off another bullet, which found its target effortlessly, sending the second man to meet his maker, but obscuring for a few vital seconds the third as he fell. Bullets whistled over McNeill's head. The adrenaline rush was the same now as his very first time, intense adrenaline-charged fear of wondering if he was going to be hit.

He rolled to the other rifle, changing position, and looked through the sight: nothing. Bullets sprayed the hilltop edge from below, AK-47 bullets – the soldier would be bearing down on the hilltop. McNeill rolled back to the M21 as bullets shattered the earth in front of him. He lay on his back, picked up Fitz's lighter and a bottle, lit the petrol-soaked rag, tossed it over the hill, and did the same with the second bottle. The Molotov cocktails exploded, sending shards of glass and a ball of petrol fire to the earth. Up sprouted a man holding a machine gun, his back alight, firing indiscriminately. McNeill squeezed off a bullet, saw it hit him in the forehead, consigning him to a more humane death. More bullets hit the hilltop from the hillside opposite about 600 yards away. He turned to see the other rifle suffer a direct hit. *Got to get off here,* he thought as he ran, M21 in hand, and jumped off the rear of the hill. Bullets peppered the hilltop as he left. *Alina!* thought McNeill as he rushed round on the hill to the side where the first kill had taken place. He settled beside the dead sniper, pointed his M21 to the road and looked through the sight.

There, running up the road towards the car, was a soldier firing his AK-47 machine gun, blasting holes in the Cortina. McNeill breathed in, held his breath, then squeezed off two bullets at the running soldier, whose one purpose was to get to the car and kill anyone near or in it. Alina was crawling up the road, bullets passing over her head; she was petrified but kept willing her body on. Then the bullets stopped. McNeill's two messengers of death had found their target. The soldier lay sprawled face down on the road, his body doing its last convulsions before permanent silence. Bullets peppered the earth at the side of McNeill and entered the dead sniper. McNeill withdrew. He counted seven bullets, or was it eight. He changed magazines and thought of Alina – surely she was back with her baby now, she should be safe. McNeill counted, *Three, man mountain; four, sniper; five, runner; six, sniper somewhere on the far side alive; officer… where the hell is the officer?*

Alina had done everything McNeill had said, carrying his instructions out to the letter. She drove the car, left it on the road, passenger side facing the ambushers, and crawled back on hands and knees, sometimes by her elbows, and she had lain face down on the tarmac as bullets whistled through the air over her head. Almost one hundred yards on hands and knees, crawling to where she left her baby. But she wasn't safe. Now, with the baby in her arms, she looked down the barrel of a Beretta pistol, just like the one McNeill had given her. Only this was held firmly in front of her, pointing directly at her head. Expressionless eyes sunk into black sockets in a wizened face looked at her. A crooked smile etched itself onto the lips of the small, thin wiry man dressed in officer's uniform, who flicked the loaded Beretta up and down, indicating for Alina to move to the road. She was rooted to the spot in fear, her eyes wide, her mouth trembling, her body shivering a cold shiver. 'Oh my God. No. Vostic,' she mumbled in fear. The crooked smile became an excited grin. 'Move!' he said sternly and began to snigger.

McNeill waited. He realised the sniper could see the dead sniper, realised he had a perfect view of the road below. The occasional bullet whistled through the air at the side of him. *He is playing with me*, McNeill thought.

Vostic eyed Alina like a wolf drooling over its wounded prey. 'You, Alina – I am going to use you to flush out that cursed American, then kill him or have him killed. Then I am going to use you for my pleasure before killing you and your baby. Now turn around and walk on,' sniggered Vostic.

McNeill knew there were at least two alive. He pressed his back to the hillside. Bullets whistled through the air on his left side. He had to move, but to where? He knew only the position of the sniper and it was a vague idea at that, but he could not recall seeing the officer. He knew the sniper would be in good cover, almost impossible to see, but obviously, as the passing bullets showed, the sniper had seen him. McNeill thought, *Why would he be wasting bullets? Is he showing off, ready to kill me when he feels like it, or is he buying time, keeping me pinned down for the officer to flush me out? I've got to get off here.*

McNeill slid down the hillside to his right, then moved around and crawled to the mound where he was positioned earlier. He nosed the barrel of the M21 over the rim, looked at the hills on the far side, moved further to his left and again looked at the hills on the far side. Trees on the far hill obscured his view, but he saw nothing. The shooting at his previous position on the large hill had stopped. McNeill withdrew his rifle and slouched down the rear of the mound. His heart banged in his chest, beads of perspiration began to emanate from his forehead and trickle down his cheeks, adrenalin-charged blood pumped through his veins. He was trying to hold his nerve. Moments earlier he was the hunter, now he felt like the hunted. He had been in this position many times before, but he always had Fitz. Now his partner was a woman and her baby. McNeill felt alone and naked. He knew he had to remain calm, stay alert, impervious to emotion of any kind; a cold-hearted, calculating killer.

He removed the telescopic sight from the M21 rifle and peered through it over the rim at the back of the mound, once again in search of the sniper, knowing if he was good he would not see him. He did not. McNeill slumped down and picked up his rifle, then made his way to a position on the larger hill, at the hill's rear side, 10 feet below the dead sniper. He looked through the sight at the hills opposite, saw the trees from earlier, but did not spot the sniper. 'I know he's there somewhere,' he said to himself, then he rolled around so his back was against the hillside. As he did, he caught a glimpse of something. He moved so he could see up the road. No, it couldn't be – what was she doing? Alina, carrying her baby, walking towards the car. *Does she think it's over?* He pressed his eyes shut and looked again; a shape was behind her, using her as cover, as bait. She had been captured. *I have found the officer.* He attached the sight to his M21 and slid off the rear of the hillside, off the bottom and into the bushes, trees and tall grass. He moved back from the edge where trees met grass, further into the trees, moving up and around to the abandoned car about 800 yards away then stopped. He was now, as he thought, directly opposite the sniper. Each could see down the road from the right-hand bend to the left-hand bend, could see each other's cover, the hillside, the trees. Neither could make out the other one.

McNeill bent down, looked through the sight at the opposite hill, hoping for a glimpse, knowing he would not get one. He figured the sniper's position would be the same. Why should he move? No shots had been fired in his direction, so he had not been seen. *But no shots have been fired recently, so as I am looking for you, you are looking for me.* However, McNeill knew it was only a matter of time before the sniper saw Alina and his colleague, and he would know she was bait.

McNeill moved. He wanted a sight of Alina, needed to see just how close they were to the car, needed to calculate how much time he had. But to do this he had to break cover. *Nice dilemma,* thought McNeill. *I cannot get to the officer quickly enough to make a quiet kill without showing myself, and to give me a sure shot at the hostage taker, I must shoot in quick succession to prevent Alina from getting a bullet herself from the officer. I must not miss, but once I fire, I give away my position to the sniper, and I don't think he will miss either. Think McNeill, think, there has to be a way out, think; what would Fitz do?*

McNeill began to explore possible scenarios in his mind. His opponents could sit on Alina for hours, or take her away there and then. *No, I have shot too many of their men and there is a nice reward for me. They will not leave me alive, and if I don't take the bait, they will kill her anyway eventually. I shoot the officer, Alina gets shot by the sniper, then we fight it out; why shoot a woman? He could catch her later. No. I shoot the officer and get shot by the sniper. I give myself up and both Alina and I get shot. Choices aren't good, are they?* he thought.

McNeill realised he had little or no option. He decided to get into a position with a good clear chance of killing the officer. That meant he had to get closer to the road. He could not miss; he had to position himself so that the kill was rapid, immediate and precise. Just below the roadside would be ideal, but to position himself so would make him very visible to the sniper and he would not miss. There was not enough ground cover near the roadside. McNeill decided to break cover and get closer to the road, then seek cover. 'One shot, one good clean shot, that's all I need,' he said to himself.

He slipped into the tall grass, then sank to the ground and crawled. He used large bushes, rocks and small mounds of earth to give a little cover. He detached the sight from the rifle and peered through at the far hill, hoping to glimpse the sniper, knowing he would not. Progress was slow. He checked the ground ahead for natural cover, checked Alina, checked the far hills. He checked Alina once more. She had now reached the Cortina. 'Slow down, for Christ's sake, slow down. Give me more time, damn you,' he whispered through clenched teeth. He saw the boot of the Cortina open, watched as the briefcases were taken out. *They are our death warrants,* McNeill thought. *I need to find cover, set up and give myself a sure shot. I will take this officer guy out, but I need to shoot partially from the front and partially from the side. A head shot to make him fall backwards.* 'Slow down, Alina,' he muttered. Then McNeill realised Alina and her hostage taker could not be seen by the sniper until they rounded the bend. He looked at the dead sniper's position on the hill. He realised both of the snipers could see each other, and that his own position earlier was a blind spot to the other sniper. He looked at the hills. *Maybe, just maybe, there is just enough time.*

McNeill retreated carefully, exactly along the path he had made to the safety of the trees. He turned and concentrated the sight on Alina, saw her baby in one arm, briefcase in the other, her captor carrying the other briefcase in his left hand. Then he saw her stumble. The briefcase made contact with the ground and so did her left knee. He watched her struggle to her feet, lurch forward, pushed from behind. McNeill exhaled, turned and ran through the trees, back to where he made the initial ascent of the hill. He reached the part of the hill level with the dead sniper, swung round and propped the dead man upright, returned to the side, climbed to the top of the hill and lay down. Repositioning the sight onto the rifle, he eased the nozzle of the rifle barrel through sparse grass at the hilltop. He lifted his right leg, grabbed the ground with his right knee, his left leg fully extended, and scouted for Alina through the sight. He saw her, her captor just behind but covered by her. They were getting closer to the bend in the road. *No time to regroup, no time to rethink, this is it, it has to work. Just a little luck is all I need,* thought McNeill, the palms of his hands now beginning to sweat.

There was an awkward silence, tense, agitating in its stillness, until it was broken. McNeill heard the faintness of a shout, a male voice. Alina's captor was speaking in a language McNeill could not understand. McNeill peered through the rifle sight, breathed in and pulled the trigger to its first position. He could see Alina, see the fear on her face, but she partially blocked from sight the wiry man behind her. McNeill realised at that point his sniper adversary was scouring through his rifle sight to find him. *Split seconds,* McNeill thought, *will decide life or death.* A bead of sweat oozed from his forehead, trailed down beside his right eye socket, down his cheek to his chin. He exhaled, his right eye glued to the telescopic sight. 'Move out of the way, Alina, for God's sake, move,' he heard himself saying.

Alina and Vostic were nearing the bend, the point of no return. *If she rounds the bend and gets out into the open, she will become a target for the sniper, then it's a catch 22. I shoot the hostage taker, the sniper shoots the hostage,* McNeill thought. 'Stall or move, Alina,' he heard himself saying. More sweat ran down his face. McNeill did not care, his attention was focussed, his brain zoned into the situation, his left eye closed, his right eye hawk-like, peering through the telescopic sight. Then it happened. Alina stumbled almost to the ground. Her captor was laughing behind her when it hit him, square in the centre of his forehead, throwing him off the ground backwards. Alina turned and looked. She went to the prone wiry man spreadeagled on his back on the ground. She saw blood trickling at first, then oozing onto the road out of the back of Vostic's head. She went to the side of the road, sat against a rock and curled up, protecting her child, and began retching.

McNeill had wasted no time. He saw his opportunity and he took it. One shot, a few more steps, and Alina would be in total openness, an easy target. McNeill was scouring the far hill when he saw it – a flash, the flash of bullet leaving rifle barrel. *Shit!* He rolled to his left twice and looked through the sight. The upright dead sniper took two more bullets to add to McNeill's knife and fell to the ground. 'Now I know where you are,' said McNeill, looking through the telescopic sight, and he emptied the magazine into the part of the hill where the flash had come from, discarded the empty magazine, reloaded his last full magazine of ten rounds and slid off the back of the hill.

Alina heard the shots. She knew McNeill was still alive. She looked up at the hills and saw nothing. McNeill was now level with the dead sniper with his knife in his belly. One bullet had hit him in the head, the other in his chest. *What would I do?* thought McNeill. *This guy is obviously very good. What would I do? Well, I would wait then break cover backwards and circle behind Alina.* The adrenalin flowing through McNeill kept him ultra-alert and continually thinking, thinking of his sniper adversary, thinking how the tables had turned and Alina was now his own bait. But what would his adversary do if he circled and saw her, would he like what he saw and want the pleasure of her, or would he just shoot her from a distance? McNeill opted for the latter; that's what he would do, professional to the last.

McNeill heard them, the faint cries of a very frightened woman. Alina was shouting. McNeill never moved. His right eye locked onto the telescopic sight with the rifle barrel laid over the dead sniper, aimed at where the flash had emanated from. A small bush shook at the side of a dark hole in the far hillside. McNeill's adversary was moving. Alina was still shouting. McNeill ignored her, his adrenalin flowing through his veins with intent, his breathing slow and careful, his body motionless, in total calm, almost a trance-like serenity. He squeezed off four rounds at the moving bush, watched, saw a shape fall and the bush shake. McNeill waited, looked through the telescopic sight and waited. Alina screamed.

McNeill slid down the hillside into the trees. He could see her standing then bending forward, hear her screaming his name, then bowing her head and holding her knees with her hands. McNeill ran through the trees and bushes, and when he knew he would be out of sight of the sniper, who he was sure he had hit but was uncertain as to how badly, he slid into the tall grass. He could see Alina, hear her crying, sobbing, her hands covering her face, watched her slump to her knees and begin rocking on them. *Well, if there were any more soldiers she would have been shot by now,* McNeill thought as he crawled through the bushes and knee-high grass, then ran across a few feet of gravel and the dirt road and came up behind her. He wolf-whistled, then whistled again. Alina stopped crying, turned to see him, stood and ran to him.

'Get down, get down, you fool, there could be more,' McNeill shouted at her. She ran towards him, crashed into him and kissed him passionately on the lips, then began sobbing and pounding her fists into his chest. McNeill pulled her to him and held her tight.

'Come on, get off the road, there could be more,' he said to her.

'No, no more, you had killed nearly all his men, he told me,' she said, pointing to the dead officer, 'apart from his Russian sniper, his Russian sniper, the best in the world. He would shoot you, then they would have a party with me, before killing me and my baby, just like Aunt Sasha.' Alina sobbed. She then threw her arms around McNeill and began kissing his face continually. McNeill just held her, put his right hand on the back of her head, drew her to him and held her tight, felt her lissom body pressed against his, felt her warm lips on his right cheek, smelled her black hair. His lips found hers. They kissed passionately, their tongues explored each other's. McNeill pulled away. 'The baby, the baby – where is she, is she OK?' he cried.

'She's OK, she is down at the front of the body where I was, she is OK,' Alina replied.

McNeill and Alina went to the baby, left just before the bend in the road. McNeill saw her, ran and picked her up. She was wrapped in a towel and he thought she smiled at him. McNeill smiled back. Alina went to the body of Vostic and kicked it squarely in the ribs with all the force she could muster, and again she kicked it, and again. McNeill grabbed her with his free hand.

'Hey, what's this all about, and who is he?' asked McNeill.

'This bastard killed my Aunt Sasha. He has murdered and tortured many people, and is one of my father's most brutal soldiers. Vostic was a psychopath; Yiddich's older brother. He is mentioned many times in the documents,' replied Alina, who then spat at the corpse.

McNeill gave Alina her baby, bent down and took the Beretta out of the dead man's hand, then pulled him off the road.

'Where's my Beretta?' he asked Alina as he went through the dead man's pockets. 'It's in the car,' she replied. McNeill pocketed the money he found in Vostic's pockets, strode off to the car, passing the body of the dead soldier. He took his AK-47. Bullet holes littered the passenger side of the Cortina. McNeill looked and turned to Alina. 'Looks like we won't be needing this car anymore. Get the bags, I will check the boot.' McNeill was met with the smell of petrol as he opened the boot. He lifted the two cans – empty, bullet-holed. He lifted the M21 rifle out and shouted to Alina, 'Get the pistol and map, I will bring the bags.' They walked away from the Cortina. McNeill stopped at the body of the soldier and started searching through his pockets. Alina looked on in disgust. McNeill felt the stare.

'I'm checking for car keys. We can't just stroll out of here and out of this country,' said McNeill as he stood up after finding nothing. They walked on. McNeill then collected the two briefcases and put them down at the roadside near Vostic's body along with the bags, and turned to Alina, saying, 'I'm just making doubly sure. Wait here, don't show your face around the bend.' And he set off and climbed the rear of the hills and disappeared.

McNeill moved quickly. He was certain he had hit the sniper. He rounded the second of two hills, and keeping low he zigzagged across 20 yards of open grassland into a thicket of bush and trees. He ran through the trees and, using boulders and ridges of earth and all the natural cover available, he arrived at the bottom of the sniper's hill. He climbed the back of it quickly. Panting for breath as he came over the crest, he saw the bushes to the right and below, pulled out the Beretta pistol he took from Vostic, checked the safety was off and began descending towards the bushes. He found him lying face down, barely alive, bullet hole in his back just below his right shoulder blade, another hole just below his right shoulder where the arm joins. His left arm was twisted around his back, blood running down his fingers, two wounds in his left arm. McNeill realised he shot him when he emptied his magazine into the hole, that the sniper was badly shot-up by that first volley, and shooting his rifle at that point was probably beyond him. The bullet in his back probably entered his lung and it was now filling with blood, consigning him to a slow, painful death. McNeill spoke to the sniper but received no answer. He bent down and prodded him with the fingers of his left hand. The sniper moaned almost inaudibly, with immense pain. McNeill stood, aimed the Beretta at the sniper's head and pulled the trigger. He had suffered enough.

Alina heard the shot and sat up, startled. She feared the worst and began to shake, then to shout. 'McNeill, McNeill, are you OK? McNEILL…' Her shouts tailed off.

McNeill collected the sniper's rifle, a Dragunov SVD self-loader, slightly longer than his own M21, but it weighed less. All in all, an AK-47 with a stock. He checked the bullets: 7.62 mm, same ammo as the AK-47 – makes sense, all the squad had AK-47s, same ammo for all. He strapped the rifle to his back, found two full magazines, each of ten rounds, one empty of twenty rounds. He brought them and walked down the front of the hill to the road.

Alina shook with fear, her mind raced. *What if McNeill is now dead, what if I go round this corner and I get shot, what if I wait here and the Russian sniper catches me? McNeill, why did you leave me here?* She waited, pistol in hand. 'McNeill!' she yelled. 'McNeill!' she screamed. Then she heard it. She listened intently: yes, she did hear it. McNeill was whistling again.

McNeill was now walking on the dirt road, approaching the bend which Alina was behind. 'Alina!' he shouted. He heard her call him and he began running. 'Alina!' he shouted again. She waited for him then held him when he reached her.

'I thought you were dead. I heard the shot and thought the Russian sniper had killed you,' babbled Alina.

'What did you say? Say it again,' demanded McNeill. Alina looked at him quizzically. McNeill shook her, demanding, 'What did you say? Say it again, Alina.'

'I thought you were dead. I heard a shot and thought the Russian sniper had killed you,' she repeated. 'The one Vostic told me about,' she added.

McNeill let her go and rubbed his chin. 'Russian sniper, Russian sniper,' murmured McNeill. 'Russian rifle, Croatian sniper, Russian rifle, Croatian sniper,' he repeated. *Oh my God. Two cars, four in each is eight – but no Russian sniper. No cars, where are the cars? No keys on any of the men so far, not even Vostic back there in the officer's coat; and he looked a little young to be in charge of such a unit,' McNeill thought. And that coat he is wearing bugs me, it's too big.*

'What is it? What's bothering you, McNeill?' Alina enquired.

'I think there is one more,' he calmly replied.

'Impossible – you have killed eight. Two cars, four in each, eight soldiers, that's what you said,' she said emphatically.

'No Russian sniper. No cars,' said McNeill icily and calmly. A stilled silence followed.

'So where would he be?' asked Alina quietly, beginning to see McNeill's reasoning.

'Somewhere near the cars,' he went on. 'If this ambush was successful, the men would walk to the cars and he would join them. If not, it's a quick getaway and lose face or he would wait, and yes, he has to be the Russian sniper. So who in your father's army is Russian and an excellent shot?' McNeill asked.

'Rasik, it would have to be Rasik.' Fear gripped her face as she spoke; she almost threw up, but covered her mouth and held her stomach.

'Would Rasik be a tallish, wiry officer?' asked McNeill clearly but softly.

'Rasik is taller than Vostic back there, but wiry like him. Rasik is a butcher, a torturer, exceptionally cruel. Possibly the highest in my father's cohorts, one of his elite, most tried and trusted, brutal and responsible for many more of the crimes in those briefcases, and yes, an excellent shot.' Alina heaved as she spoke.

'Rasik is out there somewhere, Alina,' McNeill said.

'Then where would you put him?' Alina enquired as fear gripped her body.

'To the rear. Then, just as it looks like we are home free, and on a carefree high, boom boom: both bullets for me and you are his reward. Later, he would kill you, and take the briefcases to your father alone, making him an indispensable hero, or just plain too dangerous not to have on your side,' McNeill said.

'Oh my God,' Alina said as thoughts began to race through her mind of once again being a captive slave, only this time used and abused by Rasik. Her skin crawled and shivered and she retched.

'If he is out there, McNeill, you find him and you kill him,' she said. Alina was now visibly shaking, her lips trembled uncontrollably. She was scared, but she was also angry. Vostic had told her that they had killed her Aunt Sasha and she wanted revenge. She could smell the end, almost reach out and touch it, but which way would it turn out? She looked at McNeill. She knew she was totally dependent on him. 'Find him and kill him.'

'Can you manage to bring the baby and one briefcase? It's not very far,' McNeill asked. 'I will bring the rifles, the bags and the other briefcase.'

'No problem,' Alina replied.

McNeill led the way. He crossed the road and headed towards the first hill. Rounding its base to the left they began to climb the smaller hill behind the larger first hill. The smell of burning met Alina's nostrils just before she reached the crest, where they stopped. McNeill laid down the bags and briefcase, the spare M21 and the collected Dragunov rifle, crawled to the crest of the hill and poked his M21 barrel over it. He tried to replay the scenes from earlier in his mind, tried to recollect where the bullets came from. He looked through the telescopic sight. He did not expect to see any soldiers and was not disappointed when he did not. He was looking for the cars; he looked down the road.

The road left the hills and carried straight on. Hills were set back on the left, smaller hills and an expanse of tall grass on the right. The road bent to the right, and was raised slightly on a long left-hand bend, tall grass either side, then it shot off straight again. At this point there was a small wood to the road's right. McNeill spotted one car and a black jeep, parked just off the elevated section of road on the long left-hand bend. He estimated 2 miles away. He motioned to Alina to come over. She laid down the briefcase and her baby and slid alongside him.

'What is it?' she asked.

'Look,' he said.

'Yes, I see them, black jeep and a Humber, I think. Vostic's,' she said.

'Yes, jeep holds five, Humber, four; especially with that giant in it,' said McNeill, pointing.

Alina looked around and did a body count. 'My, you were busy,' she said. 'Maybe they have the keys?' she added.

'Don't bet on it. Rasik will have the keys,' came the short reply.

They crawled back to the rear, away from the crest and slid down. McNeill spoke.

'Wait here. Look after the baby and get something to eat. I will leave the Dragunov rifle set up; keep my Beretta, too. Make sure that if or when you go to use it, the safety is off. I am going after Rasik. He will have heard all the gunfire and will be expecting someone, so he will be on his guard and alert. After I have got him, I will bring the jeep and I will flash the headlights, then you will know it is me; so watch the jeep. This may take quite a while so don't be alarmed.' He kissed her on the cheek and left.

At first McNeill moved quickly. In no length of time he had crossed the road and moved behind the rear of the hills to the position of the dead Croatian sniper with the Dragunov rifle. He took another look at the sniper and went through his pockets. He found nothing. Except he was now convinced that Rasik was out there waiting. The dead sniper was a stocky man of around 200 pounds. McNeill looked to his right. Two hills of lesser height marred the view of the overall terrain; he had seen these earlier across from where Alina was now, with a distance of approximately 100 yards from the foothills to the road, with bushes, the odd clump of small sparse trees, short grass and a number of rocks. Beyond that, a huge expanse of tall grass.

McNeill decided to take no chances; needed to map the area ahead in his mind. He left the dead sniper and slid down the front of the hill. He was now almost level with the left-hand bend in the road, and moved swiftly to the first of the lesser hills. He climbed halfway up, then moved around to its road side to reach the smaller hill. This he climbed, its slope facing the back of the larger hill. On reaching the top he slid his M21 rifle from his shoulder and crawled to the crest. He peered over the crest. He did not like what he saw.

The road ran straight and north for almost a mile. Again, hills and trees adorned its left side, then there was a 90-degree right turn directly opposite him, fields of grass, short grass, long grass, and a quarter of a mile further on the road made a long, sweeping left turn of almost 120 degrees. Here, on sparse ground between the road and field, were parked a black jeep and a cream Humber car. In front of McNeill and slightly off to his right was tall grass, at least 6 feet high in places; easy for a man to stand upright in and not be seen.

On the far right of the fields, there was the occasional cottage and house joined by trees, some of which partly obscured the houses, with rolling hills behind. But these fields were vast; three fields of at least 20 acres each. In the field furthest away, the crop was discoloured from lush green through light brown to a darker brown, the nearer fields being a continued colour of light brown. McNeill peered through the telescopic sight at the jeep; he then allowed a circle of 900 yards' radius from the jeep. A Russian sniper, the best sniper in the world, according to Vostic, and probably using a Dragunov sniper rifle: 900-yard accuracy, but certain at 700. A rifle almost 4 feet in length, from stock end to barrel tip, less than 5 kilograms in weight, ten- or twenty-round magazine. A gas-operated, short stroke, rotating bolt, semi-automatic killing machine, same 7.62-mm cartridge.

To find him would be like searching for a needle in a haystack, McNeill thought, but he kept on looking. He looked at the hills to the cars' left; too steep, too high, too close to the road to guarantee a clear shot for a good length of time. *There is something odd about the cars: they are positioned. That's it, positioned! Why didn't I see this before now? And that looks like the driver's door is open, an open invitation for someone to stop and look in. He has to be in that field. That's where I would be, too, watching, waiting, listening; and with all the time he has had, something will have been used for target practice. Flushing him out alone is going to take a lot of time and patience, and skill.* He looked on, formulating a way.

He crawled back from the hill crest and off the hill by the rear and moved away to the east to work his way around. *Ironic,* he thought, *Rasik is using the tall grass to shelter himself from me and I will use the tall grass to shelter myself from him.* He crouched low, carried his M21 in his right hand, used the trees and bushes along the far edges of the tall grass for cover. He stayed as low as he could and bent over: the tall grass was nearly 6 to 12 inches above him, but he had a long distance to travel. McNeill decided on a very wide berth as he circumnavigated, his plan being to travel around the perimeter of the fields, to approach northwards of where he thought Rasik would be. He guessed that Rasik would be 300 yards away from the jeep at the shortest, and 900 yards at the longest. He planned to circle around and position himself somewhere in between these distances, northwards, and wait.

<hr/>

Alina fed the baby the last of the bottled milk from the bag. She felt alone, frightened. A nervous tension and agitation began to take hold of her. McNeill had been gone almost two hours. In all that time there had been no sounds of shooting. The air was chilly and she only had the baby and the sound of the breeze for company. Trust kept nagging at her brain: *He needs me, he could not leave us. He cannot read the road map or the occasional signs, nor speak the language.* She consoled herself that he was a professional soldier on a short mission and he needed her to escape after the mission was done. The baby began to cry, began to fight sleep, but eventually succumbed to slumber. Alina wrapped her up to keep her warm and held her. When she was sure the baby was asleep she laid her down, and lay beside her in the grass out of the chilly breeze. She looked at her watch. Over two and a half hours had passed and in that time she had seen nothing. She felt the deathly stillness of silence.

She climbed over the crest of the hill and crawled to the rifle McNeill had positioned earlier and gazed through the telescopic sight. She never thought she would see McNeill, hoped never to see Rasik. She gazed at the jeep and car, still lying unattended at the roadside. *Am I on my own? Surely there should have been something by now.* Her mind began to race through potential scenarios. What if Rasik was not there and then all this caution was a waste of time? What if more of her father's soldiers had been dispatched to look for her? What if soldiers from the town were coming up the road this very second? What if Rasik and McNeill had killed each other? She shook herself back to reality and stopped her galloping mind and began to think of McNeill. A big guy, silent, sometimes emotionless, sometimes dead inside; and yet gentle, caring and thoughtful. He was a very good soldier – all the decisions he had made had been correct and made with some thought, every move implemented, planned, nothing left to chance. He was machine-like sometimes, and because of him, she and her baby were still alive. *Somewhere out there, he is still alive.* She returned to her sleeping baby and lay down beside her.

⇒◆⇐

Rasik waited. He had heard the shooting earlier, the sub-machine guns spluttering, then silent. The boom of some kind of explosion, more machine gunfire snuffed out. Then spasmodic rifle shots. He ran the scenario through his mind, repeated it over and over. He realised McNeill and Alina were still alive, and all his men were dead. His men were long overdue: three hours had passed since the last shots and no sign. Rasik began to think that one or both were wounded. Maybe they had returned to the town for medical attention. *I will wait longer. If the American has killed all my men, he is very good, a worthy opponent, one I will enjoy shooting when he comes to look at the jeep and the Humber car. He will know he has to abandon the brown Cortina: he will know we are looking for it.* He looked through the sight and saw the shattered side window of the Humber behind the driver's seat, the one he had used for target practice earlier. The telescopic sight atop of his Dragunov told him 450 yards was the distance.

150

⇒◈⇐

McNeill never saw Rasik stand, look through the sight at the two vehicles, nor did he see him slowly disappear into the long grass. Using the grass as cover, he had almost circumnavigated the field, had run through the bushes and trees, then sprinted across open country, his blood pumping through his veins laced with adrenalin as he moved closer to his goal. He had used the tall bull rushes as cover and sank into marshland, at times up to his knees. He heaved his legs and weary body up as the moist earth clung on, sucking them down. He walked slowly and silently between rushes and flat lowland giving rise eventually to small hills. He crouched in a hollow separating a small ridge of earth from the rushes as the ground became firmer to gather breath. At periodic intervals he had stopped like this, first to listen and then look through the rifle sight. Each time he wanted and hoped to see something, but saw nothing.

Now he was going through the same procedure. He ducked down onto his left knee, rifle stock butted into his right shoulder, right eye glued to the sight, right index finger caressing the trigger. He slowly rose, looking from left to right, paying minute attention to the field of 4-foot high crop. He was now on the north side of the field. By the gauge on his telescopic sight, he was 900 yards from the jeep and Humber. He stopped looking and sat down to wait. Behind him lay over 100 yards of flat ground before it rose to the hills. The hills then ran west almost to the roadside; a few bushes joined the two. McNeill just lay on a mound of earth contemplating, thinking, waiting. *I know you are in there somewhere with a direct shot at the two vehicles. I reckon you are somewhere near the centre – the hunter. I figure I am behind you, and the hunter is now the hunted. Patience, McNeill: patience.*

Alina lay at the side of her baby and waited. Rasik sat low in the long grass crop and waited. McNeill waited. *You don't know I am out here Rasik, but you will not show yourself. You know by now your*

151

men are dead, he thought. Another hour passed. Nobody moved and more minutes ticked by.

———◆———

Alina heard it first. The silence was broken by the far away noise of an engine, growing louder as it came nearer, then into a heavy, raucous roar. Alina crawled to the rifle as fast as she could, peered through the telescopic sight in hope and anticipation. But the jeep and Humber were still there, stood like loyal statues. 'Oh no,' she cried, 'more soldiers are coming, they will see the car and dead bodies, and they will find us.' Once again fear gripped her body; she crawled off the hillcrest and made her way to the dead Croatian sniper, McNeill's knife still in his stomach. She watched the road below.

The old van, a red box, stopped at the brown Cortina. Two men got out, one heavy, the other slight and slim. They looked inside, then went to the body of the soldier and bent over him for a few minutes, returned to the van and set off. The closer it got to Alina, the noisier it became. 'God, the racket, they will be heard for miles around. Why can't they fix the exhaust?' she asked herself. She watched them draw closer, watched them stop again, go to the body of Vostic, crouch down and roll his body from side to side. Then she saw them return to the van and drive past. She heard the van stop. It had stopped in the middle of the road, just before where the man mountain lay. She could see both men below. The smaller man collected the AK-47, and Alina watched as the older man looted the body, removing a gold chain from the dead man's neck. He ran to the roadside where two more dead men lay; again, the slim figure collected the AK-47s. The older man kicked both torsos; he had found nothing. They returned to the van and set off with a backfire. Alina let out a long, slow breath of relief.

McNeill thought he heard a rumble. He wasn't sure of the noise – he thought he recognised it but could not pinpoint what it was. He dismissed it, but the drone was still there, then a roar, then a drone; not the low drone of an aircraft or the whirr of a helicopter. He thought it might be a tank, but the ground did not shake, and he hadn't spied any tanks in the town. Again, he dismissed the noise, but it was there and it began to bug him. He rubbed the back of his neck; the uneasy itch had reappeared. Rifle sight to right eye, he rose slowly and began the sweep from right to left. He checked the two vehicles and there below them, heading this way from Alina's direction, on the straight road, was a dust cloud: someone or something was headed his way.

Rasik had heard it a fraction sooner, saw the dust cloud a fraction earlier. He returned to sitting and smiling a fraction before McNeill rose.

McNeill sat down. *If I can hear it, so can Rasik,* he thought. McNeill figured out that the roar was the driver pressing heavily on the accelerator, and the drone was the accelerator being pressed lightly. Then he had an idea – just as Rasik was using the jeep and Humber as bait, McNeill could use the droning vehicle's occupants as bait too. McNeill figured no one, in times of war, would pass up an opportunity to swap a busted up car with a jeep. He hoped Rasik would think it was him and Alina. He figured Rasik would shoot whoever went to drive the jeep first. He would wait, watch, find Rasik, and when he showed himself, shoot him. But by then the driver would be dead. *An unavoidable casualty of war,* thought McNeill.

The noisy crescendo of the exhaust drew nearer, until it stopped. The van driver opened the door, grabbed an AK-47 and got out. The smaller man, AK-47 in hand, got out the passenger's side. Rasik made ready, McNeill made ready. McNeill rose, searched the field, saw nothing, and watched the jeep. Rasik rose slowly. The big man was nearing the open driver's door from the front of the jeep; the smaller man was now at the jeep's rear.

'Keys are in the jeep. What fool would leave keys in a jeep?' the big guy said as he turned his head to his friend, then watched as the smaller man was spun through 90 degrees, arms outstretched but loose, and fell backwards. He saw no more. He felt the first bullet enter his back in the centre, between and just below his shoulder blades, and never felt it exit his chest, never felt the second bullet enter his back, his head hit the side of the jeep with a colossal thump. He felt nothing as he slid to the earth.

McNeill saw the first guy spin. There, at ten o'clock and slightly in front of him, stood Rasik. He saw the head, then the shoulders, then the long barrel, saw the head move on recoil as the bullets fired. McNeill waited, squeezed the trigger of his M21, aimed the barrel slightly lower, squeezed the trigger again, and again. Three messengers of death sped towards their target less than 500 yards away. In seconds the first bullet hit with deadly accuracy, entered Rasik's head just in front of his right ear, killing him instantly. The second and third thumped through a sweater and into soft flesh below his right arm. The lifeless body hit the tall grass then the ground. McNeill crouched down, moved position, waited, then slowly rose up, scouted around through the telescopic sight and began to make his way over to the body of Rasik.

The crop seemed to wave as he pushed through. McNeill found the body. A tallish, wiry man, approximately fifty years of age, wearing a khaki light brown jacket, light brown sweater. *Smart,* thought McNeill, *same colour as the crop in the field; obviously swapped with Vostic when he got out of the jeep.* Dragunov rifle. He bent down at the side of the body and lifted the jacket. He saw an empty pistol holster. *Obviously gave the Beretta to Vostic too. OK, clever guy, what else have you got?* McNeill went through his pockets, found money, notes and coins, and keys for a Nissan jeep. *Smart that, very smart,* thought McNeill.

McNeill picked up the Dragunov rifle, looked at his own M21, his trusted friend. 'Yes,' he said, 'it's true what they say about you: if you can see them, you can kill them.' He patted the M21 with the affection an owner would bestow on his faithful pet dog, the kind that never lets you down. Then, crouching, he carried both rifles to the jeep, heaved the dead big guy out of the way, took the keys out of the ignition and looked at them – the Humber keys. He put them in his pocket and went to the rear of the jeep. There he saw a boy, no more than sixteen years of age, blood oozing out of a hole in his chest, eyes wide open, gazing at the sky, seeing nothing. McNeill closed the eyelids and pulled him off the road, then got into the red van and drove it off the road. He went to the rear of the jeep, put two AK-47s inside, a Dragunov rifle plus magazine cases, plus his own M21, shut the door, climbed into the driver's seat, put the keys into the ignition and turned them. The Nissan jeep roared into life.

Alina heard it. She had faintly heard the raucous roar of the van in the distance, just after she had heard a few muffled cracks; six in all had broken the silence. She was filled with trepidation and loss; she was now sure McNeill was dead, that she was alone. She crawled to the rifle, looked into the telescopic sight through misty eyes. Tears obscured her vision. *Was that the sound of a jeep?* She wiped her eyes and looked again – the jeep was heading towards her. She watched and moved the rifle slightly, aiming it just like McNeill had shown her. 'OK you bastard, Rasik, I am going to kill you.' She steeled herself, finger on the trigger, now even breaths, wait, wait. The horn was blowing, the headlights flashing. She looked up, looked again, saw the headlights flash again, heard the horn blow again. She left the rifle, rose to her knees, and waved both arms over her head. McNeill saw her, exhaled a huge sigh of relief and accelerated towards her.

Alina stood, moved swiftly to pick up her baby and the two bags, and ran down the hill, dropping the bags at the bottom. She took out the Beretta from the belt at the back of her skirt. She heard his voice before she saw him. McNeill had rounded the bend and began shouting her name at the same time she was rounding the large hill. He stopped the jeep and got out. Alina saw him standing alone, dropped the Beretta on the side of the road and ran to him.

It was over five hours since she last saw him. It seemed like she had aged five years. She ran into his arms, he lifted her off her feet and spun around. She looked at him, the baby in her left arm, at the boyish grin on his face, the world's relief in his eyes. He put them down and she began to beat his chest with the fist of her right hand in anger and frustration, saying, 'How dare you, how dare you put me through that?' She began to cry, uncontrollable tears flowed from her eyes, down her cheeks. She beat him till her arm refused to beat anymore. It just folded around him and she began to shake. McNeill just held her and said nothing, just held her tight. Moments passed.

'You OK now?' whispered McNeill. She looked up at him, into blue eyes of cold steel. He looked into hers, blue eyes you could look into forever, always changing, always revealing something else more attractive, the gateway to her soul; eyes he could live in forever. Their mouths found each other's. She felt so safe, so secure in his embrace. She wanted this moment to last. *Curse this war,* she thought. But it was the war along with all its atrocities, attached to fate, that had thrown them together. The kiss was filled with passion. McNeill did not want to stop, did not want to break away, but he did. He looked at the baby, gently kissed her forehead. 'Let's get the bags,' he said.

Alina collected the Beretta, then hauled the two bags into the Nissan's boot, and saw the guns. McNeill climbed the hills, collected the other Dragunov rifle and the two briefcases and returned with them to the jeep. He looked into the bag of food for something to eat; there wasn't anything. Alina was already sat in the passenger seat and had deposited her baby on the rear seat before McNeill got in, turned on the engine and turned around. He drove up the road and stopped at the red van.

'Get out, please, and bring the baby,' he ordered.

'Don't you speak to me like that and in that tone of voice,' Alina retorted.

She got out of the jeep, collected her baby and stormed round to the front, then stopped dead in her tracks as she looked upon the body of the dead teenager. Alina felt physically sick. Her head bowed as she asked McNeill what had happened. McNeill explained the last half-hour, saying Rasik was good, extremely good. 'He shot the boy first–'

'Why?' she interrupted.

'Because he had a means of escape if he shot the big man first. One shot – so bloody perfect. He changed position and shot the big man twice before I had even fired once. I couldn't find Rasik; I used them as bait to flush him out,' McNeill said.

'Show me Rasik,' Alina demanded. 'I want to see his body,' she added firmly.

McNeill and Alina entered the field. McNeill led Alina through the 4-foot high grass crop to the body.

'Yes, McNeill, that is Rasik. Here lies a most sadistic murderer, brutal torturer, responsible for a lot of the killings and organised crime described in those briefcases. Rasik, one of my father's most trusted of officers; totally loyal to my father in life and probably death, and he is Russian, probably the best sniper in the army before my father gave him a new career as one of his paid henchmen above the law. He was feared, his name alone invoked fear in everyone,' Alina explained. Then she kicked the dead body repeatedly. McNeill stopped her. 'Come, let's go,' he whispered in her ear.

They left Rasik behind and walked through the tall grass towards the jeep. Before they reached it, Alina's right arm went effortlessly, silky smooth, around McNeill's waist and she began to lean into him. She felt his left arm move around her waist then upwards to rest on her left shoulder. They arrived at the jeep.

'I will just search the Humber for food, Alina,' said McNeill. 'Hopefully they will have had rations for an overnight stay at the very least,' he added.

He took out the keys from his pocket and popped the Humber boot. There on its left side lay a change of clothes for each member of the now extinguished platoon: shirts, trousers, jumpers. McNeill fished out his and Alina's size. He saw a small holdall which he unzipped: bread, fruit, biscuits, water, tea, a small amount of milk, cheese, bottled Coca-Cola. McNeill zipped the holdall back up and lifted it to discover magazines filled with bullets, 7.62 mm. *Smart man, Rasik, same magazine, same bullets fit both the Dragunov rifles and AK-47s,* thought McNeill. Alongside were two fifteen-round magazine clips for a Beretta pistol. McNeill brought all the ammunition. Alina came to help. She sniffed the air. There was a smell which she encountered earlier; her nose wrinkled. She sniffed the air again.

'Jesus, McNeill, where did you go earlier? You need to bathe,' she said.

McNeill looked down at his soiled trousers and socks; he smelled of the marsh. He promptly changed, threw the old clothes in the Humber's boot and shut it. They made their way to the jeep and got in. McNeill opened the holdall and removed the two bottles of coke, gave one to Alina and drank the other himself before they set off.

A few miles ahead, Alina broke the silence. 'Will there be more?' she asked McNeill.

'More what?' he enquired.

'More soldiers looking for us?' she asked pensively.

'Yes, there sure will. Your father desperately wants those brief-cases, and when Rasik does not report in, he sure as hell is going to be one angry man. Then you and I are very expendable. It's a catch 22 – to be killed either by your father's Croats or, if we make it that far, to be a target for the Serbs,' replied McNeill. 'Anyhow, there was a little fuel in that red van of the two civil-ians; that means either their house is nearby or a village that has petrol. We, however, are OK. Rasik must have fuelled up in the town back there; we have three quarters of the tank left. And like the jeep, I too need fuel. Pass me something to eat, Alina,' he said.

She gave him bread and cheese, a banana and an apple, and had the same herself. The baby woke and Alina fed her. An hour or so later they began to pass spaced out cottages, and homes grew on the roadside. McNeill slowed down and began to think. It was becoming more built-up; they were heading into a town or village. He thought of the convoy. Was this its destination? Would there be soldiers, checkpoints, police? And surely Rasik would have reported his position to Alina's father from the town earlier. Would there be someone waiting? There had to be. McNeill's mind computed on.

'General Tomelsky would sit and wait for Rasik to phone. No phone call from Rasik would mean that Alina and I are still alive, and so no briefcases. Then another phone call from his spy in the town would confirm Rasik was dead and to send someone else,' he said out loud.

Simple, but in the jungle of people who lay ahead in the town or village, McNeill knew, his chances of protecting Alina, her baby and himself were severely diminished. He knew he had a better chance of keeping everyone safe in open country. But they had to sleep and eat.

The cottages and houses set serenely on their own plots of land became rows of houses, office and apartment blocks lining both sides of the road. Shop signs became visible, then the shops themselves, but most of their windows were empty. McNeill slowed right down. People eyed the jeep and its occupants. He wasn't dressed in army uniform now. McNeill watched and he saw an old woman about 50 yards ahead exit a shop carrying a loaf of bread and a parcel under her arm. She clung to the parcel as if life itself depended on it. He watched her go by, then stopped the jeep alongside the shop door and turned to Alina.

'Alina, go into the shop and ask for what we need: food, water and anything else you can think of.'

'Why?' Alina asked, puzzled.

'Because the way the old woman left the shop, they have to be selling food on the black market and we will need more provisions. Be prepared to barter but don't waste time. There are not a lot of vehicles in the town and our presence sticks out like a sore thumb – man, woman and baby in a jeep. No doubt we have been noticed already, and if so, your father will know we are still alive. Go now; here is the money I took from Rasik. I will watch you from here,' McNeill said as he pulled his Beretta from its holster and removed the safety catch.

Alina got out of the jeep and entered the shop. It was small and sparse, with one long counter behind which an old woman stood, which ran from the front window to the rear wall. A gap in the counter enabling passage out and in was near the top, an opening behind it hidden by netting and beads. The shelves on her right were almost empty except for a few cans, bottles and odd tools. Nothing of any consequence was on display. She thought McNeill was mistaken, but whenever she doubted him something happened to prove him right. She cast the thought from her mind and strode to the counter purposefully.

'I would like to buy bread, milk, cheese, meat, baby formula, nappies and towels,' Alina said, allowing the woman to see the money.

The old woman ignored her and then told her she was in the wrong place.

Alina spoke again, forcibly repeating her demands, adding she was not police or army, and she would pay good money.

The old woman said she was still in the wrong place.

'Please,' begged Alina.

A young man in his thirties, dark hair, rather slim, gaunt face, moustache and a scar on his left cheek, came through the netting and beads to Alina's right. Alina turned to face him. 'If it wasn't for the scar, you would be very handsome, though the scar makes you attractively cavalier,' she said to him and in the same breath told him of her wish to buy food and provisions and showed him the money. The young man looked at her, watched her, his eyes calculating.

Outside, McNeill began to feel the itchiness on the back of his neck. He got out of the jeep with a towel rolled over his lower right forearm, disguising the Beretta pistol now aimed squarely at the shopkeeper through the window.

Endless silent minutes passed before the shopkeeper spoke. 'I have most but not all you want, lady,' he said.

160

Alina smiled. 'Just give me what you have, or what you can spare. We can agree a price,' she said.

'Wait here,' he said as he disappeared behind the hanging beads into the back.

Alina could hear rustling. The old woman just watched her through callous eyes. The man re-entered and put a box and bag down on the shop floor. Alina gave him what money he wanted, picked up the box and bag and left. She got into the jeep. McNeill reholstered his weapon and joined her. Alina had a great big smile on her face as McNeill drove off. He pulled off the street into a hotel car park, stopped and looked into the box and bag.

'You have done very well, very well indeed,' he said, smiling.

'Yes, I know, and a lot of promises and persuasion I had to give,' she remarked coyly.

McNeill laughed. In all their time together, Alina had never heard McNeill laugh like this and now for the first time, a deep, hearty, raucous, happy laugh was coming from him. She was pleased with herself. A good feeling swelled inside her; she felt warmed and comforted by it.

'We eat well tonight,' said McNeill. 'All we need now is somewhere to stay,' he added. He turned the ignition key and the jeep roared easily to life. McNeill headed out of the hotel car park and out of the small town.

Meanwhile, back at the shop, the old woman threw her shawl around her shoulders and walked to the hotel to use the telephone to ring General Tomelsky.

Night was beginning to creep in, accompanied with another chill wind.

'Seen anywhere to stop, Alina?' asked McNeill.

Alina was surprised. Twice, now, in the space of a few minutes, he had asked her opinion. She smiled as she replied. 'No, not yet, we must keep going north. Don't worry, if I spot something or somewhere I will tell you.'

As McNeill drove on a soft twilight overtook daylight, accompanied by a bitter wind. A few miles later, Alina spotted three houses on her right. They were equidistant, separated from each other by small fields. Two had smoke emanating from their chimneys and lights flickered from behind curtained windows. The last house looked dark and empty. 'There, there,' Alina called as she pointed to it. McNeill pulled off the road, dimmed the lights and drove up the lane to the small house. He reversed the jeep round to the rear out of sight of the road and the other two houses, took out his Beretta and said, 'Wait here, Alina.'

McNeill crept all around the house looking into the four windows carefully as Alina watched. He saw no sign of life. The house was simple; two windows set 6 feet from either side of the doors, front and back. The front door was solid wood, the back door was in two halves – solid wood at the bottom and glass in the top half. The glass was of 6-inch squares set into a wooden frame, four panes up, four panes across, and it was thick. McNeill smashed the pane of glass nearest the door handle with the butt of his Beretta pistol and let himself straight into the kitchen. Inside were a small table, four chairs, a stove with a kettle on top, a sink under the window, and cupboards either side of the sink, below it, and on the wall between the window and door.

He turned left down a small corridor. There was one door on his left, one door straight ahead and one door to his right, which he opened first, walking into a bathroom with a bath, washbasin, toilet and cupboard. He went back out and opened the door to his left and let the door swing right around to the wall. It was a bedroom: a double and single bed, two wardrobes, a chest of drawers, lockers, a dressing table, a lone chair by the window. McNeill went on ahead through the last door to find another bedroom, more or less the same as the other. He could see neither bed had been slept in for quite some time. He returned to the kitchen-living area then went outside to Alina in the jeep.

'Wise choice. The house is empty and has been for a while. We stay here tonight and leave early in the morning. I will bring the food, you bring the baby and whatever you need,' said McNeill.

162

McNeill went inside, left the food on the table, made and lit the fire and the stove, then went outside to the jeep.

Alina looked around the kitchen and noticed there was a washing machine, a small fridge freezer, baskets of wood either side of the stove and a couch against the far wall. Alina placed her baby next to the box of food on the table. Her mind skipped to a place of happiness and serenity. She imagined herself married to McNeill, who came in from a day's work and bent down and lifted the now four-year-old girl and hugged her and herself. Her daydream was shattered by the harshness of reality in McNeill's voice as he demanded, 'Does the cooker work? Have we water in the taps, or shall I fetch some from the well outside? Do the lights work? Black out that window.'

'Orders, orders, orders – don't you ever relax, or are you always a soldier?' she shouted.

McNeill was taken aback. 'OK,' he said as he put the guns and rifles on the sofa, adding 'Sorry' as he turned the taps on and got nothing. He found a large pan and went outside to fill it with water and returned.

'The cooker is gas. There is gas but I don't have anything to light it,' said Alina.

McNeill put his hand into his pocket and thumbed Fitz's lighter out and gave it to Alina. She lit the cooker. McNeill emptied some of the water into a smaller pan and placed it onto the stove. They then searched the cupboards. Alina checked the fridge, which was bare, but she found two tins of beans, one tin of peas and one tin of pears. Cutlery, plates, glass tumblers, mugs, tea, mouldy coffee, sugar and a tin of powdered milk was what McNeill found. Alina opened the bag on the table and took out two pounds of cooked ham, a small block of cheese, bread, milk, six eggs, yoghurt, baby food, nappies, fruit, salt and a towel.

'How did you manage to get all that?' asked McNeill politely, smiling at her.

'I batted my eyelids, promised I would meet him for a date,

163

told him you were my big brother, and some other promises I had no intention of keeping, and which are not for your ears,' she replied wistfully.

But McNeill had seen that mischievous glint in her eye, the kind that nearly all men find irresistible. Alina, the contemptuous flirt. She made tea for herself and for McNeill, warm milk for the baby. McNeill prepared a dinner of ham, eggs and cheese on toast, with pears for dessert for good measure. McNeill ate the last of the cheese on a slice of bread. They looked at each other across the table and both smiled. 'Any need to wash up?' Alina enquired.

'Not really, one job less. Let's leave the washing-up in the sink,' replied McNeill.

McNeill went over to the rifles, began to dismantle and clean them and took off his boots. Alina made more tea. The baby slept after feeding.

'When will they come, McNeill?' asked Alina.

'Not tonight. There were few soldiers in the town, although I am sure your father knows we are still alive. So really, they will come as soon as they can, sent from wherever they are, and it will be another crack force of men. So it's a matter of where this crack force is or his best men are and despatching them. You say his army is based in the south and west. I think his crack force will already be mobilised, so you may like to think which group of men were as good as if not better than Rasik's,' McNeill said calmly.

She handed him his tea and sat sipping her own on a small chair she had moved to sit by the fire. McNeill finished cleaning the weapons, got up, opened the fire door on the stove and put some logs in, then put some logs on the fire. He turned and placed his right hand on Alina's left shoulder, patted it and gave it a gentle squeeze, then collected the sleeping baby and sat beside Alina. Alina watched the flames flicker and lovingly lick the wood, and turned to look at McNeill. He was almost trance-like, looking into the fire, reflecting; a tormented reflection. He could see his own cottage burning in the fire, burning from the explosion as Molotov cocktail met gas violently.

The baby stirred in McNeill's arm and wailed. McNeill rocked her gently, caringly. Alina looked at this big man, so kind, so gentle, so caring with the small living child, yet so brutal, detached, a killer of fellow human beings. But she could see a bond, a strong bond had formed between McNeill and her baby girl and vice versa. The child lay in the crook of McNeill's left arm, wanting to sleep but fighting to stay awake: a small battle which she would eventually lose and succumb to slumber. McNeill went into the larger of the two bedrooms and placed the baby on the single bed and wrapped blankets over her, and left her to sleep.

He returned to the kitchen. Alina had just made more tea for herself and had removed the mouldy coffee from the top of the coffee jar and made coffee for him. She offered the coffee to him, strong and black. McNeill took it, took a small sip from the mug, liked the taste and put the mug on the table. Alina did likewise. She looked at McNeill, went the three paces to him, held out her arms and hugged him. She held him tight, felt his arms engulf her. McNeill could smell her scent, felt her soft hair wisp against his face. She turned her head to look at him, her eyes wide. McNeill looked into them, watched her pupils dilate just before she kissed him.

Then she broke away, but never retreated, wanting him to kiss her passionately. He did not disappoint. Their lips met, tentatively at first, small kisses until he could not resist any more. His open mouth met hers, his tongue relentlessly searched for hers, found it and the two tongues embarked on a samba dance. She felt his right hand holding the back of her head, and her own right hand found its way to hold the back of his neck, pulling him closer. She felt her nipples begin to enlarge and protrude. He broke from his kiss but her breathing was heavy and seductive, her mouth wanted more.

She felt McNeill's lips press to hers, gentle and firm, then felt his lips begin to caress her neck. She could feel her erect nipples rubbing against the inside of her bra and could feel McNeill's hands on her buttocks. She pushed him away and pulled at his woollen jumper, lifting it over his body and head, then the same with his T-shirt. McNeill threw the T-shirt on the table and Alina's hands found the flesh of his chest, feeling his pulsating heartbeat. She began to kiss his chest. McNeill began to pull her jumper up. Alina lifted her hands above her head as McNeill lifted the jumper all the way up and free of her hands. Their lips met again. McNeill's hands searched for the clasp of her bra at her back. She pressed her hands into his chest and pushed away. McNeill found the clasp at the front, undid it to release her breasts from the captivity of her bra. McNeill covered her breasts with either hand, began to gently squeeze and rub them, accentuating her nipples. Alina let out a moan.

He kissed her mouth, then her neck. Cupping her right breast in his left hand he took the nipple in his mouth. His tongue licked and playfully tormented it. Alina held the back of his head and again moaned gently. McNeill's mouth made it back to hers, then she felt him lift her off her feet and begin to carry her from the kitchen as she kissed his cheek. McNeill entered the bedroom and put her down. Alina's feet touched the floor and they kissed passionately, topless skin to topless skin. She felt the fingers of his hands slide slowly down her spine and into the small of her back, then unfasten the zip of her skirt. She parted from him marginally to let her skirt fall to the floor, stepped out of her shoes and began undoing his trouser belt, then she slid down the zip and slipped her hand inside, feeling his aroused manhood.

McNeill swept her hair from the front of her shoulders to her back, then his hands began exploring her hips and her svelte figure. She gently swayed back to allow his hands to move up and find her breasts, then the cheeks of her face. Her mouth opened slightly, provocatively. McNeill's mouth found hers, his tongue met hers. She pushed his trousers down over his firm buttocks. His trousers fell to his ankles just before they both fell onto the bed.

McNeill removed his trousers and his socks and Alina pulled off his boxer shorts and began stroking his manhood with her hands, her tongue licking his mouth and lips. She felt McNeill's hands on her hips, felt him turn her sideways and in doing so began to slide her panties down her thighs, then beyond her knees. She kicked them away from her and immediately his hand began to feel the top of her left thigh. He pulled her to him, kissing her passionately as he slipped his hand between her legs. Alina moaned.

He twisted so that he was on his back, but in doing so he had pulled her on top of him. She felt him guide himself into her and she moaned with intense pleasure as she made love to him, throwing her head back at her climax, her mouth open and soft murmurs followed ecstatic moans. She felt his right arm slip around her back, holding her in position as he rolled her over.

They lay in the afterglow, totally contented, exhausted but happy. She lay on top of him, her head tilted slightly back, McNeill caressing her hair. McNeill reached up and she raised herself. McNeill began kissing her and laid his head back onto the pillow. Then they just lay there, entwined in each other's arms.

Eventually they got under the covers, and once again McNeill made love to her. Afterwards, Alina slept in his arms. McNeill looked at her sleeping, so serene, so beautiful, so content, then sleep caught up with him.

Alina woke to the crying of the baby and she went to her. McNeill felt Alina leave him, woke and followed her out of the room to the next bedroom. He peered through the open door and looked over at Alina, who was now sitting on the bed breast-feeding her child.

'Bring her, she can sleep with us, you will both catch your death of cold in here,' McNeill said. Alina rejoined McNeill in the next bedroom and finished feeding her baby, then placed the baby girl in-between them in the bed. The baby girl cooed with contentment and duly fell asleep. Alina and McNeill slept.

McNeill woke early. The familiar sound of mortar fire rang his alarm bell. He listened intently; it was faint, very distant, but nevertheless, mortar fire was what it was. He woke Alina. She heard the steady muffled explosions, looked at McNeill and asked what the sounds of little thunder were. McNeill explained. 'Our journey is nearly over?' she asked with a hint of sadness. 'We are nearly there – the other side of the thunder is safety,' she added solemnly.

She looked at McNeill and she knew that not only was she reliant on him, she had fallen in love with him. McNeill watched the expressions on Alina's face, a face that told him she was eagerly anticipating being out of the chaos, but also that she wanted to remain in the chaos with him.

'Tell me again, McNeill, what are my father's options as a soldier now? He would not have expected you to wipe out one of his best crack assassination squads. What will he do?' asked Alina.

McNeill checked his watch and replied, 'Like I said to you earlier, by now your father knows we are still alive and Rasik is dead, his crew also. If he sends his best men from the south, it is going to be a race against time, a race he cannot win as we are too far north, and by the sound of things we don't have much further to go, although this is by no means going to be easy. Your father's options are such: either men will be taken from the front line with orders to intercept and kill us, or some of his men are already positioned on our route with orders to shoot on sight. He will know our route as he will have mapped it out from the reports relayed to him. Or another crack squad is already close with orders to identify and execute.'

'But McNeill, we are so far north now. I know my father is owed favours and he is a total bully, but surely the front line defences will be of utmost importance to his co-commanders,' put in Alina.

'No, definitely not! Your father wants those briefcases extremely badly, and now will stop at nothing to get them; he can't have them fall into the wrong hands. Your father sees that you are defying him, sticking your finger up in his face with the audacity to be alive, still. Me – he will surely want me dead now. So more soldiers will be on the lookout; there may even be a nice reward for us. It's a question of how close his best reliable men are,' McNeill countered.

⟫◆⟪

At that moment, Alina's father was being given a slip of paper. 'This came through to your office earlier, general, sir,' the soldier announced before being dismissed. General Tomelsky unfolded the slip of paper:

'Rasik not showed. Your daughter plus American were in Rasik's jeep in the next town. Ambush failed.'

The general read it again with disbelief, then clenched his fists, crumpling the slip of paper. He flew into a rage, hammering both fists into the desk. He flung the desk lamp across the room, stomped and kicked the rubbish bin. His face reddened as he cursed under clenched teeth, then bellowed, 'Darned American!' A look of vile hatred flushed his face. He yelled for his sergeant, who entered the room almost immediately, took one look at the general and began to quake. The general's dark snake-like eyes burned into him. 'Get me Radlinsky, NOW!' the general boomed.

The sergeant disappeared and soon afterwards the phone rang on the general's desk. 'Radlinsky, sir,' said the sergeant's voice.

'Radlinsky, where are you?' the general demanded.

'I am now three hundred kilometres from the front line and then the border. Do you still want me to proceed?' a cold calm waspish voice said.

'Comrade Rasik is dead, his men too. Do whatever it takes: stop them, kill them all, bring me those briefcases,' the general

169

spat, then silently dropped the phone into its cradle, ending the call.

Radlinsky was an athletic soldier, a veteran of many skirmishes, loyal only to his general, Alina's father, and he enjoyed the immunity his loyalty gave him. He rolled a cigarette, put it in his mouth and lit it. Half smiling, he drew on it and inhaled the sweet smoke, then exhaled. 'Do whatever it takes,' he kept saying: that meant no survivors in his dictionary. He finished the roll-up, stubbed it out in the ashtray and marched out of the hotel to his red and grey Toyota jeep, shouting, 'Ready, move out!' The Toyota left town in a cloud of dust. Radlinsky and his three colleagues were in hot pursuit of his general's daughter, her baby and an American soldier.

<hr>

McNeill decided it was time to go, time to take from the house whatever suitable provisions it held and leave. Alina packed what little tinned food was in the cupboard; McNeill took extra blankets, towels and clothes. They both filled empty bottles with water and climbed into the jeep. Alina put the wrapped-up, sleeping baby on the back seat padding extra blankets and towels around her.

McNeill drove steadily north in sombre silence. His mind was calculating, analysing, exploring all options. He knew Alina's father had no intention of letting them have a safe passage, he knew he was desperate for the briefcases and he would kill to get them. They were all expendable, worthless, considered good-for-nothing nuisances by the general. A sarcastic smile slipped across his lips. *A safe passage,* he thought. *A war in front, crack soldiers behind, and by now he knows that Rasik is dead, and we are in Rasik's jeep.* McNeill decided open country held a slightly better chance for survival than the towns, where they would be hunted. At this moment he was an awful pain in the arse for General Tomelsky. He had killed too many of his men, his most loyal and trusted soldiers, some of who, like Rasik, may have been personal friends. *A festering boil is how the general would perceive me*, he thought. 'How far is it to the border?' he asked Alina.

'About two hundred kilometres,' she replied.

'How many towns and villages between here and the border? And can we avoid them by going around?' asked McNeill. Going around was going to use fuel and swallow valuable time. He checked the fuel gauge; the needle was pointed at a space in-between half and a quarter full. Maybe enough for a small detour, but not enough for a major one, or more than one, he calculated.

Alina's voice broke his thoughts. 'Two major towns between here and the border, one of which is quite near. I suspect that is where the explosions are coming from,' she said.

McNeill began to calculate a possible detour around the first town. If Alina's father had men there looking for them or his spies watching out for them, by going around they would not be spotted, and it may give them more time and a head start, because by the time the general realised they had diverted round the town, they would be hours further ahead. Maybe this would allow them to reach the last town and travel through using a bombardment as cover; surely if the nearest town was under mortar fire, then the next should be in the thick of it. Unless it had been taken. *Risky*, he thought but it just might work.

The baby woke, crying. Alina fed and changed her and nursed her to sleep. 'How far to the next town, how much money have we left, how much food do we have left and where can we go to get more?' asked McNeill.

'Fifty to sixty kilometres, we have a small amount of money left, a few possessions and clothes to bargain with, but not enough food to reach the border,' replied Alina.

McNeill was now making a mental note of how much ammunition he had left. *Not enough for a major skirmish*, he thought.

He began to worry, a discomforting emotion for him, an emotion which had been alien to him for quite some time, until now. Since the death of his wife and daughter he had only thought of himself. He thought of Fitz. Fitz worried about him, but he hadn't worried about Fitz – he was reliable, self-reliant. That was the way they worked, that was how it was. Since Fitz's death, it only confirmed in his mind that he was alone, there to face the world in solitude, disrespect and hate; nothing to live for, nobody to care for. He felt neither obligated nor attached to anyone, did not care if he lived or died. A professional soldier, another statistic. But now, now he realised he cared; he cared for Alina, cared for her baby girl, wanted freedom for them and himself. Wanted to be a part of them, wanted to belong with them, wanted Alina and her baby to belong to him. He looked at Alina. Alina squeezed his hand. 'What's troubling you?' she enquired.

McNeill began, 'We are still rats in a trap. Ahead is a war, the front line which we have to pass through. We could be killed by enemy or friendly fire; the shoot-first-ask-questions-later kind. Behind, more of your father's men who will shoot to kill, and maybe on our flank, a detachment of your father's men from the front line sent specifically to wipe us out. Not a very comfortable position to be in for us. I'm sure you agree?'

'But McNeill, we are free rats. You are a good man and a brilliant soldier. I, for one, would not like their chances,' remarked Alina, who began to laugh. McNeill laughed with her.

Rain hit the windscreen, a light drizzle at first, subdued, but the beating of the raindrops against the glass got louder and more intense. The wind picked up and drove the rain head first at the jeep.

'If the rain is like this for us, I sure hope it is this bad for whoever is following behind,' commented McNeill.

'Tell me about Rasik,' McNeill asked as he slowed the jeep.

'Rasik,' Alina began, 'a personal friend of my father's, extremely loyal to him and vice versa. They had to be – it was a marriage of consequences but they were loyal to the core to each other. Rasik was a killing machine, a sadistic assassin; he would be around fifty years of age or so. Rasik was given a life sentence for the killing of his mother and father; my father bought his freedom. He stood by him, told everyone it happened because Rasik had had a neglected childhood, a brutal childhood at the hands of his father, and his mother beat him for crying. He also said Rasik was an unwanted, unloved child and treated as such, like an animal. My father traded on people's sentiments and enrolled Rasik into his army. Rasik was a crack shot, who just enjoyed killing, no matter what. He enjoyed the destruction of living things, absolutely brutal. My father used him to either exterminate or control his enemies, and there were not too many left who needed controlling, courtesy of Rasik being over-indulgent and too heavy-handed.

'But Rasik and another, Radlinsky, were my father's favourites; both killing machines, above the law, answerable only to my father. My father's rise to general was very quick, aided undoubtedly by the removal of what he would call obstacles by either Rasik or Radlinsky. My father bullied his way to general, and the further up the ladder he got, the better the positions of authority for Rasik and Radlinsky. Both Rasik and Radlinsky used my father's first name, Gregor, and he theirs; that in itself was a measure of the standing and regard they had for each other, and always they never shouted at each other. Each had total respect and loyalty to each other.

'The atrocities are in the files in the briefcases. Not only the general public but my father's own soldiers and officers were very frightened of Rasik, and are of Radlinsky. They have had a free hand to do as they please, and often did, with complete disdain and disregard for anyone except my father. As I said, the three were loyal to each other, each needing the other – it's all in the briefcases.

'Both Rasik and Radlinsky have their own men, or had in the case of Rasik, hand-picked by them, loyal to the last. Rasik would have known my father for twenty-five years, Radlinsky a little less,' Alina ended.

McNeill frowned. It was as he had thought, it was his most

loyal, trusted men that the general had sent. Not only were the briefcases of the most utmost of importance, but this would now become a personal vendetta for the general.

'Tell me, Alina, would Rasik and Radlinsky ever work together?' asked McNeill.

'Sometimes both would be sent; as I told you, both Rasik and Radlinsky had their own men, and often there was rivalry as to which were the best, the most loyal, most brutal, most efficient. But if it was of grave or vital importance to my father both would be sent, depending on where they were in relation to each other. One acted as cover for the other, but the cover was never needed. They would be my father's best,' Alina replied.

Mmm, OK, thought McNeill, *a lucky break, that's maybe how we got out of the town.* Maybe Radlinsky was there, probably in some hotel room, just waiting for Rasik to show. Up until yesterday he always had, and so Radlinsky and his men would have been having a good time for themselves while he and Alina slipped through. Now Radlinsky knew they were ahead and Alina's father knew that Rasik was dead and their position was somewhere ahead of Radlinsky. 'Which was the best, Rasik or Radlinsky?' asked McNeill.

'Neither, both are master planners, clever, devious, brutal, mechanical in getting the job done. I suppose you are saying Radlinsky is behind, and if he knows Rasik is dead he will be very, very careful,' Alina replied.

'Yes, he sure will. He and your father want those documents, and by now your father knows we know what is in them,' McNeill replied.

Alina spoke with an air of realisation. 'Oh my God, they are going to just kill us. We are all expendable.'

'Listen, Alina, this is not going to be easy. Radlinsky is behind us. If we get delayed in the town ahead he will catch up; if we divert around it, he will either be just behind or in front of us, depending on how much time we waste and how far behind he is. Nice catch 22 situation coming up,' McNeill said purposefully.

'Which is better, us in front or behind?' asked Alina.

'Well, you know what he looks like – you can identify him, I hope – and it is similar to the last time; it's always better to know how many are in the opposition,' said McNeill.

Alina retorted with her voice raised, 'What are you suggesting? To use the same tactics that nearly got me killed yesterday? McNeill, you are insane!'

'How many men does Radlinsky have? Do you know? Unlikely,' snapped McNeill.

'No, no I don't!' Alina shouted. 'Can't we outrun them?' she added, her voice beginning to waver.

There was a long silence before McNeill spoke. 'What if we tried to outrun them, and at the front line we get delayed? War in front, Radlinsky behind. Rats in a trap who cannot identify Radlinsky's men. Sitting ducks, we would be.'

'OK, McNeill, what do you propose?' asked Alina.

McNeill knew he had her full attention and co-operation. He began, 'We will pull into the town ahead and wait, maybe ditch this jeep, but definitely hide it, but we wait or, better still, we pull into the town, get food and leave in a hurry, hide and wait. We should reach the town in just over an hour. We eat, spend a little money. We make sure we are seen but we act naturally, don't overdo this. Then we leave in a hurry. Firstly, we circle the town, find somewhere to lay up later. Then retrace our steps and head in. Once again, the hunter will become the hunted, and it may be that the war ahead may be our opportunity to dispose of Radlinsky and his men. You got that?'

'OK, McNeill,' she said, nodding her head in agreement to the last few words. She liked the idea of disposal.

⇒•◇•⇐

McNeill approached the town, but swung off to his left 2 miles before it, slapped the jeep into four-wheel drive and headed off down a dirt track. It was bumpy, potholed, but hidden from view by bushes and trees which grew on either side. Rain still pelted the windscreen. The lane narrowed and the jeep lurched from one water-filled pothole to another, but eventually the lane ended at a small road. McNeill turned right. His aim was to arc the town from south to north, and find somewhere to hide on the north side of it. At times he left the roads and drove over and through fields of short grass and mud. An hour passed before he located the northbound road out of town. He drove north. Alina spotted and pointed at a boarded-up cottage set off the road in a hollow, visible for only a moment half a mile before it, and almost invisible when upon it. McNeill pulled off the road and drove up the narrow lane to the cottage, garage at the rear.

He halted the jeep but left the engine running as he got out. 'Turn it around,' he ordered as he went to the cottage's rear door, hitting it with his shoulder forcefully. The old timber door opened without too much resistance. McNeill drew his Beretta as he entered. Ten long minutes passed before he returned to the jeep, his Beretta now holstered. 'Welcome to the Plaza,' he said to Alina as he passed by on his way to the garage. He forced the garage door, looked in, saw it was empty, shut the door and returned to the jeep. 'Move over, I'm driving,' he ordered. Alina did as she was bid without fuss.

McNeill drove back to the south-side road he had left some one and a half hours earlier and headed into town, checking his watch. 'Time, time is essential,' he kept on muttering, his brow furrowed. Alina began to worry. They drove past houses on either side of the road. Some had little gardens in front, others had none. The mortar fire had abated. They reached the main hub of the town. McNeill eyed ahead: shops, hotels, cafes, houses, flats, disused restaurants, boarded-up clothes shops and other abandoned shops which had their windows smashed. The town's main thoroughfare had rows of parking spaces on either side. McNeill slowed and pulled over, not bothering to reverse in – he just drove the mud-spattered jeep across three parking spots facing north. He noticed his was the only vehicle on that side of the

176

road. Alina got out with her baby and joined the queue waiting for bread outside the shop across from the jeep. McNeill got out and sat on a bench. The air was damp but the rain had stopped.

McNeill checked his watch and looked behind, back down the road. He waited forty agonising minutes, his palms sweaty, calmness turning to anxiety, his mind examining every scenario as he waited for Alina and watched for Radlinsky. The tension in him grew, only to subside a little once Alina was back at his side with a loaf of bread, milk and a small amount of cheese. The milk was for her baby and she made a cheese sandwich for both her and McNeill. McNeill sat on the bench and stared at the small shop from where Alina had come earlier, then at the jeep, then the road. He watched and waited. There had been an occasional car pass by, civilian drivers, soldiers on foot and in cars, but these were all too young to be Radlinsky and his cohorts. He estimated Radlinsky's age was about the same as Rasik's from what Alina had related earlier. More young soldiers in a group of six walked the pavement on the opposite side to Alina and McNeill.

Alina began shouting at McNeill in her native tongue, telling him what a bone-idle, lazy man he was, how he was worthless, useless, how he would never do anything for her and her baby, just used her for sex and beat her. 'Shut up, shut up you fool!' McNeill whispered through clenched teeth. Alina began waving her arms and pointing, still shouting. McNeill grabbed her. Two soldiers, having watched what was happening, broke away and began to make their way towards McNeill and Alina. 'OK, that's enough, don't go overboard, I don't want to be arrested or shot,' he whispered to her. Alina turned to see the two soldiers, smiled at them and gave the baby to McNeill and began to walk to the jeep with him. The two soldiers stopped, turned and headed back to join the rest of their group. 'That should have been noticed, McNeill,' said Alina with a cheeky grin as she got into the jeep.

'Superb,' replied McNeill with a relieved smile.

The smile disappeared as quickly as it came. McNeill started the engine, squealed the tyres as he gunned the Nissan out of town. Outside he stopped and slowed down, made a right turn and slowly meandered back around the outskirts, returning to within touching distance of the main street on the east side, where he parked. 'Wait here,' he said to Alina as he got out, removing his jacket and throwing it in the back seat. He grabbed a pullover and put it on as he walked the 50 yards to the main thoroughfare. He stopped when he reached it, looked left and right. To his left it was almost empty, apart from the old man and lady making their way up the town. To his right were apartment blocks on either side, three storeys high and sparsely used. On the left-hand side was a small green, and the little bench where he had sat earlier. Soldiers were still milling around the shops opposite but there were cars and jeeps abandoned outside now, and more people, young and old.

He turned right and headed towards more young soldiers, more cars and more jeeps, which were abandoned in the parking places. McNeill walked past the baker's and butcher's, boarded-up shops, and he passed an electrical store with bars on its broken window, protecting empty shelves. Soldiers milled around and McNeill made his way silently, apologetically through. His pulse raced, adrenalin pumped, his nerves taut. He crossed the street to a bench, sat down and exhaled slowly. In front of the bench was a small parking area large enough for four cars, if they pulled in nose first.

He looked across to a small green surrounded by the concrete masses of two-storey apartments, and five detached houses. Most of the apartments were derelict, some were boarded up. He turned through 180 degrees. Soldiers were milling about, eating, laughing and smoking. It appeared to McNeill that this town was a respite for them, a safe haven. They seemed and looked relaxed. Most of the vehicles in the street were commandeered cars and a reliable amount of jeeps, six in total. More soldiers were across in an entrance to a shopping mall; a hotel was next door. *More than a hotel*, thought McNeill as he watched soldiers going in and out of the building. At the side of the hotel was a roadway leading to a rather large car park, which served both the hotel and the shopping mall. At the other side was a bar and next door a ramshackle coffee, tea and soup parlour. *Perfect,* McNeill thought as he began the walk back to Alina.

He went down a small lane behind the soup parlour, leading to the large car park. Some people looked out of their houses with blank expressions on their faces; others looked frightened. He passed children playing with marbles. At the corner he turned right down a small alleyway, with apartments either side. Washing lines loaded with laundry linked the two sides overhead. Further down he found himself stooping to avoid the washing. An occasional shout broke the silence, some woman ranting and raving at McNeill as he brushed past her washing. McNeill strode on, arriving at the end and there, 30 yards up and to his right, was the jeep.

McNeill quietly came upon the jeep's rear and opened the door, giving Alina a fright. 'Sorry, didn't mean to alarm you,' he said softly. She was relieved to see him – startled, but very relieved. McNeill watched as the tension in her dissipated. He too was glad to see her and to see her nursing her child. A strong bond now existed between mother and daughter – he could see that – and a strong bond existed between mother, daughter and himself; he could feel that.

'OK,' said McNeill, 'you ready to listen to what we are going to do?'

'Yes,' said Alina attentively.

McNeill began, 'We are going to park the jeep near a coffee shop in a lane facing out of the car park, walk a few yards and order soup or tea in the ramshackle parlour, and we are going to sit in and wait. You are the only one who can recognise Radlinsky. He will enter the town and want to know if we were spotted and how long ago and he will ask and that show you put on will be relayed to him. We watch, we find out how many men he has with him, and what kind of vehicle he is driving and then we follow. Alina, you can recognise him, but he can also recognise you and this may put us in jeopardy. We have to see him but not allow him to see you. My guess is Radlinsky and his men will enter the town and park near the bench were I sat just now and approach the soldiers at the front of the hotel, maybe the shops, maybe the hotel itself. We can see the bench partially from the coffee shop. Right now, we have to get to the coffee shop unseen, and remain inconspicuous until Radlinsky shows. I reckon we will not have long to wait. Feed your baby – we need her to be sleepy. I hope she will oblige.'

Alina undid her top and began to breastfeed her baby, who suckled contentedly as she covered herself up as best she could. After feeding, Alina passed the baby girl to McNeill and expertly dressed. The baby looked at McNeill and he smiled. Alina began to reach for her daughter but refrained and watched as McNeill made goo-goo eyes and cooed at the baby. Alina smiled. *Yes, McNeill, I love you,* she thought, *we both love you.*

McNeill returned the baby to Alina. 'Ready?' he enquired. 'Yes,' came her reply. He started the engine and turned the jeep around, returned to the small intersection, made a left turn and drove slowly to the T-junction, then headed left again. Minutes later he saw the lane he had walked earlier, containing the low-strung washing. Shortly he spotted the lane ahead which led to the large car park. He arrived in the large car park, turned full circle, re-entered the lane and stopped the jeep. He checked his Beretta pistol – fully loaded – and he reholstered it under his pullover. 'So far, so good,' he said, adding, 'OK let's get to the coffee shop and order soup, maybe a cup of tea after and ask for milk for the child. Have we enough money?' he asked.

'Think so,' came the reply.

'OK. I will go to the end of the street, you stay five yards behind. I will look to see if it's clear and you go to the shop and place the order. Sit so you have a good view of the bench and the road, but choose somewhere not too conspicuous. I will join you,' he said.

They got out of the jeep and walked to the main street without any fuss. McNeill checked and waved to Alina, who passed McNeill and entered the coffee shop. McNeill waited, watching, checking, looking at the soldiers ahead, looking out for something out of place, checking the parked cars and jeeps, eyeing the people: nothing. He entered the coffee shop. Soldiers drank tea and coffee at the back. Alina had found the perfect view point, or so she thought, but as McNeill sat alongside he realised she could be seen as well, very easily. They changed seats and watched out through the shop's front window. A young boy passed their table and shortly after appeared at the coffee shop owner's side behind the counter and then brought soup to Alina and McNeill. Alina smiled and thanked him. As they began to drink the soup the boy once again passed by, but this time on the shop's outside. *Going back to play with his friends,* thought McNeill. Soldiers passed by, townspeople old and young, children played on the tiny green behind the bench. Alina and McNeill finished the soup. Alina ordered tea as her baby slept. 'How much longer?' she asked.

'I don't really know, but if he is an expert hunter-soldier, then soon, very soon,' McNeill said quietly. The tea was hot. Alina and McNeill drank slowly. Just as McNeill lifted the mug to his lips to take the last mouthful a red and grey mud-spattered jeep came to a rushed halt near the park bench. All four doors opened simultaneously and four men disembarked and moved to the jeep's rear. Alina's eyes widened, her jaw dropped. 'That's him – tall, green jacket, shaven head, and that one beside him is Jarowiscz, professional assassin.' She began to stand but McNeill grabbed her arm. 'Sit still, no quick or sudden movements, don't alert the soldiers in here, don't let them get suspicious. Wait,' he said quietly and firmly.

'I'm scared,' said Alina.

'So am I,' replied McNeill calmly.

Outside three of the men received their orders and headed off down the street away from the cafe. Radlinsky headed towards the cafe. 'Don't move till I say so, keep your eyes firmly down on the table and don't look up,' said McNeill. The six soldiers at the rear stood and left the cafe.

Radlinsky crossed the street and reached the pavement. His head jerked up and then down the street, and he moved off down towards the soldiers gathered on a corner, the direction the soldiers from the cafe were headed towards.

'Up,' McNeill whispered sternly. Alina stood. McNeill held her arm forcefully and led her behind the counter, where she glimpsed a startled coffee shop owner as they went past him. The coffee shop owner shouted at McNeill, who turned, Beretta pointing at the man. 'Rear door!' Alina demanded. The coffee shop owner pointed. The rear door led onto the street at a right angle to the main street. McNeill could hear the shouts and screams of a small boy.

—⟫◆⟪—

Radlinsky's men had wasted no time. They'd gone into the baker's and butcher's, guns ready, demanding of all the people inside whether they had seen a black jeep, American soldier, dark-haired young woman and a baby. They were told of the row in the street earlier and how a black jeep had roared out of town, heading north. As Radlinsky walked down the street he watched a young boy run through a group of soldiers and fall to the ground, struggle to his feet and begin running away from where his men were and towards him. Radlinsky caught the boy. 'In a hurry, are we? Where are we going, and what have we to tell?' he asked. Radlinsky's burly cohorts arrived and began relaying how a large man and a young woman with a baby had an argument at the park bench, and how the black jeep screamed out of town northwards about one hour ago. Radlinsky held the boy in an iron grip. 'What have we to tell?' he asked the boy as he began to squeeze his arm tighter. Jarowiscz lifted the boy's legs off the street by the ankles and began to twist them counter-clockwise.

As Radlinsky squeezed tighter, the six soldiers who had just

182

left the cafe approached Radlinsky. His two other men pointed their AK-47s at them. The soldiers stopped. 'They're... they're in the coffee shop... in the coffee shop!' the boy cried in agony.' Jarowiscz dropped the boy and Radlinsky let his hold loosen, shouting. 'Go! Go!'

Two men with AK-47s burst through the front door of the coffee shop, followed by Jarowiscz and Radlinsky. The coffee shop owner pointed out the back.

'Move, move quickly,' said McNeill to Alina as they emerged onto the side street, dodging past people heading to the main street wanting to know what the commotion was. Alina and McNeill moved past an elderly couple and began running to the jeep, only to find a Land Rover was blocking its exit and two men were admiring the black jeep.

'What the hell do they want?' demanded McNeill. Alina shouted at them to get away from their jeep. The two men sneered and one began slapping a wheel brace against the palm of his free hand.

'Tell them we will swap,' said McNeill.

'Are you crazy?' Alina shouted.

'Tell them!' McNeill answered forcibly, his eyes wide. Alina relayed the message, just before they reached the jeep. McNeill went to the boot of the black Nissan and took out a long green bag and a small holdall, threw the keys to the larger of the two men and shut the boot.

'Land Rover, quick – you drive,' he whispered to Alina. Alina got in the driver's seat. 'Move this junk heap out of their way, let them go ahead,' said McNeill, throwing the bags into the rear seats. He climbed in and took the baby from her.

The two men started the black jeep, rammed it into gear and screamed up the lane to the main street, made a right turn and sped off out of town. McNeill lay down in the back. 'Take a right then head left and east, drive slowly,' he instructed as Alina started the engine.

Radlinsky exited the coffee shop the same time the black jeep completed its right turn onto the main street. All four men ran to the corner, then left to their red and grey Toyota, jumped in and followed the black Nissan out of town.

Alina saw Radlinsky in her rear-view mirror and froze. McNeill looked out of the rear window and watched it all unfold. The red and grey Toyota roared past the lane end in pursuit of the black Nissan.

'Turn round and follow them,' McNeill said.

'What? Are you crazy? Have you taken leave of your senses? You want to follow them. We were nearly caught, we or you could be shot dead now, and you want to follow them?' Alina said, horrified.

A calm voice of steel came from the rear of the Land Rover. 'Turn round and follow them; drive slowly out of town.'

Alina found herself following McNeill's instructions. McNeill opened the green bag, took out his M21 rifle and the Dragunov rifle and checked the magazines. Full ten rounds on the Dragunov and six in the M21. *Not much room for error,* he thought, *must not miss.* Alina began to cry.

'Hey, what's the matter? What's up? Keep driving slowly, we are nearly out of town,' McNeill said.

'Yes, out of town and on our way to certain death. Radlinsky is smart, very clever; special operative Jarowiscz is exactly that, exceptional soldier; the others, Masny and Lukas, they hate me and are also exceptional soldiers and assassins. Along with Rasik, these would be my father's best. The top, toughest men in his army. If you had to hand pick four of his elite, these would be them. I'm frightened, McNeill, scared for you for the first time and for me and my child. We are so close but we are not going to make it,' Alina said, wiping tears from her eyes as she spoke.

'Shut up, drive and stop whingeing; we are still alive,' McNeill retorted. *Which is more than can be said of the two in the Nissan when Radlinsky catches up with them,* he thought.

Alina headed northwards out of town, past the cottage. It was just after midday. They felt every bump on the road, the Land

Rover's rock hard suspension made sure of that. Alina drove on through a light drizzle. Bushes and trees began to creep into view, and hard bracken-like foliage; they were heading towards a forest. 'Don't worry about throwing us around in the back, drive faster,' urged McNeill. His mind was racing, wondering whether Radlinsky had caught up with the Nissan and its occupants. If he had, he would know a switch had taken place and he would head back to the town.

Radlinsky was in the passenger seat of the Toyota. Lukas was driving; they had reached the forest almost half an hour before Alina. Lukas slewed the Toyota around the road and into the forest, driving the jeep expertly like a rally driver. He went round and through the corners; men on a mission men in a hurry. 'Faster, Lukas,' called Radlinsky. 'The sooner we have them in sight the sooner we can finish this; and before dark I want this over.' Lukas tried to speed up but realised that the road through the forest was not going to let him; too many turns and tight bends, not enough straight road. He drove to his limit and eventually exited the forest. The heavy gorse and bracken and trees gave way to a rocky side on Lukas's left and a drop on Radlinsky's right. He drove into a long right-handed hairpin bend, dipping down the hillside. As they turned they saw their black quarry at the bottom of the hill. Two more hairpins, one left, one to the right and a 90-degree bend to the left, before open, straight road across a lowland of lush valley stretching for at least 2 miles.

'Hurry Lukas, step on it!' screamed Radlinsky in fevered anticipation.

'Yeah, step on it,' said Jarowiscz, adding, 'We don't want to be caught up in the front line ahead.'

Lukas eased the accelerator down a tiny fraction. He knew around the hairpins he had to be careful and at this speed a small error of judgement and none of them would live to see the quarry, never mind the front line. Lukas negotiated the hairpins and the 90-degree left-hand bend, then gunned the accelerator to the floor, rapidly changing gears and driving the jeep to its limit down the valley plain and off after the black Nissan jeep. The drizzle gave way to a chilly overcast grey sky.

Alina drove the Land Rover as fast as she could into the forest. *Too slow*, thought McNeill. 'Speed up, we are falling too far behind.' Steam began to emanate from under the bonnet of the Land Rover. 'Shit,' she heard McNeill say. 'The engine is overheating, slow down and turn the heater to red hot and the fan blower to its maximum,' he added. They exited the forest a good half-hour after Lukas. 'Stop!' McNeill yelled. Alina jammed on the brakes and brought the Land Rover to a standstill. McNeill got out, the vein on the side of his head pulsing to the rhythm of every thought.

Radlinsky should be with the Nissan by now, and at this stage the two bums would be dead, or if they were still alive, he had been duped. What would he do? Would he track back to the town or try and head them off? He didn't know which way they would go. He knew he was recognised, he would be sure he had been spotted and that Alina would be very frightened. He would expect them to go off in another direction to avoid him, but which way? He would have to go back; he had the briefcases which were still in the boot. One thing for sure was that he would not have expected them to follow him. *So what do we do? Hide, let them drive by and make a run for it, and when he hits town and finds out which direction we took he turns round and comes after us to tie up all loose ends. Mmm*, thought McNeill as he rubbed his chin.

'Can you shoot?' he asked Alina.

'What?' she replied.

'Can you fire a sniper rifle and can you hit what you aim at?' asked McNeill.

'Are you crazy?' she replied.

McNeill was beginning to lose patience. 'Look, stop dallying, Alina and answer me. Can you shoot?' he repeated sternly.

'Of course I can shoot. I am a butcher general's daughter. I can shoot but I hope I have a big target to aim at,' Alina replied curtly.

'How about a muddy Toyota jeep? Is that big enough? But it will be moving towards you rapidly. You shoot straight at it, could you hit it?' McNeill enquired.

'McNeill, it is a long time since I fired a rifle. You're a marvellous shot, why can't you hit the Toyota?'

McNeill broke in before she could add anything more. 'Stopping it is one thing, killing its occupants is another. We cannot let any of its occupants escape, especially as these are the best soldiers your father has. If we leave one alive, he will hunt us down. We have to totally incapacitate them, dead or severely wounded. Severely wounded, I don't mind, although I would prefer dead. This is not a game, they will kill us, so it is simply kill, or be killed, survival of the fittest, first law of the jungle. I cannot guarantee if I stop the Toyota from that ridge there that all its occupants will be killed. If one or two get out alive, it could take hours flushing them out or them flushing us out. Either way, if they have sniper rifles like we do we could not outrun them. I think they will bring both jeeps back, two men in each.'

'What do we do? I am frightened, these are crack assassins, the elite of my father's personal bodyguard. What do we do, McNeill?' interrupted Alina anxiously.

'Pray,' said McNeill with a smile.

'How can you be so flippant?' shouted Alina angrily.

'Look, Alina. Radlinsky is not stupid. He gets to the Nissan, sees we are not in it. He stops it, interrogates the two in it, and finds out we have a dodgy Land Rover with a burst head gasket. He knows we cannot get too far. Either he kills them or not. The briefcases are in the back so they are as good as dead. If I was him, I would bring Rasik's jeep as well, head back to town, find out which way we went and come after us, figuring using Rasik's jeep may catch us out as we would be expecting his own Toyota and we would be sitting ducks in a busted up Land Rover which cannot be driven too fast. So once again, do you think you could shoot up a jeep heading towards you from that ridge there?' McNeill's voice was harsher.

'Laying an ambush. You're not going to give them a chance, are you McNeill? You are as bad as them,' shouted Alina.

'Oh please, spare me the moral talk; if they kill me and capture you, then what? Each will take his pleasure of you then slit your throat. As for your baby girl, she will be left to starve to death, or die at their hands. Maybe they will kill your daughter before your very eyes and then kill you. They cannot let either of us live. If your father survives this war and becomes a big-shot politician, you and I know too much, and what scandal would that cause him? You are as dead as I,' retorted McNeill coldly, adding, 'Now, do you think you can hit a jeep from there?' He pointed with his right arm.

'Yes, I can hit it,' said Alina meekly.

'Good. Aim for the windscreen, driver's side first, and shoot the hell out of it, don't let anyone get out,' said McNeill.

'And where will you be?' asked Alina.

'Down there. The second jeep will be a short distance behind, and will stop as soon as you fire. That's my target and if you miss the first jeep, I may still have a chance to stop it as it climbs the slope. Feed the baby, we don't have much time. I will hide this scrapheap.'

McNeill sat in the Land Rover, his mind toying with the idea that he could save one of the jeeps as the Land Rover would not get much further. While he hid the sick vehicle, Alina began to feed her daughter.

Lukas was driving like a man possessed, like a cheetah after an antelope. 'It's slowing down,' said Masny. 'I'm sure of it,' he added. He was looking through the rifle sight on a sniper rifle in the Toyota's rear seat. 'OK, close up, Lukas, then ease off; be careful, this may be a trap,' said Radlinsky.

'There are too many of us, sir,' Jarowiscz exclaimed, excitedly thinking of the pleasure of taking the general's daughter, making her submit to his every sexual whim, then killing her slowly. His blood pumped through his arteries faster.

Lukas eased off. The Nissan was pulling over, then it stopped.

Two doors opened at the same time as two AK-47s were trained on them. Two men got out and began to relieve themselves. Lukas stopped the Toyota in front of the Nissan. Masny exited the rear door like greased lightning, AK-47 at the ready, pointed at two now frightened young men. 'In your own time,' laughed Masny.

Radlinsky, Jarowiscz and finally Lukas joined Masny. Lukas and Jarowiscz trained their AK-47s on the two men. Radlinsky removed his Glock pistol from its holster and told the men to turn around, then fired one round each in-between their feet.

'Don't kill us, please,' they begged.

'Shut up. Answer the questions only,' said Radlinsky, a twisted smile upon his face.

'Where are the American, woman and baby?' he asked.

'We don't know,' they replied. A volley of sub-machine gunfire over their heads from Jarowiscz accompanied the babble of the two men.

'Quiet!' shouted Radlinsky. 'Answer the question. Where are the American, woman and baby?'

Radlinsky was now circling the nearest man to him. Then he stopped an arm's length away and behind him.

'Don't know,' said the man, and Radlinsky shot him in the back of his head. The man fell to the ground and in one movement Radlinsky aimed the Glock at the other man's head. The man, arms aloft, began to weep.

'Please, please, don't shoot, we swapped the jeep for our busted out Land Rover in the town back there. We were going to take it anyway, when a big guy and woman carrying a baby burst round a corner into the street. The woman yelled we could have the jeep for the Land Rover as long as we headed north rapidly. We laughed to ourselves as we were going this way anyway. We both live near the next town, which is now under siege, and we needed a better car or jeep to get our families out. The Land Rover's gasket was blown and the town would probably be as far as it would go before it broke down completely, and that's my brother you have just shot there!'

'Not your lucky day, is it?' Radlinsky said as he shot him. He strode to the Nissan, saw the keys still in the ignition, opened the boot and saw the briefcases. Radlinsky smiled. 'OK, back to town. Lukas, Masny, take the Toyota; Jarowiscz, get in the Nissan, I will drive. And Lukas, do take it easy. You know I cannot keep up with you, the way you drive, but do hurry, you heard what that guy said; the Land Rover was breaking down, so it cannot have got far and the American may have had to go back to town to steal another car or they are on foot.'

⟹·◇·⟸

Alina had fed her daughter and wrapped her up in blankets on the rear seat of the Land Rover. McNeill opened the green bag and removed the two sniper rifles. 'Come on, Alina we must get into position quickly,' McNeill said. They ran to the roadside before it disappeared down, meandering round the hillside. McNeill looked down and round, eyeing the terrain. 'OK, see those bushes higher than the road?' asked McNeill.

'Yes,' said Alina, already moving towards them. They lay behind the bushes. McNeill looked through the sight down at the bottom of the hill, then told Alina to lie down and look. 'OK, when the first jeep hits here, see through the sight, you squeeze the trigger. It's a two-stage trigger and you only have six bullets. You can discharge the magazine all at once or one bullet at a time.'

'I know,' interrupted Alina. 'I have fired an M21, but my father preferred Dragunovs. I have knowledge of the two-stage trigger. What is it that's said? Oh yes, if you can see it, you can kill it, the M21 is deadly accurate,' she said, mimicking her instructor's squeaky voice.

'True,' said McNeill, 'and this is my best friend I am entrusting you with.' Alina smiled as she looked at him across her left shoulder. McNeill looked into her eyes and saw the provocative smile on her face, and the smell of her was his addiction. They kissed and he picked up the Dragunov and was gone.

190

McNeill had set the sight on the M21. All she had to do was pull the trigger and empty the magazine into the windscreen. *No problem, I hope.* But he felt uneasy. He stopped at the bottom of the hill just to the left of Alina's line of fire and looked back, then moved forward and off to his left. He lay down in tough, thick grass, stretched out and nestled the Dragunov's barrel between two rocks, invisible from the road. He checked the magazine: ten rounds. This was a gas-canister-fired, semi-automatic sniper rifle, almost an AK-47 with a stock. The stock was almost nonexistent, merely a frame that nestled neatly into McNeill's shoulder. Which was the better of the two sniper rifles? Hard to know, it was just a matter of personal choice. McNeill would have preferred his old friend, his M21, but it might not have enough bullets in the short time he anticipated to knock out the second jeep. His plan was formulated; all he and Alina had to do was wait.

McNeill saw it first, a shivering shape driving towards them in the distance, a red Toyota. 'Surely,' McNeill said as he took his eye from the sight, 'surely she has spotted this. I hope to God she has.'

Alina saw the shimmer. Her heartbeat quickened and she bit her bottom lip to try and calm her nerves. She looked down the rifle sight, eased her index finger to the trigger. Her body shook but she calmed herself.

McNeill waited. He saw it a few seconds later, a black shape a little behind, almost hidden but there.

Lukas was driving fast and furious along the last straight stretch before the climb, a 90-degree right turn dividing them. McNeill checked the red Toyota through his sight as it drove towards the bend. 'Shit, it's travelling very fast and without much let up in speed,' he mumbled. Alina squeezed the trigger. The first bullet smashed through the windscreen and hit Lukas in the right shoulder, exiting out the back and into the driver's seat. Alina fired again, fired until all six shots were gone. She was sure she had put all six into the Toyota but it did not stop it. It slowed around the bend, careering across both carriageways and wobbling from side to side, but it still came ahead. She looked through the sight. The windscreen was smashed out and a body was slumped in the front. She squeezed the trigger but the magazine was empty; all she heard was click, click. She dropped her head to the ground.

Lukas was still alive, alive and hurting badly, wounded in his right shoulder. Blood trickled down his arm and oozed down his back. Masny was at his side, slumped down onto the dashboard. Three bullets had hit him, the first in his right shoulder as he tried to plug Lukas's wound, spinning him face forward in his seat, ready for the next two to smash into his chest, killing him.

McNeill never blinked, never looked round at the Toyota. All he could see was the Nissan, the only thing he focussed on was the Nissan braking, stopping. He squeezed the trigger of the Dragunov, which pumped into action. He watched through the sight as the windscreen shattered then vanished; saw the driver sat prone in the driver's seat, moved the sight just in time to see the passenger door open and a body lurch out. McNeill never hesitated, he squeezed the trigger, saw a big man slap backwards onto the ground.

Alina panicked. The Toyota had rounded the second of the hairpins and was still making its way up. Only one more hairpin bend to go. She tried to get up but bullets whistled through the air overhead and smashed into the earth in front of her; Lukas was firing somehow. She threw herself to the ground. Lukas rounded the last hairpin and climbed to the last bend. Alina pushed herself backwards away from the M21. Lukas stopped the jeep and fired his AK-47 at the bushes. Bullets whistled over Alina's head as she pressed herself into the ground. Lukas got out of the jeep with his AK-47 spluttering bullets. His right arm hung limp, blood dripping from his fingers. He headed for the bushes.

He never saw them hit. He felt them enter his back, felt them explode out of his chest. He fell forward to the ground. His noisy AK-47 discharged its last bullets wildly in the air before silence and his life slipped away.

Alina was gripping the ground and shaking. Her breaths were short and hurried, her mouth open, her eyes clamped shut. She heard him, heard her name, heard his voice. *McNeill!* she mouthed silently until her voice returned. 'McNeill!' she screamed as she got up and ran to the road, passing Lukas's body. 'McNeill!' she screamed again. She reached the road and saw him kneeling, pointing his rifle towards where Lukas had fallen. She waved with both arms vigorously, watched as he stood and began running to the road, towards her. She fell to her knees. McNeill ran to the road, up the steep climb; it seemed like an eternity before he reached her. She was shaking and weeping uncontrollably, her knees held into her chest by her arms, her head buried in her knees. McNeill crouched down beside her, dropped the Dragunov to the floor and held her. He kissed her hair on the top of her head. She heard his soft voice whispering, 'Hey, it's OK, it's over.'

'Don't you ever put me in a position like that again and don't you ever, ever leave me,' she said through tear-streamed eyes which looked deep into his.

She kissed him, warmly, lovingly. McNeill rose to his feet and helped her to hers. He collected the Dragunov rifle. 'OK, bring the Land Rover, I will check this mess.'

McNeill walked to his M21 and picked up his old friend, then walked to Lukas and removed the AK-47 from his left hand. He turned him over to face the sky and removed a spare magazine from inside his tunic. He went to the Toyota and looked in; Masny was slumped on the dashboard. McNeill pulled him backwards to rest in the seat, took his spare magazine and his AK-47, along with the Dragunov rifle on the back seat. The Toyota was still running, its diesel engine pumping life under the bonnet, where death was inside the cab. McNeill checked the fuel gauge; just above empty. He pulled Masny out, and pushed his lifeless body over the ridge where roadside met slope. He dragged Lukas's body and did the same.

Alina arrived in the Land Rover. 'OK, I'll transfer everything into here. How is the baby?' he enquired.

'Awake and calling for you to change her,' replied Alina.

McNeill smiled as he heard the baby's cries, and began transferring everything from the Land Rover to the Toyota. 'Turn this around, Alina,' he said, pointing to the Toyota. Then he pushed the Land Rover over the edge. Alina turned the Toyota round and McNeill got in.

Alina drove on as the baby cried. McNeill pointed an AK-47 out of the gap where the windscreen used to be. They approached the black Nissan. Alina could see Radlinsky sat upright in the driver's seat, and a motionless body slumped outside an open passenger door. She stopped short of the Nissan. McNeill handed her a spare AK-47. 'If it moves, shoot it,' he said. McNeill moved to the driver's side of the Nissan. Radlinsky was dead; two bullets had hit him, one in the chest and one in the head, both fatal. McNeill pulled Radlinsky out and as he did so a packet of American cigarettes fell from his pocket. McNeill picked them up and took his Glock pistol from its holster.

Alina was over at the passenger side. 'Jarowiscz is dead,' she said. McNeill went over and bent down to see, his fingers checking for a pulse in his neck. Machine gunfire broke the silence, then the click, click of an empty gun. McNeill spun around. Alina had emptied what was left in the magazine into the dead body of Radlinsky. 'Alina!' roared McNeill. Alina jumped, startled. She turned, a look of pure hatred in her eyes. 'That's for all the times you groped me!' she yelled at the lifeless body of Radlinsky. McNeill stood and put his AK-47 on the Nissan's bonnet and took the one from Alina.

'Check the Nissan for anything useful. I will try and start it.' Alina waited as McNeill turned the ignition key. There was fuel but the gauge read less than a quarter full.

'Looks like you shot and killed the engine too, McNeill, there are bullet holes in the front,' Alina said. McNeill went to the Toyota and began removing as much glass from the front as he could. Meanwhile, Alina changed the baby and covered her with the blankets and towels she collected from the Land Rover. McNeill brought the two briefcases from the Nissan.

'Have you seen anything that may hold liquid, Alina?' he asked.

'There is an empty cola bottle in the driver's door here,' she replied.

McNeill got the bottle and removed the lid. He walked over to the dead body of Radlinsky, searched for and removed his knife, then approached the Nissan and crawled underneath. He located the fuel pipe and cut into it with the knife. Diesel began to flow. He filled the cola bottle. Alina came and he passed the bottle to her and she deposited its contents into the Toyota's diesel tank. McNeill drained the Nissan of diesel and climbed out from underneath.

'OK, everything in the Toyota?' he asked Alina.

'Yes,' came her reply.

McNeill went to the body of Jarowiscz and removed his tunic and jumper, which he threw to Alina. 'Here, put this on, it's going to be cold with no windshield,' he said .

They headed north and the overcast sky began to deposit light rain. McNeill turned to Alina and said, 'We need somewhere to sleep, food and water.' An hour later the sky had darkened, the drizzle had turned to rain. Alina spotted a ramshackle old barn with remnants of hay bales in it. She drove towards it.

The barn was in need of repair. The roof was good but the side facing the road and the front were open to the wind. McNeill began to manhandle the rectangular hay bales into a square, throwing loose hay in the centre. He formed a small square made of rectangular bales, three high. Alina came to look. 'Mmm, looks cosy, not exactly a penthouse suite, but cosy,' she said coyly. McNeill brought the baby, Alina brought as much food as she could find and the holdall and climbed in. They ate the fruit which Alina found in the Toyota. Alina covered her baby with hay and lay down. McNeill covered her with hay, then snuggled in beside her. She rested her head on his shoulder. 'What happens now, what will my father do now, McNeill?' she asked. 'Get some sleep,' was his reply.

He could smell her, could feel her pressed to him. He swept a few loose hairs away from her cheek, tucked them behind her ear and as she slept she murmured, softly and delightfully. McNeill just gazed at her luscious lips, wondered at the little nose which came to a point, the high cheek bones. He smiled and dropped into slumber.

⇒•⇐

McNeill woke just before dawn. Alina and her baby were sleeping. He got up. Light was beginning to crack the darkness of sky. He went outside and leant against the barn, opened the cigarette packet he had taken from Radlinsky's dead body and pulled out one of the five remaining cigarettes. He put it to his lips and lit it with Fitz's lighter. The first pull felt heavenly, stress relieving; he inhaled and exhaled through his nose, took another drag and moved to the Toyota's passenger door and opened it. He climbed into the passenger seat and opened the glove compartment, started going through its contents. Steyr hand pistol, seven rounds, identification papers, command papers with a stamp of authority from Alina's father, and a map. He took out the map and unfolded it; highlighted on the map were the towns and places in which Alina and he had been. A large cross was at the tunnel where it all began. A line then traced from there to yesterday's town. 'Easy,' said McNeill aloud. *Easy to see where we are headed, easy for Alina's father to track us and send people after us. The last town is nearly on the front line; I wonder if he has any more men in there?* he thought. McNeill finished the cigarette and flicked the butt away. He stood up and felt the cold morning air as the sun rose. The baby began to cry.

He went inside the barn and climbed into the centre of the hay bales. He saw the baby's bottle in the holdall, put the map down, reached for the bottle and picked up the baby. The baby stopped crying, looked at him and smiled, her eyes wide. McNeill sat down with his back to the bales, stretched his legs out in front of him and placed the teat of the bottle into the baby's mouth, who began to suckle. 'Easy little one, patience. Easy, take your time,' McNeill said as the baby gulped down the milk. Alina heard, turned over but made out to be asleep, then coyly opened her right eye. She watched as this brute of a man, who had taken so many lives in their short time together, gently, apologetically nursed this fragile little baby with tenderness, respect and great care. She watched as the baby girl giggled as McNeill patted her on her back with his big hands but surprisingly dexterous fingers to wind her. Those same hands took life so rationally, brutally, calmly, and yet he wanted to preserve the baby's life with such gentleness. Alina looked from him to her baby; a tremendous bond was evident between the two. One she desperately wanted to make three. She realised she loved him, realised she loved her baby also.

She opened her other eye and raised her head slightly, smiling as she said, 'Good morning.'

McNeill smiled back. 'Morning, hope you slept well.' Then he added, 'Now that I have fed her, you can change her.'

'Sorry, I am having a lie-in, you may carry on as you are doing such a great job,' said Alina. McNeill tossed the now empty baby's bottle at Alina and laughed, then promptly changed the baby's nappy. 'See, I knew you were doing such a great job,' Alina added with a wry smile.

'Seriously? Oh, I didn't think you had noticed,' replied McNeill.

'My, how could I fail not to? I mean, this is not the Grosvenor Hotel Presidential Suite where I could be lost in a bathroom, you in the main living area and her in a bedroom, now is it?' Alina replied with a slight tilt of her head and raised eyebrows.

McNeill collected two handfuls of hay, moved a step closer to Alina and threw the hay at her. As she fenced off the hay he dived towards her, landing by her side and brushed the remains of the hay gently from her face and pulled her towards him. He kissed her gently at first, then hard but without too much force. Alina responded wilfully, her tongue exploring his mouth, her arms locked around him. She wanted him there and then and for always. They made love and lay together in the afterglow, her eyes dancing and glittering with delight, a permanent smile on her lips, ecstatic joy on her face as she propped her head on one arm and gazed at McNeill. McNeill put his left arm around her slender waist and eased her on top of him.

'But my darling, we have only just finished, surely you can't go again so soon?' Alina said, her eyes flirting. McNeill put his right arm around her and let it rest on the back of her right shoulder blade. He could feel her hair touching his cheeks, feel her naked bosom resting on his. He looked into her mischievous eyes, kissed her and rolled her over onto her back.

McNeill got up and dressed. 'Time to go, fun's over for now.'

Alina got dressed as McNeill watched. He watched her cover her back with her shirt, watched it dance and tickle her bare skin. He saw the sublime movement of her bottom moving side to side poetically as she pulled up her skirt. He reached for the map. *Duty first, pleasure later,* he thought, although he knew he wanted it the other way round. He opened the map on the floor and called to Alina, who turned, brushing her hair back with her fingers.

'Look, Alina, the line on the map –it's where we began from and are now. Your father has followed our every move, plotted where we are heading. Is there any way – and by the way, I think Radlinsky is the last – but is there any way he could have more of his men in the last town before the lake and then the border? Think: has he got anyone else he could send? Any more of his personal assassins, groups of men, solo hitmen, snipers just like me?' asked McNeill.

'Never have I ever seen anyone shoot like you, McNeill, not even when I was growing up and watching the shooting on the rifle ranges and the shooting competitions on the army bases.

No, truly, never have I ever seen anyone like you. No, I don't think he has any solo hitmen, as you put it. Rasik the Russian sniper would have been his finest sharp shooter, his best sniper. Radlinsky's brutes were his finest soldiers, especially urban and close quarters. Both Rasik and Radlinsky would have been the most trusted of his personal guard, also his most ruthless and best. But McNeill, that does not mean to say there have been no more additions; after all, I left when I went to find Slavan.'

McNeill watched her as he listened attentively, pondered and spoke. 'Alina, we could probably go around, but we have not enough food ,nor money, and most travelling would have to be done at night. The jeep will run out of fuel at some stage, so that means plenty of walking, and the fighting ahead may be fierce. According to this map the front line is beyond the town. I am assuming that line there is the front line, would you agree?'

'Yes,' she replied.

McNeill went on. 'If the Croatian Army get pushed back they will retreat and regroup in the town. However, if they hold out and push on, which is what I hope they do, then our most direct route is to that lake which has the border across it. It may be a little bit easier and we may just make the lake on what fuel and provisions we have left. We may be able to enter and exit under cover of mortar, rocket and machine gunfire. People will not be out but we will be conspicuous as we will be moving, albeit slowly, when we should be sheltering. It is very difficult and dangerous to move through a bombardment for obvious reasons, but also we would be an easy target for a competent sniper of your father's. However, I have a feeling Radlinsky was the last throw of the dice for an armed group – why else would they be in such a hurry to get to us? I think they were despatched by your father almost at the same time, possibly from near to where he is. As you can see, it has been easy to forward think and plan where we are heading just by looking at the ink line and crosses on the map here. Your father knows where we are heading. He also knows if he survives the war he will need the protection of his army, especially as you have the briefcases, and his political ambitions will be dead in the water, and that, for you, is deadly dangerous.'

'Why, McNeill? We will be in another country and we could never return,' remarked Alina.

'A war hero going into politics would have the landslide vote of the people. They would see him as a saviour, a man of trust, a patriot. He would be afforded tremendous prestige, comfort and money; but you Alina, you, his own daughter, would be his nemesis. Imagine the scandal if you survived and could give an account and proof of what he has done, his personal assassins, unlawful killings, protection rackets, corruption, selling arms to the Serbians and so on, all done, as you say, on his behalf. You cannot be free, Alina. His own daughter has to be controlled; in a prison, namely, where he can keep an eye on you; married to a person who will control you and be controlled by your father; or better still, dead. That way, silence is guaranteed.

'So please, try to remember. Where your father was the fighting was only sporadic, a kind of boxing without the desire for a winner or knockout punch; a kind of arranged war, rather lackadaisical. But ahead this is real, uncompromising, unyielding, savage to the extreme, no quarter asked, none given, no prisoners wounded or alive, two heavyweights beating the hell out of each other, each striving to kill or maim the other. We will be sitting ducks if he has snipers in the town and I don't think we have fuel or time to go round and I personally would like to live longer than the next two days, which is about what it will take from here to the border, one to the lake and one to cross over and yes, I want both of you to share the rest of my life with me so think, cast your mind back and think, think slowly and think hard – both for you, your baby and me. Our lives are in your hands,' McNeill concluded.

McNeill put the bags into the Toyota as the sun came out to greet him, but a chill was in the early morning air. *At least it looks like it will be dry today*, thought McNeill. Explosions ahead broke his trail of thought. 'Oh shit, closer to the town than I hoped,' he murmured, an anxious look on his face. He put the baby girl on the back seat, padded her in and threw away a wool nappy. 'We will not be needing that anymore,' he said. 'You drive, Alina, and take your time thinking.'

Alina got into the driver's seat and turned the ignition key. The engine sprang to life and she set off. McNeill was in the back. He had reached into the boot and taken an AK-47, a spare magazine, the Dragunov rifle and his best friend, the M21.

He put the AK in the passenger well, the two sniper rifles from floor to ceiling in the well too, resting against the front seat, and climbed into the front. Alina drove towards the next town. The closer she got, the louder the explosions, and the higher her own expectations. McNeill dismantled the M21 and began to clean it. He did not know why he did this; he had no ammunition left for it, but it seemed he had a duty to it. He hummed a nonsense tune as he dismantled the rifle, cleaned it and rebuilt it. He placed it on the floor in the rear. He did the same to the Dragunov; there were only two bullets in its magazine. He removed them and held them in a clenched fist, a priceless collection of two bullets, held them as if life itself was dependant on the two life-takers. He put them down on the seat between his legs, cleaned his Beretta and the Glock and checked the ammunition: seven rounds for the Glock, eight for his Beretta. He then ordered Alina to pull over.

She stopped the jeep and McNeill got out and removed the two remaining AK-47s and the spare magazines and he brought them to the passenger seat and got in. Alina drove off, and McNeill checked the AK-47s. They were both well oiled. He checked the magazines; one had eight rounds remaining, probably the one from Jarowiscz, and one was full. 'Expecting trouble?' asked Alina.

'Being prepared. Any conclusions on our problem?'

'I cannot think of anyone else, nobody as efficient as you, but that does not mean he has not got anyone, maybe another paid mercenary from another country, I don't know. I told you, I left to find Slavan. All his best men are dead and by your hand,' Alina replied.

'OK. As I see it, your father would expect Radlinsky to report sometime today, maybe noon-ish. By early evening he will guess we are still alive and Radlinsky and his men are dead. That gives us till mid to late afternoon to get through this town and out the other side, and by that I mean a few miles beyond. If we get through today alive, the chances are we will make it across the border.'

Alina began to cry, not tears of sorrow, but tears of joy. She took one hand off the steering wheel and squeezed his. 'Drive with care and keep your eyes peeled,' came McNeill's cold response. The closer they got to town the more frequent and noisier the shell fire; sporadic machine gunfire mingled with it. Alina looked at McNeill. She was frightened. 'McNeill, you have two bullets for your sniper rifle and spare magazines for the AK-47s, but I have never seen you in combat and street fighting.'

'Yeah, I'm anxious too, it isn't my forte. All soldiers are different, even though they act as a team a unit. Me, I am good at target shooting, not too bad with a machine gun, it's basically aim and fire. Don't worry about bullets for the Dragunov rifle, Alina, the bullets for the AK-47 are the same. So, you see, we have plenty of armoury. It's just we have to be extremely careful ahead, just do as I say and try to relax.'

Knowing that the Dragunov bullets and the AK-47 bullets were interchangeable seemed to have a relaxing effect on Alina, who stopped the jeep.

McNeill looked around. The shell fire was noisy yet he was silent, contemplating, his mind ticking like a chess grand master's, exploring every move and every consequence. 'Why are we stopped?' he asked.

'I am going to feed my daughter. We are only a couple of kilo-metres from the town suburbs ahead, see for yourself. And it's better if she is content, she will sleep longer through all this shell fire and therefore will be one less worry,' Alina said.

Smart thinking, clever, but I cannot see her sleeping through all this noise, thought McNeill. Alina breastfed her daughter. McNeill seemed like he was in a trance. He looked through blank eyes as Alina removed her jumper, opened her shirt and began to feed the baby, changing after a while to her other breast. The baby was content and she put the baby down. Her upper body was naked, but still McNeill did not notice. He was consumed by his thoughts.

The mortar fire and shell bursts were now beginning to lap at the town's west side. The gunfire was becoming continuous. 'Ready?' asked McNeill. Alina took the steering wheel and drove on. McNeill picked up a spare magazine from the AK-47s and loaded it into the Dragunov sniper rifle; perfect fit. Simple Russian technology, so efficient, so effective in its brilliance. 'Watch out for roadblocks, anything strange,' he said to Alina. 'No people – we have seen no people, no people running away from the town, no refugees, no trucks or vans with all worldly possessions strapped to their roofs, no cars bursting at the seams crammed with people. No PEOPLE!' shouted McNeill.

'If they had any sense they would have left days ago, evacuated northwards across the border. We are so close, McNeill, I can almost smell freedom,' said Alina excitedly.

'Stay calm, stay focussed, stay alive,' McNeill said, 'and remember this: there will be desperate people ahead. It is us or them, regardless of uniform or side. All soldiers we meet who stand in our way are the enemy. This jeep, when soldiers or people see it, they may see it as a means of escape, and may kill to get it. The only country you have, Alina, is me and your daughter: us or them.'

Alina looked at McNeill, who was totally focussed, totally zoned in, cold, hard, ruthless. She knew in that instant he would lay down his life, if the need arose, to protect her and her daughter. She knew they were his country. 'Roadblock ahead,' said McNeill as he saw upturned cars strewn across the road, leaving a narrow passage in-between.

Rockets were beginning to hit near the town's centre. From

their slightly elevated position McNeill saw the town below, and wondered why there was no really heavy fighting to their right. *You could lay siege to the town from here, the position here is strategically excellent,* he thought.

'Approach the roadblock slowly, Alina,' said McNeill as he opened the window then ducked down and climbed into the back. He slumped behind the passenger seat, picked up an AK-47 and clicked off the safety. 'Stop twenty yards short, Alina. Drive slowly.' McNeill put the baby on the floor behind Alina in the driving seat. Alina was becoming nervous. A knot was forming in her stomach, her throat becoming dry. 'Give me your hand,' she heard McNeill say. Alina removed her right hand from the steering wheel and dropped it to her side. McNeill squeezed it in his then placed his Beretta pistol into it. She put the Beretta in her lap. 'Us or them, kill or be killed,' McNeill said, adding, 'Stop short, open the door slowly and put your legs out; they will see you are a woman.'

'Any fool can see that,' she interrupted.

'Yes, but they will relax. Just show me how many by the fingers on your right hand. I will know where they will come from. Do everything slowly. Take the Beretta in your hand, put your left hand on the door, keep the door open and remain behind it. If anyone comes towards you, shoot and don't hesitate,' ordered McNeill.

Alina stopped 20 yards short, slightly to the left of the narrow passage between the upturned cars. She noticed a rifle pointed at her from an overturned van on her right. She shook her hair, opened the jeep door and put one bare leg outside. 'Woman alone,' a voice to her left rang out. The soldier lowered his rifle. The owner of the voice came from behind the overturned wreckage of what was once a Volvo truck, and slung his rifle over his shoulder. Alina was now standing, both her legs visible under the jeep door, her left hand holding the door at the top, her right hand by her side holding the Beretta. Two more soldiers came from the side to Alina's right. Both were smiling. All four soldiers came into view. They were grinning and talking amongst themselves. She overheard them say, 'First we have the woman, then we take her jeep and we leave all this shit behind.'

Alina motioned with her fingers; three to the right, one to the left. 'Take the one on the left,' whispered McNeill, who sprang up and sprayed the death sentence to the three men on the right. Alina brought the Beretta over the door and fired three bullets into the soldier on her left. At the same time McNeill was firing what was left in the AK's magazine into him. Mortars and rockets and machine gunfire erupted ahead. As the soldiers fell to the ground so did some of the tall buildings in the town. 'Back into the jeep and drive, drive into the town, Alina,' shouted McNeill.

McNeill realised time was vital, essential, and he knew it was in danger of ebbing away. He assumed the fighting would soon be hand-to-hand in the town. He knew the Serbians were pushing the Croatians back. He knew they had to get through, and as quickly as possible before the town was surrounded and fell. He knew they could not be in the town when that happened. The risk of capture was becoming greater every minute. He discarded the empty magazine and snapped a full one into the AK-47, his brain, with the rapidity of an overworked computer, assessing, analysing any would-be scenarios. Alina was full of adrenalin, which pumped through her with every loud heartbeat, fuelled by McNeill; who looked at her and thought, *Yeah, she is going to be OK, tough lady, solid companion, all doubts removed, she will do what is necessary.*

'When you reach the town, keep left. Going in is far easier than coming out. Keep left and try and circle to the north. The fighting is getting fiercer; that means shortly it may be hand-to-hand. Whoever is in the town will push reinforcements to the centre and then the west side, where the fighting seems to be currently at its worst and that seems light and sporadic. I think they are fighting north and east, and the north is holding better than the east. It also means the defending HQ is somewhere on the west. I noticed another main road out of town to the west;

maybe that's their escape artery – maybe falling back westwards gives a better opportunity to regroup,' said McNeill.

'Why is it easier going in, McNeill?' asked Alina.

'Men and machines will be moving in the same direction, we will just fade into them. But coming out we will be going against the flow of men and arms and this may raise suspicion,' he explained.

Alina made the south side of the town. Buildings crumbled to her right, mortar shells exploded, bombarding her ears, and machine gunfire prickled the noise. The baby woke and began to cry. Neither McNeill nor Alina noticed, they were too focussed, their attention honed. 'Stop! Stop!' yelled McNeill. Alina hit the brakes. Before the jeep stopped he was out running. A dead soldier lay at the roadside. McNeill ripped off his tunic and ran back to the jeep. 'Put this on and step on it,' he shouted. Alina turned left, then hit a major T-junction on her right. She flung the Toyota into a wide road, with high apartment blocks on both sides the dull grey colour of depression, empty and faceless. Soldiers had exchanged places with civilians and were now running in the street. Jeeps moved ahead of Alina. 'Close up, but not too close,' McNeill said quietly.

Alina narrowed the distance between her and the Land Rover ahead. 'Tag along,' McNeill said. Rocket explosions away to their right brought more tension. Both Alina and McNeill heard the 'boom' as buildings were hit, buildings which were once tall and erect. Alina saw part of the convoy turn left 100 yards ahead and others turn right. 'Which way?' she asked. 'Right, turn right,' came McNeill's reply. Through a furrowed brow and fraught, tense eyes Alina looked ahead and turned right. She was remembering McNeill saying 'Do as I say' to try and focus, to try and remain calm. More buildings, two-storey, three-storey, empty and different coloured houses and apartments. What had been shops now had smashed windows and bare shelves interspersed between houses. The road forked ahead into two lanes either side of a central aisle. *This must be, or we are quite near, the town centre,* she thought. Empty shops with nameplates came into view, larger and wider pavements, some filled with soldiers, soldiers running around like worker ants all heavily armed, going about their duty and paying no attention to Alina or the jeep.

More explosions on her right, only this time ear-splitting; and this time she heard the building split and cry out before part of it crumbled to the ground. After the deep hollow thud machine gunfire crackled. A rocket launcher burst into life ahead, catapulting its load into the sky rapidly. Still she tagged along, but they had slowed. 'How many in front, can you make them out?' McNeill asked.

'I make it four jeeps, one van, one trailer with gun on it,' she replied.

'That's what I make it,' said McNeill. Rockets hit the building 100 yards ahead. Alina saw the devastation first hand. The building was on an intersection, and it took two direct rockets into its roof, then exploded from within, bursting and billowing out fire, smoke, rock, twisted metal and other debris onto the ground below as it crumbled to dust. Large pieces of concrete were strewn across the road, blown like feathers on the wind before thudding into the ground. Soldiers dived out of the way, more soldiers crouched in doorways. She drove the Toyota closer.

She heard the screams before she saw them; prone on the ground were the wounded. A medical team was present, searching for the worst hit, only to leave and go on to another; she counted five men injured. Mortar fire. Boom, boom! Rockets fired from launchers, concrete-dust-laden air and the smell of smoke was all she encountered for the next 50 yards. 'I'm scared, McNeill.' McNeill had no time to answer. The large four-storey hotel about 30 yards ahead to their left exploded when the rocket hit it, showering everything and everyone below. Alina instinctively braked forcefully and ducked her head down. McNeill ducked his head and half turned to cover Alina with his arm and upper body. Bits of concrete and a cloud mass of dust hit the jeep. The rattle of tiny fragments of what was once a monolith of the town cascaded over the jeep and danced on its bonnet. More rockets hit buildings around the hotel, a shopping mall was obliterated. They raised their dusty heads only to see two jeeps and a field gun leap into the air before them and explode into a sea of flame. 'Drive, Alina, quickly. Pull out, cross the aisle onto the other side of the road and drive. Now, Now!' screamed McNeill.

Alina slammed the gear stick into first, rammed the accelerator to the floor as she let out the clutch and hurtled the jeep over the raised central reservation. She sped past two stalled Land Rovers, the twisted wreckage of what was once a field gun and the unrecognisable mass of steel that was pulling it, past what used to be a hotel with a now gaping hole from floor to roof, past wounded and dead soldiers amidst the rubble, and onwards just before rockets smashed into the stationary Land Rovers, twisting them airborne and landing them roof first. Rockets smashed into the empty shops alongside, taking out the shop fronts effortlessly, strewing debris across the road as the shops crumbled and fell into dust.

High-pitched whistles ripped the air, followed by a sickening, hollow thud and then a huge bang. McNeill was shouting at her, but Alina did not hear him. It was like her head was immersed in water and the people talking above her were indecipherable,. She could see his open mouth moving, his eyes wide, then she felt his strong arm shake her right shoulder vigorously, shaking her back to the present. 'Slow down, slow down, you will get us both killed. Slow down!' he was screaming. Alina's body shook. 'No need to shout,' she retorted.

As they passed a church on her right she slowed. The church stood there, defiant against the onslaught, untouched, unharmed, unbowed, while all around it buildings were crumbling, succumbing to the screaming rockets. Alina looked at the church in awe, and wondered if it had an impenetrable shield or was it God's will that kept it unharmed. 'Escape,' she heard herself say. 'Which way, McNeill, which way do we need to go?' she bellowed.

'North, we need to turn left somewhere,' he replied.

Alina, blood rushing through her veins in a tsunami, manoeuvred the Toyota past rubble, overturned vehicles, mangled wreckage and craters in the road, then swung hard left into more dust-filled air and grey debris which carpeted what once was tarmac. Buildings stood nervously, other buildings stood with portions missing, windows blown out, people and soldiers lay motionless in the dust. 'Slow,' McNeill said as he saw soldiers in front facing them, ushering them to the roadside and up onto the pavement.

There were pickup trucks with mounted machine guns on their rear, two more Land Rovers and two truckloads of heavily armed soldiers that approached them head on and squeezed past. Then soldiers waved them forward, beckoning urgently. 'Move,' McNeill said forcibly. Machine gunfire crackled over the sound of more mortars exploding. 'Keep moving, Alina, keep moving; we are right in the middle of both town and war,' he said as rockets exploded a short distance behind them. Rockets flew overhead and crashed into buildings beside them, the explosions rocking the jeep. Alina looked fraught and nervously at McNeill, her eyes pleading. McNeill just replied, 'Keep moving, keep going, don't stop unless I say so,' in eerie calmness. Alina drove on slowly to the soldiers.

McNeill's hand went to the AK-47 on his lap. The baby's cries joined forces with the whistles and screams of rockets. 'No, no!' screamed Alina at the soldiers. 'Important personnel for HQ. Get out of my way, get out of my way, NOW!' she yelled.

A round-faced soldier lowered his pistol-bearing arm and let them through. 'Third right, old hall,' he shouted. Alina drove on. A massive explosion hit behind them, lifting the rear of the Toyota off the road. Two missiles had found targets behind them; one into a building which used to be a shoe shop, the other into the road. The bodies of the patrol littered the ground under debris. 'Drive on, don't think or look, keep going,' McNeill said heartlessly. Alina began to cry. The baby was crying on the rear seat. McNeill heard heavy artillery machine gunfire on his right. 'Getting closer,' he said to Alina. They passed the turn-off for the old hall and 50 yards further on two soldiers jumped from two doorways on either side, their arms out, beckoning Alina to stop. Alina stopped and watched as two trucks of men, two mobile rocket launchers, two pickup trucks with heavy machine guns on the rear of each, another truckload of men and a truckload of rockets for the launchers passed across from left to right. A jeep slowed and the soldiers got in. The two jeeps sped off.

'Straight ahead,' McNeill said. Alina set off. Minutes seemed like hours, the day seemed never-ending. Progress was extremely slow and fraught with danger from all sides and all personnel. She looked across at McNeill, the AK-47 resting across his lap, finger never off the trigger, his face stern, his eyes flicking and darting in every direction, his mind computing, alert to every situation, adjusting to and with it. She saw beads of sweat slowly trickle down the side of his face, although at this time his heart was ice cold. She realised he had been in and seen this situation before, realised that although he was experienced, it still scared him. She noticed the difference; out in the open with his sniper rifle he was calm, ruthlessly efficient, in a controlled environment under his control, but here in the town there were too many scenarios, too many outside interferences, too many things to happen and alter course, too many annoyances and too many things that could go wrong. McNeill was uncomfortable in his experiences, but she trusted him. He had got them this far; she was not going to doubt him now. She remembered his words again, 'Do as I say and we will be OK', and that is exactly what she intended to do.

She swung the jeep around overturned cars, past buildings with their fronts disfigured beyond recognition by rocket fire, slowly manoeuvred around masses of brick and concrete, and saw ahead what looked like the roadblock they passed earlier. Two cars lay either side of two central ones across the road. No way through. As she was about to ask what to do, McNeill's voice rang in her ears. 'Push the middle of the two upturned where they meet, push them out of the way gently.' She hit the two cars exactly where McNeill had said, pushed metal to metal and eased her way through. She felt the jeep scrape against the car on her right, but kept going. A few more yards ahead was a major intersection. She approached the crossroads slowly. 'Straight on,' said McNeill, 'and go around those cars on the other side. This is a main exit if they need it, that's why it's blocked; if needed for a retreat, they will fly down here like bats out of hell.' Alina mounted the kerb and edged past the next barricade. She looked puzzled. McNeill filled in the blanks in her mind. 'The cars will have petrol in them. Either they will be used for escape or they will be crashed together and set on fire when the last of the retreating forces leave, to buy time for retreat and regrouping.'

Alina noticed that the bombardment of the town had not had the same demolishing effect in the area they were now in, as though they had missed this part. Nearly all the buildings were intact, except a few shops missing their front windows where the looters went in before fleeing. It seemed calm, a surreal calm, untouched, whilst the approach to it was almost obliterated. Trucks carrying soldiers were heading towards them. Suddenly, they veered left. More soldiers ran across the road from left to right, following the trucks. The sound of rockets hitting buildings was away to their right along with the machine gunfire and mortar explosions. Alina reflected on what she had just survived.

'Drive on slowly,' came the deadpan voice to the side of her. 'We have to be out of here, and find somewhere safe to stop before nightfall. We will need to sleep, and stay awake and be vigilant. Night patrols will be sent out,' he added.

'I don't follow,' Alina said.

'One sleeps, one takes watch and vice versa till dawn; then we move. We cannot drive at night, a lone jeep with headlights on is asking for trouble,' McNeill said.

'Too easy to spot?' said Alina.

'Clever girl, what a quick learner you are,' replied McNeill, and for the first time that day they smiled at each other.

'Alina,' McNeill said with agitation in his voice. 'Do you know who is in charge in the town, who is the highest ranking officer directing operations – and if so, does he know your father?' he enquired.

'No, but I would be sure that whoever it is has met my father in military circles, so they would know of each other. I need a name,' Alina replied.

She watched him, watched his breathing relax at the same time his muscles in his body did. *Very astute,* she thought as she followed his line of thought. *He is exploring all possibilities, wondering if the commander in the town has direct contact with my father, and wondering if men are looking for us.*

⇒•◇•⇐

General Tomelsky had been in contact with the garrison commander, Major General Slavic. He had waited for Radlinsky to contact him and he was long overdue. His military mind told him Radlinsky and his men were dead. 'Blasted American, blasted American!' he had boomed, while his fists once again crashed into the desk in front of him. Tomelsky was enraged, enraged to the point of desperation, and he had ordered Slavic to organise a manhunt, to which Slavic had had the audacity to reply, 'Are you crazy? We are in the middle of some of the bloodiest, toughest fighting I have ever encountered. We are stretched to our limits to defend this strategic shit-hole. Most of my men have not slept in days, and as we speak mortars, rockets and machine gunfire are hitting the west side of this would-be concrete grave with ceaseless monotony and accuracy. We are close to being breached, then surrounded as our belly would be bare, then captured, then shot by a firing squad – and you want me to spare men to go and search for a man, woman and child! What do you think this is, sir, a teddy bears' picnic?'

This had enraged Tomelsky, and through clenched teeth, his voice as poisonous as a viper, he had ordered Slavic to send out a platoon to find his daughter, her baby and this Yank, and to kill them if they resisted arrest, saying, 'I want to know before this day is out that you have them, dead or alive. That's an order, Slavic. Do your duty, soldier.'

Slavic had heard the line go dead. He turned and looked at himself in the mirror situated in the main room in the town hall, battle HQ. He saw a man, dead if he survived at the hands of Tomelsky, dead if he was captured at the hands of the enemy. Slavic had heard of Tomelsky's private guard, the brutal rapes, killings, murders of anyone in his way, military or political.

Reports came in through the large oak double doors. Officers, both male and female, brought them; all had eyes of admiration for him. They were all utterly reliant on him to save them or as many of them as he could. 'Main arteries in the town open still?' he asked one.

'Yes, sir, strategic blocks in place as you ordered, sir.'

'Many casualties?' he asked.

'North side holding, minor casualties, nothing too serious. North-east – more or less the same, but the fighting is fierce.'

'And the east?' interrupted Slavic. 'Tell me as it is, major, please,' he added.

'Heavy fighting, often severe in its intensity. We are being pushed back into the east side of town. Heavy rocket fire. Many buildings are damaged and we have sustained losses in the town. The road southwards is now unusable as it is destroyed in many places. Reinforcements have been deployed as you ordered, sir; and at this moment we seem to be holding the advance – just, sir.'

'Major, what about the men outside the town on the east side, what of them?' Slavic asked.

'Heavy losses, sir, but morale is high,' the major reported.

'Thank you, major, thank you,' Slavic said as he dismissed him.

Major-General Slavic turned and made his way to the large table in the centre of the room and looked at the detailed map of the town spread over it.

'OK, people, listen up. At some stage our opposition will realise that the majority of our forces are situated on the north, north-east and east sides. Our anticipation of their attack here has been correct and our defence successful up to now. Our east flank has to hold till nightfall. This is imperative and paramount to our survival, for the reinforcements which we re-route from the north side to position and deploy. Who is in command here?' asked Slavic, pointing at the map.

'Major Grassic,' came the reply.

Slavic smiled a warm smile. He and Grassic were loyal to each other, a loyalty of respect and devoted friendship. 'Good. Tell Grassic to hold on; I need him to keep the Serbs out. Tell him reinforcements are being sent to him from the north.'

A young female officer ran from the room to relay the message to Grassic. Slavic abated for a moment. His thoughts turned to his good friend Grassic. *No better man for the job,* Slavic thought.

'OK, back to it. Withdraw a third of our forces from the north side and send them to Grassic. Tell them to use the route out west then south, then in along these arteries here, tell them they are clear. Order them out at nightfall. Get them into here and here and ready before dawn.' Slavic jabbed his finger, pointing east and south-east on the map. 'Then pray or hope, whichever you do, that once again we have anticipated their next move, and that they think the forces of resistance are a lot greater than what they actually are. And if the north side comes under severe attack be prepared to rush the reinforcements back at Major Lukas's call.' Slavic turned and left the room.

He walked into his office and closed the door, opened the top buttons on his shirt and sat behind his desk. He took out a bottle of vodka from the lower drawer in his desk and poured himself a drink. A knock disturbed his relaxation. 'Come in,' said Slavic. He was joined by his friend Petric. 'Something is bothering you, my friend. Even at this time, which may turn out to be a turning point in the holding of this town, something outside these manoeuvres is troubling you,' said Petric.

'I hope I have anticipated correctly, otherwise we will be overrun from our spearhead,' Slavic said.

'My friend, you cannot protect everyone all the time, as you always try to do. Everyone in this army here serves you first; you are their country. Rest assured, everyone will do their duty to you and will not waver. We are a team, all of us, and you are its leader. You have looked after all of your men like a proud father looks after his children and, my friend, you have mighty fine children, loyal to you to the last, but only to you. Your decision to remove some of your strong point to the weak point is very sound. I, like you, think our opposition will now try and break through our east and south-east side and try to get underneath us, deploy an attack on our north side to keep it occupied and we both know how able Major Lukas is at our north side. You predicted days before that the Serbs would bombard our southern escape routes with rocket fire, which they did, but you removed most of the men and people from these areas beforehand. You avoided heavy losses and casualties and your actions have saved many lives. So the Serbs will see the south-east and east as our weakest points now, especially as they are close to the town on that side, but once again they will meet stern opposition,' Petric said, adding, 'But no, this military decision is not the thing that troubles you, my dear friend. I hear you had a telephone call from General Tomelsky?'

'OK, Petric you wily fox,' Slavic said, smiling. 'You are ten years older than I and therefore ten years wiser in your reading of a man's concerns; however, at this time my duty is to my loyal people, men and women who serve with me here in this town, fighting the enemy to survive, to live. We have to be stubborn; stubbornness brings endurance, endurance brings survival, to survive means to live. But here before you is a dead man. Tomelsky's daughter, her child and an American are here in this town; they have come a long way if they have escaped from him. Obviously, they are heading for the border and mean to cross our front line into Serb territory and then make the torrid journey through to freedom. Tomelsky has ordered me to search the town to find them, take them dead or alive; he wants them dead. Whatever she knows is extremely damaging to him – worth killing your own daughter to silence her. I, in the interest of all my loyal people here, am going to ignore this order to search the town, and if any of your men in this vicinity come across them–' he leaned closer to Petric and whispered '–let them go. Spare a bit of food if you have it, but let them go. They have got this far – they deserve a chance.' Slavic slumped back in his chair. 'We cannot spare any men to search this town, north to south, east to west. Grassic is holding out by his fingernails. He needs help and support, and he is going to get it, Petric.'

'But Slavic, Tomelsky will have you killed,' Petric said.

'I know,' said Slavic, 'but he said "Do your duty", and my duty is to my men,' Slavic said as he rose from the chair. 'Now, please bring some tea, coffee, biscuits; whatever those people outside need. We have a long night ahead,' Slavic added, putting his arm round his trusted friend. 'Remember: if any of our soldiers find or stop Tomelsky's daughter and the American, let them through,' he whispered.

Alina drove slowly through an eerie, silent street. Rockets, missiles and shells fell into the town behind them, the noise of impact abating slightly. The street looked deserted, an oasis in the midst of a battle, accompanied by a cocoon-like, unnerving stillness which surrounded McNeill, Alina and her child.

'This doesn't make any sense,' Alina said to McNeill.

'No, it's too quiet, no movement,' he replied cautiously.

The street turned 90 degrees left and then 90 degrees right and landed them straight in the jaws of a military patrol. 'Oh shit!' Alina murmured. 'Keep calm,' urged McNeill as they slowed to a stop. A huge army truck faced them. Guns and rifles of all kinds pointed at them; faces young and old peered down. 'Out!

Out!' two men motioning from behind semi-automatic machine guns shouted. Alina got out. 'Important personnel for HQ!' she bellowed.

'Wrong way, you passed the HQ two miles ago; try again,' retorted one of the men.

McNeill eased his finger away from the trigger of the AK-47 on his lap and placed one hand high on the driver's seat to his left; the other he rested on the windowless ledge of the passenger door, through which a rifle muzzle was now being pushed. 'Out!' a voice said. McNeill pointed to the AK-47 with the index finger of his right hand before opening both hands. The soldier holding the rifle shouted and stepped back a pace and McNeill was faced with rifles and machine guns from every direction. A young officer appeared on McNeill's right, leaned in and removed the AK-47 from McNeill's lap; on the rear seat the baby began to cry. 'Out! Arms where we can see them,' the officer said to a seated McNeill. 'Check the rear,' the officer ordered one of his men. McNeill got out, hands and arms held high and wide. 'Search him,' ordered the officer. A soldier removed the crying baby from the jeep's rear seat, walked round and gave the baby to Alina. Alina then moved to McNeill's side. 'Come with me,' a voice said in Croatian. Alina tugged McNeill's side.

McNeill and Alina were brought to a waiting Land Rover and ordered into the back. Two soldiers and the officer climbed in and sat opposite Alina and McNeill, who stared at two machine guns and a hand pistol pointed at them. The officer barked an order and the driver sped off. 'At least we are going in the right direction,' McNeill said to Alina as they travelled northwards through the town, through a platoon of soldiers and then an oncoming convoy of men and machinery. Alina looked quizzically at McNeill. 'Where are they taking us?' she asked him. 'I don't know, but we cannot escape yet, not with all this going on around us; we will just have to sit tight,' replied McNeill. The driver expertly sped around and through the machinery and through the streets laden with weaponry and men. 'A small army,'

Alina said to McNeill. The Land Rover halted outside a hotel. The officer and soldiers jumped out and gestured to Alina and McNeill to do the same. Alina and McNeill were shown into a room and locked in. Guards were positioned outside the locked door.

The room was small, with two single beds, two lamps on two small lockers and a small television on a shelf opposite the beds. Off to the back, complete with shower attached to a bath, a washbasin and toilet was a small bathroom. No windows. McNeill lay down, saying to Alina, 'I suggest you do the same.'

'But McNeill, isn't there anything we can do to get out of this?' she asked, her voice quivering with anxiety.

'No, not yet,' came the stony reply. 'Lie down and rest,' he added. Alina lay down on the bed with her baby.

McNeill woke when he heard the key being put into the door. He heard the click as the lock went back, heard the door open. In walked two men, both armed. One spoke English. 'Come with me, please, Miss Tomelsky, and you, sir, please bring the baby.' They were joined outside by two more soldiers carrying submachine guns who drew up the rear. McNeill and Alina followed on down a corridor and then down a flight of stairs, passing other soldiers going about their duty like worker ants, sublime in their efficiency and never once meeting amid the chaos. McNeill and Alina were ushered into what was once the dining room where a captain was saluting a major, who then turned to face McNeill and Alina. 'Come, friends,' he said in perfect English. Alina looked with nervous confusion towards McNeill, who nodded.

The major came over to them and then spoke. 'Miss Tomelsky, American – I'm sorry, I do not know your name, but you command my utmost respect as a soldier. Allow me to introduce myself. I am Major Slavan Lukas, or Slav to my men.' Alina was petrified. She was trembling with fear. *So close, so close to freedom,* she kept on saying in her mind, *and now caught like rats in a trap, and surely McNeill is going to be shot.* But at that moment she saw the tenseness dissipate in McNeill, saw him relax. She wondered in confusion as McNeill held out his hand and told the major his name. 'McNeill, just plain McNeill,' she heard him say and looked on in bewilderment as the major shook McNeill's hand.

'Good choice of weapons – AK-47s, Beretta Steyr and Glock pistols, M21 and Dragunov sniper rifles. The best,' said the major. 'A fine collection.'

'Thank you, sir,' said McNeill.

'Please be seated. Can I get you anything? Coffee, tea, biscuits, sandwiches; milk for the baby?' asked the major. 'You must be hungry.'

'Yes please, all of the above,' said Alina. McNeill nodded in agreement. With a nod of his head the major sent one of the guards to bring the food. He returned a few minutes later with tea, biscuits, ham and cheese sandwiches, coffee, sugar and milk, all on a large tray, and placed it on the table in front of McNeill and Alina.

'Please eat,' said the major. 'Martina here will feed the baby with the bottle of milk.' But Alina was reluctant to let her baby go. Martina pulled up a chair and sat down beside Alina, took the baby from her and promptly put the teat of the bottle of warm milk into the baby's mouth. The baby sucked hungrily and contentedly.

The major spoke. 'You must both be wondering, and I must put you both at ease. The delay is that we are awaiting your jeep. The news of your capture, or shall we say bumping into us, was relayed to Major General Slavic, the commander of the army here and defender of this town. It seems your father, Alina, is desperate to get his hands on you, and to have you killed, McNeill. However, my orders from Major General Slavic are to let you both go. The bags at the end of the table have food and drink in them. The two briefcases alongside are what was in the jeep's boot and your arms – pistols, sniper rifles and AK-47s – will be in the jeep. I cannot spare ammunition or any fuel, it is becoming very scarce, and if the east side falls – which I do not think will happen, as Major General Slavic is very adept, I can assure you, but it may – we will need all the fuel we have for our own safety. I am sure you will be aware and appreciate our situation, McNeill.' McNeill nodded. 'You have free passage to the end of the town and to our front line; after that, you are on your own. God speed and good fortune be with you both,' Major Lukas said, rising from his chair.

Alina stood, went around the table, arms outstretched and trembling – not with fear, as earlier, but with joy – her tears of trepidation changing to tears of anticipation and hope. She hugged the major. 'Thank you, sir, and please thank Major General Slavic for us,' she said. McNeill blew a huge sigh of relief, stood up and saluted the major, who then nodded and held out his right hand. McNeill took it in his, shook it and said, 'Thank you, sir.' Martina gave Alina back her daughter and they left the hotel dining room, passing by the two guards at the door. Martina led McNeill and Alina back to the reception area, where she gave them a carry cot, more towels and blankets. Alina thanked her as McNeill watched the soldiers, both women and men, rushing around but orderly in their chaos. Outside stood the Toyota jeep, with the young officer from earlier sat in the passenger side, cradling an AK-47 and looking at the Steyr in the open glove compartment. 'Nice,' said the officer. McNeill did not understand. Alina translated: 'He said the gun is nice.'

'Tell him to keep it – looks like he will have more use of it than we will.' She passed on the message. The soldier smiled as he alighted, nodded and left.

Alina scowled at McNeill. 'Jesus, you gave away a bloody AK-47 – what are you thinking?' she asked sternly.

'The magazine needs replacing. We only have two magazines left and a few bullets. We have two AK-47s left; that's a magazine each and the rest of the bullets will fit into the Dragunov's magazine. That's it, that's all we have, that and our lives. Come, we must go,' he replied.

'Shall I drive or will you?' Alina asked. 'You drive,' McNeill said.

McNeill sat in the passenger seat. 'Take it easy, Alina, we have safe passage to the end of town and beyond. No point in careering into another platoon or breaking the jeep up,' said McNeill. Alina slowed down and deftly manoeuvred the jeep along narrow passages through overturned vehicles, passing soldiers on foot and army personnel moving munitions southwards. This side of the town, the north side, stood defiant. McNeill sat deep in thought.

Alina broke the silence. 'You have not spoken a word in over forty-five minutes. What's the problem, McNeill?'

McNeill replied, in droll fashion, 'Just thinking.'

'About what? What are you thinking? Tell me McNeill, please,' she added.

'Well, I hope what Major General Slavic is doing is correct. I am just exploring the options.'

'Which are?' she interrupted.

'Option one: the enemy has removed some of its forces from the north front and will redeploy them to attack the town's east side, a point where they have been successful and they have almost made a breach in the resisting forces. By moving some of his forces from the north side, Slavic is counteracting this scenario. Option two: Slavic has made a mistake by weakening his north side forces to defend his weakest point, the east side of town, if the enemy hasn't moved any of its forces at all from the north, leaving the north weak and at risk of being overrun. Anyhow, Slavic has to reinforce his east side. From our point of view, option one may make our passage a little easier.'

'Oh, I see – fewer soldiers, a slightly lower risk of capture by the enemy,' said Alina.

'We are approaching the end of town. When we leave, we become a target, a target for both sides. There will be patrols both day and night and they will not be friendly. This jeep is a prize, easier to ride back to camp than to walk, so be extra vigilant and careful. There will be a roadblock ahead at some stage:

approach with caution. I am sure Major Lukas has given the orders to let us pass, but just in case, be careful. After that we fight to survive, both sides.'

Alina drove along the concrete-house-lined roadway and, sure enough, came to a roadblock. The sentry was very cautious; behind him a heavy machine gun was aimed at the jeep. Alina pulled the jeep slowly to a halt just in front of the sentry. The sentry moved round hesitantly, then moved closer to the jeep, passed by Alina in the driving seat and looked into the rear and saw the baby. 'Let them through!' he shouted. Alina breathed a huge sigh of relief. McNeill, though, was agitated. 'What's up?' asked Alina.

'Something is wrong; that was too easy. No questions, no searching,' McNeill said.

'Like you said – free passage,' Alina said, smiling, her breathing returning to normal.

'I know, I know; but that was too easy, too simple,' McNeill replied.

'You always doubt, McNeill,' she replied abruptly.

'I know, I know, but it's kept me alive so far,' he retorted.

They left the roadblock behind, Alina driving carefully at first, then with increased speed as her caution decreased and the real-isation that the border was almost in sight. A short time elapsed and McNeill took one last look at the town, now in the distance, then to either side. He looked out at openness, fields of nothing but grass, sparse in most places. He looked ahead; the road seemed to rise above either side, as if the fields had met like the earth's plates and forced the road above them. *Oh shit. No cover, nothing. We could be absolute sitting ducks, perfect for an ambush, easy target for either side,* thought McNeill. 'Slow down, Alina, I don't like this.' Alina looked at McNeill. She could see the worry on his face and it made her feel uneasy.

A small bead of sweat trickled from his temple, down by his eye, over his cheek, past the side of his mouth and hung from his jawbone, clinging to it like life itself was dependent on it, before dropping onto his open-necked shirt. There was a stony silence. Alina remembered what McNeill had said earlier: a target for both sides. She looked at McNeill, who squinted ahead, his features set. Alina followed his line of vision and saw nothing. 'McNeill, there is nothing there,' she said.

'I'm not looking for anyone or anything,' replied McNeill without moving.

Alina began to shake nervously. *Why am I shaking? Why am I questioning him? Has he not kept us alive so far?* she thought as she slowed down. They both stared ahead, thinking, as Alina drove on. The silence was deafening.

Salvos of rocket fire obliterated the silence. Streams of smoke lined the sky from their right, heading towards the town. 'Drive, drive!' shouted McNeill. 'Floor it!' he yelled as he reached into the rear, taking the baby from the back seat, placing her on the floor behind her mother and padding the blankets and towels around her. The jeep skewed from left to right as its rear tyres sought grip, before plunging them head first along the road. 'Quicker, quicker, faster, faster!' screamed McNeill as explosions erupted from the road behind them. Stone, dust and pieces of tarmac belched upwards into the air, before splattering to the ground. 'We are being fired on!' screamed Alina.

'Yeah, we are being used for target practice, by the ones who are not firing on the town. Drive like hell, get us out of here,' McNeill replied anxiously, as more explosions came from the earth just behind and below them to their right. 'Too close for comfort,' he said as he heard the screams of the missiles before the thunderous thuds of rocket hitting earth.

'Get off the road on your side. Move!' McNeill screamed. 'Keep the pedal to the metal and don't stop.' Alina obeyed. She yanked the steering wheel to her left and tarmac and stone gave way to grass and earth. She motored on parallel to the road. The comfort of the road was replaced by the unevenness of earth. The baby screamed. 'Not now, please not now,' said McNeill as they all shook, bounced and rocked in unison with the jeep.

Missiles hit the road in front and below them. Alina drove on through falling debris and smoke, her arms straining at the steering wheel, her body being bounced in and out of the driver's seat. The jeep bandied about like a ping-pong ball between the shock waves of the exploding missiles and the rough terrain underneath. She sat driving as hard as she could, like someone on a pogo stick. 'Drive, Alina, drive – keep going,' she heard McNeill's yell of encouragement. The baby cried as she bounced behind the driver's seat; neither Alina nor McNeill heard her.

Onward the engine of the jeep propelled them. The air stung their faces as it came in through where the windscreen should be. Stones from the rocket-shattered road hit the jeep like hailstones. The noise of the exploding missiles deafened. McNeill was shouting at Alina. She felt his hand grip her right arm; she turned, she could see his mouth open and close, but she could not hear what he was saying. McNeill pointed; Alina swung the jeep to the left and drove at a right angle to the road. The explosions continued but the noise lessened. Twigs began to scratch the underside of the jeep. Alina slowed down. 'Pull up over there,' ordered McNeill, pointing. Alina obeyed.

The baby's cries brought Alina to her senses. She had no time to reflect on what had just happened, no time to acknowledge the fear, the adrenalin rush, the extreme apprehension, nor the knowledge of what had happened and what she had left behind. She looked for McNeill, but saw an empty seat and wide open door. He was outside peering through the telescopic rifle sight at the town behind, watching rockets exploding, seeing dust clouds form where buildings used to stand. He saw missiles leave the town, heading for their oppressors. He looked up at the sky; what was blue was now lined with white trails. He looked on at the town, and saw rockets leave from the grass outside of the town. 'Mmm, good,' he murmured. McNeill surveyed a full 360 degrees, then let the rifle down from his shoulder and looked back at the jeep. Alina had got out and was clutching her baby girl to her chest. McNeill moved towards them.

'Don't you think she has had enough of being shaken around?' he remarked as he came to them. Alina gently bounced her baby in her arms and he asked if they were OK. Alina began to sway to and fro and screamed at McNeill in Croatian, her face like thunder. McNeill hugged them, held them tight, and Alina's anger melted as she looked at him. He kissed her forehead. 'I'll drive,' he said.

McNeill put the rifle behind the front two seats and climbed behind the steering wheel. Alina, holding her baby, got into the passenger seat and closed the door. McNeill drove off, turned right and took a further right turn and headed in the direction of the road. His aim was to meet the road further up from where they were forced to leave it.

'That was a bit hairy, frightened the shit out of me.'

'Me too,' came her reply. 'God, McNeill, don't turn soft on me now; don't tell me you were scared?' she added playfully.

McNeill laughed. 'I have feelings as well, you know,' he said, smiling. Then, in a more serious tone, 'This is going to be a long evening. Have we any blankets for a night in the open, Alina?'

'No, not for you and me – we only have blankets for the baby,' she replied.

'OK, then we need somewhere to sleep which will keep the cold chill of night off us, and when I looked round through the sight earlier all I saw was a wooden shed,' McNeill said.

'Maybe that's a farm outpost? Shall we go and take a look?' Alina enquired. McNeill swung the jeep in the direction of the shed. The day began to surrender to night. He drove on, resisting the urge to use the dipped headlights, eventually arriving at the shed. He stopped the jeep and got out. A cold damp chill greeted him as he walked cautiously to the battered shed door. He pushed it open and looked inside. He returned to a shivering Alina in the jeep. 'Welcome to the Ritz,' he said.

The timber shed was a makeshift affair, put together with little care and few tools and had not stood the test of time well, either.

It was empty, but the floor was dry. Alina, holding her baby, entered and McNeill went off to take a look around. Alina stood in the middle of the floor. The shed gently moaned in time with the chilled breeze. She shivered as the shed creaked. Her senses were gripped. There was a sound there which shouldn't be there. She listened again, her ears tuned. It was there – a grating sound behind the back of the shed. She looked round for somewhere to hide, but there was nowhere. It was a small, rectangular empty shed. 'McNeill,' she whispered. Her voice met with a louder grating sound. Suddenly the door opened and in strode McNeill, pulling a large rectangular bale of straw. 'Found this under a sheet of tarpaulin outside, which I will get now and put on the floor, spread the straw on it and fold the tarp over us,' he said. Alina blew a sigh of relief.

Shortly afterwards McNeill had made the sleeping quarters, and he went outside to the jeep. He returned to the shed carrying his rifles, pistols and the bags of food. 'We eat now, sleep a little, and just before daybreak we leave.' Alina fed and changed the baby and then along with McNeill she ate some sandwiches, leaving some for the next day. After drinking some water they lay on the straw bed. A little while later Alina was sound asleep and McNeill got up and went outside into the night. It was dark, getting darker; an occasional rocket lit up the night sky. He checked around, saw nothing, felt the chill of the damp night and went back inside.

He climbed into the straw beside Alina and pulled the tarpaulin cover over them. The baby slept. Alina turned to McNeill and put her arms around him, snuggling closer. McNeill held her. She woke and looked into his eyes. He could smell her, wanted her. She kissed him, and they locked in a passionate embrace. He broke away, saying, 'Get some sleep, tomorrow is going to be one hard, slow day and we both need to be very alert.' He kissed her forehead. She laid her head on his chest and slept. McNeill the soldier lay awake, thinking of night patrols; fatigue finally caught up with him and he slept.

———❖———

McNeill woke up a good half-hour before the baby's cries broke the night silence. He woke Alina and passed the baby to her. She began to feed the crying child. McNeill went outside as she did so, his eyes constantly peering in the dark, seeing nothing untoward. He figured daybreak to be less than an hour away. Time to move. He felt his pockets for a cigarette, took out the packet; two left. He took one and lit it with Fitz's lighter, then looked at the lighter as he rolled it round in his hand. His mind drifted to his dead friend as he smoked the cigarette. He took the last pull and dropped the butt to the floor and stamped on it. *That should have given Alina enough time,* he thought and went back inside. He saw the little baby girl happily feeding on Alina's breast. *Lucky bugger,* he thought. 'Time to go. I will drive first, then you,' he said. 'OK, I will be lookout then,' Alina replied coyly with a mischievous grin.

Alina finished feeding and fastened herself up before taking her baby outside to the waiting jeep. She put the baby on the rear seat, noticing the Dragunov rifle on the floor, and climbed into the passenger seat. Her eye was caught by the AK-47 lodged at the side of the passenger seat facing McNeill as he sat in the driver's seat and another across McNeill's lap; his Beretta pistol was shoved under his left thigh. He leaned over and gave the Glock pistol to Alina. 'Expecting trouble ?' said Alina worriedly, taking the Glock and making doubly sure she had the Beretta in her belt.

'This could be one hell of a nightmare day. We haven't that far to go – the lake and hence the border isn't that far away; however, to get there we have to cross Croatian and Serbian territory. We will be the enemy in each. Sooner or later we have to come into contact with a patrol or patrols and in war there are no prisoners. You know this yourself; if I get killed, you will be the spoils, then they will probably kill you too. Today is going to be one long, cautious day. I bid you good fortune,' McNeill said.

They set off. Daylight was replacing the night sky. McNeill headed across the fields for the road. Plumes from rockets and missiles began to decorate the sky. Explosions could be heard in front and behind them. McNeill had hoped for a cloudy, rainy day. God delivered a sunny one.

McNeill sped across the grassy fields, the jeep bucking and jumping across the hollows in the terrain. He could see the elevated road a few hundred yards ahead. He slowed the jeep to a halt. 'You drive and wear that combat jacket,' he said to Alina as he got out, AK-47 in one hand, Beretta in the other. Alina climbed into the driver's seat, leaving the Glock on the passenger seat. McNeill walked across the front of the jeep and opened the passenger door, tossed the Glock to Alina and deposited both the Beretta and the AK-47 onto the seat. He checked his wristwatch: 6.30 a.m. He opened the rear door and picked up the Dragunov rifle. He circled the jeep, peering out through the rifle sight in all directions. The baby slept.

The surrounding fields and terrain looked clear and natural in the morning chill. He breathed out slowly, put the Dragunov back behind the passenger seat and climbed into the passenger seat. Alina spoke. 'Why do you want me to wear the jacket?'

McNeill replied, 'Simple: we are still in Croatian territory, so it stands to reason that they may not shoot at us.'

'Good logic,' she replied. 'Ever heard of friendly fire?' she added.

'Yeah, and I hope we don't meet retreating Croatian soldiers – the jeep may be commandeered,' McNeill said.

'Oh no, we cannot let that happen,' Alina replied, her eyes filling with fear.

'Exactly, so you drive alongside the road, underneath it if you can, keeping as much as possible from being seen. The missiles and rockets are still being fired by both sides – tit for tat, if you like – judging by the plumes in the sky. So let's make time and progress while we can. Sooner or later, we will meet something, it's inevitable, so go,' said McNeill. McNeill sat in the passenger seat peering through the telescopic sight as Alina drove. The influx of air through where the windscreen was cool and chilly, and its eerie whistle disturbed the silence. Shortly, McNeill spoke. 'Slow down and pull over.'

Alina stopped. 'What's wrong? Did you see something?' she asked.

'The grass is much longer ahead and could hide an ambush. If we venture onto the road, or drive on the far side, we will be seen and used for target practice. If we stay this side, the road hides most of the jeep; however, it's short grass and open fields on the far side, long grass and corn on this – much easier for an ambush. I think running the gauntlet on the other side of the road may be the better option. Patrols which have been out all night will use the ground cover to return to base. Also, I am sure that whoever fired at us yesterday has a marked distance from rocket launcher to the road. What do you think, Alina?' McNeill said.

Alina was astounded as she looked at him. McNeill had asked her opinion in his search for an answer. She felt a warmth cross her face. Flushed, she asked, 'If the patrols are returning to the town, would they open fire on a jeep going away from it, especially with me wearing this jacket? And we will make better time on the road.'

'I don't know for sure – maybe not if the patrols are from the town. But, not to overstate the obvious, Serbian patrols will fire, and whether we are on the road or the other side, missiles and rockets will be fired at us. Dilemma!' replied McNeill, adding, 'Your choice.'

'Worried about the cornfields, McNeill?' asked Alina.

'Yeah, that's where I would be; impossible to spot anyone in there from the ground. A little easier from the air, but I don't see anyone flying around up there, do you?' he replied with a wry smile.

'At least that is one thing in our favour: no planes or helicopters. But how can you be so flippant, McNeill? This is deadly serious, our lives are at stake here and it calls for intelligent rational decisions based on what you see and your experiences and training as a soldier, not a devil-may-care, come-what-may philosophy,' Alina angrily replied.

'Worried and scared, are you?' McNeill enquired.

'Petrified and terrified,' Alina retorted.

'OK, run the far side of the road opposite the cornfields. If we get shot at by rocket fire, move to the road and drive like hell. What happens then will determine our actions,' McNeill said in a deadpan military tone.

'Don't you mean, the side from which we get shot at will determine the side of the road on which I drive?' Alina said.

'That's about it and let's hope we don't get shot at from both sides, or we are in big trouble,' said McNeill matter-of-factly.

Alina drove alongside the road towards the cornfields. The grass and corn grew taller the closer she came to them. She could now hear grass clutching at the jeep's underside, scratching and clawing. 'Cross the road,' McNeill urged. Alina pulled the steering wheel down to her right and the jeep leant to one side as it rode the embankment on a diagonal before straightening out on the road. Bullets hit the rear of the jeep on the left-hand side behind Alina, but high up. She pulled the steering wheel to her right a little more, then felt McNeill's left hand pull her down in the seat, his other hand reaching for the steering wheel, which she released. The baby slid along the rear seat behind McNeill to the far door, stopped and fell to the floor as the jeep lurched and began to cry.

McNeill was holding the steering wheel firmly in a lying position over Alina, his head turned, his eyes looking out of the corner of the jeep's nonexistent windscreen and passenger window. Bullets hit the jeep in streams, smashed the driver's side rear window and left through the roof; smashed the passenger side rear window, showering Alina and McNeill with glass. Alina tried to curl up but McNeill's body weight on top of her prevented it. She heard the fizz of bullets overhead, heard the metallic clunk of bullets hitting the metal of the jeep's roof on the inside. McNeill never flinched. He moved his left hand from Alina to the steering wheel, jerking it left as the jeep hit the join between man-made tarmac and God's earth, hammering the accelerator to the floor with his right hand. 'Get up and drive!' he shouted. 'Get us out of here!'

Alina sat up in a hunched position and grabbed the steering wheel. The jeep careered from side to side, flinging its occupants about as McNeill held the accelerator pedal to the floor. Alina regained control of the jeep off the road on the short grass and stones and returned to the tarmac. McNeill pushed himself up. Alina's foot replaced his hand on the accelerator. McNeill's big hand reached into the rear for the baby and pulled her through onto his lap as he slouched down. She was crying. McNeill searched for bullet wounds, found none and heaved a huge sigh of relief, then put the baby behind the driver's seat on the floor, and reached for the AK-47 down at his feet. He took the wedged AK-47 from beside the driver's seat and placed it on Alina's lap. He did not hear the machine gun crackle to life from the soldier on the road behind them, nor did he see the dust rise where the bullets hit the road beside him, but he heard the clink of a bullet hitting metal on the rear of the jeep. 'Keep your head down, Alina!' he bellowed.

'They are firing at us!' she screamed in panic.

'Drive, drive faster, get us out of range!' came McNeill's shouted reply.

Alina had the accelerator glued to the floor and the jeep slewed from side to side as she pulled at the steering wheel, first one way and then the other, gripping it with all her might. The palms of her hands began to sweat and her arms ached from correcting every movement of the jeep, bucking and skidding on the rough terrain, eventually driving on the grass and pebbles. The Toyota wanted a life of its own; Alina was not about to let it have one. The soldier on the road kept firing until the magazine emptied, without further success. The jeep disappeared out of range.

'OK,' said McNeill. 'OK, slow down a little. I would rather be shot than die by your driving,' he added.

Alina scowled. 'What's wrong with my driving?' she retorted angrily.

'Nothing, absolutely nothing – as a matter of fact, it's brilliant. Well done,' he replied.

'You men, you men – you think that women cannot reach your standards, let alone surpass them,' Alina said.

'Not hurt, then?' McNeill sarcastically asked as he smirked.

'Only by your tongue,' came Alina's witty reply.

McNeill laughed. Alina began to laugh also.

'Life's never dull with you around, Alina,' McNeill said.

'Kettle calling the pot black, arse,' she replied and they laughed more.

A high-pitched scream ended the laughter there and then. 'Shit, that's a rocket!' bellowed McNeill. The rocket flew overhead and over the road before exploding on the far side, billowing dust clouds after the almighty thud. 'Get up onto the road. The embankment slope is levelling out and we will have no cover anyway. Get up on the road and drive like hell; that's only a tracer that has just landed,' McNeill shouted urgently.

Without hesitating, Alina swung the jeep up the embankment and onto the road, flooring the accelerator as she did so. 'Zigzag, just in case,' said McNeill. McNeill heard the high-pitched scream once again, then the agonising wait before the ear-splitting boom of rocket meeting earth. 'They are hitting the embankment just behind us. Floor it, Alina!' he shouted. Alina now stopped zigzagging to drive as fast as the Toyota would go to try to outrun the barrage that was to come. McNeill clutched at the AK-47 and listened to more high-pitched wails; he felt naked and helpless. He prayed silently. A salvo of rockets hit either side of the road, spewing dust and grit skywards. Alina drove on through like a woman possessed. Rockets hit the road behind them, the jeep trembling with the shock waves.

Holy shit, it's only a matter of sooner rather than later, the rockets are getting mighty close and a direct hit is looking inevitable, McNeill thought. He glanced at Alina. She was gripped with steely determination, her face steadfast, her thin arms taut, her grip on the steering wheel vice-like. She concentrated dead ahead, unflinching. McNeill looked ahead, looked for a bend in the road, something which could make the rocket launchers readjust, re-aim – a mound of earth, a hill, a hollow of road, anything. But there was nothing, only straight road, a road slightly raised above the ground level. *Sitting ducks.* More wails, more ear-splitting explosions, more dust, more shock waves, more grit to either side and behind. Alina powered on, immersed in her own focus and concentration.

The short grass was giving way to sparse rocks and longer grass, more rocks, small boulders and larger ones. Another salvo of rockets bombarded the road, only this time they landed in front of the speeding jeep. Clouds rose and tarmac and grit rattled against the jeep. Alina zigzagged, rocking McNeill side to side. Alina drove on. Machine gunfire erupted on McNeill's right, rockets pounded the road. Soldiers stood 30 yards or so ahead in front of the speeding jeep, rifles ready. 'Shoot, for God's sake, shoot, McNeill!' screamed Alina.

McNeill had seen the soldiers and at the same time as Alina yelled, his AK-47 spat to life, to end life. He watched two soldiers fall, felt the whistle of a bullet as it flew by his left ear, saw another soldier fall backwards as they sped past amongst a hail of bullets. Moments later three rockets hit the road in front; Alina swerved to her left to escape the newly formed crater and dust cloud. Then it all seemed to happen in slow motion. She heard McNeill shout, 'Down!' She glimpsed two rockets screaming in, watched in horror as the first hit the ground at the roadside, ripping the earth and road like tearing tissue paper. She saw the second hit the road just in front of the jeep, parting the road like Moses parting the waves. She felt an echoing numbness, felt McNeill pulling her down, and as he did she pulled the steering wheel down with her left hand. The shock waves, dust and bits of road did the rest.

The jeep hit a large chunk of exposed tarmac with its right front wheel, immediately bursting the tyre and sending the right-hand side of the jeep into the air. Shock waves hit the underside, pushing the jeep away from the trench-like crevasse in the road and off to the left of it. The jeep and its occupants were upside down and flying through the air, Alina clinging to McNeill. The jeep began to dip. The bonnet hit the earth first, then the roof above the two front seats, crumpling the struts on either side of the vacant windscreen. The jeep slid on its roof and sparks flew off in all directions before it crashed into a boulder, spinning the jeep through a full circle clockwise before resting it against another boulder 20 yards further on. 'Out, Alina, OUT! Bring the guns,' she heard through muffled ears. Alina clambered out of the upturned jeep and took the AK-47 from McNeill's grasp. 'My baby, my baby!' she cried.

'Get the hell into the cornfield. NOW!' yelled McNeill. Alina turned and ran into the cornfield. McNeill clambered out, blood dripping down the right side of his face, clutching the other AK-47 and dragging out the Dragunov rifle from behind the front seats and ran into the cornfield at Alina's right-hand side. Both of them heaved for breath.

They heard them first, heard their shouts, then saw them – three soldiers either side on the road, running towards the jeep and firing their rifles at it. McNeill lay and pointed to his left, then pointed at Alina. Alina was sure her baby was still in the jeep and did not need an invitation to open fire. As soon as McNeill pointed to her she lifted the AK-47 and began spraying bullets at the first soldier nearest the jeep and to both his sides, back and forth. McNeill did the same, only aiming at the soldiers on the jeep's right. Alina watched the three soldiers fall from her hail of bullets. McNeill saw his fall from more precise shooting as he released the trigger.

He could still hear the firing mechanism of the AK-47 in Alina's arms, but the magazine was now empty. She was trance-like, in a state of euphoric delusion. McNeill grabbed the AK-47 and shook it and her; she was momentarily startled and stopped squeezing the trigger, making a move to stand up fully. McNeill pulled her back down. 'Don't move. Where is your Beretta or Glock pistol?' he asked quietly. Alina showed the two empty palms of her hands and shrugged her shoulders. McNeill reached inside his jacket and took out his Beretta, clicked off the safety and gave it to Alina and whispered, 'There are still more soldiers out there. Be quiet, lie still and don't waste bullets.' McNeill removed the magazine from the AK-47 and counted them; five in all. He then removed the empty magazine from the Dragunov and replaced it with the magazine loaded with five precious bullets, saying to Alina, whose face carried a quizzical expression, 'This fires one at a time every time I squeeze the trigger. Like I said – save ammo. Now move back slowly and try not to disturb the corn.'

McNeill found himself going backwards in a track where a tractor wheel had cut the earth. Alina was twenty paces ahead. They were now 50 yards from the jeep. McNeill stooped on the ground, right leg bent at the knee, rifle butt jammed into his right shoulder, right eye peering through the telescopic sight barely above the corn tips. Alina was now 10 yards in front, heading towards him. He motioned to her to stop and get down on the ground. Alina lay down and began inching her way to him. Then she stopped, rooted to the spot. McNeill had swung the rifle round, off line with the jeep, and remained rigid, statue-like, controlling his breathing.

He had spotted two men heading toward the jeep on the road, now hunched down on one knee. Both had machine guns and both guns were trained on the jeep. *That puts them near their dead colleagues,* he thought. McNeill gently squeezed the trigger. He saw that both enemy soldiers bore the weight of the machine guns on their left arms and he aimed at the soldier to the left first. McNeill then readjusted and sent another two bullets at the soldier on the right. The first soldier fell backwards, hit in the chest, the second heard the muffled cry of his colleague and half turned, baring his chest to the two oncoming deliverers of death.

Alina began to get up and as she did so she looked at McNeill, who removed his hand from the trigger and signalled to her to stay down. McNeill surveyed through the telescopic sight: nothing. He waited and surveyed again: again, nothing. He waited and the sun beat down. Once more he looked, and then he began to crawl up the tractor track, using elbows and knees, shuffling from side to side. Alina watched him draw level with her and then proceed further, stopping every now and then to rise and peer through the telescopic sight. McNeill signalled her to follow. Thoughts of her daughter now enveloped her mind as she followed McNeill, still so cautious.

McNeill reached the cornfield's edge; 20 yards or so more to the jeep, same distance again to the road. He looked behind at Alina, some 20 yards away holding the Beretta as she crawled. He waited for her to draw level and motioned to her to watch the road as he ran to the jeep. McNeill broke cover and ran to the jeep, clambered into the front and picked up the Beretta pistol from the floor, stuffing it into his trouser belt as his eyes searched the rear for the baby. His rifle was on the floor. Then Alina saw them: two men approaching. She did not know what to do. She had never been in this situation before and only had a handgun. If she shouted, McNeill would be shot instantly. She watched as the two men began to converge on the jeep. She saw McNeill, still inside the jeep, but motionless. She saw him pointing something, but she had seen him leave the Dragunov on the floor outside the jeep.

The soldier behind McNeill shouted something. McNeill focussed on the soldier in front of him. The soldier behind fired a shot into the jeep's engine and moved closer. Caught like a rat in a trap, McNeill only watched the soldier in front. McNeill pulled his right sleeve down to conceal the Beretta pistol now held in his right hand, then watched as the two soldiers came more into view. Alina, petrified, confused, aimed at one and then the other, then waited. McNeill waited. The soldier behind stopped and waited, then aimed at the jeep. The soldier in front of McNeill was uttering something but he kept moving in, moving towards McNeill. 'Close enough, close enough,' McNeill heard himself repeat as he shot him. Alina fired at the soldier behind McNeill – when he had stopped moving in, she had concentrated her aim solely on him. She fired three times after she heard McNeill shoot, but bullets had already hit the jeep to McNeill's right, one ripping through the top of his left thigh. Then they stopped. Everything was silent.

———≫◆≪———

McNeill eased himself out. Alina rushed towards him, saw his bloodstained trouser leg and bloodstained face. 'Oh my God! No! No!' she cried and bent down beside the now seated McNeill. 'You're hurt badly. And my baby, is she inside?' she asked. 'No, no baby. I'm OK, it's only a flesh wound by the looks of it and the blood on my face is where I wiped my hand. But it looks like I will need a new pair of trousers,' came the stoic reply.

Alina was torn. She wanted to find her baby and she wanted to tend to McNeill. She looked at the bloodstained McNeill, who saw the division in her eyes. 'Take off my left boot while I rip the trousers,' McNeill said. 'We need to tend my wound. Use the ripped trousers as a bandage, then we look for the baby. She must have been flung out when the jeep overturned. She can't be far away,' he added. Alina removed McNeill's boot and pulled off the ripped trouser leg, making it into a bandage. She wrapped it tight around the wound and replaced his boot. 'Help me up,' he said.

With Alina's aid McNeill stood, then bent forward.

'You OK?' Alina asked.

'Yeah,' came the reply. But every time he put weight on his leg he felt blood seep into the makeshift bandage.

'Can you walk?' she asked.

'Yeah, but nowhere near as good as you,' McNeill said with a cheeky smile, eyeing her cute derrière.

'OK, tough guy, OK. Where do we start looking?' she replied and knew he was in pain.

'Get the pistols and the rifles. You keep the Beretta. Take off that jacket – these guys ain't wearing anything like that. I will carry a rifle and this pistol too. We go back from where we landed to where we took off and look around on a wider angle back to here, till we find her,' McNeill said.

Alina and a limping McNeill set off. Alina arrived at where she thought the jeep began to flip and turned to see McNeill a little way behind. She looked around as he came closer. Her search revealed nothing. 'What now?' she asked, McNeill now standing beside her. 'Simple – we walk back at a wider angle, eyes and ears peeled.'

Alina turned, looked at the chasm dividing the road, marvelled at the hole the missile had created and surveyed where the dust and debris had fallen. She turned to face McNeill and said, 'Jesus Christ, we were very lucky,' with tears welling in her eyes. 'Get on with the search,' he replied.

Alina moved off, listening and searching. McNeill laboured on. By the time Alina arrived at the jeep, McNeill was only halfway there and using his rifle as a walking aid. She turned and watched him for a few minutes. Tears ran down her cheeks as she began to run back to him. 'You look awful,' she said with crying eyes.

'Yeah, thanks for the compliment. You don't look too good yourself,' he replied, adding, 'Now you go back to the start and walk back further out.' Alina did as she was told.

On her way back she saw him collapse down onto one knee in the brush grass. *Jesus, he is in such pain, his leg must be horribly sore and his face was devoid of all colour moments ago,* she thought as she marked where she was. She abandoned her search and ran towards McNeill. She began wondering if she would find her baby, if she was still alive or badly hurt; she could not control the tears that streamed down her face. She came closer to McNeill, then stopped a few paces from him. He was holding something, holding something close to him and looking at the sky above. 'Is she… is she… alive?' she asked tentatively.

'Yeah, sure is,' McNeill replied as he turned to face Alina. It was Alina's turn to go down on bended knee. Uncontrollable tears streamed down her face as she took her baby from him. McNeill wrapped an arm around her. Alina held him and her baby together, then kissed him.

They parted. McNeill spoke: 'Come on, we better get back to the jeep and see what we can salvage – maybe one of the dead guys has a medical pack. Then we had better start walking. It's not yet noon and I already feel like it's been a week from daybreak to now!' Rocket streams broke the blue sky – one of man's tools of destruction heading for the town, countered by another directed at the launching sites.

McNeill reached the road edge near the upturned jeep. He saw the bodies of the soldiers, looked at some of the faces; so very young. He began the search for a medical bag and checked each gun for ammunition. All were almost empty of bullets but he collected what precious few he could. Alina was waving and shouted from below and past the jeep. McNeill hobbled down. It was the soldier Alina had shot with the Beretta, three times in the back. He had fallen forwards and she had turned him face upwards. The AK-47 he held had almost a full magazine, and she had found another full magazine on him. Better still, she had found what McNeill had been searching for – a first-aid bag, intact. McNeill took the medicine bag and removed the morphine injection, sticking it into his leg above the wound. Alina removed the makeshift bandage and replaced it with one from the medicine bag, which she loaded with antiseptic powder.

McNeill sat with the baby in his arms. Alina left him there and went off. Later she returned with a pair of trousers, roughly McNeill's size. 'Put these on,' she told him, adding, 'I have two AK-47s. Clip the magazines on.' McNeill clipped the magazines into place and Alina took one. She picked up her baby and with the AK-47 swinging off her shoulder, walked towards the over-turned jeep. McNeill looked at her. She looked like a terrorist mother; he smiled. He picked himself up and hobbled to the jeep where Alina was now waiting. 'Don't suppose you can turn it over and see if the engine will start?' she inquired. 'Nope, the engine has been shot up so there's no point. Get as much food and drink from the dead soldiers. I will search the jeep, then we go.'

The sun was directly overhead. McNeill reached inside the jeep for the bag he saw earlier, a small travel bag which contained the baby food, nappies and a change of clothes. Alina returned with a packet of cigarettes of various kinds, which she had collected from each soldier and deposited into one packet, three bars of chocolate and four bottles of water. 'Not much, but that's all,' she said.

'More than we began with,' McNeill replied.

Alina put two bottles of water and a chocolate bar into the baby's bag, and gave McNeill a bottle of water and a bar of chocolate, keeping the same for herself.

'How are we going to do this?' she enquired.

'I will carry the baby in my right arm, bag and rifles over my right shoulder, Beretta in my belt, AK-47 over my left shoulder, then lean on you for support,' replied McNeill.

'Oh yeah! So I carry my AK-47 and your other Beretta and the briefcases and support you? So basically I am carrying the lot,' Alina retorted.

'That's just about it,' said McNeill with a smile. They set off.

It was easier for McNeill to walk on the road; off the road, the surface was uneven and although he chose his footing care-fully, darts of pain shot up and down his left leg. Half an hour passed in silence. They walked on. A further hour passed. The rocket fire had ceased and the quietness had begun to bother McNeill when Alina spoke. 'McNeill, it seems very quiet here, shouldn't it be noisier? And why no soldiers?'

McNeill looked at Alina. 'Look, whoever we meet or whatever we meet now is your natural enemy. Your own people behind cannot come past that crater in the road where we went off; therefore, the only vehicles will be coming towards us. We are in a kind of no-man's-land and there is a lull in exchanges while strategies are thought through and questioned. Different plans, but I think the Serbians will make a push for the town when the sun recedes. At the moment the weather is too good but there are clouds coming and shortly I think we will have to leave the road as it will be too dangerous. I know we are making good progress but that is going to change. It will become slow and cautious, with even no progress at all if there is a push for the town,' he said.

It made sense to Alina, explained once again matter-of-fact by McNeill. They walked on in silence, waiting and wanting for the silence to be broken. The feeling of the closeness of freedom began to rise in Alina with every forward step, followed by doubt, worry and the fear of failure. Clouds began to wrap around the afternoon sky. Alina spoke. 'Hey, McNeill, what are you going to do when we reach and cross the border? I mean, will you go somewhere or will you stay with us?'

McNeill replied slowly. 'You mean, look for another war to survive in? No. We can count ourselves extremely fortunate if we get out of this one. Try not to think of tomorrow; today is far from over.' McNeill went on, 'If we do make it, I would like to stick around; I don't know what you will have me do, but I'm sure whatever it is I will have a darn good try.'

Alina was thrilled. She squeezed him with her supporting arm and smiled. A joyful spring entered her step. 'Slow down. Take it easy on my bad leg. Wounds lessen considerably your chances of survival, and at this time I need all the blood I have in my body, so stop bursting into a trot and depositing more and more blood with each step,' McNeill said, but Alina was happy, happier than she had been for along time. She wanted McNeill, wanted him to stay. Not only had she come to rely on his cool sensible judgement; he was a good man, always doing or trying to do the right thing for them, putting them first, giving without taking. She knew she loved him. They walked on.

The cornfields disappeared, giving way to large grass separated by large boulders, and the road which was once elevated above the fields was now flanked on either side by slight mounds of earth which disappeared into thickets before trees. The road began to climb, slowly and steadily; the baby woke from slumber. 'Time for a feed,' McNeill said to Alina. 'For all of us,' he added. They moved off the road to the left.

McNeill sat on a boulder drinking a bottle of water. Alina used it to support her as she fed the baby girl, then she ate half her bar of chocolate and drank water. McNeill got down from the boulder and picked up the rifles and bags; Alina kissed and hugged him. They made their way back to the road and once again began the steady climb.

Alina and McNeill felt it near the top of the incline – they felt the road shudder, then the bushes and trees on either side began shaking, then there was a dull hum, a deep, dull murmur, and still the ground shuddered. 'What's that? What the hell is happening, McNeill? Is it an earth tremor?' asked a visibly shaken Alina.

'Tanks, more like – heavy artillery tanks, and a few of them coming this way. Let's get off the road and find some deep cover, then lie still, no sound, complete silence till this convoy has well and truly passed. The tanks will be first, followed by infantry, then trucks and jeeps, field guns, mobile rocket launchers, engineers – and soldiers aplenty. It will take a good bit of time for it all to pass by. We must find good cover. Soldiers will be in these trees watching for enemy patrols or the possibility of attack,' McNeill hurriedly explained.

'How long before they get here?' asked a terrified Alina.

'About twenty to thirty minutes,' replied McNeill. They turned off the road to the left. Nature had made that side more hilly and added bushes and tall grass. Boulders and rocks had been deposited haphazardly amongst the wild grass.

'Keep going, we are not yet far enough away from the road, and I am sure their patrols will be this deep. Keep going,' McNeill said.

Fifteen minutes passed. The solid, dull drone of engines drowned out their voices. Alina pointed to her left wrist. McNeill held up the palms of both hands: *ten minutes, tops.* Alina was beginning to panic.

McNeill tapped Alina's shoulder and pointed to a large rock with an overhang about 2 feet from the ground. They moved to it. Bushes, gorse and leaves filled the void between the earth's floor and stone ceiling. 'Get in, get in under the bushes – break them, if you must – and lie down,' ordered McNeill. Alina climbed in. McNeill passed her the baby, bags and rifles, then covered them with more bushes and leaves, smoothing the earth over with a branch, leaving no trace of footprints. He got in beside Alina and covered the front from the inside. Pulling the last bush into place he looked at Alina. Alina stared back as he put his left arm round her, squeezing her to him. 'Now, we wait,' he said.

The ground underneath was shaking violently. McNeill heard voices; one from the right above them shouting. Alina's eyes widened in horror. She placed one hand gently over the sleeping baby's mouth, closed her eyes and held her breath. McNeill grasped the Beretta and breathed slowly through his mouth. He could define three men in close proximity. The voice above carried on shouting. McNeill heard scraping as the soldier slid down from the rock, landing on his feet. He stood, legs slightly apart, black boots laced just above the ankle, dark green trousers tucked into his boots. McNeill could even make out the creases in his trousers, he was that close. The soldier waved his arms, shouted and marched on.

The drone became deeper and louder, the ground stilled momentarily, then came the clang and squeaks of the tanks. McNeill had detached the sight from the rifle and was now peering through it, watching the tanks with their hatches open, senior officers peering through binoculars, searching ahead. McNeill

243

could not smell the exhaust fumes but he could see them, great puffs and clouds of black smoke. He could hear the groans of the road when the tank tracks moved over it, and there were five tanks in all, all in single file, joined by soldiers in jeeps. Each jeep was minus its doors and soldiers sat with machine guns across their laps. Trucks came next, trucks pulling field guns, trucks carrying munitions, trucks carrying soldiers; rocket launchers passed. Alina lay perfectly still as McNeill watched.

Alina mouthed a prayer and crossed herself when she had finished. *Amen to that,* added McNeill solemnly. The baby murmured. Alina turned to see her child push out its arms, smack its bottom lip against its top one, cry out and return to slumber. Tension gripped Alina, McNeill looked fraught and anxious. Had the soldiers heard the cry? Were they coming to investigate? McNeill looked nervously out as Alina held her breath. He gave the all clear. Alina let out a long sigh of relief; they had been in the hole for almost an hour. McNeill lay on his back. She manoeuvred to look out through the bushes; all she saw was more soldiers and machinery. She returned to lie beside him, resting her head on his right shoulder. Together they lay as an eerie silence descended. *McNeill is waiting, but waiting for what?* pondered Alina. She looked at McNeill, who just smiled at her.

'Hey, you big lovesick puppy, what are we waiting for, why don't we leave?' she whispered. 'These are professionals; there will be a group behind doing a sweep. After they have gone, we wait some more then slip away,' he whispered back.

Ten minutes later they heard them, laughing and joking. Alina watched as they came into view, guns thrown round their young shoulders, some resting them on the backs of their necks, folding their free arm round the barrel. McNeill saw them. Quietly and patiently, he waited, while Alina held the baby, her hand ready to silence any cry. The soldiers passed on.

Ten minutes later Alina went to remove the bushes at the entrance, but McNeill stopped her. They waited another ten minutes, both listening intently to the sounds outside, strained their ears for one misplaced noise, an alien one that did not belong. They waited. The baby let out a cry which startled McNeill; again he looked nervously out, searching. Alina held her breath.

McNeill pushed the first bush out of the way, then another and another. 'Wait till I give the signal,' he whispered to Alina and he crawled out. Alina waited.

McNeill scanned the front, then to left and right. He moved in a crouch position to his left and came up onto the top of the boulder; saw and found nothing. He slid down and called to Alina to come out. She passed all the rifles and bags before her baby and clambered out. The ground still shuddered but not as violently and the dull hum of the tanks could still be heard as she loaded herself and McNeill up. Shortly, they moved off through the trees.

Alina heaved a huge sigh of relief. 'That was close, McNeill, very close,' she said.

'Don't worry, it's over. But more close encounters lie ahead,' he replied, adding, 'Base camp must be near, so keep a sharp lookout; patrols will be despatched if they are not already out. How's the baby?'

'She is awake. I will feed and change her,' Alina replied.

'Use leaves to wipe her, and you must bury that dirty nappy. I will keep watch,' said McNeill.

'Have you a name for her, Alina?' asked McNeill as she fed and changed her baby.

'No, not yet. I was thinking of naming her after my mother, but I'm not sure. Have you thought of one, McNeill? You name her,' Alina replied.

McNeil looked at Alina. Her eyes were wide, her head tilted slightly to one side, mouth slightly open. He wanted her, wanted to take her with every fibre of his being, wanted to kiss her and hold her: but the soldier in him stopped the man in him from doing so.

'Thank you, Alina, that's a great honour but if I am to name her, we both have to agree on her name, OK?' said McNeill.

'Done,' said Alina as she finished changing her baby and then she buried the nappy. They set off warily. 'Shall we head for the road?' Alina asked. 'It was easier on your leg.'

'OK, let's go,' came McNeill's reply.

Boom, boom, boom!

Alina and McNeill dived to the ground.

Boom, boom, boom, whoosh!

Then, the whistle of rockets speeding through the air.

'Shit, rocket launchers – mobile – and where there are rockets there are soldiers; and where the rockets are fired from, the opposition aims at,' McNeill said. 'We go left. They are probably on the road and by the sounds of it a little ahead. Going left we circle around them. Quietly now,' he added.

They edged left as more rockets were released. McNeill counted: six released, then a pause, three times, eighteen in all. 'How many rocket launchers are there, McNeill?' Alina asked.

'Two, I think, each letting a full barrage of nine rockets off in three sets of three; they are reloading now,' he whispered to Alina. 'Keep going,' he added as she slowed.

The further west they went away from the road, the lighter the density of the trees; bush and grass became the terrain, long grass which reached and lapped at Alina's waist. Soon the tall grass gave way to short grass, rocks and stones. They reached a hillside and stopped. They could still hear the rocket barrage continuing from behind them and to their right. 'McNeill, what now? If we go up, we may be seen, and there are more hills to our left, which may take too long to go round with your bad leg. It was hurting you crossing the stony ground. And if we go round to the right we may come into contact with the soldiers.'

'Yeah, that's it in a nutshell. So, my military commander of a brainbox, what say you, what shall we do? Please take into account: woman, baby and injured man,' McNeill said between heaving breaths.

'Sarcastic pig,' retorted Alina.

'OK, OK, I'm sorry. First, we rest; it's comparatively safe here for now,' he replied.

McNeill's leg was hurting, bleeding slightly, which he considered a good thing. He sat down and lit a cigarette, rolled Fitz's lighter around in his hand. He could not help thinking that where the rockets were, there were more vehicles and wouldn't it be nice to steal one. Alina could drive and he could rest his leg. He drew on the cigarette.

He never finished the cigarette. As he exhaled the sounds of cracking and splitting wood splattered through the air, followed by the ear-splitting bangs of rockets exploding. The rocket launchers were being fired upon by the town defenders, only the aim was slightly askew and overshot. Shock waves bent and shook the trees like flickering candlelight, before they rested upright once more.

'Which way?' cried Alina.

'Into the trees. Let's head for the rocket launchers. If there is a patrol they will see us in the open, they will not expect anyone to head for the rocket launchers. And the major's rockets will get closer to their intended targets, I hope,' McNeill replied.

Alina looked at McNeill, her face contorted in disbelief. 'You want us to go into the skirmish? We will be killed,' Alina said.

'Look, if the next salvo from the town is nearer the rocket launchers then maybe one of Major Lukas's patrols are out here directing the town fire. If that is the case they will be up high, so they have visual – far enough away but close enough to see through binoculars, maybe on that hill over there. And they will not want anyone heading in their direction as it may give them away. So it's back to the launchers,' McNeill said, trying to console Alina and convince himself.

Thirty or so minutes later they re-entered the trees. Where moments before had stood full-grown trees, huge trunks had been uprooted and deposited to earth as if they were matchsticks. The noise, the ear-splitting, headache-thumping boom as the rocket launchers set off their deadly, destructive loads continued. Return fire had left craters for Alina and McNeill to negotiate. McNeill was a few yards ahead of a frightened Alina carrying her baby. Suddenly, he stopped and crouched down behind a sturdy tree, signalling to Alina to get down.

McNeill gave her the signal to join him, but to keep low. She reached McNeill, her heart pounding in her chest, her eyes now wandering, her thoughts on the immediate future, her breathing short and fast, her baby clasped to her chest. McNeill whispered, 'Three right, four left, moving in towards the road, the same direction as ourselves.' Alina looked but could see no soldiers. Puzzled, she looked at McNeill, who gripped her arm and moved quietly another 20 yards further ahead, still crouching. Releasing her arm he nodded in the soldiers' direction. Alina looked and saw exactly what he had seen. McNeill gripped her arm again and zigzagged through the trees a further 30 yards. Crouching low, he listened. Both he and Alina could hear voices, barely.

BOOM!

The three men to the right were thrown into the air, silhouetted arms outstretched against a red flash. Trees cracked and fell. McNeill covered his ears, Alina crossed her arms behind her baby and pulled her into her chest, covering her ears also. The earth trembled uncontrollably before returning to solidity. Alina released her ears and relaxed her arms. The baby cried. McNeill was already looking ahead, his head darting in rhythm with his eyes as they searched all around. He saw the four men on the left run to the road and could now hear the shouting voices more clearly. Alina, stifling the crying baby as best she could, joined him and began to translate. 'They are being called in; they are moving out, the rockets are landing too close.' She quietly added, 'Do we sit tight?' McNeill smiled as he nodded a yes, whispering 'For Christ's sake can you get her to shut up?' Alina did the only thing she knew, she began to feed her. McNeill watched the shouting soldiers.

They heard the engines of the rocket launchers and another

truck, a troop carrier, spring to life. They heard more shouting, heard the drivers cram the trucks into gear and reverse before turning and moving towards their base. They sat still as they heard the engines of cars and jeeps scream and doors slam, then their tyres squealing to get away. Two more booms followed. Both hit the far side of the road in quick succession. The dust settled, the noise abated, and stillness and silence prevailed.

McNeill waited a full half-hour before he stood and flung the AK-47 over his shoulder. Then he turned and looked at Alina, the baby in her arms, AK-47 strapped to her back. 'You OK?' he asked. 'Yes, I do this every day for a laugh, you big lummox,' she retorted before bowing her head and beginning to weep. McNeill hugged her then kissed her hair on the crown of her head, then just held her. Eventually she raised her head and looked at him. Their lips parted and he kissed her. Then he said, 'I love you, Alina.' She kissed him before replying, 'I love you too, McNeill.' He held her, then the soldier in him took over. 'We must move on, head north back towards and up the road.'

Missiles zoomed across the sky overhead. Alina and McNeill watched the white plumes. McNeill spoke. 'The town is still firing – that means it's stalemate, or maybe the crevasses in the road behind us delayed the tanks, but they should be able to cross. Maybe the convoy of trucks didn't cross?' He rubbed his chin, he did not like that last remark.

'What's up, McNeill, what bothers you?' Alina asked.

'If the trucks cannot cross the crater, they will have to turn back. That would mean a whole regiment of men coming along behind us and getting closer.' He checked his watch, and then hummed as he digested his thoughts. 'It was noon when we were leaving the jeep, the search for water and medical pack maybe took another half-hour... it's gone four in the afternoon now. They should have reached the crevasse well over an hour ago; they must have got through, otherwise the ground would be trembling and we would hear the dull drone of tank engines now and we cannot, so the tanks are through. We wait another half-hour before I can relax about the trucks, just in case,' McNeill said with an air of caution.

McNeill had forgotten about the injury to his leg. The adrenalin surges of the past hour or so had masked the pain and thinking of a plan of action had been a distraction, but God did it hurt now. Alina looked at McNeill and knew he was in agony. She made her way to him and supported him, before telling him to sit and hold the baby whilst she went back for the briefcases – she had left them as they entered the trees.

Shortly she returned. 'Come on, we have to go. So get up, I will carry you,' she said to McNeill, adding with a playful smile on her lips, 'And I will not let you forget that I carried you.' McNeill winced with pain as he leant on Alina to walk. 'The macho tough guy is now like a whimpering baby with a splinter in his finger.'

'Just shut up and move ahead,' McNeill countered.

'Oh, touchy, are we?' teased Alina. McNeill smiled. They moved to the roadside.

'Strange… Odd,' said McNeill.

'What is?' asked Alina.

McNeill went on, 'Strange, we have not seen a house, sheds, cars, people or animals since yesterday. I know it is a war, but has everyone hibernated or evacuated?'

'Probably the latter,' replied Alina.

'How so?' asked McNeill.

'If the Serbs are here, or were here, then the people would be afraid of their ethnic-cleansing programme; better not to be here,' Alina stated.

'Oh, I see. With speeches like that you would make an honest politician,' McNeill replied. They both laughed. McNeill lit up another cigarette. Alina spoke. 'Strange, when you hardly had any cigarettes you saved them, and now you have a few you cannot wait to smoke them. Why is that?'

With a smile McNeill replied, 'That's the Alina effect; the more I see you, the more I want you.'

'Come on, you brute – move!' she said, smiling happily.

'OK. But we stay off the road as much as we can, walk through the trees at the road's edge,' McNeill said.

Alina supported McNeill as they moved along. McNeill was grateful of the support at times but at others he pulled away and stubbornly refused Alina's offer of help. He knew relying on Alina to walk severely diminished their chances of survival. He knew he would have to acclimatise to the pain, or just downright put it out of his head. He knew to survive he could not let the pain get the better of him. The road began to decline downhill. Alina became agitated, excited, animated. 'What's got into you?' asked McNeill.

'Take a look: go on, take a look through your telescopic sight,' she urged him. McNeill looked at Alina, who smiled, then at her baby, who seemed to smile too. McNeill removed the Dragunov rifle from his back, crouched and looked through the sight; then he did a curious thing. Still crouching, he made his way to the middle of the road and spreadeagled himself on it, peering through the sight for ages.

He could see a vast lake. He got up to the crouching position and remained like that as he returned to Alina. 'Did you see it, did you see it? Did you see the lake?' Alina excitedly enquired.

'Yes, I saw the lake,' came the stoic reply.

'Yes, McNeill, and on the far side of that lake lies freedom. We will all be together, you, the baby and I. A new life – free,' Alina said, eyes dancing.

'Pass me your AK-47,' McNeill demanded. Alina gave McNeill the weapon. He unclipped the magazine and removed four bullets, then clipped the magazine back. He unclipped his own AK-47 and took out three bullets for a total of seven. He then checked the clip in the Dragunov – two rounds, which he removed and replaced, then loaded the other seven into the magazine. Nine in all.

Alina's euphoria diminished rapidly as she watched McNeill. 'What else did you see, McNeill? What else? Tell me,' she demanded sternly.

'Yes, I saw the lake. It's over to our left, hills either side of it, four, five miles away, maybe. I also saw a roadblock about a mile ahead. There is a little village away to our right with Serbian flags in it. Also, there is a whole bloody army in there too, with practically every infantry weapon that's needed for an assault, except helicopters and airplanes. Obviously they are waiting for nightfall to move out. Patrols have left the village, I saw them leave. They will comb the outlying lands to make sure that the convoy does not get ambushed and gets to where it is heading. Slavic's town is about to be heavily assaulted.

'Five patrols left the village,' he continued, 'each with what I estimated between seven and nine men. It is not possible for us to avoid a patrol, we have to meet or cross paths at some stage, and I figure we have to be at the lake before the convoy leaves for the town. If the convoy is still in the village in the morning, we will have been captured by then. Patrols will be sent out during the night at regular intervals and in different directions to protect that convoy; and there just does not seem like there is anywhere to hide. I reckon we have about… mmm, what time is it? Quarter past five – that's two to four hours tops… four hours may be extreme… three hours to reach the lake. That's basically when that convoy will move out for a night push on Lukas's north side of the town. Lukas will also have patrols out, but I severely doubt they will come out this far. They will probably lie in wait and communicate back to the town. The right information will be priceless for Slavic. Basically, for us, the further away from here that convoy gets, the fewer personnel there are around, the fewer patrols, the easier it will be to avoid capture. Catch my drift?' McNeill imparted.

'McNeill, don't let them catch me, please don't let them catch me,' pleaded Alina.

'I don't intend dying, and I sure don't intend on losing you and the baby; you both are all I have. We have come this far and I am not giving up yet; besides, I love you, Alina,' said McNeill firmly. He went on, 'Now listen, the patrols left in a five-fingered fan, one for the lake, one for the trees and the road here, one for the road to the level land, like this. Alina looked confused as McNeill explained, so he grabbed a stick and drew in the earth at his feet. Alina followed the pattern made by the stick.

'The patrol for the lake will move up from the lake, through the forest at the back, combing the hills to our left. This patrol will come through here, the third between the road and here, this side. Our side is the one that gives a potential ambush more cover; that's why three patrols will come through,' said McNeill as he prodded the earth with the stick to demonstrate the point. 'Any questions?' he added.

'Yes. You have nine bullets – which patrol are you planning on meeting?' asked Alina. 'None, I hope, but at walking pace and with diversions the lake patrol will be the last to get here. All the others will have passed and it is essential and imperative that we miss these. If one patrol gets hit and the bodies are found by a following patrol, they will think they are under sniper attack, a sabotage attempt on the convoy by an elite force, and more men will be deployed. If we encounter a patrol, it has to be the lake one. I reckon two hours before we are in the same area. The road is now out of the question; it will be watched and surveyed constantly. We must stay in the forest, and we have to go through the forest to the hills on the other side,' McNeill said.

'I see,' said Alina, 'you are aiming to confront the lake patrol as it will be behind the other patrols and cannot warn anyone behind as there will be no one. What if the best men are in this patrol?' Alina added.

'Alina, the best patrols are the ones given the most perilous manoeuvres. So take your pick – the best patrols are all on this side, our side, and I expect they will all be thoroughly professional and very good. These people seem pretty well organised, from our spell in the hideaway we saw that, and the way they retreated when under fire was quick and efficient. Also, the first convoy, the smallest by far, did not turn round when it reached the crater in the road, did it? So yes, this army is very well organised and competent,' McNeill said.

'So we go back through the forest to the hills, then what? Lie in wait?' asked Alina.

'That's about it. In the forest, the chances of our survival if it comes to a skirmish are slim; the trees make it hard to get a clear shot and we would be overrun. But out in the open and on high ground, and as long as the ground cover is sparse, the advantage, although small, lies with us and this Dragunov rifle,' McNeill explained.

'OK, McNeill, what's so super about that rifle? I know you are a great shot, you have proved it time and time again,' asked Alina.

'As you saw, Alina, the bullets are interchangeable with the AK-47's, and the AK-47 seems to be a preferred choice. Basically, it's an AK-47 with a shoulder stock and slightly longer barrel, and it's effective at a mile away, so they say. Like the old M21 – if you can see your prey, you can kill it. So we move through the forest to the hills, watch and wait, and if we encounter a patrol and destroy it we use their ammunition.'

They moved through the forest, McNeill walking slowly. His stubbornness meant he resisted Alina's offer of support, so he trudged on with Alina and her baby by his side, each sharing carrying the rifles, bags and briefcases. At times the footing underneath was uneven and Alina could see McNeill wince in pain, but undeterred he kept on going. Tough, solid, reliable, dependant, stubborn, caring were words that entered her mind. Thinking about McNeill, she began thinking of their future. McNeill, who was watching her, spoke: 'OK, smiler, what's so funny?'

Alina replied, 'Nothing.'

McNeill carried on watching her. 'Well, nothing has certainly put a spring in your step these last minutes,' he remarked. Alina looked at him and continued to smile.

'How's the baby, Alina?' McNeill enquired.

'Fine, she has been awake since we left the road,.' Alina replied.

'OK, then let's all eat whatever food we have.'

They sat down and Alina foraged in the bags for the last morsels of food for herself and McNeill, then began to breastfeed her baby.

McNeill watched as the baby girl contentedly suckled, and he began to think and reflect; never at any stage had the baby been a problem. Never had she wakened and cried when silence had been imperative. Never had she cried when bullets and rockets were falling near her. God's little gift, a child to whom her mother wanted no attachment when she was born; a child he thought would be a burden and sure to make their survival an impossibility; a child for whom he did not want responsibility, though it was thrust upon him. She was a child who had been an absolute joy, both to care for and look after and still was; a child with whom he had bonded, but more importantly, a child whose mother had now bonded too.

Alina finished feeding and, using leaves, cleaned her baby's dirty bottom the best she could. McNeill looked at the baby in Alina's arms, and with his right forefinger he touched the baby's chin gently. The baby giggled and smiled in recognition. McNeill hobbled on and Alina followed.

They reached the end of the trees, passed through the wild grass and began to climb to the top of the hill. Alina, carrying her baby and the bags, passed by McNeill on the way up. 'Stop just before you reach the top, wait and let me look around. I will be along shortly,' he said. Just before the crest of the hill, Alina stopped, sat and nestled her baby in her arms. The baby smiled. Alina returned the smile and gently caressed her cheeks. McNeill arrived and deposited rifles and briefcases beside them. 'OK, maybe if the baby becomes thirsty we can give her some water, maybe if she becomes hungry... well, that's your department,

Alina. I will look around.' He took the Dragunov and climbed to the top.

Once more he spreadeagled himself on the floor and peered through the telescopic sight. He could see the village and the convoy which merged into the suburb. Occasionally, he could make out patrol members to the convoy's left and members of the patrol to the road's right, the central patrol. He could see soldiers milling around the trucks in the stationary convoy, but to his disappointment he could not see the one patrol he was looking for, because in front of him, blocking his line of sight, was a taller hill. Alina crawled to his side. 'We have to get on there,' said McNeill, pointing at the hill. To their right rockets flew, heading for the town behind, but both Alina and McNeill were oblivious to them; their focus was on the hill in front. Alina and McNeill returned to the rifles, bags, briefcases and baby.

'Rest a while, McNeill, you are pushing yourself so hard, and I see specks of blood on the new trousers I got you. Let me have a look at your leg,' Alina said worriedly. 'No time,' came the stark reply.

McNeill loaded himself with the rifles, briefcases and bag and asked Alina if she wanted a break from carrying the baby. Alina replied with an emphatic 'No'. They moved round the hill to face the next and began to descend. Thoughts entered McNeill's mind. He knew his injured leg would be of no use to him if he had to run. He remembered that there was one more phial of morphine; the pain was growing, but he intended to save the phial for later when it may be more useful. Alina watched as McNeill's face contorted with pain, 'Stubborn, aren't you, McNeill? You are in a lot of pain and you will not give in, and there is morphine and you will not take it. Just grit your teeth and carry on,' said Alina.

'Me? Stubborn? What about you, independent Annie? You are worse than me; as for the morphine, it will be of greater value later, you will see,' McNeill replied. Alina was a little bemused; yes, she was stubborn, but what did he mean by later?

'What's going to unfold later?' she asked tentatively.

'The patrols lie between us and the lake; contact is inevitable and unavoidable. And when a full patrol or part of one goes missing, more soldiers will be sent to investigate and more searches will be done. Sooner or later we will come into contact with the lake patrol. Even if we take them out, we have to be at the lake, find a boat, and be hidden before they realise the patrol is missing and headquarters sends out search parties. You follow, Alina?' asked McNeill.

'So cut the unavoidable crap! You aim to shoot up that patrol and be so deep into their territory that they will not think of looking for us there. How many men? You put nine bullets in that rifle – has each one got a life inscribed on it? Don't you think we have killed enough soldiers, taken enough lives of such very, very young men? Can we not slip through?' said Alina resolutely.

'Don't get all righteous, and don't go soft on me, not now! You said earlier "Please don't let them take me", and I am not coming this far to get captured. Have you forgotten? We are dead regardless of which side captures us, be it Serbian or Croatian. Your father will see to that. So it's dog eat dog,' McNeill retorted, sterner than ever, his face set into a scowl.

'Stubborn PIG!' said Alina, her voice raised.

'Stubbornness leads to endurance, endurance leads to survival, survival leads to living,' replied a focussed McNeill, who walked on by Alina without breaking stride.

In her heart of hearts Alina knew McNeill was right. She knew the patrol stood between them and the border, she knew he would try to avoid them, but his military brain told him contact was inevitable. However, she knew if he could avoid them it would make perfect sense to do so. If they could slip by unnoticed and all patrols returned unscathed, then no one would look for them. They would not know they were there. Her mind raced as she walked behind McNeill. She hoped against hope that they would slip by, but deep down she realised that once again the fight to survive was beginning. Clutching her baby to her she caught up

257

with McNeill, and grabbed his left arm. McNeill stopped and turned, and as he did so Alina kissed him and smiled. McNeill smiled back and winked with his left eye. They continued on. Intermittently, McNeill would wince with the pain from his leg; Alina would squeeze his arm and look at him with growing concern. Every look was met with the answer, 'I'm OK.'

⇒◆⇐

Ascent followed descent, and on occasion McNeill leant slightly on Alina for support. Suddenly, a horrifying thought came to her. 'McNeill, we are out in the open. If they see us, they could shoot us at any second.' She began to tremble.

'Relax, it will not happen. The patrols are a group of men who specialise in short hand-to-hand combat, or information gathering, not necessarily sniper patrols. We will be OK. Moreover, we know they are there, they don't know we are here. The element of surprise is with us; I hope we don't have to use it but fear we may have to,' McNeill said in a consoling tone of voice.

For Alina, the tension rose in tandem with the gradient of the hill climb. She could feel herself tremble in the pit of her stomach, the agitation of her nerves making her body shake coldly, like someone had walked over her grave. She hated this feeling; life-threatening actions usually followed. They reached the summit. The whiteness of the clouds had evaporated into the blue of the sky. The sun was up but not warm and a light breeze had begun to blow. 'Chilly up here, isn't it?' said a spreadeagled McNeill, peering through the telescopic sight down the sniper rifle barrel. He was looking once again at the village and the convoy, searching the layout for the patrols, seeking out the lake patrol as he had named them. Alina watched intently as he swung back to his right, then back to his left, a manoeuvre he repeated three times more, sometimes quickly, sometimes very slowly and cautiously. *What is he looking for? Or what has he seen?* she pondered. McNeill peered on. Alina wondered, had he found a way through unnoticed? Whatever the outcome, she knew McNeill's decision would be the decision which would give them the best chance of success. She waited for McNeill to finish.

McNeill laid the rifle in the short grass and rolled onto his side to see her lying beside him, holding her baby. Concern was there for all to see. 'OK. Tell me as it is,' she said matter-of-factly. 'Looks bad,' he said. Alina's body slumped and her shoulders dropped. All hopes of slipping through unnoticed evaporated into thin air there and then. Her eyes fell to the ground. Then she looked at her baby and discovered a new strength and inner steel. Finally, she spoke: 'OK, McNeill. As you say, we have come this far, they are not going to stop us. My baby is going to be free, free of this war, and you and I are not only going to make sure she grows up in freedom, but will be together to make sure she does. Now give it to me straight!'

McNeill's heart missed a beat. The three of them together, a new life – that sounded excellent and it gave him a longing. Now she had given him something to live for. Not only was he fighting for his own survival but theirs and she did not want to part from him when it was over. He began, 'The lake patrol is a little behind the others, but in what resembles a semicircle formation and therefore it's too close to the road patrol for us to slip through unnoticed. Also, they are too tight to one and other, which means I will not be able to pick them off without the other one knowing his colleague is no longer beside him. It's the same for the road patrol nearest the lake patrol; however, the far side – I could shoot them now as they have drifted out of position. I count an eight-man patrol in the lake patrol and nine in the road. If we have to resort to hand-to-hand fighting we cannot defeat seventeen men, the odds are too great. We cannot slip down the hills and around to our left, as there are small fires on this side with more soldiers, trucks and jeeps at the edges of this line of hills. We may wait a while and see if they stretch out, but not for too long.'

'Don't you mean hope they stretch out?' said Alina.

'Or become detached,' added McNeill almost apologetically.

'How near do they have to be so you can shoot them, McNeill?' asked Alina.

McNeill rolled back to peer through the sight. 'Accurate to a mile with a clear shot, so they say; half that, much better,' said McNeill coldly.

The lake patrol was still behind the road patrol. McNeill knew he could pin them down, but that would be pointless; neither he nor they would progress and he only had nine bullets so sooner rather than later more soldiers would come, flush them out and kill them. He rolled away from the rifle. 'Take a look, Alina.' He beckoned.

Alina looked. 'OK, it looks hopeless. Soon they will come and we will fight. How much time do we have, McNeill?' she asked.

'They are just over a mile away, so about twenty minutes or so,' replied McNeill. Alina continued looking through the sight and listened to his voice. 'Do you see the trucks over to your left, and the fires? If I take out the two men of the lake patrol nearest those, do you think you and the baby could slip by the rest?' McNeill asked.

'I am not leaving you, McNeill. I am not leaving you here alone. No way! We go, we all go together. DO YOU HEAR ME? And are we very clear!' Alina had rolled away from the rifle and was hammering her index finger into McNeill's chest as she spoke, forcibly instilling her point.

'OK, OK. And you say I am stubborn,' said McNeill. McNeill looked through the sight.

He watched and waited. 'OK, Alina, make sure the safety is off your Beretta and the AK-47 on your back; you are going to need them. Put the briefcases into the bag and strap the bag to your back, but before you do, get the last phial of morphine and stick it into my leg. I will carry the rifles and tuck the baby under my arm. Make sure she is very well wrapped in case I have to carry her on the run in one hand; and stay low and out of sight. This is not going to be a nice party and we will be moving fast, then stopping, then moving again fast, so keep up and keep your AK ready when we have to move.'

'Move, move where?' asked Alina.

'Just stick to me like glue; I will make spontaneous decisions at the time. I just hope they will be the right ones,' McNeill said. He watched the lake patrol come into the semblance of a straight line across his vision. 'Ready, Alina?' There was a pause and before she could reply McNeill added, 'Our first move is from here down there to the left, out of their sight, then around to come between the patrol and the line of trucks and fires. We will be in the middle, and the road patrol will come through the forest on our right and up these hills for a vantage point at the sounds of gunshot. I think there is a stream or small river which runs to the lake on our left; if it is so, we follow it. Water will be below ground level and it's hard to spot from up here. I am not quite sure what is there. Hopefully we will be through before the two patrols meet or are confused and frightened enough that they fire on each other. Although daylight would render that improbable.'

Alina could almost touch the tension in the air, could feel her blood pump through her arteries, her veins beat with the rhythm of her heart. She crossed herself and prayed. 'Say one for me,' said McNeill. McNeill saw his chance. He had waited till he was sure of his first target and kill, waited till they approached to less than 800 yards away. He could see two soldiers together on his far left, in a small clearing talking, about to light cigarettes. They were stopped while the rest of the patrol kept moving forward. The two stood side by side now, smoking. Alina was saying AMEN, when she heard the rifle fire, two sets of two bullets in quick succession. She crossed herself once again. McNeill watched and saw the two men fall backwards. He turned his rifle sight to the rest of the patrol; they had not seen their colleagues fall and came ahead, walking slowly. McNeill said, 'Go.' It had begun.

McNeill moved backwards on hands and knees, pulling the Dragunov with him. Alina was already at the point where McNeill said they would leave the hill, carrying her baby. McNeill caught her up and took the baby from her as they moved off the hill. He was running but dragging his wounded leg. Alina was close behind; they rounded a smaller adjoining hill and headed towards bushes at the far edge of a sparse field. 'Quick, we have to cross this twenty yards and not be seen. Keep low,' he instructed.

They hit the bushes running in a crouch position; the gorse needles ripped at their trouser legs and arms. Suddenly McNeill fell into a shallow ditch hidden behind the bushes, rolling on and landing, the baby in his left hand, Dragunov in his right, the other weapons strapped to his back. Moments later Alina landed beside him, bags strapped to her back, Beretta in her belt and AK-47 in her two hands across her chest.

They moved quickly and as silently as possible down the ditch towards the fires. McNeill was in an adrenalin-infused, morphine-induced, painless and trance-like state, totally focussed on getting through and staying alive. Then he stopped, Alina stopped. McNeill pushed out the barrel of the Dragunov through a gorse bush thicket and peered through the telescopic sight at the trees slightly below. He saw two members of the lake patrol moving back to where their dead colleagues were. He pulled the rifle back and slid the long barrel over the earth ridge to his right, and saw what he thought was the road patrol, slightly below their own position but a distance away. 'Damn!' he uttered as he removed his rifle and pushed it back through from the gorse and looked. 'Damn!' he repeated as he shook his head, blinked and pressed his right eye to the sight. He saw it just ahead and to his left: a little narrow valley-like channel between the rising of two small mounds of earth.

'In there and up round the back, quickly,' he ordered, pointing. Alina was already moving and led the way through; she crossed the small channel and started the ascent. McNeill overtook her and at the top he flung himself to the ground and desperately set up the rifle. He could make out the two dead men and the two soldiers on foot heading towards them, then another four in a line but well detached from the two nearest their dead comrades and further forward. McNeill moved to where he reckoned on spotting the road patrol; from where he was, he could make out parts of the road. He looked at the trucks on his left. His position was wide open to the trucks across sparse ground, only they appeared to him to be approximately one and a half miles away. The sun was over to his right and in front of the sky. 'Give me your jumper quickly, Alina, quickly,' he said without removing his face from the rifle sight.

Alina dropped her weapons, unstrapped the bag, took her jumper off and gave it to McNeill. McNeill took it and covered the top of the rifle sight with it, leaving the end clear so he could see through. Alina lay down with her baby at McNeill's side. McNeill focussed his attention on the two men searching for their stricken colleagues.

The two soldiers were walking back, shouting the names of their dead colleagues, making their way through thick forestry to light. The underfoot terrain had turned from a springy surface, where the forest floor had caught the droppings of the trees over many years, to a sample of grass and stone. They had entered the clearing and had not seen them at first, but after a few paces into the almost cylindrical oasis in the woods they saw their colleagues lying sprawled on their backs. One of the men ran over to them, the other dropped to one knee and readied his weapon.

They did not know they were dead. As soon as they entered the clearing a mark of death had been put on them. McNeill despatched the first life-taker at the moment the soldier bent down on one knee. The second life-taker had already been fired at the soldier who stood upright, looking down at his dead friends. He heard the fall of his compatriot just before the messenger of death entered his back and blew an almighty hole out of the front of his chest. He fell forward to join his friends. His life ebbed away and was gone before he lay with them.

McNeill turned through 90 degrees, looked at the road and waited for the first soldier to enter his view. His one clear shot.

He squeezed the trigger and the bullet left the barrel. He pulled the Dragunov back and returned the jumper to Alina, picked up the baby, bag and M21. 'Move, move!' he commanded. They ran down the nearside of the large mound and back into the ditch, crouching and stumbling. Alina stuffed her jumper into her belt. She was panting for breath, her lungs burning. She was confused but followed McNeill blindly. McNeill began to slow, eventually stopping and walking. Alina caught up. 'Take the bag, Alina,' he said softly. Alina did so. McNeill's face was white.

The soldier on the road was part of what McNeill termed the road forest patrol; he was the second in from the forest. He had stood in full view of McNeill for only a minute whilst he was talking to his comrade below him in the trees. It was a minute when life changed to death. The deadly bullet entered his chest just left of centre and spun him round as he fell, lifeless. His patrol colleagues dropped to the ground in an instant after he hit the ground. The remaining members of the lake patrol hit the floor in a domino effect, the one nearest the road patrol first.

McNeill slowed, held the baby to his chest. She was awake and simply coo-ed at him. 'Stay quiet, my little darling, for God's sake not a sound, please,' he whispered to her. He turned his head to Alina, who came up beside him. 'Be careful now, not a sound,' he whispered. Alina, breathless, nodded in agreement. McNeill stopped; once again he pushed the nozzle of the Dragunov through the bushes over the shallow ditch rim and peered through the sight. He moved the rifle round left and right and saw nothing. He looked at Alina and jerked his head in a forward motion, putting his right index finger to his pursed lips as he did so. Alina moved ahead slowly; McNeill followed a few yards behind. Shortly, McNeill increased his speed and caught her up, caught hold of her left arm and gently pulled at it. She turned. He motioned for her to lie down and he gave her the baby.

McNeill had seen that the shallow ditch rose to the level of the ground and was coming to an end. Again, he slid the rifle barrel out over the rim, but this time there were no bushes, only grass. He rose slowly so he could see through the sight, combing ahead then to the right, then behind and finally the left before slinking down. He saw two of the patrol moving up through the forest cautiously from tree to tree in the opposite direction to them, fires and trucks and a few soldiers on foot ahead and to their left. He carried the rifle in his right hand and took the baby from Alina with his left and moved ahead. At the ditch's end McNeill stopped and turned to Alina and quietly said, 'We crawl from here. Use your elbows and knees, keeping the AK across your arms, and put the Beretta in your belt at your back.' McNeill shouldered the Dragunov and, with the baby now in his right hand, crawled out of the ditch and into the grass. Alina followed suit.

Alina gasped. She looked to her right and saw the last beams of daylight shine in the clearing where three dead soldiers lay, two face up and one face down. McNeill motioned to her to hurry up and keep moving. Alina looked again at the illuminated clearing in the forest and imagined three dead soldiers with their mouths agape, lying there, four empty eyes open, looking skyward, two looking earthward, all seeing nothing. She caught sight of McNeill's arm waving vigorously for her to move ahead. She crawled on and tears began to fall down her face as she thought of the dead soldiers' mothers' impending grief.

McNeill had stopped when he waved, but now he began to move on and slightly leftwards. He looked back and saw Alina coming closer. For Alina, the minutes seemed like hours. Crawling on hands and knees and shuffling her body from side to side to keep low was hard work for her. A few times McNeill had stopped and waited for her to catch up. McNeill could now see that the grass was becoming entwined with bush and he made his way through a small hole between bush stems. Then the earth gave way under his left elbow and he plunged forward. It was a hollow in the ground and he hauled himself in. Alina followed, exhausted, and turned and lay on her back. Panting for breath she asked, 'Well, are we through?'

McNeill gave the baby to her and said, 'Let you know in a minute,' as he removed the Dragunov from his shoulder.

He smiled at her and kissed her on the cheek, before pushing the barrel of the Dragunov through the bushes and grass and gently rising up. He searched through the telescopic sight and saw the patrols climbing the hills which they had descended earlier. He looked around in a 360-degree circle. He saw glimpses of the village with the convoy still there, he made out the hills which enveloped the lake, saw the smoke from the fires of the soldiers and trucks. He ducked down slowly, put the rifle down and lay at Alina's side.

'Well? Well?' she forcefully whispered, digging her right elbow into his ribcage for an answer.

'Steady on,' said McNeill. 'OK, the situation is such: that way, the soldiers are patrolling and combing the hills we left earlier; to our left and ahead, are the soldiers' trucks and fires with nothing doing; the convoy is silent in the village still. There looks to be a roadblock between us and the lake,' he reported.

'So we are stuck in the middle,' Alina said apprehensively.

'Only if the patrols come back this way, and they are more likely to stick to the road, Alina,' McNeill said reassuringly.

'OK, and what about the convoy and the town's north side defended by Lukas, McNeill?' Alina asked.

McNeill replied matter-of-factly, 'That convoy has to move. There are too many weapons and men in such a tiny space – it's a military disaster waiting to happen if they remain like that for long. The tanks we saw earlier must be within range of Slavic's town and will probably have some success, but will just test the town's resistance without being able to breach the fortifications, and so they will wait for the convoy before an assault. Lukas was well set up for an advance on his part of town, we saw that. These people are clever and are waiting for the all-clear from the patrols before moving out. Slavic is very clever; if he knocks out

266

the tanks and machinery, what is to stop him breaking out of town and making a push to surround this army and disable it in this village and still defend the east side of his town? Nothing – that's exactly what he will do if he gets a chance. Our shooting of the patrol may be put down to a far out patrol from the town – I hope – and soon the convoy will move. What bothers me is the soldiers and trucks with the fires on this side – are they part of the convoy or will they move into the village to guard it when the convoy leaves? Of that, I am not sure.'

Alina listened intently to McNeill the soldier. 'So the convoy moves when it gets word from the patrols, how does that happen? It then catches up with the patrols and then what, McNeill?' she asked.

'Maybe one or two men will be sent back to the village to give the all-clear, or maybe it will be done by flare. At some stage someone will be sent to bring in the bodies when they realise part of a patrol is missing, but that will more than likely be tomorrow, in daylight,' McNeill replied.

'Then how long do we have? We can't stay here – the patrol may come back this way to collect their dead, and to carry them even to the road will require a lot of soldiers,' Alina stated.

'Yes, Alina, very true; we cannot stay here,' he replied.

'Go on, McNeill, what are you planning?' Alina enquired.

'We could hide, and hide right where they would not think of looking; over there with the soldiers, trucks and fires – even amongst them, if we have to,' McNeill said.

Alina was dumbfounded. 'Are you crazy? You are crazy. Have you lost your senses? Has the morphine got you out of your mind? All this way to hide amongst a Serbian army – a man, woman and baby – to escape a Serbian army?' she said, dismayed.

'Ironic, isn't it?' McNeill uttered.

'Well, you have got us this far, and this kind of warfare is definitely your expertise, so whatever you ask, I will do, with one exception – just do not ask me to leave you,' Alina imparted.

'OK, we wait a while and we watch. It's already getting darker.

Have we much left in the way of food and drink? And our smiler here may need a feed,' McNeill gently said, touching the baby's cheek.

Alina looked through the bag and found water, two apples and precious little else. She passed them to McNeill, keeping an apple for herself, and began to feed her baby. McNeill looked away. Alina smiled as she looked at the back of McNeill's head while the baby contentedly suckled. She could hear a clicking. 'What are you doing?' she asked.

'Well, the magazine in the rifle is nearly empty and I'm just taking some bullets out of my AK's magazine to put into the rifle's magazine, just in case we have some unwanted guests on their way towards us, my dear,' McNeill replied nonchalantly.

Even now when Alina was being a natural mother, McNeill's inner soldier was calculating and preparing. Alina pondered this thought. She realised that as much as she wanted to get to freedom, so did McNeill. He too could smell the end, but a few obstacles stood between them and it, and she knew that calm, calculating brain would master the excitement and programme itself to the situation. Freedom, to McNeill, was when he walked through the border crossing; until then, he was still escaping to it. She also realised that if she had to choose anyone to get them there, it would be him. She began to dream, dream of what civilian life would be like for McNeill. How would he adapt? She now had a link to McNeill, a chain link she did not want to sever or break. She was deeply in love with him and began dreaming of living in a city or the country. Which would he prefer, she asked herself. She carried on dreaming. Before the war she had been a journalist; politics was her field. Would she go back to it, or would she go further and become a politician? If she became famous, McNeill could be head of security. *I'm sure he would not mind looking out for me and if he looked at me all day, surely isn't that OK for your husband to do?*

The baby stopped suckling and began to cry, bringing Alina back to reality. McNeill turned to them, took the baby and began gently tapping her back to bring up her wind. The baby gurgled and cried. Alina watched as she fastened the buttons of her blouse and replaced her jumper. McNeill gave her the baby and took out of his pocket the last half of a chocolate bar and gave it to her. Alina gratefully took it and began to devour it. McNeill checked his watch: twenty-five minutes had passed since his last scout. He picked up the Dragunov and, looking through the sight, scanned the horizon as before, doing a full circle. Smoke from the fires was barely visible, the convoy was still unmoved and what looked like a roadblock was still there, but he saw no patrols. He lay down, waited five minutes and checked again. He repeated this manoeuvre five more minutes later. No patrols, everything the same, except the twilight was fading rapidly to darkness. 'OK, Alina, let's pack and go,' he said.

They left the safety of the hollow. McNeill crawled out in front, using his elbows, AK-47 and M21 rifle on his back, Dragunov in his right hand, baby in his left, Alina in tow with bag strapped to her back, Beretta in her belt and AK-47 across her arms. McNeill gently pushed his way through thicker gorse and Alina followed. The twenty minutes of crawling through the gorse was slow and arduous. McNeill's left leg began to ache and he heaved a huge sigh of relief as grass slipped by under his elbows. He waited for Alina, who came along gently cursing under her breath. 'Ssh!' He looked ahead for cover and moved off to his left.

His back against a 10-foot rise of earth, he waited for Alina and handed her the baby. He looked through the rifle sight. 'Nothing. Wait till I look over the top,' he said in a low tone. He crouched low against the slope and peered over the edge in a full 180-degree scan, and slipped back down to Alina's side. Her mouth dropped open; blood was running down the side of his boot and onto the ground. 'McNeill, are you OK? You are bleeding,' she said.

'Come on, we go alongside a line of gorse and small mounds of earth for about thirty yards, then it looks like there is a break and we go through to the other side. There are rushes, so there must be water. There is an expanse of rushes between the other side of the hills and the ground where the trucks are. The soldiers will never expect anyone to be in there,' McNeill said.

'But your leg – can't we at least have a look?' pleaded Alina.

'Not here, we get to somewhere much safer,' came McNeill's curt reply.

Crouching low, they crossed the 30 yards quite easily, and as McNeill had surmised, there was a smaller mound of earth between two larger ones linking them together. 'Wait here; I will go up. Go over there, stop by the rushes and wait for my signal to enter, and stay low,' McNeill ordered.

⟫•◆•⟪

Alina waited by the rushes, eyes fixed on McNeill as she held her baby girl in her arms. McNeill climbed the larger mound to the left, and once again looked through the sight at the fires, trucks and soldiers. He watched and waited, then signalled to Alina to enter. She did so cautiously. McNeill checked again through the telescopic sight. She had not been spotted by the soldiers on guard at the trucks. He looked at the convoy, still stationary at the road-block, then he lowered himself back down the rear of the mound and checked behind for anything. He looked in the direction of the road, unable to see the road, saw nothing. *Still, if I cannot see them, it doesn't mean they are not there, but if I cannot see them, then they cannot see me.* He focussed on the large hill from where he shot the first two soldiers in the distance behind him, and he saw them silhouetted in the starlit darkness, two men, machine guns at the ready, beginning the descent, moving slowly down. *Mmm, the patrol must have reached the shot-up jeep; these two are either coming back looking for something or looking for their dead colleagues,* he thought. He waited. Alina waited.

Once again the two men were silhouetted against the sky, only this time closer. McNeill's index finger moved to the Dragunov's trigger as he took aim at the soldier on the left. He waited, relaxed

270

and took a breath, but the two men turned and headed for the forest and the road. McNeill trained the rifle on them at every stage, but the two men disappeared into the darkness of the forest. He waited, peered through the rifle sight at the forest, scanned it, but saw nothing. He descended the rest of the mound, shouldered his Dragunov, crouched low and entered the rushes by the same route Alina had taken earlier. Alina could hear the rushes move behind her. 'McNeill, is that you?' she cried in a hushed voice.

'Ssshh!' came to her ears. 'What the hell took you so long?' she whispered angrily. McNeill told her of what he saw, then said, 'We wait here.'

'Wait here! For what?' she inquired.

'For the light to dim some more. And give me your AK-47 – I want to double-check the magazine,' McNeill said. They both dropped to one knee on the damp earth. McNeill removed the rifles and AK-47 from his back. Alina gave McNeill the AK-47. McNeill took four rounds from her AK and put them into his own. Alina watched and spoke softly. 'Tell me why, if you are so worried about our weapons and ammunition, and I know by the frown on your face that you are, why did you not take the weapons from those dead soldiers back there?'

'Simple,' replied McNeill. 'If we took the weapons from the dead, they would know someone was here and had penetrated that far, and they would comb the area from the dead soldiers looking for intruders through all the ground from there to the lake, to the village and beyond, and more so if that convoy stays put – that's too many soldiers to slip through. This way, they know the arms were taken from the men we shot at the jeep. A medical bag is missing, so they will know one was wounded, and hopefully they will surmise that there was a deep patrol which saw the convoy and retreated with the wounded to warn the town and Lukas.'

'Makes sense. I hope you are right. But what of the two soldiers you recently saw?' Alina questioned.

271

'My guess is that the convoy will move when they have been debriefed, and either a patrol will come out to look or they wait till daybreak. And when they find them? Well, nothing was taken from them so they may just collect them and return to the village,' McNeill explained. 'So we wait a while, have a look and move accordingly. How is the baby, and how are you?' he added.

Alina began, 'Baby is fine, she is wonderful, has just dropped off to sleep. You would swear she knows what's happening and what's required. I'm bearing up and now, tough nut, let me see that leg of yours – so come on, trousers off.' Just then the baby stirred and began to cry.

'Oh, what a proposition. I never thought you would ask. But are you sure we wouldn't be heard or spotted?' whispered a smiling, mischievous McNeill. McNeill undid his belt and slid the trousers to his knees. Blood had stained the bandage, oozed out from underneath and run down the side of his thigh to his knee and down the outside of his leg.

'If you remove that bandage, have we another one to replace it, Alina?' whispered McNeill.

'No,' came her short reply.

'Then leave it be.' And he pulled up his trousers and fastened his belt, picked up the Dragunov rifle and rose slowly up. He began to scan in a full 360-degree circle starting with the soldiers and trucks. After that he saw nothing and slipped back down. 'Wait here, I'm going back to the mound. I can't quite see the convoy or village from here and the two soldiers must be back in the village by now,' he said as he turned and left. Alina tended to her baby.

Back at the large mound he scanned through 360 degrees, giving more attention to the shapes of the convoy. There was a faint drone. He peered through the sight; starlight appeared and disappeared. What was it? Could it be...? He blinked and looked again. Could it be exhaust fumes, he wondered. He watched and waited. Minutes passed and seemed eternal, but the convoy began to move. McNeill watched and surveyed; the convoy was moving out. Then he felt the unmistakeable shudder of the ground. Tanks glistened in the starlight, four in all, rocket launchers, heavy machine guns, heavy field guns, trucks, trucks and more trucks, more mounted heavy machine guns, more trucks. He watched them leave the village, moving westwards before turning and heading southwards up the road towards the north side of town defended by Lukas and his men.

McNeill descended and carefully returned to an ashen-faced Alina. 'Convoy's on the move,' he said.

'Yes, I know. I could and can still feel it. Were there tanks?' she enquired. McNeill nodded in agreement. 'I hope Major Lukas is ready for what's coming. What do we do now?' she said.

'We wait, wait to see if this lot move into the town or with the convoy,' McNeill said.

The dull hum of the tank engines turned to a constant drone, the ground underneath their feet shook more violently. McNeill rose and looked through the telescopic sight at the trucks and soldiers across the marshland and wasteland in front. The trucks had begun to move, all but one at the rear side, which was being bypassed. *Maybe it's broken down,* thought McNeill. 'Wait here, I need to get a better look,' he said to Alina as he moved slowly past her.

He went back to the mound and surveyed. He saw the tanks, and turned his attention to the roadblock. Here he saw the trucks laid out in single file from the marshland to the roadblock. Intermittently, the queue moved as a lorry loaded with soldiers joined the convoy. Two out of the last three truckloads headed for the village when the convoy had passed; the other remained at the roadblock. He checked the compound and located the bypassed truck.

He descended the mound and was heading back to Alina when his gut wrenched and an urge to return to the mound gripped him. He retraced his steps and once again looked through the rifle sight. Soldiers had dismounted from the truck at the roadblock and began heading towards him, but still a way off. A jeep with a mounted machine gun remained at the roadblock.

McNeill returned to Alina. 'We have to move now, quickly,' he whispered harshly.

'Move? Move to where?' she asked.

'Across to where that truck is. Take off your jumper and wrap the AK-47s in it – you carry both. We go into the marsh, into the water. Try to keep them dry. I will bring the rest. Quickly now, do as I say.'

McNeill hurriedly strapped the bags and M21 rifle to his back, lifted the baby and Dragunov in either hand and strode off deeper into the rushes. The moist earth soon gave way to mud, then cold water. Time was essential. McNeill knew they had to cross the marsh and be in position at the front of the disabled truck, so they could not be seen from the mound which he had recently left. McNeill figured that once the soldiers had found the bodies, they would look around, see and use the hills to communicate with the jeep and check the compound too.

The water was cold. Alina's teeth began to chatter now the water was just above her waist. She was alongside McNeill, who was now struggling, dragging his leg. The cold water was good for his leg but the footing underneath was uneven, and he winced with pain. 'Go ahead, move to the left of the compound and come round near the front of that truck, but not too close – there may still be a few soldiers in there,' he told her, and she moved on ahead.

The almost empty compound's edge where the trucks had been was raised above the ground by 4 to 6 feet, supported by stone – larger stone at the bottom with layers of smaller stone and shale on top. The solitary truck sat on the far side, the rear pointing to the marsh where McNeill was now wading, chest deep. Alina moved through the water with two AK-47s across the back of her neck, held there by each arm. She strode on purposefully and carefully. McNeill fell a little further behind. He began talking to himself in a low voice, trying to motivate himself to move faster. He looked at Alina, the water lapping at the tops of her shoulders, but still she kept going for a further five minutes, slowly striding out to make fewer ripples and less sound.

The water began to recede, but not the coldness. The water slipped down to waist height, then below her hips, and she encountered rushes again. She pushed slowly through, heading for a clearing at the water's edge. She was gasping and shaking with the cold. She came out of the water and onto the shore, walked up a few paces in a crouched position and sank to her knees, exhausted, putting the guns on the floor at her right side. A voice calmly told her to get up. She turned her head to see a pistol barrel, then a soldier. He beckoned with the pistol for her to get up. She stood, arms raised slightly above her head, her left hand clasped tight, her right hand clasped except for the raised forefinger, pointing skywards, her back to the marsh, her eyes shut in prayer.

The soldier flicked away his cigarette and moved towards her, saying, 'Take off those wet clothes.' He walked three paces and Alina heard a thump. The soldier lay dead at her side a few feet away, blood oozing out of his head. McNeill had shot him. Alina picked up the AK-47s and unwrapped them, holding hers at the ready, looking towards the compound. McNeill made the shore and came alongside her and put the now wet baby down beside her bent leg.

'You OK?' he asked.

'Fine – you answered my prayers,' came her reply.

'Keep watch,' said McNeill as he pulled the dead soldier into the deep rushes. Satisfied he would not come loose and float, he returned to Alina, who sat trying to soothe the crying baby.

'Take off your jumper and wring out as much water as you can. Do the same with your blouse and bra before you freeze to death, and dry the baby. I'm going to take a look to see if the rest of his comrades heard the shot or the cries of the baby,' McNeill ordered as he passed her by.

McNeill crouched low and went cautiously and carefully to the compound perimeter, rose up and looked in. He watched, then returned to a semi-naked Alina. He picked up her jumper and wrung out as much water as he could. 'Here, put this on and bring your blouse and bra: we move now.' Alina slipped the jumper on. They moved down the edge of the compound, both McNeill and Alina crouching low to stay out of sight. McNeill led the way. The soil underfoot had now changed to gravel, which crunched under McNeill's boots. He held out his left hand and Alina gave him his AK-47. Suddenly, he stopped. Alina stopped and heard voices, but they were too far away to decipher what was being said. McNeill pointed to the grass.

Alina entered the knee-high grass, and heard McNeill whisper, 'Find cover and get down.' They lay in the grass behind a small mound of earth, and not a moment too soon; from across the marsh and high on a hill a soldier began to shoot bullets into the sky in volleys. One shot may have been unrecognisable against the drone of the tanks leaving the village, but with volleys of gunfire crackling through the night sky it was impossible not to hear them. The men in the compound began shouting and running to the north-west side of the fence. McNeill whispered to Alina, 'Wait here.'

He left her and made his way to the compound's edge and slipped the barrel of the Dragunov through the diamond wire and peered through the sight. He began counting, one, two, three and two, is five...plus six legs visible from underneath the truck, making eight men. He made his way back to Alina. 'What's the fuss?' she asked.

'They have found the dead soldiers in the clearing. How is the baby and how are you?' he replied, taking the bullets from the Dragunov's magazine, and checking both AK-47s.

'I'm cold but fine and the baby is out of the wet towels and asleep,' she said.

'Good, leave her here. Give me a ten-minute head start – I am going off in a loop across the top to come around. Here is my little knife, called little helper. These jaws will cut that wire if you need to, as in some places it's just hanging free. The truck is almost dead ahead and the sides of the engine are off. Three soldiers are at the back. You come up from behind and remember: shoot to kill, no prisoners, and don't take any chances. Do I make myself clear? Your magazine is full.' Alina nodded, then he left carrying only his AK-47.

Although his leg ached, after being in the cold water for some time it did not feel as bad. He crouched low. Every once in a while he would stop, look and listen. He checked his watch: seven minutes had passed; he moved on.

<hr />

The minutes seemed like hours to Alina. She wrapped her baby up as warm as she could until fear gripped her and made her body shake. She would be leaving her daughter alone, except for a couple of bags and rifles for company. She would be going to kill, to murder, to take a life or lives. She steeled herself and came to terms with her conscience; killing was a means to their survival. She grabbed her AK-47 and watched the seconds tick to ten minutes past. She set off, moved to the gravel below the ground level of the compound, searched for where the diamond wire had become detached from the sparse tarmac and used McNeill's tool to cut a way underneath. She looked through the underneath of the truck's rear axle and saw bare legs, six in all, meaning three soldiers, as McNeill had said, and the engine was bare under the night sky.

Without making a sound she entered the compound, squatted then began to approach the truck. She breathed slowly, and bit her bottom lip as she exhaled. Her blood pumped rapidly through her veins. With each nervous step her adrenalin rose and so did the tension inside her. She could hear muffled voices; the closer to the truck, the clearer the voices became. She moved carefully, selecting every step to keep the gravel in silence. She was almost at the truck and the voices were goading and laughing. Alina moved away from the front of the truck and around the side and they came into view: men, some clothed, others half naked, waiting for their turn at three naked women they held spreadeagled on the floor. Alina filled with rage and opened fire. She sprayed bullets at the soldiers, who fell like pins in a bowling alley.

McNeill stood at the far side of the compound, AK at the ready. 'Damn it, I told her to wait!' Crouching, he made his way toward her from slightly off to her right.

Alina had not shot all the soldiers. Three men kneeling still held the women's arms over their heads, the women trying to wrestle free. 'Stand up!' Alina barked at the men. The men stood, 6 feet apart from each other, their trousers falling to their ankles as they did. 'Hands high so I can see them and turn round so I can't see your ugly faces,' she ordered. Two of the soldiers spun round and did as she ordered. The soldier in the centre just turned and then yelled, 'Why, bitch – you are just going to shoot anyway.' Then he turned his head to see if he could ascertain where her voice was coming from. As he moved his head his right hand began searching under his jacket, finding his pistol and removing it from its holster. The baby's cries broke Alina's concentration, she half turned in their direction giving the soldier the time and opportunity to turn.

McNeill squeezed the trigger of his AK-47, killing the three soldiers instantly. He ran to the dead soldiers and women. Pointing beside him he yelled 'Get here, NOW!' at Alina. The naked women pulled their legs together and pulled their knees up to their breasts, and shook. McNeill tossed some of their clothes back to them. 'Get dressed,' he said. The women thanked him for their clothes but had confused looks on their faces. Alina bent down on one knee, level with the women, and said to them, 'It's OK, please get dressed, it's all over, you are OK now.'

McNeill grabbed Alina's arm and pulled her to her feet. 'What the hell were you doing? I told you no chances, no prisoners. You could have been killed – lover boy there had his gun out. What the hell were you going to do with those three anyway? Invite them to dinner? Don't let these three women go yet either, and tell them to put the dead soldiers' jackets and trousers on just in case the shots were heard and someone comes looking. And you get out of those damp and wet clothes too! I'm off to get the baby.' And an angry McNeill strode off.

McNeill returned, carrying the crying baby, bags and rifles. Alina took the baby and removed the clothes she had wrapped her in. McNeill noticed Alina was wearing a skirt, given to her by one of the women, who were now grouped round Alina and her child. One of the women began to cry, then another began kicking the dead body of a soldier; the other went to the one crying and comforted her with a hug. The woman stopped kicking the dead soldier, came to Alina and took her baby. Alina turned round. McNeill was looking at the soldiers and in the truck.

What's he looking for? she asked herself and a frown grew on her forehead. She looked at the soldiers. Except for the one that McNeill had shot, none of them had a weapon. She had just murdered five unarmed men in a rage. Alina looked again at McNeill, who was now lying down under the truck, exchanging magazines onto his Dragunov rifle before looking through the telescopic sight. At intervals he checked his watch. *What the...? What is he expecting?* she thought. Then she realised – the shooting; he is expecting soldiers to come. Alina turned to see two of the women removing jackets and clothes from the dead soldiers and anything of value from the pockets. The third cooed at the baby.

Forty minutes passed before McNeill returned to Alina. He looked at the pile of clothes and saw a pair of trousers his size. Alina helped him take off his boots. McNeill exchanged trousers to the accompaniment of cat calls and wolf whistles. Alina blushed and gave him a shirt and vest, helping him out of the damp ones he wore. She kissed him lovingly and passionately to more wolf whistles. McNeill broke away. 'Food – these have to have food, ask the women,' he said. 'Ask the women to check the truck. They are wearing uniform and if anyone from the roadblock decides to have a look after all the bullets flying around then it will look normal.' Some of the fires had now burned out, the embers glowing only, but the one near the truck was still alight. The women returned with a large box and a bag, which they opened. Inside the box was a frying pan, milk, eggs, cheese, tea, bread and fruit. One woman had found water.

'Good, ask one of the women to cook, Alina, and you feed the baby. A feed for her and food for us all, we eat and eat quickly,' he said. Alina asked the women if they had eaten: no, was their reply. 'OK we share all the food that's left after I feed my baby.' The women stood round, then one grabbed the pan and poured milk into it; another went back to the truck, while the other began peeling oranges. Alina fed her baby while the women made omelettes and drank tea from metal mugs. McNeill watched the compound perimeter through the sight in-between eating. One of the women then gave him a packet of cigarettes which she had taken from one of the soldiers. They both smoked one. Another brought him a mug of tea. McNeill thanked them. The two women returned to Alina, where they were joined by the third. The women began to talk to Alina, turning their heads to glance at McNeill, then giggling. Alina smiled.

McNeill got up and joined them. He took Alina's AK-47 and spoke to her. 'Find out how many men are between here and the lake.' Alina watched as McNeill checked the magazine: empty. He checked the magazine on his own AK-47 and the Dragunov rifle. Then he went round the dead soldiers, searching for ammunition.

'Not a good rifle on them – only these four handguns,' said McNeill, tossing them at Alina's feet and shaking his head from side to side. Alina got up and went to him. 'What's the matter?' she asked.

'Not a single round for the Dragunov or the AKs between them, just those pistols,' stated McNeill.

'Are we out of ammunition? Surely my AK has enough bullets in it,' said Alina.

McNeill showed her the empty magazine. The happiness on

her face was immediately replaced with shock, horror and fear. 'If you had not shot those men I would be...' She tailed off. McNeill brought her to him, his arms surrounding her. 'Don't think about it,' he said to her softly. She raised her head and looked up at him. The realisation that she could now be dead or wounded numbed the muscles of her face. Her mouth was agape, her eyes trance-like, totally absorbed in the thought of what might have been. McNeill kissed her gently. She blinked as she returned to the reality of life and she responded to his kiss. Their lips parted to the sound of gentle wolf whistles from the women. McNeill and Alina went over to them.

McNeill spoke to Alina, who translated and asked the women about rifles and guns. 'The truck broke down. The soldiers with rifles went on the other trucks, and took guns out of that one. These are mechanics, mostly, who remained to fix it and go back to the roadblock. We were walking from the lakeside and when we got to the roadblock the three there forced us to go with them or they would shoot us. We had no choice, and you saw what they were doing.' One of the women pointed to Alina as she spoke. Another began to weep, before adding, 'Yes, when they had finished we were given to the rest. Thank you for saving us from more.'

McNeil, deep in thought, said to Alina, 'Ask how many men at the roadblock and if there are too many, can we get to the lake without those at the roadblock seeing us?'

Alina continued to translate: 'There are some men at the road-block; these were to be dropped back and then others were to take their place with us. The land to the lake is sloped away from the road.' One woman began to draw a map in the gravel and sand. 'The river here runs into the lake, but it narrows ahead to go under a small bridge. You cannot swim under as it gets very shallow on the far side as the river diverts into two sections. The roadblock is at the side of the bridge closest to the village, just before the road junction. There is another roadblock just before you enter the village which you cannot see from here.' The woman who had been silent now spoke. 'Our families are in the village. We have to return, but the men at the roadblock saw us and will recognise us. When they find these dead soldiers we will be sought out and shot. What do we do?' she pleaded with Alina.

'Tell me how to get to the lake. McNeill here will tell you what to do, and don't be afraid,' Alina said to the woman.

The woman, in her late twenties like the other two, began describing how on the far side of the bridge, furthest away from the roadblock, there was a lane which cut off from the road to the right. The lane was wide enough for one vehicle at a time and seemed to be cut out from the hillside on the left of the lake. It was invisible in parts from the roadblock and it was the route they always took as it was not much frequented by soldiers. From the roadblock soldiers could see the main route on the right-hand side of the bridge and a machine-gun post on the far side of the hill to the left of the main road. McNeill perked up. 'Go on, go on,' he urged. 'The machine-gun post is in front of a fuel dump, which is heavily guarded; but once in the lane you cannot be seen, and this lane leads to a small sandy beach where some of the menfolk who fish the lake leave their small boats, usually five or six. The boats are basic sailboats for one or two people.'

McNeill spoke to Alina. 'Where is the best place to cross the road at night?' She relayed this to the women.

'A searchlight is shone from out of the fuel dump and another on the right in the dump and they criss-cross. There is a curfew and anyone caught in the beams is shot. If you pass the little bridge below here,' she said, pointing, 'your passage to the lake is safer but until you reach here—' she pointed once again '—you can be seen from the roadblock, and they too have searchlights which they use. It's mostly short grass from bridge to lane and it offers very little protection and no hiding places.' The other two women nodded in agreement. She went on, 'Our husbands and children will be wondering where we are. There has been a massive amount of soldiers in our village of late and we would like to be safe in our homes; homes which we have to leave now.

So what are we going to do? Patrols are sent out and they shoot to kill.'

McNeill gave the women a pistol each, then turned to Alina and said, 'Tell them to get to their families and get the hell out of there as quickly as they can and don't wait till morning. They were seen by the men in the roadblock, and those three brought them up here and were alive. They will be interrogated, tortured and probably shot, and their families too. Victims of war, Alina. And we have a problem – for the women to get to the village they have to get past the roadblock. If they are seen trying to sneak by it, they will be shot. It may be best for them to walk to the roadblock crying and weeping and hope they let them through. Usually, if they are human they will. Their lives have been altered by what has happened here; to survive they must leave the village.'

Alina passed on what McNeill had said and then shivered. One of the women stood and gave Alina her brown coat and another gave her back her baby. The women changed out of the uniforms and back into their clothes then hugged her and thanked her and McNeill. McNeill turned to Alina. 'Pack up quickly, it's getting darker. If the women keep the roadblock occupied we may be able to cover the open ground between the bridge and the lane,' he said.

'If you are going to put their lives at risk by using them as a distraction, we should at least tell them,' Alina said.

'What if they get stopped and questioned and tell the soldiers on the roadblock what happened here to save their lives?' McNeill broke in. 'We don't know them; OK, you saved them from a terrible ordeal, but is that enough? How is the baby?'

Alina answered, 'The baby is fine.' She then thought for a while before saying, 'OK, I agree, we cannot take the chance and tell them.'

The three women left. Alina and McNeill could hear them talking and the gravel crunching beneath their feet as they walked. 'OK, come on. We follow the compound's edge, keeping low. When we get to the bottom the compound's edge levels with the earth around it and we have fifty to sixty perilous yards to that lane and we have to find it. It's dark enough now,' said McNeill.

The women made their way diagonally across the compound as Alina and McNeill slipped along the opposite side unseen. There was no fence around the compound so close to the road and, like the compound, the road was manmade, of stone built on more stone and gravel over the top to make it level. The forlorn broken-down truck was alone in the compound, hiding its news. The women made it to the road faster than McNeill had envisaged. McNeill, crouching, had rifles strapped onto his back, the baby in his left hand, an AK-47 in the other. Alina, also hunched over, had a bag and AK-47 strapped to her back, Beretta pistol in one hand and a Glock from one of the dead soldiers in the compound in the other when the searchlights came on.

McNeill froze. Alina froze. They were out in the open, stood where compound met field on the same level, equidistant from the small cutting and the bridge. McNeill dropped to one knee, adrenalin charged his blood, pumped in his veins. 'Shit!' he cursed. He waited with bated breath, frozen to the spot as he watched the searchlights, one from the roadblock and the other two from the fuel dump, criss-cross, just like the woman had described. McNeill watched to see if there was a sequence in the searchlights' movements. A terrified Alina joined him and saw the cold sweat on his face, saw the anxiety in his eyes. 'Stay out of the line of sight between the three women and that searchlight. Move when I move,' said McNeill sternly and quietly. Alina nodded.

McNeill passed the baby to Alina and took the Dragunov from his back. He exchanged the magazine from his AK-47 with the magazine on the Dragunov. 'How many bullets?' asked Alina tentatively. McNeill never answered, he just spread one hand. The searchlight from the roadblock found the women. 'Down! Down!' he ordered and they collapsed to the floor. Searchlight beams ran in front and behind them and located the three women from behind. 'OK, we wait, pray and hope God listens,' he said to Alina.

The women held up their hands and began crying, and walked to the roadblock. The other two beams from the fuel dump trailed off as the roadblock searchlight held them captive. The women walked towards it, as if they were hypnotised by it, drawn to it. One of the other two beams trailed round the compound, almost lighting up the truck, then returning to search the terrain nearer the fuel dump. Statue still, McNeill exhaled heavily, watched the other searchlight creep over the compound and then search the road back towards the roadblock. He watched and he counted, and waited. Suddenly he lurched from prone to hunched and began to half run. 'Keep up!' he urged Alina.

The women were at the roadblock, crying and swearing abuse at the soldiers, who just laughed. With a slight delay they were let through. McNeill was now at the roadside. He gestured to Alina to hurry. McNeill could see the searchlight returning over the compound. She fell to the ground at his side and watched the light beam slowly pass a few yards behind her. 'Phew, that was close,' she panted. She looked at McNeill then at the road-block and began to grab his arm. She was frantic in silent panic. McNeill looked behind at the roadblock. 'McNeill, if that search-light is turned onto us now we are sitting ducks,' she nervously said.

'Yeah, I know. I just hope the women put on a good show, and the soldiers keep that light on them whilst they head to the village a little longer,' he said.

The searchlight from the dump passed by on the far roadside and lit the road momentarily. McNeill grabbed Alina's arm, pulling her to her feet, and they ran across the road lit by the search-light moments earlier and down its far side on hardened earth to make less noise. Alina could hear McNeill counting as she ran alongside him, his bad leg keeping him labouring. Then he pushed her to the ground at his right and jumped on top of her. The searchlight had returned, passing on its journey, its rays almost lighting up their feet. Alina, petrified, looked at McNeill; McNeill anxiously looked back at the roadblock. Then he got up. It was a race against time with death awaiting the loser. 'Come on, one last push for the lane. We are going to make the lane, don't stop, don't wait, get into the lane, Alina.'

Alina set off running, hunched and clutching her baby to her. Her body ached, her arms ached, her legs wanted to surrender, but her heart drove her on. Alina ran into the lane first and then into a cutting where the lane had been etched from the hillside and hit the ditch side. McNeill followed; the searchlight from the roadblock followed. McNeill and Alina hit the floor, out of sight as it passed overhead. McNeill saw the searchlight from the fuel dump light the road. Exhausted, her lungs hurting, Alina asked, 'Are we… Are we…?' She could not finish. The night air hurt as she breathed in. '… safe?' she finally blurted out. McNeill, head back, chest heaving, forehead sweating, ashen-faced in pain from his left leg, replied, 'So far, so good.' He blew hard, regained some control of his breathing and added, 'We must get to the lake or near it and find somewhere to hide and sleep.'

They kept close to the ridge. Frequently the roadblock searchlight flicked at the ridge. McNeill had figured the roadblock searchlight to be haphazard, the only one without a set pattern; it went where the controller wanted it to go. He had noticed earlier the dump searchlight stayed to the road and the compound side of it; the other dump searchlight searched the top of the compound weakly and the terrain around the dump. He had calculated the positions of the dump searchlights in his mind before he set off. The only searchlight which may have located them was the roadblock searchlight and the women immobilised it long enough to reach the lane safely. The lane was cut out of the hillside, in parts 6 feet lower than the land above, but in general about 3 to 4 feet. Occasionally, the searchlight hit the ditch on the far side and lit it up, but McNeill and a smiling Alina didn't care; they knew if they kept to the nearside they could not be found by it. The only one with a semblance of a chance of spotting them was the dump searchlight which was now totally concentrated on the road and it sporadically lit the hillside which ran down to it further up the road from the lane to the dump.

Alina and McNeill kept moving. The lane appeared to be manmade, dug out from the earth, and what soil and sand had been removed dumped on the edge. The lane was a good 12 feet wide in places. In some areas the removed soil and sand had been levelled out. McNeill and Alina remained crouched until the lane sank to its lowest. Here, the pair stood upright. McNeill's back ached, his leg ached. He placed both hands onto the small of his back, pressed his shoulders back, pushed his stomach out, breathed out and took three deep breaths, his head tilted slightly backwards. Alina joined him. Her baby awoke in the cool night air and they both smiled at him. McNeill looked at the baby and smiled back. It was as if the baby knew. It punched the air in front with its arms and kicked with its legs and murmured happily. Alina looked from the baby to McNeill. McNeill looked at Alina. They kissed, then McNeill swung his left arm across her shoulders and Alina slipped her right arm around his waist and they walked on. Alina looked at McNeill and then broke the silence. 'What will they do now, the soldiers in the village?' she asked.

'Depends. It looked like they were pulling out to lay siege for a few days but if they are taking heavy losses at the town, parts of the army will be back sooner and will make ready for retreat, which means fewer patrols. However, stalemate and or progress means the army stays and pushes for the town, so there may be two night patrols before a dawn patrol. Rest assured, they will patrol the lake to the dump to the road and go back through the roadblock. The soldiers will have some kind of signal to the searchlight operators, so they don't get shot at. I don't know what their signal would be.

'Now, it seems a lot of men went with that convoy, so patrols may be less often, or have fewer men in them. Regardless, I only hope that they find the dead men in the compound tomorrow, the later the better. As soon as they find them they will realise their lines have been breached. Their prime concern will be the fuel dump, but the more men they send out looking the more danger we and those women are in of being detected. If the women are caught, they will be tortured and they will talk and then be shot, but the Serbs will know to look for a woman, a baby and an American soldier. They will know where we are going – we asked about this lane and the lake and they will concentrate their search around it. Hopefully, we will be gone before they start searching. The quieter it is now, the better it is for us. The noisier, the chances are that the men in the compound have been found. Let's hope for a quiet rest of the night,' McNeill said.

They continued on, crouching low as the lane turned to the right then slightly left and another slight left followed. The night was becoming darker; helpful to both Alina and McNeill. The cutting of the lane reduced to 2 feet in places and they had to crawl: McNeill was leaving nothing to chance. They both smelt the moist night air, the fresh air, the moistness giving a revitalising chill of tasting freedom. The lane turned to the left, and they swapped over the sides they walked.

Fifteen minutes further on they found sand underfoot, and soon they moved through an opening onto a small, sandy beach. Alina sank to her knees. McNeill moved to his right. He felt the sand getting sloppier and heavier. The beach was disappearing into marsh. He stopped and looked; marsh in front, lake to the left, road and sand dunes to his right. Also on his right in the distance the searchlight beam cut the night sky. He watched and followed the beam. By watching the beam he knew his exact position in relation to the fuel dump, the roadblock and the village. All he needed now was to find somewhere to sleep and to locate a boat. He looked round. What was that? Then he saw it: a light, small at first, but then a sweep of a beam flicking at the night air, coming from near the roadblock and moving out into the lake. He ran to Alina, dragging her to her feet. 'Come on, we have to hide, and hide in the marsh,' he commanded.

An exhausted Alina replied, 'Why? What is it?'

'A lake patrol boat, who may drop men here to patrol back to the roadblock via the lane, as they know it is only partially visible to the searchlights. It's the only way of patrolling it. Stay low,' he said as they made their way into the middle of the marsh.

The searchlight flicked over the rushes. The motor on a boat became audible, and voices filtered through. McNeill removed his guns and covered them with sand, leaving a stick as a marker, and said to Alina, 'Break a rush; if you need to sink underwater, put the rush in your mouth, leave the tip above the water's surface and breathe in and out slowly through it. Give me the baby.'

'Can we not just shoot up the boat and make a run for it?' Alina enquired.

'Gunshots will be heard from miles away in the still of night and besides, which direction would we go, and what if there are more boats ahead combing the lake? No, it's better to hide,' McNeill explained as they sank into the marsh.

McNeill wrapped the baby and waded in. Deep into the marsh he stopped and placed her above the water level on a small bed of rushes. An unusual nest, he thought, as he covered her with more rushes. He prayed that she would stay asleep and moved away. He heard the voices before the searchlight scanned the rushes. McNeill sank into the water and let it lap at his chin. The light passed overhead. The engine roared and then slowed. He heard splashes and shouts – soldiers were alighting from the boat.

He looked at Alina, over to his left and not in such deep water. She had thickset rushes between her and the shore and was crouching in the water and she could see the silhouette of the soldiers against the night sky. McNeill noticed the water only came to her waist. McNeill began to worry. Firstly, he thought she was in too shallow water. He began to move towards her slowly. Suddenly, he stopped and slipped underneath the water line, put the rush pipe in his mouth and let it through the surface. Two members of the patrol had split from the main group; the boat's searchlight was illuminating them. Alina watched McNeill slip below the surface, and slipped down onto her back and let the rush pipe up through the water. The two soldiers walked to the marsh edge in line with Alina a few yards away, separated by bulrushes. They stopped, relieved themselves, turned and rejoined the patrol.

She lifted her head above water slowly without letting her hair out of the water and let the water drain off her face without a sound. She looked over to McNeill and watched the searchlight pass tamely over his head. She could see him, one finger over his mouth, the left forefinger telling her which way the patrol was going – around behind her and back down the lane. Then the palm of his hand motioned downwards. She slipped below the surface of the water and began breathing through the rush pipe. The boat's engines revived. McNeill could see the boat, see the searchlight directly on the patrol as it made its way down the lane. Then the searchlight scanned the marsh before the engine roared to life and the boat sped off into the lake.

McNeill waited, then surfaced and waded to collect the baby. Alina surfaced and waited. McNeill passed her the baby girl, waded to shore and dug up the rifles. Alina joined him. 'Whatever next?' she asked.

'It may be safer in the dunes. The boat circled and went up the lake, so it will come back. Where did you hide the bags?'

'I wrapped them in my coat and buried them. What about the patrol, McNeill?' she enquired.

Smoothing back the sand he replied, 'Probably will make its way to the village.'

Alina dug up the bags and coat and smoothed the sand and they headed deep into the dunes. The water dripped from their wet clothes. 'OK, let's get out of these wet clothes and wring as much water out as we can,' he said.

Alina put the baby down on the sand, wrapped in her coat, slipped off her jumper and began to wring it out. She watched McNeill take off his shirt. She made her way over to him and the palm of her right hand found his chest. She flicked her wet hair to the side and provocatively her mouth opened slightly as she craned her neck upwards, her hand moving from his chest to the back of his neck, pulling his head gently towards hers. Their mouths met gently at first, encouraging each other's lips, her left arm moving under his right arm, her left hand gently resting on the skin on his back. He began to caress her neck with his mouth, kissing it, then reaching her ear he toyed with its lobe with his tongue before kissing her neck and returning to her mouth. Her tongue flicked inside his mouth and began to explore. Her mouth was pressing firmly against his and she began to invite his tongue to dance with hers.

His hands slipped down her back, one finger finding its way down the length of her spine. He undid her skirt and pushed it slowly down over her hips, gently moving his midriff away from hers, allowing the skirt to fall to the floor. He felt her bottom and squeezed it, his lips never leaving hers, his heart and mind wanting her. Her lips parted from his. He kissed her neck and she moaned delightfully. She wanted him with all her being. She undid his belt and his trousers, then slipped her right hand inside the zip, feeling his manhood. It was McNeill's turn to moan as she gently squeezed. He kissed her forehead and undid her bra, sliding the straps down her shoulders. Her mouth once again found his as the straps fell down her arms. With both her hands inside his trousers, she slipped them over his hips and her bra and his trousers fell to the ground. She put her hands inside his shorts as she began to kiss his chest, then ribs as she slid the shorts down his thighs. Once past his knees she let them drop.

McNeill slowly bent down. Their mouths found each other's. His left hand located her right breast, cupped it and squeezed it gently, in tune to her right hand squeezing and rubbing between his legs. His mouth left hers and began exploring her right breast, his tongue toying with the nipple, his teeth gently biting as his tongue flicked across it. Alina's right hand was now holding the back of his head as she moaned with delight and pleasure; her nipple was so erect it ached. His hands began to explore her thighs, rubbing, caressing, tickling, feeling her moisten. She wanted him inside her, wanted her arms around him and his around her. She sank to the ground, dragging him with her. He kissed her and rolled onto his back. Without hesitation she mounted him, felt him deep inside her. She moaned in ecstatic pleasure as they made love.

McNeill just held her in the afterglow, gently caressing her head, letting her hair slip through his fingers, their legs entwined. Occasionally, he would kiss her forehead and she his chest. Then she lifted her head from his chest, turned it to him and looking deep into his eyes said the words, 'I love you, McNeill.' McNeill kissed her gently and replied, 'I love you too, Alina.' She flung her arms around him. He squeezed her tight with his and they held each other without speaking, wallowing in the closeness.

McNeill broke the silence. 'We should get out of here. I need to keep watch on that boat especially and any patrols which may be out. We don't want to get caught with our pants down, now do we?' Alina chuckled. McNeill smiled and began wringing the water out of their clothes before dressing.

They moved further up the dunes, arm in arm in carefree fashion, McNeill carrying the extra burden of her wet clothes by his side, always keeping sight of the lake shore. 'I wonder where this pathway we have stumbled upon ends, Alina?' he said.

'The border, I hope,' she replied, snuggling into the coat. Small dunes were now on either side, but the lakeside ones began to reduce in size and eventually stopped. Once again sand met gravel as they hit a dirt track which widened and ran on ahead, turning left between high dunes. They followed the track and came to a small junction. Turning right they followed the track which led them to a beach. McNeill went ahead. There were six boats scattered in a semicircle around the entrance; two on his left side, four on his right. *OK, so this is where the patrol boat ran to before going back,* he thought as he began checking the small boats. Alina began to shiver. Under her coat she wore only her bra and knickers. McNeill beckoned her to him.

Alina bent down at McNeill's side and put the baby between her legs. They were near to the first boat on the left. McNeill gave Alina her damp skirt and jumper, which she put on and began to feed her baby. The first boat was a small fishing dinghy 24 foot in length, attached to a large outboard motor with very little diesel in its tank. He knew this craft was too far up the shore for him alone to push it to the water. It probably required four men to get it into the water and as it wasn't tied down he assumed the water did not rise high enough or come close enough for it to float. The next one was covered at the front, not as big as the first and had nets and oars in, and no outboard motor, but it was located quite close to the water's edge. He looked under a timber seat which linked both sides and found what at first felt like a wool rag. He opened it up to find a woollen jumper. He returned to Alina and gave it to her, and began looking in more detail at the last four.

The one nearest the lake was much the same as the first: same size, outboard motor on the inside under a wrap, no fuel, but with nets, pots and buoys attached to the outside. Again, he surmised that four people would have to push this into the water. 'Maybe the fishermen all turn up at the same time and help each other,' he thought out loud. His mind raced as he looked closer. 'Only thing is, they don't look like they have been in the water for some time,' he continued and he searched two more, found ropes on one, nets, another jumper, oars in both under full covers. The furthest away from the shore and a little detached had more of its hull showing as McNeill approached it from the lake. It too was covered with tarpaulin. It wasn't quite dilapidated but it was worse for wear. The boat was shorter than the largest two but a little longer and slimmer than the other three and with being upturned slightly deflected the breeze from the lake over it. McNeill returned to Alina and gave her the jumper.

She pulled the jumper over the one he had given her earlier. McNeill spoke. 'Are you and the baby OK?'

Alina replied, 'Baby's fine. I'm tired, cold and hungry, but I will be fine.' She shivered.

'OK, we sleep there,' he said, pointing to the dilapidated boat.

'There? Why not that one? The one you have chosen looks a wreck,' she said.

'Then we sleep in the wreck,' McNeill said assertively.

'Anything you say – but just you wait till we cross this lake, I will then determine where we sleep,' she said, wagging her right index finger, before picking up the baby and grabbing him by the hand, heading off to the wreck. McNeill loosened the tarpaulin cover enough for Alina to put the baby in the boat towards the bow. She took off her wet skirt, lay down her coat and climbed in. McNeill fastened the tarpaulin to cover them, and began wringing her damp clothes by hand. He removed as much of the water as he could. He carried them to the next boat down towards the lake, dropping her jumper, and hung them on the boat's lane side. He lay down the rifles and began to undress, wringing out the water from his own clothes.

All the while, unknown to McNeill, Alina watched him. A now naked McNeill was hanging his clothes on the boat's lane side out of view from the lake when Alina undid the tie of the tarpaulin and got out, went and collected her jumper and tiptoed behind McNeill. McNeill sensed her behind him, turned and took her into his arms and lifted her up. They kissed each other passionately before making love once again under a night sky. Then he just held her.

He was stroking her hair when he saw it, unmistakeable as it flicked over the dunes. He was totally naked, lying on his back; she wore briefs and a jumper. There was no time, no time to reach the boat where the baby and pistols lay and the Dragunov had five bullets in total loaded. The searchlight of a boat began to meander slowly from boat to boat, the engine cut. The searchlight lit up the tarpaulin on the boat where Alina had been lying and the baby lay. 'The baby,' they both whispered in unison. Alina's head sank into McNeill's chest and she prayed, hard.

McNeill held the back of her head, closed his eyes and whispered, 'God, please don't let her waken and cry.' Then he opened his eyes. The searchlight beam was now on the boat which they lay behind. Alina shook and shuddered in his arms. The beam left the boat and focussed on the others one by one, and made a sweep of the sand in-between; the engine gunned into life and the patrol boat left.

McNeill exhaled first, Alina followed. 'Jesus, thank you, but that was close, McNeill,' said a relieved Alina as she again rested her head on his chest. 'Too close. Thank God you collected your jumper. Now go get some sleep and don't distract me anymore. I will keep watch,' he said.

'Why, don't you like my distractions?' Alina said cheekily.

'Like them? I love them,' he replied, smiling. McNeill got dressed, removed Alina's clothes from the boat's side, collected the rifles and went to the boat which hid the baby. He helped Alina climb in and gave her clothes to her, saying, 'These will dry in here.' He laid the rifles at Alina's side, except for the Dragunov. He fastened the tarpaulin loosely and asked, 'How is the baby?' adding, 'I'm going for a look, be back shortly. Do not leave this wreck.' Alina replied, 'Baby's fine, absolutely fine, bless her. Be careful. I love you.' McNeill strode off into the night.

Alina soon realised she was alone, except for her baby. Alone, without sight of McNeill for the first time in a long time. She had grown accustomed to him always being there. She liked the safety and security she felt when she was around him, loved his reliability, loved the joy in his eyes when he looked at her, loved the joy in his eyes when he looked at her baby. And he was so gentle for a solid, muscly guy, so gentle and sincere. They had come a long way from the day he saved her in the tunnel when she would rather have died. Now she wanted life, desired it, willed it – a life with McNeill and her baby. She loved him wholeheartedly and hated being parted from him, but she knew he had gone to check that the patrol did not come in their direction and she knew he was looking out for their safety.

She rested her head but did not sleep. The length of time he had been gone seemed an age. It seemed time was travelling in reverse. She began to worry. Worry led to being agitated. The thoughts in her mind began to race, conjuring worst case scenarios. She wondered if she should go and look for him. She turned, restless in the boat. *Where is he? I hope he is not in trouble. Why is it taking so long? What is he doing – has he been shot? Is he dead or wounded? Has he been captured?* She realised she was thinking irrationally. 'Stop this, stop this, and think clearly,' she said to herself. 'God, I love him so much!' she exclaimed in realisation. She controlled herself. Breathing became easier and she began assessing. *I haven't heard any shots. As he said, sound travels further at night-time – how ridiculous is that? It travels no further, it just has much less accompanying sound to drown it out. He is careful, he will not give away his or our position; in fact, he would lead them away from here.* 'Oh my God! Oh my God!' she whispered, as she began to fumble at the knot on the tarpaulin tie put there earlier by McNeill. 'You have to be OK, you have to be alive; you cannot run out on me now!' she said to herself. She freed the tarpaulin and began to climb out.

'Hey, where the hell do you think you are going?' came a low voice. Alina turned and saw McNeill coming towards her. He got to within a yard of her. The prodded finger was accompanied by a voice slowly discharged from between clenched teeth: 'Where the hell am I going?! Where the hell have you been?' The prod of her finger gained in intensity. 'Steady on, steady on, Alina, that hurts,' McNeill said, grabbing her index finger and pulling her to him. She just folded into his arms and kissed him. 'Glad to see me, then,' he whispered. She nodded her agreement. 'I love you too, now into the boat.' They got into the boat. She demanded to know what he had seen. 'Say something, tell me, McNeill.'

'OK, the patrol does not come up this far – it checks the dunes as far as that half cutting about fifty yards away. From there they can see all the boats clearly except this one, just the end piece of the hull. They then turn and head back along the lane. The patrol boat did not come up, it just headed back. Sorry I took so long,' he said. Alina thought and then spoke. 'Boat, then patrol. What next – boat?' she asked.

'I'm not sure – remember, we were in the water. It could be boat twice, patrol twice, but I think you may be right. However, we should have a couple of hours of nothing. Get some sleep, and no distractions, please,' replied McNeill. Alina laughed contentedly and she laid her head on McNeill's shoulder. Sleep overtook her. McNeill lay awake and checked his watch, remembering the times of the patrols. He resigned himself to two hours' sleep, and he closed his eyes.

$$\Longrightarrow\!\!\!\bullet\!\!\!\Longleftarrow$$

The cries of her baby woke Alina. She reached up and brought the baby to her and fed her. She looked at McNeill, who was deep in sleep. The heat generated by their bodies under the tarpaulin had dried the clothes. After feeding her baby and watching her fall contentedly back to slumber she opened the tarpaulin and let some of the heat out and the cold early morning air in. She carefully poked her head out and looked outside. She got out, bringing her clothes with her: a mist had fallen, blanketing the lake, and it was still quite dark. She looked at the baby now beside McNeill as she tied the tarpaulin down. She walked northwards and barefoot along the lake shore, her skirt flowing. She walked into the water and felt the cool water around her ankles. She bent down and began to scoop the refreshing water onto her face.

Alina was splashing water onto her face and gently rubbing her skin and daydreaming when she heard it. McNeill never heard it; the baby never heard it – the clang of metal on metal. A truck had reversed almost to the edge of the gravel. Orders were being shouted; people were alighting from the rear of the truck and being ushered onto the beach. The commotion snapped Alina back to reality. A jeep screeching to a halt behind the truck woke McNeill, voices outside stunned him. He felt at his side for Alina and felt her baby. His eyes blurred into vision. *Where the hell is she?* was the first thought which ran through his mind. He moved quietly and silently to where she had lain, felt for the Dragunov rifle and found it; he began disconnecting the sight. He placed the sight to a small hole in the tarpaulin cover above the wood frame of the boat and looked through.

He saw a group of people being forced to the lake shore at gunpoint. He counted twenty at least, old men but mostly women, both young and old, and four young children. He searched for Alina amongst them. A wave of relief swept over him, seeing she wasn't there, but concern grew when he could not see her. Frustrated by the restricted vision, he resigned himself to checking the soldiers. They were heavily armed, all with machine guns. He counted six on his side and two on the other, and wondered how many more. Knowing he could not kill all of these soldiers his thoughts strayed to Alina. *Where the hell is she?* was his repeated thought. He watched as the group were forced into the lake and made to get down on their knees in the shallow water.

The soldiers aimed their guns, the women held their offspring close. 'Stop!' yelled a deep booming voice. 'Don't waste bullets.'

Alina had heard the voices. She turned and looked through the mist and saw the people getting off the truck at gunpoint. She stopped washing herself, collected her jumper from behind her, put it on and entered the water. The mist dissipated intermittently and she could see the backs of the soldiers. She waded carefully but quickly out into the water. Her pulse raced as the shallowness at the lake edge seemed to be eternal, but soon the water depth increased rapidly and she let out a controlled sigh of relief. From a distance she looked at the men, women and children on their knees in the lake as the water lapped at her nose. Her thoughts raced to McNeill and her baby. She felt helpless, isolated and alone, even though she could faintly see the boat containing them. Clouds of mist descended across the lake to obscure her vision.

The soldiers began looking into the four boats on the other side, some sweeping the covers back and looking underneath, then shooting holes in the hulls, laughing as they did so. Tears ran down Alina's face in silent fear for her impending loss.

McNeill watched the soldiers on the opposite side, saw them toss the nets and ropes out of the boat nearest the lake, watched as they peppered the hull with bullets. He withdrew the sight and picked up the pistols.

Through a break in the mist, Alina saw what was happening. Anguish and apprehension etched itself onto her face; she wanted to scream but could not. She covered her mouth and felt nausea in the pit of her stomach. The people in the lake began to sing. The owner of the low booming voice came into view, a huge, burly, man mountain of a soldier, shouting at his men. 'Stop playing games with the boats and guard!' he ordered and he entered the lake.

Alina watched in horror, retching at the sight, her empty stomach surrendering nothing. The burly soldier stood behind an old man, raised his right hand above his head fully and brought a lump hammer crashing down onto the old man's skull, sending the old man forward into the water and oblivion. He did the same to the next, a young, beautiful blonde woman, who fell head first, dead before she hit the water.

Two soldiers sat on the boat in front of McNeill, tossed the cover, sat down and began to smoke cigarettes, watching their commander in the lake. Alina looked on. She sobbed, she retched; her tears met the water of the lake. More of the people met their deaths but still they sang a lullaby. McNeill looked on in disgust, horrified by it all, till a fire of hatred and anger welled in his stomach. His face set, granite-like, his eyes burned with malice.

The two soldiers finished their cigarettes, walked round the boat and with their backs to McNeill began laughing as they shot holes into the hull. Still laughing, they began the walk towards the wreck housing McNeill and the baby. The baby stirred and made a small cackling sound. McNeill placed the pistol onto the floor at his knees and with his left hand scooped up the baby, brought her to his chest and covered her mouth with his hand and held her tight. His right hand held his Beretta, aimed at the two soldiers. He heard shouting and alarm gripped him. He steeled and steadied himself, ready to fight and to meet his maker.

Alina watched as the burly soldier stopped clubbing. She saw what he was looking at. Panic and dread made her body shake uncontrollably below the water. Terror and horror cemented on her face at the fear of losing her baby and seeing the man she loved shot dead. She wanted to scream, but her voice did not answer her brain's command and she just watched, sobbing in petrified silence.

The burly soldier, hands on hips, was bellowing furiously at the two soldiers walking, getting ever closer to finding McNeill.

McNeill could almost smell them; he envisaged their faces, played the scene over in his mind. *They open the tarpaulin and pull it back and that's the last thing they will do before they depart this life.* Then he would toss the baby out of his hand and shoot his pistols till he could shoot no more. In his mind's eye he could see bullets ripping into him, spinning him, blood oozing from the holes, then falling dead. Alina was crying silent tears; the soldiers were approaching the boat. McNeill stilled and clutched the baby tighter, making sure she could make no sound. His heart pounded in his chest as he gritted his teeth, finger poised on the Beretta trigger. More shouts, but this time from below his feet, yards away.

A terrified Alina watched on through the mist. The soldiers were so close to the boat she thought they could taste what lay inside. Her eyes moved to the burly figure in the water gesticulating with both hands. She saw some of the people still kneeling in the shallow water, still singing the lullaby, others prone. She looked on, her eyes transfixed on the boat containing McNeill and her baby and prayed for their salvation.

The two soldiers were only a few feet away and laughing.

McNeill felt the sinews in his face tighten as he gritted his teeth and set his jaw. More shouts came from the direction below his feet. McNeill knew the two soldiers were very close, and he knew his position was desperate. He waited, baby clutched to his chest, Beretta held firm and poised by a death grip in his right hand. He inhaled and waited for the tarpaulin to fly back, waited for that moment to silence their laughter, waited to still the voice below his feet, waited for the bullets to come to end him. The voice below his feet shouted at the two soldiers. One of the soldiers shouted back. The voice that returned was stern and commanding. The soldier stopped, his compatriot stopped. McNeill held his breath. Alina prayed and held hers. The soldiers turned away. Alina could not believe what she was seeing. She closed her eyes tight, then opened them. The soldiers were making their way away from the wreck back to the lake shore. She looked and saw a mounted machine gun on the jeep swivel and point into the water. The burly soldier resumed his clubbing.

The mist was beginning to lift. McNeill waited, motionless, eyes transfixed on the tarpaulin, which remained covering him. He waited, listened, let minutes pass until he realised the soldiers were walking away. He peered through the hole in the tarpaulin, taking care not to disturb it, straining his eyes to see out, to see what was happening outside. His ears strained as he heard soldiers muttering; he could not understand their language anyway. He waited, steeled and ready.

Alina saw them: two soldiers detached from the others and walked beyond the four boats in the direction of where she had entered the lake. She remembered what McNeill had told her, what now seemed an eternity ago: 'If you can see them, they can see you.' She watched the lump hammer descend for the last time on the skull of a young girl and she took a deep breath and slipped under the water, holding her nose between finger and thumb.

The soldiers looked out across the lake, the mist clearing. Alina held her breath. She waited, counting. Her lungs began to burn.

They wanted to burst, but she waited, telling herself just a few seconds more. She waited till she could hold her breath no more, threw her head back under the water, held her hair and slowly penetrated the surface with her nose and forehead, breathed out and in and sank below again. She repeated the procedure five more times. Once more she broke the surface, only this time she opened her eyes. The cold water that lapped into them stung them. She again breathed deeply. The water in her ears muffled the sound, but she was sure she had heard it – the phut-phut of an outboard engine.

She raised her head and let the lake lap her nose and below her ears once again. Her eyes focussed on the two soldiers now walking back to the others. She saw the burly soldier, arm aloft, holding his lump hammer like a trophy. She heard it again, the phut-phut, louder now, off to her left, but the mist had not lifted enough and it was cloaking the boat, keeping it secret from her sight. She heard loud shouts and saw the soldiers on the lake shore wave, heard the phut-phut become a continual loud purr. She took a deep breath, squeezed her nose tight between thumb and forefinger of her left hand and, clutching the hair to her head with the palm of her right hand sank to her knees in the water and prayed.

She felt a small force on her back, gentle but firm, heard the muffled drone in her water-filled ears. She waited and steadied herself against the force of the water pushes, waited for the pushes made by the boat's outboard motor propeller to dissolve. Her lungs once again were on fire, the air in them burned. The pushes ceased. She rose up, half turning in the direction of the patrol boat as she did so, stopping with the top of her head breaking the surface, then her nose. Tilting her head backwards to allow her mouth out of the water she exhaled and gasped for air. She brought her head up, her mouth slipping below the water once again; her lungs ached as she watched through the breaks in the mist the rear of the patrol boat slipping away. She spun round and looked at the wreck hiding McNeill and her baby.

McNeill lay in the boat, waiting. He heard the tones of cheery voices and laughter, the voices speaking a language foreign to him. Still, he waited. He heard the clanging of metal on metal, listened as the jeep engine sprung to life to be drowned out by the whirring of the truck engine. He strained his ears, listened attentively as the truck engine revved, his body and mind taut, still expecting the tarpaulin to lift.

Alina watched the soldiers get into the rear of the truck, saw the plumes of exhaust fumes as the truck burst to life, watched as it drew forward, stopped, reversed a little and sped off.

McNeill heard the truck stop, the whoosh of the air-brakes, the grating as the driver forced it into gear, heard it speed off. He relaxed, exhaled and lay back and in doing so released his hand from the baby. No sound! 'Oh my God, the child,' he muttered. He shook the baby girl gently; no sound or movement came from her. He shook a little firmer; still no sound or movement. Panicking, he put the baby down beside him and rolled over to her, pinched her tiny nose, placed his mouth to hers and gently blew, released and pressed her little chest gently but firmly with the fingers of his right hand to the rhythm of the count: one, one thousand; two, one thousand; three, one thousand; until he made fifteen. He stopped and waited: nothing. He pursed his lips to hers and repeated the sequence. He watched. Was that her hand that moved or was he seeing things? He put his ear to her tiny chest, heard a faint heartbeat. *She is alive, she is alive,* sped through his mind. McNeill lifted his head from her chest and the baby gave a little cough and burst into tears. He held her and kissed her. His own tears rolled down his face as he lay on his back with the baby on his chest.

Alina waded towards shore. Her apprehension for the safety of McNeill and her baby, combined with the dismay and disgust at what she had just witnessed, made her immune to the cold of the water. Reaching the shallow water she began to run to shore, then up through the hard and soft sand to the wreck.

McNeill heard her shouting, yelling his name. 'I'm OK, Alina, she's alive,' he replied as he began to untie the tarpaulin. Suddenly he stopped, held the crying baby, lay down and picked up his Beretta, the soldier in him thinking it was a trick.

Alina reached the boat, yelling, 'McNeill, my baby, McNeill!' She ripped the tarpaulin free. Light came into the dark for McNeill. Alina sank to her knees. 'Thank God,' she said, her tears flowing. McNeill relaxed the grip on the pistol and gave Alina her baby. She clutched her baby to her wet bosom. Water from her hair mingled with the baby's tears. McNeill got out of the boat, knelt in front of Alina and held them both. She looked up at him and kissed him passionately.

The mist began to recede into the lake. 'Help me pull this boat into the water, Alina. The others have holes shot in them,' McNeill asked.

'But McNeill, this looks like its best days are behind it,' she replied.

'I will take my chances with it, rather than stay here all day and end up like those poor people,' said McNeill emphatically. He went on, 'Tie back the tarpaulin, throw out what's not needed – those old pots and nets, anything to make it lighter – then let's roll it onto its hull. Put the baby in the stern, we can use that rope over there and the oars. We tie the rope to the front, I pull, you push.'

McNeill collected the rope and tied it to the bow. McNeill then went to the boat's side and heaved while Alina shoved. Every muscle in their arms and legs strained as they righted the boat onto its keel. McNeill took up the rope, wrapped it around his body like a tug-of-war anchor man and pulled; the boat began to edge through the soft sand. Alina pushed: inch by inch, foot by foot, yard by aching yard.

McNeill's injured leg burned and started to leak blood. His muscles bulged, sweat showered out of his body, tendons and ligaments taut, almost at snapping point: still, he pulled. 'Push, Alina, push. We don't want to be here if that truck gets back with more victims. Push,' McNeill said in-between huge gasps for air. Alina did not need any encouragement – she pushed for all she was worth. The veins in McNeill's head swelled, his calves ached; his arms had locked in position and ached, his whole being ached. His heart pumped fast, ready to burst at any moment, but the sand underfoot was getting firmer and the pulling became easier.

Alina stopped pushing, ran and collected two oars and put them in the boat and resumed pushing. Her baby cried. Progress over the soft sand had been slow, but it was much better on the firmer sand. McNeill's body cried 'Stop!', but he dug in and pulled, keeping the boat moving, not wanting to stop and have the strenuous effort of getting it to move again. Blood trickled down his leg.

The sand became wet and water began to lick his boots. He stood, motionless, caught in a void. 'Pull, damn you!' screamed Alina; but McNeill could not move an inch. He stood, statue-like, looking at the blood-red water lapping at his ankles. He surveyed the still, lifeless bodies floating in the lake, arms outstretched, some gazing skyward through eyes that saw nothing, others face down in the red water, drifting aimlessly. His eyes rested on a young boy of around ten years of age, his skull mangled on one side of his head, disfiguring his face. McNeill retched. Alina came to his side, saw the horrific sight and threw up.

Alina throwing up seemed to act like the clicking of fingers that ends a hypnotic trance. McNeill picked up the strain on the rope and began pulling, pulling the boat through the gaps in the water of the lifeless bodies. The baby still cried, yelled at the top of her voice. Alina cried tears of sorrow as she pushed on. The water began to turn blue and the boat began to float. 'Jump in, Alina!' he shouted as he kept pulling.

Alina jumped in, took up her baby and started to breastfeed, all the while looking back at the dead in the water, replaying in her mind how they were bludgeoned to death. She replayed the scene of the old man on his knees in the water singing, the burly man mountain standing behind him, hammer raised in his outstretched right arm high over the old man's right shoulder, then 'Bang!', onto the side of the old man's head in one movement, toppling the old man over, depositing him face down in the water. She saw in her mind's eye the beautiful blonde lady, the little girl next, and the rest of the people singing the lullaby before death. She shivered. 'Oars!' shouted McNeill, just before the body of a boy no more than twelve years old drifted past, face down. McNeill closed his eyes, crossed himself, bowed his head in a token of respect and hoisted himself into the boat. Alina was mesmerised by grief. 'Alina, snap out of it!' he barked. Alina shook. 'Pass me the oars!' he demanded. Alina slid them down the boat. 'I will row, you keep watch through the rifle sight, all round. We head into the mist,' he added assertively.

The boat was a good 14 feet long, made of timber, about 5 to 6 feet wide at the centre, with two half-cup pieces of metal attached to its sides which McNeill put the oars on and began to row, striking a rhythm quite quickly with his feet jammed against the seat in front of him. His broad back rocked forward and backwards; the pain in his injured leg worsened and blood seemed to ooze from it with every stroke but the boat began to glide through the water.

Alina saw it as she turned from stern to bow – the redness of McNeill's trousers at his thigh and the trickle of blood over his boot. 'Your leg – it's bleeding again,' she cried woefully.

'Can't stop now,' came the matter-of-fact reply as the mist engulfed them.

'Sshh, be quiet, shush, stop rowing,' she demanded. McNeill stopped, and there it was – the unmistakeable phut-phut of an outboard motor. 'The patrol!' she said, fear in her voice.

'Get the handguns,' said McNeill, his mind beginning to focus.

'This Beretta has been in the water,' she said as she removed it from the belt of her skirt at her back.

'OK, take the one there. Pass me yours, and I will keep the Glock,' he said pointing at his Beretta. Alina exchanged pistols.

McNeill quickly dismantled the Beretta, wiped it dry and reassembled it. 'Keep low,' he said, his voice hushed. The phut-phut of the outboard motor became clearer, louder, but the boat was still out of sight in the mist. 'McNeill, what are we going to do – what's your plan?' Alina whispered.

'Don't have one. We wait – see if the patrol boat slips by and we remain unseen; however, I think the engine noise is coming from just in front and to our left a little, kind of ten o'clock. What do you think?' he asked quietly. She listened intently then nodded in agreement.

'Now what?' she whispered.

'We let it come almost level but with water between it and us. My guess is that it will be very close and on our left. If they see us, they may shout, then if that boat draws level and side on we shoot whatever is on it, like galleons delivering a broadside, OK Alina?' reported McNeill adding, 'Now stay low, out of sight. Leave the baby at the bow, it's safer there. They are going slow, probably cannot see too far ahead in this mist.'

McNeill had pulled in the oars when he first heard the outboard engine; now the rowing boat rocked ever so slightly. The phut-phut was loud and clear now. McNeill, lying down, raised his head and looked in the direction of ten o'clock. Intermittently through the mist he glimpsed the patrol boat on an opposite direction parallel course. He lowered his head. 'Ready, Alina?' he whispered. She tapped his left ankle. McNeill lifted his head, steadied both forearms on the boat side, held firm the two pistols. Glock in his left hand, Beretta in his right, he recognised the shapes of men on the patrol boat through the mist about 25 feet away. A voice on the patrol boat shouted; cue for McNeill to open fire. He aimed at the shapes, saw two men fall backwards into the water, another two slump forward. He kept shooting at the boat till the Glock clicked empty. Bullets flew over his head. Alina raised herself above McNeill's legs, aimed the Beretta at the boat and began shooting. McNeill stopped shooting. With his left hand holding his right at the wrist he steadied his right hand holding

307

the Beretta and he aimed at the soldier holding the tiller and squeezed the trigger. Bullets whistled by him. Alina screamed and fell against the far side of the boat. McNeill took careful aim and squeezed off four rounds into the boat. Screams of pain emanated from the patrol boat. No more bullets came McNeill's way and the patrol boat drifted on its return journey.

McNeill turned to see Alina lying in the small boat, blood oozing from a wound on her left side. She looked pale. He ripped her jumper at the seam over her left shoulder and tore the sleeve off the jumper, plunged it into the water, lifted it out and squeezed it, then pressed it onto the wound situated above her left breast, just below her left shoulder blade. He pulled her to him. She moaned in pain. 'Talk to me, talk to me, Alina,' he called. The bullet had passed straight through, taking part of her shoulder blade as it exited, the exit hole being much larger than the entry hole. He removed his shirt, plunged it into the water, squeezed it, folded it into a pad and placed Alina flat on her back with the exit hole resting on the shirt pad. He pressed the sodden jumper into the front of her wound, pulled over her right hand and placed it in the jumper to keep pressure on. 'Talk to me, damn you, sing to me if you like,' he said. She was shivering. He put her coat over her. 'Talk to me, swear at me, swear at whoever,' he said to her, frustrated. 'God, sometimes you never shut up and now you have the chance to speak, you stay silent!' he added.

'Shut up, can't you see I have been shot and I am in pain?' she lambasted him.

McNeill heard the outboard motor pick up. He reeled, finding the Glock on the hull floor, but the Glock was empty and the engine began to fade. He grabbed the oars and resumed rowing. 'How long before they return, McNeill?' Alina asked.

'About one hour, tops,' he replied.

'We are not going to make it, the lake is too long. We will not reach the border on the far side. What are we going to do?' Alina asked.

'We fight. We are dead if they catch us now anyway and I for one would rather be shot than clubbed to death, thank you,' he replied. The baby began to cry.

'She is hungry,' Alina said.

'At least we know she is still alive and just for now she can stay hungry a while longer,' McNeill replied sternly.

The patrol boat was shot to pieces. Five men were dead, three wounded, one badly; the two others had flesh wounds, one to his left arm, the other a graze on his head. The soldier with the wound to his left arm had reached the outboard and kept it from stalling, then gunned it out after the skirmish whilst the man with the head wound lay unconscious. They headed for the bridge near the roadblock.

The bodies of the men in the compound had been discovered. There was chaos; soldiers in jeeps drove around the compound and its environs, sometimes shooting at nothing. Suddenly, an officer with a wizened face was driven into the compound and he shot bullets into the air from an AK-47 and brought them to order. He sent four men to the roadblock with instructions to find out who passed them from the compound road last night, if anyone, and to return to him, pronto. The four men sped off in the jeep. Twenty minutes later they returned. 'Three women, sir, just before curfew,' relayed one of the four.

'Find them, bring them to me,' he said forcibly. Turning to more soldiers he shouted, 'You men, search the fuel dump', and pointing to another group, 'You men, come with me.' Ten men crammed into two jeeps which set off through the compound to the road, turned and sped off in the direction of the fuel dump. The wizened officer and three others mounted another jeep and sped to the roadblock.

The baby cried. Its crying was getting to McNeill, making him edgy. 'OK, can you feed her?' he asked Alina. 'Think so,' came a weak reply. He pulled in the oars, passed Alina and went to the bow of the boat, collected the baby and gave her to Alina to feed, without rocking the boat too much. He resumed rowing and looked on as a bloodstained Alina breastfed her baby. She looked at McNeill. 'They will be back,' she said, feeling deflated and defeated.

'Yes, nothing surer,' he replied matter-of-factly.

'It seems all is lost; how can you defeat them or get us to the border?' She was sounding beaten and depressed.

'Not going to be easy, but they shot up all of the boats back there and maybe they only have one patrol boat. Maybe we shot that up pretty bad? What worries me, Alina, is the mist is lifting – it's going to be one sunshine of a day,' explained McNeill.

'We are both wounded, in dire straits and you talk about the bloody weather,' she sarcastically stated.

'Well, we have a sniper rifle with five rounds and a couple of rounds in two of the pistols. More than enough, wouldn't you say?' said McNeill cheerily.

'Do not jest. You have a wounded leg, I have a wounded shoulder – you know our chances of survival are slim. You cannot row this boat to the border in less than an hour. For that matter, you will not row the lake. Don't be stupid!' she said, but McNeill had noticed that fire had returned to her voice.

'When lake meets shore is that the border, Alina?' McNeill asked.

'No, it's a kind of no-man's-land, an in-between zone, if you like.'

McNeill interrupted, 'OK, that's enough, that means they can't go in and neither can the guards on the other side, but we can be shot at by both sides. Not exactly fair, is it?' he finished, trying to add humour. Alina was humourless and in pain. Her shoulder ached, burned, oozed a sticky liquid and she was hungry. She struggled but eventually sat up.

McNeill could see the pain on her face. 'Make yourself comfortable. Lie down, if you like, and rest your head,' McNeill said as he dipped the bloodstained shirt from her back into the water, washing it out. He did the same with the jumper which they again used as a pad for the front, and he laid her on her back, saying, 'Rest, Alina, if only for a short while. Gather your strength.'

'Here, McNeill, take the baby. Put her at the bow where she is safe,' said Alina.

'No, keep her with you.' He checked his watch and he began rowing.

Twenty minutes later he stopped rowing and pulled in the oars and listened. He heard nothing, so he dismantled the Dragunov rifle, cleaned it and reassembled it and stroked it gently as you would a loving pet. He placed it along the boat with the stock facing him. The mist continued to clear, the sun was beginning to break through. McNeill was deep in thought. He knew the patrol boat would reach the roadblock base or wherever they had set out from. He envisaged men taking off the wounded and dead, could see how the survivors would be questioned, sense the replies to the questions – *but it was a surprise attack; we had no chance, we are lucky to be alive, we could not see them in the fog but they saw us and opened fire. No, sir, it was just a rowing boat.* He could see more soldiers with machine guns being ordered into the boat to seek and destroy. Again, he checked his watch.

⇒•◇•⇐

The patrol boat reached the small beach just below the roadblock. One of the wounded screamed in pain as the boat ran ashore. The soldier at the helm shot three rounds overhead. The wizened officer and his three men jumped up from a little table, spilling their drinks onto the floor. Grabbing their guns, they went outside. The roadblock machine gun was now trained onto the patrol boat. Other soldiers appeared from three cars and made their way over. The wizened officer and his three men got to the patrol boat first. The wizened man began bellowing orders, shouting at the other soldiers to get over here and help the wounded. 'Get a medical officer,' he demanded of one.

The wizened man bent down and began to question the soldier at the helm, whose arm was still bleeding from his bullet wound.

'We did not have a chance, sir, they were lying in wait, silent in the heavy mist. They ambushed us. We lost four men before we could return fire. The shooting was fierce and deadly accurate.'

The officer intervened. 'Machine gunfire?' he inquired.

'No, sir, small arms fire.'

The wizened officer asked, 'How many men would you estimate, soldier?'

'Four, sir,' came the reply.

'And the boat they were in?' asked the officer.

'Rowing boat, sir, no engines, no outboard, either,' replied the soldier.

'ARE YOU SURE?' the wizened man asked definitively and with purpose.

'Yes, sir. We drifted after the skirmish and then sped off, then I killed the engine to listen to see if they were coming after us or going the other way. There wasn't a sound; it had to be a rowing boat. It wasn't as long as this patrol boat, either,' relayed the soldier.

'And where did the ambush take place? Explain your patrol detail,' said the wizened man.

'We set off to patrol the lake shore as usual, past the far beach and up to the point. We usually rest there for twenty minutes before heading up further; however, the mist and fog was very thick and heavy, visibility was very poor and we returned to the point of rest instead of down the far side of the lake and then down to here in a straight line. We ended up at the point and we headed towards the middle of the lake, keeping the shoreline as a guide, but we had to stop the engine or put it on tick-over to see through the gaps in the mist to keep our bearings. It wasn't our usual pilot; he has gone missing. There was no other sound of a boat – we would have heard its engine, so it had to be a rowing boat, sir,' the wounded soldier reported.

The wizened man spoke again. 'OK, soldier, get that arm seen to.'

The soldier asked, 'My patrol members, Kuscak and Ivanovich —how are they, sir?'

'Ivanovich is dead and Kuscak is badly shot up, touch and go,' replied the wizened man empathetically.

'This boat's badly shot up too, sir, it's shipping water badly,' added the soldier.

'Before you go, soldier, how long to the ambush point?' the wizened man asked.

'Half-hour on full throttle, sir, that's how long it took for us to get back here,' replied the soldier.

'Mmm, I see, thank you, soldier,' said the wizened man.

The wizened officer turned to the soldier on his left. 'Get that dinghy from over there,' he ordered.

'You can't have that – that's the colonel's personal craft,' a voice said from the background and a huge man began effortlessly pushing through the soldiers to survey the scene. More men came.

'Get the dinghy, Petrov,' the wizened man said to the soldier who accompanied him as voices shouted, 'Fuel dumps OK, sir.'

'Thank you, help Petrov get that dinghy,' the wizened man said quietly.

The booming voice spoke, 'Did you not hear? That is the colonel's personal boat; you cannot commandeer that dinghy. Who the hell do you think you are?' the booming voice added with a sneer.

The wizened man, with his hands folded behind his back, stood in front of the man mountain and calmly said, 'It is not who *I* am, but who *you* are that matters, sir.'

The man mountain sneered and boomed, 'I am Lieutenant Colonel Brostic.' Looking down his nose and towering over the wizened man and with wild eyes blazing he asked, 'And who are you?'

The wizened man calmly stood his ground as the man mountain pushed his bulk to rest against him and replied, 'I, sir, am Major General Asimovic. Perhaps you have heard of me?'

The lieutenant colonel stopped in his tracks before backing off and coming to attention. Then he began mumbling, 'My apologies, my most humble of apologies, sir.'

'Shut up. Shut up while I think,' commanded the major general. The lieutenant colonel was in awe of the wizened man in front of him, the leader of the forces which had pushed so far into enemy territory from the east. Asimovic spoke.

'Listen to me, Brostic, I travelled non-stop these last two days and nights to come here and see why we are meeting so much resistance from the town, to see first-hand why we cannot take it. I have moved men around to their weakest points and attacked and back again, trying to make their strong points their weakest so the army would be able to attack their weakest areas and break through. This has not happened; the resistance in that town is of the most heroic and well organised that I have ever encountered during this dirty, stupid war. I have to take a town of heroes, men willing to stand shoulder to shoulder, lay down their lives for each other. Men fighting for their cause, sure – but more than that, fighting for their commanding officer. An officer like myself who puts men's lives before all else: an officer who grieves with his men, for his men and I have to take that town with jumped up little bigots, upstarts and bullies like yourself, Brostic.

'Do you know who we face? Do you have any idea who is in command in that town? That town has held out and resisted and is hopelessly outnumbered, but it is not out-fought, nor is it out-manoeuvred, nor is it out-thought, and the bravery and courage of those men is far above what I have at my disposal. Yes, our nemesis in that town is the brilliant Major General Slavic, with his brilliant team of officers and most courageous of men. Slavic is their country, Brostic, do you understand that? No, I don't think you do. For Slavic, these men would die. He treats all the same, from colonel, major, captain to private, has the same regard and pride in them all and they in him.' He eyed Brostic and continued.

'Yesterday, and last night and this morning, Brostic, a boat patrol and foot patrol have been heavily shot up. Your tanks found bodies of our men in a crevasse in the road. Those tanks were sitting ducks for a time and we suffered heavy losses. We were informed that the road was crystal clear and it would be a cake walk, Brostic. Yet this was not the case. The first wave came under such an attack that the second wave had to go in and rescue them. Buffoons like you are leading to the tragic heavy loss of life on our side. You would rather take charge of a dinghy than your own men; out for personal gain at the expense of your compatriots and your compatriots are leaving their blood on the ground, while you and your kind chew on the fat of life. Anyway, I digress. Back to the foot patrol – shot up men found in the compound along with one truck, all dead, shot to pieces. We have reports of three women who have now vanished into thin air along with their families—'

'Yes, we found the men in the foot patrol and steps were put into place, sir,' Brostic interrupted.

'Quiet, don't be so insubordinate!' Asimovic yelled. He went on, 'These steps, Brostic – was that the slaughter this morning of the men, women and children?'

Brostic was stilled, his arrogance abated.

'Well, Brostic, what have you to say?' asked the wizened Asimovic.

'I will follow orders and do my duty as I see it. I serve my country. Those people were arrested, questioned, found to be spies and paid the consequences, sir,' Brostic replied, chest blown out.

'Sir,' came a voice, 'I have the dinghy and have fuelled the outboard motor on it.'

'Thank you, Petrov. Get four or five men,' said Asimovic politely.

He then turned to Brostic. 'It seems, Brostic, does it not, that the people who shot up the foot patrol, the compound, the men found in the crevasse in the road and the boat this morning are on their way to the border in a rowing boat on this lake,' he said.

315

Petrov returned with four men. Asimovic nodded his acknowledgement. Brostic boomed, 'Major general, sir, I will apprehend those men and have them shot as a reprisal.'

Asimovic halted, pondered; Petrov looked on from behind Brostic. The major general spoke. 'OK, lieutenant colonel, as you wish.' He nodded to Petrov. Petrov and his four men came alongside Asimovic. Brostic turned and shouted to three others, calling each by name, to man the dinghy and bring machine guns. They climbed aboard the dinghy and roared off into the lake.

'Jumped up fool,' Petrov said under his breath. Asimovic smiled at Petrov, turned and then asked, 'Well, my loyal friend, what makes you say that?'

Petrov replied, 'Sir, whoever is on that boat are crack professional soldiers – look at the damage they have caused.'

Asimovic studiously replied, 'Ah, Petrov, my friend. It could be it is the American who has constantly been a thorn in Tomelsky's side – he despatched nearly all of his most brutal assassins to their maker and we know he was headed to the border this way. Remember how you accidentally heard of this news a couple of days ago and the reward Tomelsky was offering for their deaths? Anyhow, whoever it is may only have handguns and if so they will probably be shot by Brostic, who will acclaim himself a hero for the Serbian cause. However, if he is shot dead, at least the Croatian people will have a small recompense in atonement for the atrocity of this morning's barbaric executions.'

Petrov listened and smiled 'And which do you wish for, sir?' he asked nonchalantly.

'The latter,' replied Asimovic instantly.

'In that case, you have sent him to his death, sir,' Petrov said.

'After what happened this morning before we got here, either under his command or his doing, my conscience is clear, Petrov; besides, you are too loyal a friend and too good a man to waste,' Asimovic imparted.

Petrov went on, 'For your ears only, sir; I think that's the last we will see or hear of Brostic.'

'So do I, Petrov; for if it is the American, he will use his sniper rifle and Brostic and three of his kind will meet their death,' Asimovic said.

'But sir, how do you know the other three are his cohorts?' asked Petrov.

'Brostic pointed, nodded to them, called them by name,' replied Asimovic. 'You know, my friend,' he added philosophically, 'we fight to remove bigots like Brostic from power, and sure enough, eventually we replace them with others like them.'

Petrov spoke, 'I too now think the American is in the boat, and I wish him well in his quest to the border.'

'So do I, Petrov, and so I think we can now call off the search of the town,' said the major general.

Brostic roared off in the dinghy, eyes wide, salivating at the thought of the impending slaughter. He started to laugh. His cohorts asked him why he was laughing. 'Bloody fool Asimovic has sent me to kill these soldiers. I will return a hero. They have hand-guns only – we have machine guns.' They all started laughing. Brostic sneered. His thoughts turned to hoping for it to be the American his friend Tomelsky wanted dead. Tomelsky would give him power and riches after this stupid war. 'Hurry, hurry!' bellowed Brostic eagerly. Either way, he was a winner: four men slaughtered in a rowing boat and used as trophies to proclaim him a hero, then a political life in the upper echelons of government, or the same end for killing a man, woman and child, with the added reward. His eyes widened in anticipation, his nostrils flared; he could smell his prey and his success.

McNeill rowed then stopped, looked at his watch, listened, looked through the rifle sight. He gave the rifle sight to Alina lying in the hull beside him as he rowed, saying, 'Every few minutes, look through the sight. If you see anything, you tell me.' She made herself as comfortable as she could, raised the sight

317

to her right eye and looked out over the narrow stern. 'They are coming, aren't they?' she said, seeing nothing.

McNeill rowed on. 'Yes, and soon you will see them,' he answered.

The mist had all but lifted. 'It's going to be a beautiful day,' McNeill said again as he watched the sunlight flicker and dance on the water in the lake. The sun began to warm the back of his head. The only ripples on the water were caused by his oars. A deep serene calm descended.

'Faster!' screamed Brostic excitedly. 'Faster, faster!'

'But sir, we are going all out – it will not go any faster,' replied one of the men.

Brostic did not feel the heat of the sun – the excitement, the anticipation of easy pickings had him enthralled at fever pitch. The dinghy sped on, Brostic kneeling at the front, flanked by one man either side, and the last at the helm. 'Give me the binoculars,' Brostic shouted, eyes aflame. The man on his left removed them from around his neck and passed them to him. Brostic snatched the binoculars, pressed them to his eyes and began to search right to left. Sunlight suddenly hit his eyes, blinding him temporarily. He pulled his face away from the binoculars, put his head to one side and squeezed his eyes shut. His eyes watered. He then resumed his search and saw nothing. 'Can't this thing go any faster?' he bellowed.

Alina gave a short gasp, then took a rapid intake of breath. She lay the sight down. 'OK, what did you see?' asked McNeill, the sun still warm on the back of his head as he watched her.

'Nothing at first, then a flash on the water from over there, nothing either side of the flash, and you seem to be going off course,' she said, pointing as best she could.

McNeill swung the boat further round, pulled in the oars, rested Alina's head low in the boat and placed her crying baby beside her. He took the sight and attached it to the Dragunov and eased himself into a comfortable firing position, letting the barrel rest on the boat's narrow stern.

'You were heading for the sun, that's the reason we are off course; you were waiting for me to spot the glint of sunlight on glass, McNeill,' Alina said weakly.

'Yes, I figured they would be constantly looking through binoculars to try and spot us, and hopefully the sun will have blinded them for a split second and we will not have been spotted,' he replied. Suddenly, in the despair of her situation, McNeill had given her hope. She prayed for deliverance and hugged her crying baby.

McNeill looked through the telescopic sight and saw the dinghy making rapid headway towards them. He saw the bulk of a man at the bow, two either side and a helmsman. He took aim and fired once.

Brostic was half turned when he felt it whistle past his stomach. He was still half turned when he saw a red blotch appear on the helmsman's chest and he watched as he released the throttle on the outboard motor and fell backwards into the lake. The dinghy slowed and careered uncertainly in the water.

McNeill watched the panic and waited for another clear shot. Brostic was shouting, 'Get the motor, get the helm,' and gesticulating. The dinghy rocked. The man on Brostic's left was lying in fear; the man on the right was trying to reach the helm. He crawled to it and grabbed it, steadied the rocking dinghy only partially as the throttle began closing. The engine did not stall, and he remained lying on the dinghy floor, fumbling for his AK-47.

'Get the throttle,' Brostic hissed to the man on his left; the man refused to move. 'Get the throttle,' he screamed, 'or I kill you here and now,' Brostic threatened, eyes bulging in their sockets, burning with hatred, contorting his face. The man looked and felt revulsion for this sick, brute bully of a man as he moved to the helm. He knew when he steadied the boat he invited a bullet. 'Move, get us moving, I can see them,' bellowed Brostic, frantically waving his big arms. 'Move!' he screamed in anger, his back to the new helmsman. But the dinghy did not propel forward.

The two in the dinghy turned to see and watched on as the helmsman took the bullet in his chest with open arms. The other soldier needed no telling; he had located his AK-47 and let off a volley as he moved to the helm.

McNeill lowered his head. The bullets fell short and to McNeill's right. McNeill cursed himself; he had the choice of two easy hits and hit the man at the helm, the easiest shot of the two, a man with both arms outstretched. McNeill realised the soldier wanted the bullet, probably to absolve his sins, to repent, and he had left alive a competent, dangerous soldier. Alina broke his thought chain. 'McNeill, McNeill,' she called anxiously.

'It's OK, I am still here,' he replied, peering through the telescopic sight. McNeill thought, *Three rounds left, and after that mess, they will definitely shoot up the rowing boat.* The dinghy sped towards them; bullets began to hit the water just in front and off to the side of McNeill, still just out of range, but not for long, fired by the man in the front, a huge man. Was it? Could it be? He could only surmise but it looked like the man with the lump hammer from earlier. The dinghy lifted and swayed. Bullets passed over McNeill's head, others hit the water in front of the rowing boat. No clear shot.

McNeill waited, a pressurised wait. He fired twice. The first hit the rubber just at Brostic's left, passing right through. Brostic never had the time to look around to the yell from behind as the second hit his left side just below his ribcage, laying him full out on his back. He heard another moan and the revs on the outboard subside. Brostic clambered to his compatriot, and on reaching him his huge hand lifted him up. The soldier's last breath brushed Brostic's face as his life ebbed away. Fear, hatred and anger gripped Brostic. He used the body of the dead soldier to jam the throttle on the outboard open and set the helm on a collision course with the rowing boat. He ripped the soldier's machine gun from him and staggered to the bow of the dinghy where he began firing at the rowing boat, screaming and yelling at the same time.

McNeill ducked his head. Bullets whistled over his head. Alina's lips offered prayers at a rapid rate. Brostic was wild with anticipation. He was now within range. He began yelling, bellowing, taunting, screaming, his black eyes wide and bulging, his mouth salivating, like a hyena stalking wounded prey, his ribcage bleeding. 'I'm going to run you over, smash you to pieces with my bare hands, then shoot you to pieces,' he yelled as he fired. Bullets hit the boat behind McNeill. Splinters of wood hit Alina, who screamed.

'It's OK, hang in there,' said McNeill, who was waiting for a gap in the fire, waiting for the magazine to empty. The boat began to ship water. McNeill raised his head, peered through the sight and reset it. The dinghy was almost upon them. McNeill pulled out his Beretta, raised it over the rim of the boat, aimed at the dinghy and fired the Beretta till it could give no more.

Brostic's delight became wilder, the excitement had him possessed. 'No bullets, have you no bullets?' He began to laugh a sadistic laugh.

'Show yourself, fool, and I will show you if I have no bullets. This one is for you. Come on, show yourself, one clear shot is all I ask,' whispered McNeill.

Brostic slid down to the outboard motor on the dinghy and unjammed the throttle. The engine stilled to a phut-phut. *No need to run them down now,* he thought. *I have them, I have them, I will coast alongside and empty this machine gun into them, watch any wounded beg for mercy before I shoot them.* His eyes gleamed, his mouth watered.

McNeill peered through the sight; sweat rolled from his forehead, his finger began to ache on the trigger. 'Don't miss, McNeill, you have one left; for God's sake, don't miss,' said Alina softly, praying to heaven.

The big hulk peeped up and then ducked down. McNeill waited. Brostic did the same again. McNeill waited, beads of sweat now running down his face, his concentration astute and totally focussed. A life or death shot; from McNeill's point of view, their lives and the man mountain's death, but time was running out. The dinghy moved ever closer; his finger moved to the trigger. The big man's laughter echoed to the rowing boat. 'We are sinking, and he's laughing at us,' called Alina.

'Yeah, he thinks we are out of bullets but isn't sure,' said McNeill calmly as he took aim.

The dinghy moved closer. The man mountain knelt up, cradling the machine gun in his huge hands. McNeill squeezed the trigger. 'Bye bye, murderer,' he whispered. The big man's mouth was open before the bullet entered his head between his eyes. McNeill watched through the sight, saw the blood spurt from Brostic's forehead, saw the huge man fall backwards. The weight of the big man falling lifted the dinghy's bow out of the water, and Brostic tumbled to the rear, resting on the body at the helm, jamming the throttle open once again.

No time to waste. McNeill released the Dragunov and clambered to the seat, pushed out the oars and began heaving at them, pulling for his life. He wheeled the boat around to his left, heaved on the oar, pushed with his legs, feeling excruciating pain in his left leg as blood oozed out with every stroke. *Got to get out of the dinghy's path – if it hits us it could rest on our boat and bring it under water.* He pulled at the oars to disperse the water, heaved them through the water again. He felt like passing out. He pulled backwards again and shouldered the right oar. He heaved the left through the water and the dinghy passed by the stern.

Alina had her eyes tight shut and was holding her crying baby close. McNeill saw the bodies: the man mountain sprawled on the dinghy floor; the other, draped across the throttle, he recognised as one of the soldiers who nearly uncovered the tarpaulin on the boat earlier, one who shot holes into the other boats whilst laughing. 'They will laugh no more,' he said as the dinghy shot by, spraying water on McNeill and Alina.

McNeill turned the rowing boat around and began rowing at a pace which was easier on his aching leg with the sun shining on the left-hand side of his face as water from the lake leaked in. He allowed himself a glimpse of the future and breathed in with the coming of a new and different life with Alina and her baby; it frightened him a little and he exhaled with relief and refocused on the job in hand. He looked at the wounded Alina, her baby now resting on her chest, many times as he rowed the lake. Every time she caught him looking she would smile at him, a warm, content, loving smile.

McNeill rowed till the boat ran ashore. His wounded leg ached and bled, his stomach yearned with hunger. He climbed out of the boat. Standing in shallow water he bent down, cupped his hands in the lake and put the cool, fresh water onto his face, then his wounded leg. He picked up the empty rifles and strapped them to his back, put the empty pistols into his belt and strapped the bag to his back. He bent down, picked up the baby, wrapped her warm in a jacket and carried her to shore. He placed her down on the sand and he returned to the boat. Alina was murmuring with pain. 'Hey, give me a hand here as I try and lift you, or do you want to go down with your ship, captain?' he said. Then, with as much help as Alina could muster, he lifted her onto her feet in the water. The water in the leaking boat had soaked into the back of her jumper and her skirt. 'Can you walk?' he asked her. 'Yes!' she replied stubbornly through gritted teeth.

She leant on his left shoulder for support and paddled slowly to shore. McNeill steadied her and bent down to retrieve her baby. He scooped the baby up in his right hand, turned and looked at a weary Alina, who looked pale. He placed his left arm round her and she her right arm around him, supporting each other as they began to walk off the sand. Alina began to sing. She sang the same lullaby the people sang before being clubbed to death. They climbed the small sand dunes and came on to a narrow tarmac road moving in both directions, left and right.

'OK, which way?' asked McNeill.

'Any way you like,' she replied, carefree.

'We go left,' said McNeill.

Instantly she replied, 'In that case, we go right.'

They turned right onto the tarmac. The road headed off and turned left between some more sand dunes and headed inland.

Alina was bleeding, her left arm limp by her side. Occasionally, McNeill would lift her by his left arm, holding her waist and Alina would moan with pain.

The sand dunes had turned to fern and grass. McNeill looked ahead. The road was getting wider and he could see that the road bent to the right 50 yards ahead. They reached the bend and a large black dog came running towards them, barking. McNeill began talking to the dog, trying to calm the dog with his voice, but to no avail; the dog continued to bark loudly. Presently, an old man pushing a pushbike with a basket attached to the front came into view and he almost fell over at the sight of them. He stopped and walked toward them, commanding the dog to stop.

He spoke to McNeill and Alina in a tongue neither recognised. Alina began to cry. Tears of joy ran down her cheeks as she flung her arms round the old man and kissed him on both cheeks, her blood staining his shirt as she did so. McNeill grabbed his hand and shook it vigorously before giving them both a bear hug. The dog growled and barked. He released his grip and Alina flung herself around him. Once again McNeill shook the old man's hand. The old man looked at his own shirt, then at McNeill's bloodstained trousers and Alina, blood gently oozing again from her chest wound. He reached into the basket on the front of the pushbike and gave them a parcel, gesturing for them to sit down – he would be back in thirty minutes. McNeill and Alina both sat down, McNeill holding the baby as Alina opened the parcel. The old man mounted his bike and headed off in the direction from where he had come.

Alina opened the parcel. It contained four cheese sandwiches. McNeill and Alina ate them slowly, savouring every morsel.

The old man cycled to the lookout post and the four sentries he had passed through twenty-five minutes earlier. The sentries lifted the barrier to let him through as always. Only this time he stopped, dropped his bike, made his way to them hurriedly and began shouting and waving his arms vigorously, making no sense whatsoever to the sentries. 'Whoa, slow down,' said one. The old man explained: 'One soldier, one woman and a baby, both wounded – look, I have her blood on my shirt – are in need of help twenty minutes down the road and speak a language I have no comprehension of.'

One of the sentries started a Land Rover, another jumped in, machine gun at the ready; the old man and his dog got into the back. The remaining two sentries stayed on guard.

The Land Rover slowed before it reached McNeill and Alina. The driver spoke to the old man in the back and the soldier in the passenger seat took aim. The Land Rover stopped 20 yards from McNeill and Alina; the old man and his dog got out and began walking towards them. Alina handed him her baby and McNeill helped Alina to her feet. The sentry kept his gun pointed at McNeill. McNeill leant Alina against the Land Rover; he then stood, arms aloft, legs slightly apart. The driver removed his pistols and checked them: both empty. He removed the bag, opened it, saw papers and baby clothes and closed it, and signalled for McNeill to take off the rifles. Again, the soldier checked the rifles: both empty. He gave the rifles and the pistols back to McNeill and held out his hand, which McNeill took into his. They shook hands and the soldier patted McNeill's arm.

The other soldier relaxed his stance as the driver called him over. The two soldiers and McNeill lifted Alina into the rear of the Land Rover, and one of the soldiers got into the back along with McNeill, who dangled his legs off the back of the Land Rover. The old man, carrying Alina's baby and his dog, got into the front. McNeill took out the last of the pack of cigarettes and offered one to the soldier, who took it; then, with Fitz's lighter, McNeill lit both cigarettes and threw the empty packet away. McNeill pulled on the cigarette, allowing the smoke to circulate in his lungs. He looked at the lighter as he rolled it round in the palm of his hand. He exhaled and he thought of Fitz, thought of the times they had shared; the good, the bad, the ugly and the lonely. Loneliness is only felt by the heart, he could remember

Fitz saying. McNeill put the lighter in his pocket and finished his cigarette.

The Land Rover stopped at the checkpoint, where the old man gave the baby to McNeill and the soldier got into the front. McNeill and Alina were driven to a Red Cross refugee base, where they were rushed in. The baby was taken from McNeill and promptly fed by a nurse. McNeill and Alina were laid in separate beds alongside each other. A doctor spoke to them both in English, first to McNeill. 'Your leg is infected but you will be OK.' Turning to Alina he said, 'You, my dear, are a little more complicated. The bullet passed through but in doing so has broken and removed parts of your shoulder blade. You are weak because of your loss of blood.'

'And my baby?' she interrupted.

'Fine, just fine – in much better shape than the both of you.'

Alina reached over to her right towards the bed where McNeill lay and grabbed his extended left arm. Tears swelled in her eyes as they looked at each other, until she could hold them back no longer. Tears rolled off her face as she said, 'We are free, McNeill, you have brought us to freedom. You are an amazing man and I love you so very much. Thank you, thank you so much.' She squeezed his arm and he caught hold of her hand as her head lay back on the bed and she drifted off into unconsciousness.